IN THE MIDST
of WINTER

IN THE MIDST

of WINTER

ISABEL
ALLENDE

Translated by Nick Caistor and Amanda Hopkinson

SCRIBNER

LONDON NEW YORK TORONTO SYDNEY NEW DELHI

First published in Great Britain by Scribner, an imprint of Simon & Schuster UK Ltd, 2017
First published in the USA by Atria Books, an imprint of Simon & Schuster Inc., 2017
Originally published in Spain with the title *Más allá del invierno*, 2017
A CBS COMPANY

1 3 5 7 9 10 8 6 4 2

Simon & Schuster UK Ltd
1st Floor
222 Gray's Inn Road
London WC1X 8HB

Simon & Schuster Australia, Sydney
Simon & Schuster India, New Delhi

www.simonandschuster.co.uk
www.simonandschuster.com.au
www.simonandschuster.co.in

A CIP catalogue record for this book
is available from the British Library

Hardback ISBN: 978-1-4711-6687-7
Trade paperback ISBN: 978-1-4711-6688-4
eBook ISBN: 978-1-4711-6689-1
Audio ISBN: 978-1-4711-6702-7

Interior design by Amy Trombat
Printed and bound by CPI Group (UK) Ltd, Croydon CR0 4YY

Simon & Schuster UK Ltd are committed to sourcing paper
that is made from wood grown in sustainable forests and support the Forest
Stewardship Council, the leading international forest certification organisation.
Our books displaying the FSC logo are printed on FSC certified paper.

Excerpt from *Summer* by Albert Camus. Copyright © Éditions Gallimard, Paris, 1954

To Roger Cukras, for unexpected love

Au milieu de l'hiver, j'apprenais enfin qu'il y avait en moi un été invincible.

—ALBERT CAMUS

In the midst of winter, I finally found there was within me an invincible summer.

Lucia

At the end of December 2015 winter had not yet reached Brooklyn. As Christmas approached with its jangle of bells, people were still in short sleeves and sandals, some of them celebrating nature's oversight and others fearing global warming, while to the confusion of squirrels and birds, artificial trees sprinkled with silver frost appeared in house windows. Three weeks after New Year's Day, when no one gave any further thought to how out of step the calendar was, nature suddenly awoke from its fall torpor and unleashed the worst snowstorm in living memory.

Lucia Maraz was cursing the cold in her Prospect Heights basement apartment, a cement-and-brick cave with a mountain of snow blocking the doorway. Blessed with the stoic character of her people, accustomed as they are to earthquakes, floods, occasional tsunamis, and political cataclysms, she grew worried if no disaster occurred within a given length of time. Yet she was unprepared for this Siberian winter that seemed to have struck Brooklyn in error. Storms in Chile are limited to the Andes Mountains and the deep south of Tierra del Fuego, where the continent crumbles into islands torn to shreds by the austral wind, where ice splits bones and life is brutal. Lucia was from Santiago, undeservedly renowned for its benign climate, although its winters are damp and cold, its summers hot and dry. The capital lies nestled among purple mountains that at dawn are sometimes covered in snow, and then the purest light on earth is reflected from their dazzling peaks. On very rare occasions a sad, pale dusting falls over the city like ashes, never managing to turn the urban landscape white before melting into dirty slush. Snow is always pristine from a distance.

In Lucia's Brooklyn cave, largely below street level and with poor heating, snow was a nightmare. The frost-covered glass impeded light from entering through the small window, and the inside gloom was hardly dispelled by the naked bulbs dangling from the ceiling. The apartment contained only the essentials: a jumble of shabby second- or thirdhand furniture and a few kitchen utensils. Richard Bowmaster, the owner, was not interested in either decor or comfort.

The storm began on Friday with a heavy snowfall followed by a fierce squall that lashed the nearly deserted streets. The force of the wind caused trees to bend and the freezing weather killed many birds who had forgotten to migrate, fooled by the previous month's warmth. When the cleanup operation began, sanitation trucks carted away frozen sparrows along with the scattered debris. However, the mysterious parakeets in Green-Wood Cemetery survived the blizzard, as was confirmed three days later, when they reappeared intact, pecking for crumbs among the gravestones. On Thursday, television reporters with funereal expressions and the solemn tone usually reserved for news about terrorism in far-off countries had predicted the upcoming storm as well as dire consequences for the weekend. A state of emergency was declared in New York, and the dean at NYU, where Lucia worked, had heeded the warning, informing all faculty that Friday classes were canceled. It would have been an adventure to reach Manhattan in any case.

LUCIA TOOK ADVANTAGE of that day's unexpected freedom to prepare a life-restoring *cazuela*, a Chilean soup that lifts downhearted spirits and sick bodies. By now she had been in the United States more than four months, eating mostly at the university cafeteria and with no reason to cook for herself except on a couple of occasions when she did so out of nostalgia or to celebrate a friendship. For this traditional dish she made a hearty, well-seasoned stock; she fried onion and meat, cooked vegetables, potatoes, and pumpkin separately, and finally added rice. Although she used all the pots in the kitchen and it looked as if a bomb had exploded there, the result was well worth it. For it dispelled the feeling of loneliness that had overwhelmed her since the storm began. That loneliness, which in the past used to arrive unannounced like an unwelcome visitor, had now been relegated to a distant corner of her mind.

That night, as the wind roared outside, whipping up the snow and filtering in impudently through the chinks, she felt a visceral childhood dread. She knew she was safe in her cave, that her fear of the elements was absurd, and that there was no cause to disturb Richard, apart from the fact that he was the only person she could turn to in circumstances like this, because he lived on the floor above. At nine in the evening she gave in to her need to hear a human voice and phoned him.

"What are you doing?" she asked, trying to conceal her apprehension.

"Playing the piano. Is the noise disturbing you?"

"I can't hear your piano. The only noise down here is the crash of the end of the world. Is this normal here in Brooklyn?"

"There's bad weather every so often in winter, Lucia."

"I'm scared."

"What of?"

"Just scared, nothing specific. I guess it would be stupid to ask you to come and keep me company for a while. I made a Chilean soup."

"Is it vegetarian?"

"No. Well, never mind, Richard. Good night."

"Good night."

She drank a shot of pisco and buried her head beneath her pillow. She slept badly, waking up every half hour with the same fragmented dream about being shipwrecked in a substance as thick and sour as yogurt.

BY SATURDAY THE STORM had continued on its raging path toward the Atlantic, but the weather in Brooklyn remained cold and snowy. Lucia did not want to venture out as many streets were still blocked, although efforts to clear them had begun at first light. She would have plenty of time to read and prepare her classes for the coming week. On the news she saw that the storm continued wreaking havoc wherever it went. She was pleased at the prospect of some peace, a good novel, and a rest. Eventually someone would come and clear the snow from her door. That would be no problem, the neighborhood kids were already out offering to work for a few dollars. Lucia appreciated her good fortune, realizing she felt at ease living in this inhospitable Prospect Heights cave, which wasn't so bad after all.

As evening fell, she began to feel bored with being shut in. She shared some of the soup with Marcelo, the Chihuahua, and the two of them settled down together in the bed on the floor, on a lumpy mattress under a mountain of blankets, to watch several episodes of their favorite TV crime series. The apartment was freezing. Lucia put on her wool hat and gloves.

In the first weeks, when her decision to leave Chile had hung heavy on her—there at least she could employ her sense of humor in Spanish—she had consoled herself with the certainty that everything changes. By tomorrow, all of today's misfortunes will be ancient history. In fact, her doubts had been short-lived: she was enjoying her work; she had Marcelo; she'd made friends at the university and in her neighborhood; people were kind everywhere; after going three times to any coffee shop, she would be treated as one of the family. The idea Chileans had that Yankees were cold was a myth. The only person she had to deal with who was somewhat cold was Richard Bowmaster, her landlord. Well, the hell with him.

Richard had paid a pittance for this large Brooklyn brownstone, which was similar to dozens of other houses in the neighborhood. He bought it from his best friend, an Argentinian who suddenly inherited a fortune and returned to his own country to administer it. A few years later, the same house, but more run-down, was worth over three million dollars. He became the owner just before young professionals from Manhattan arrived en masse to buy and refurbish these picturesque dwellings, raising the prices to ridiculous levels. Before this, the neighborhood had been an area of crime, drugs, and gangs where no one dared to walk at night. But by the time Richard moved in, it had become one of the most sought-after areas in the country, despite the garbage cans, the skeletal trees, and all the junk in the yards. Lucia had joked to Richard that he should sell this relic with its rickety stairs and dilapidated doors and grow old living like royalty on a Caribbean island, but Richard was a gloomy man whose natural pessimism was reinforced by the demands and drawbacks of a house with five large empty rooms, three unused bathrooms, a closed-off attic, and a first floor with such high ceilings that you needed an extension ladder to change a lightbulb.

Richard Bowmaster was Lucia's boss at New York University, where she had a one-year contract as a visiting professor. Once the year was over, her life was a blank slate: she would need another job and somewhere else to live while she decided on her long-term future. Sooner or later she would return to end her days in Chile, but that was still quite a way off. And since her daughter, Daniela, had moved to Miami to study marine biology, and was possibly in love and planning to stay, there was nothing to draw Lucia back to her home country. She intended to enjoy her remaining years of good health before she was defeated by decrepitude. She wanted to live abroad, where the daily challenges kept her mind occupied and her heart in relative calm, because in Chile she was crushed by the weight of the familiar, its routines and limitations. Back there she felt she was condemned to be a lonely old woman besieged by pointless memories; in another country, there could be surprises and opportunities.

She had agreed to teach at NYU's Center for Latin American and Caribbean Studies in order to get away from Chile for a while and be closer to Daniela. Also, she had to admit, because Richard Bowmaster intrigued her. She was just emerging from a failed romance and thought Richard could be the cure, a way of definitively forgetting Julian, her last love, the only one to leave any kind of imprint on her since her divorce in 2010. In the years since then, Lucia had learned how few suitors were available for a woman her age. Before Julian appeared, she had had a few insignificant flings. She had known Richard for more than ten years, while she was still married, and had been attracted to him ever since she met him, although she could not have clearly said why. They had contrasting characters and little in common beyond academic matters. Although they had met here and there at conferences, spent hours talking about their work, and kept up a regular correspondence, he had never shown the slightest romantic interest in her. Uncharacteristically, as she lacked the boldness of flirtatious women, Lucia had even hinted at it on one occasion. Before she came to New York, Richard's thoughtful, shy demeanor had been a powerful attraction, for she imagined that a man like him must be deep and serious, noble spirited: a prize for whoever succeeded in overcoming the obstacles he placed in the way of any kind of intimacy.

Lucia still entertained the fantasies of a young girl despite the fact that she was almost sixty-two. She had a wrinkled neck, dry skin, and flabby arms; her knees were heavy; and she had become resigned to watching her waist disappear because she did not have the discipline to combat the process in the gym. Although she had youthful breasts, they were not hers. She avoided looking at herself naked, because she felt much better when she was dressed. Aware of which colors and styles favored her, she kept to them rigorously and was able to purchase a complete outfit in twenty minutes, without ever allowing curiosity to distract her. Like photographs, the mirror was an implacable enemy, because both showed her immobile, with her flaws mercilessly exposed. She thought that if she had any attraction, it lay in movement, for she was flexible and had a grace that was unearned, since she had done nothing to foster it. She was as sweet-toothed and lazy as an odalisque, and if there had been any justice in the world, she would have been obese. Her forebears, spirited and probably hungry people, had bequeathed her a fortunate metabolism. In her passport photograph, where she was staring straight ahead with a dour expression, she looked like a Soviet prison guard, as her daughter, Daniela, said to tease her, but nobody ever saw her looking that stiff. She had an expressive face and knew how to apply makeup.

In short, she was satisfied with her appearance and resigned to the inevitable damages of age. Her body was growing old, but inside she still kept intact the adolescent she once was. She could not imagine the old woman she would be. Her desire to get the most out of life grew greater as her future shrank, and part of that enthusiasm was the vague hope of having someone to cherish, even if this clashed with the reality of a lack of opportunities. She missed sex, romance, and love. The first of these she could obtain every so often, the second was a matter of luck, and the third was a gift from the gods that would probably never happen, as her daughter had told her more than once.

ALTHOUGH LUCIA WAS SOMEWHAT SAD that she had broken off her affair with Julian, she never regretted it. She wanted stability, but even though he was seventy years old he was still flitting from one relationship to another, like a hummingbird. Despite the advice of her daughter, who advocated the advantages of free love, for Lucia intimacy was impossible with a man distracted by other women. "What is it you're after, Mom? To get married?" Daniela had laughed when she learned her mother was finished with Julian. No, but Lucia wanted to make love in a loving way, for the pleasure of her body as well as the tranquility of her spirit. She wanted to make love with someone who felt as she did. She wanted to be accepted without concealing or pretending anything, to get to know the other person deeply and to accept him in the same way. She wanted somebody she could spend Sunday mornings in bed with reading the newspapers, somebody to hold hands with at movies, to laugh with at nonsense, to discuss ideas with. She had gotten beyond any enthusiasm for fleeting adventures.

However, now that Lucia had grown accustomed to her space, her silence, and her solitude, she had concluded it would be a high price to pay to share her bed, bathroom, and closet, and that no man would be able to satisfy all her needs. In her youth she had thought she was incomplete without being in a loving couple, that something essential was missing. In her maturity she was thankful for the cornucopia of her existence, although she had vaguely thought of turning to an Internet dating site simply out of curiosity. She gave this up at once, because Daniela was sure to find out from Miami. Besides, Lucia did not know how to describe herself so that she seemed more attractive without lying. She guessed that the same thing happened with others; everyone lied.

Men around her age wanted women who were twenty or thirty years younger, which was understandable since she herself would not want to get together with an ailing old man and preferred a younger Romeo. According to Daniela, it was a waste she was heterosexual. There were more than enough single women with rich inner lives and in good physical and emotional condition who were far more interesting than the widowed or divorced men of sixty or seventy out there. Lucia admitted her limitations in this respect but thought it was too late to change. Since her divorce she had had a few brief intimate encounters with one friend or another after a few drinks at a disco, or with strangers on her travels, or at a party. These were nothing to write home about, but they helped her overcome the embarrassment of taking her clothes off in front of a male witness. The scars on her chest were visible, and her virginal breasts belonged to a young bride. Having nothing to do with the rest of her body, they mocked her current anatomy.

Her fantasy of seducing Richard, which had seemed so enticing when she received his invitation to teach at the university, had evaporated barely a week after she moved into the basement apartment. Rather than bringing them closer, their relative proximity—meeting regularly at work, in the street, on the subway, or at the front door to the house—had quickly distanced them. The once warm camaraderie of international

meetings and electronic communication had frozen when put
to the test of physical closeness. No, there would definitely
be no romance with Richard Bowmaster, which was a shame
because he was the kind of tranquil, reliable man she would not
have minded being bored with. Lucia was only a year and eight
months older than him. As she often told herself, this was a neg-
ligible difference, although in secret she admitted that she was
at a disadvantage. She felt heavy and was shrinking steadily as
her spine contracted, but she could no longer wear very high
heels without falling flat on her face. Around her, everyone else
seemed to be growing taller. Her students towered over her, as
gangly and aloof as giraffes. She was fed up with seeing all the
nose hairs of the rest of humanity from down below. Richard
on the other hand wore his years with the awkward charm of a
professor absorbed in his studies.

As Lucia described him to Daniela, Richard Bowmaster was
of medium height, still with enough hair and good teeth, and
with eyes somewhere between gray and green depending on the
reflection of light on his glasses and the state of his ulcer. He
seldom smiled without a real reason, but his permanent dim-
ples and tousled hair gave him a youthful look, even though he
walked along staring at the ground, loaded down with books
and bent under the weight of all his concerns. Lucia could not
imagine what they could be, because he looked healthy, had
reached the pinnacle of his academic career, and would be able
to retire with the means to ensure a comfortable old age. The
only financial burden he had was his father, Joseph Bowmaster,
who lived in a senior residence fifteen minutes away, and whom
Richard phoned every day and visited a couple of times a week.
Although Joseph was ninety-six and confined to a wheelchair,

he had more fire in his belly and mental lucidity than many half his age. He spent his time writing letters of advice to Barack Obama.

Lucia suspected that Richard's taciturn appearance hid a store of kindness and a well-disguised wish to help without any fuss, from discreetly serving at a charity soup kitchen to volunteering to monitor the parakeets in the cemetery. Richard must surely have owed that side of his character to his father. Joseph would never allow a son of his to go through life without embracing some worthy cause. In the beginning, Lucia studied Richard to try to find any openings to secure his friendship, but as she was not drawn to the charity soup kitchen or any species of parrot, all they shared was their work, and she could not find a way to insinuate herself into his life. She was not offended by Richard's lack of interest, because he equally ignored the attentions of his female colleagues and the hordes of young girls at the university. His hermit's life was a mystery: Who knew what secrets it concealed? How could he have lived six decades without any unsettling challenges, protected by his armadillo's hide?

By contrast, she was proud of the dramas in her past and wished for an interesting existence in her future. She mistrusted happiness on principle; she found it rather kitschy. She was content to be more or less satisfied. Richard had spent a long period in Brazil, where, to judge by a photograph Lucia had seen, he had been married to a voluptuous young woman, yet neither the exuberance of that country nor that mysterious woman seemed to have rubbed off on him. Despite his odd behavior, Richard always made a good impression. In her description of him to her daughter, Lucia said that he was *liviano de sangre*— light blooded—a Chilean expression for someone who is good natured and makes himself loved without meaning to and for no obvious reason. "He's a strange sort, Daniela. He lives alone with four cats." She added, "He doesn't know it yet, but when I leave he'll also have to look after Marcelo." She had thought this over carefully. It would be heart wrenching, but she couldn't drag an aged Chihuahua around the world with her.

Richard

Whenever Richard Bowmaster reached home in the evening, by bicycle if the weather permitted, otherwise by subway, he first attended to the four cats. They were not exactly affectionate and had been adopted from the Humane Society to solve his mouse problem. He had taken this step as a logical measure, devoid of any sentimentality, and yet the felines became his inseparable companions. He had obtained them neutered, vaccinated, with a chip injected under their skin. They also had names, but to simplify matters he called them with numbers in Portuguese: Um, Dois, Três, and Quatro. He fed them and cleaned out their litter tray, then listened to the news while he made his supper on the large multiuse kitchen table. After eating he would play the piano for a while, sometimes feeling inspired, other times simply as a discipline.

In theory, his house had a place for everything, and everything was in its place, but in practice the papers, magazines, and books proliferated like phantoms in a nightmare. Every morning there were more of them, and occasionally publications or loose sheets appeared that he had never seen before, and he had no idea how they had ended up in his house. Later on he would read, prepare his classes, correct his students' homework and his essays on politics. His academic career was based on his persistence in researching and publishing rather than on his vocation as a teacher. This meant he found it impossible to explain the devotion his students showed him, even after graduating. He kept his computer in the kitchen and the printer in an unused room on the third floor, where the only piece of furniture was a table for the machine. Luckily he lived alone and so did not have to explain the curious distribution of his office equipment, since few would understand his determination to get exercise by going up and down the steep stairs. In any case, he was forced to think twice before printing anything unnecessary, out of respect for the trees sacrificed to make paper.

During nights of insomnia, when he could not manage to seduce the piano and the keys seemed to play whatever they wished, he gave in to the secret vice of memorizing and writing poetry. To do this he used very little paper, writing by hand in school exercise books, which he filled with poems he later abandoned, and a couple of luxury, leather-bound notebooks where he copied out his best verses with the idea of polishing them to perfection in the future. But that future never arrived: the thought of rereading them made his stomach twinge. He had studied Japanese to be able to enjoy haiku in the original, and while he could read and understand the language, he would have thought it presumptuous to try to speak it. He was proud of being a polyglot. He had learned Portuguese as a child with his mother's family and later perfected it with his wife, Anita. He had acquired some French for romantic reasons and some Spanish out of professional necessity. His first great passion, at the age of nineteen, had been for a French woman eight years older than himself whom he met in a New York bar and followed to Paris. The passion quickly cooled, but for convenience they lived together in a garret in the Latin Quarter long enough for him to attain the basics of carnal knowledge and of the language, which he spoke with a barbarous accent. His Spanish came from books and the street; there were Latinos everywhere in New York, but these immigrants rarely understood the Berlitz school pronunciation that he had studied. Nor could he follow them much beyond what he needed to order food in a restaurant. Apparently almost all the waiters in the country were Spanish speakers.

BY DAWN ON SATURDAY, after the worst of the storm had moved on, Richard awoke with the sour aftertaste of having offended Lucia the evening before when he coldly dismissed her fears. He would have liked to be with her while outside the wind and snow lashed the house. Why had he been so abrupt with her? Afraid of falling into the trap of romanticism, which he had avoided for twenty-five years, he never asked himself why he rejected love, because the answer seemed obvious: it was his inescapable penance. Over time he had grown used to his monkish habits and the inner silence of those who live and sleep alone. After hanging up the phone with Lucia he had felt an urge to appear at the basement door with a thermos of tea to keep her company. He was intrigued by this childish fear in a woman who had experienced a fair amount of drama in her life and who seemed invulnerable. He would have liked to probe this breach in Lucia's fortress but was prevented from doing so by a sense of danger, as if by giving in to this impulse he would find himself on uncertain ground. The feeling of danger was still there. Nothing new in that. Every so often he fell prey to an irrational anxiety, which was why he had his green pills. At such times he felt he was plunging unavoidably into the icy depths of the sea, with no one nearby to stretch out a hand to pull him back to the surface. These fatalistic premonitions had begun in Brazil, brought on by Anita, who lived on the lookout for any sign from the Great Beyond. In the past he had often suffered from these attacks, but had learned to control them.

The instructions given on radio and TV were to remain indoors until the streets had been cleared. Manhattan was still semiparalyzed, with most stores closed, but the subway and buses were running again. Other states were in a worse situation than New York, with houses destroyed, trees uprooted, neighborhoods cut off, and some areas without gas or electricity. The inhabitants had gone back two centuries in a few hours. By comparison, in Brooklyn they had been lucky. Richard went out to clear off the snow from his car before it turned to ice and would need to be scraped off. After returning, he put out food for the cats and made the breakfast he ate every day: oatmeal with almond milk and fruit. He settled down to work on his article about the economic crisis in Brazil that international observers had detected in the run-up to the Olympic Games. He had a student's thesis to review but would do so later, since he had the whole day before him.

At around three in the afternoon, he realized that one of the cats was missing. Whenever Richard was at home, they made sure to stay close by him. His relationship with them was one of mutual indifference, except with Dois, the only female, who took advantage of the slightest opportunity to jump up and settle herself near him so that he would stroke her. The three males were independent; they had understood from the outset that they were not pets and that their duty was to hunt mice. Richard could see that Um and Quatro were prowling around the kitchen, but there was no sign of Três. Dois was stretched out on the table next to his computer, one of her favorite spots.

He looked throughout the house for the missing male, giving the whistle they all recognized. He found him sprawled out on the second-floor landing, with pink froth around his nostrils. "Come on, Três, get up. What's wrong with you, my boy?" He managed to set him on his feet, and the cat staggered a few drunken steps before collapsing again. There were flecks of vomit everywhere, which often happened, as sometimes the cats did not properly digest the rodents' tiny bones. He carried Três to the kitchen, where he tried in vain to make him drink water. While in the midst of doing this, Três's four legs went rigid and he started to convulse. Richard understood these were symptoms of poisoning. He quickly ran through a mental list of the toxic substances in the house, all of them safely stored. It took him several minutes before he found the cause in the cabinet under the kitchen sink, where he had stored the car's antifreeze. Some of the fluid had leaked, and Três must have licked it, because there were paw prints on the floor. Richard was sure he had closed the container and the cabinet door properly. He could not understand how the accident had happened, but he'd worry about that later. For now what was most urgent was to take care of the cat; antifreeze was lethal.

Traffic was restricted except for emergencies, which was exactly what this was. He looked up the address of the nearest veterinary hospital, which he remembered passing by at some point. He wrapped the cat in a blanket and put him in his car. He was glad he had brushed the snow off that morning, and relieved the disaster had not occurred the day before while the blizzard was raging. Brooklyn had become a Nordic city, white on white, the angles softened by the snow, empty streets, and a strange peace, as if nature were yawning. "Don't you dare get the idea of dying, Três, please. You're a proletarian cat, you've got steel guts, a bit of antifreeze is nothing, hang in there," Richard encouraged him as he drove with painful slowness through the snow, conscious that each extra minute could prove fatal for Três. "Stay calm, pal, hang on. I can't go any quicker, because if we skid we're done for. We're almost there. I'm sorry I can't go any faster . . ."

A journey that would normally have taken twenty minutes took twice as long. By the time he finally arrived at the clinic, it was snowing again and Três was being shaken with fresh convulsions, bringing up more pink froth. The cat was seen by an efficient veterinarian of few gestures or words. She showed no optimism about the cat or sympathy for his owner. His negligence had caused the accident, she told her assistant in a low voice, although not so low that Richard did not hear. On another occasion he would have reacted to this caustic comment, but a powerful wave of bad memories caught him off guard, and he remained silent, humiliated. This was not the first time that his negligence had proved fatal. From that terrible moment on, he had become so careful and had taken so many precautions that he often felt he went through life walking on eggshells. The vet explained that there was little she could do. The blood and urine tests would show whether the damage to the kidneys was irreversible, in which case the cat was going to suffer and it would be better to give it a dignified end. It had to stay at the clinic; there would be a definitive diagnosis in a couple of days, but he should prepare himself for bad news. Richard nodded, on the verge of tears. He said goodbye to Três with his heart in a knot, feeling the vet's hard look from behind: an accusation and a sentence rolled into one.

He handed his credit card for the initial deposit to the receptionist, a young woman with carrot-colored hair and a ring in her nose. When she saw how he was shaking, she took pity on him, reassuring him that his pet would be very well looked after, and pointed out the coffee machine. Faced with this gesture of minimal kindness, Richard was overwhelmed by a disproportionate sense of gratitude and let out a deep sob. If anyone had asked him his feelings toward his four pets, he would have answered that he fulfilled his duty by feeding them and cleaning their litter tray. His relationship with the cats was no more than polite, except with Dois, who demanded affection. That was all. Never had he imagined he would come to appreciate those aloof felines as part of the family he did not have. He sat on a chair in the waiting room and drank a cup of watery, bitter coffee while the receptionist looked on sympathetically. After taking two of the green pills for his nerves, and a pink one for his stomach acidity, he gradually regained control. He had to get home.

THE CAR HEADLIGHTS REVEALED a desolate cityscape as Richard drove cautiously in the twilight, peering out through the semicircle free of frost on the windshield. The streets seemed like those of an unknown city; for a minute he thought he was lost, even though he had taken this route before. Time seemed at a standstill. The hum of the heating blower and the relentless back-and-forth motion of the windshield wipers gave the impression that the car was suspended in a fog. With the unsettling sensation of being the only soul alive in an abandoned world, Richard was talking to himself as he drove, his head filled with sounds and gloomy thoughts about the inevitable horrors of the world and of his own life in particular. How much longer was he going to live, and in what state? If a man lives long enough, he gets prostate cancer. If he lives longer, his brain starts to disintegrate. Richard had reached the age of fear: no longer attracted by travel, he was tied to the comfort of home. He did not want any shocks and was scared of getting lost, or of dying and no one finding his body until a couple of weeks later, by which time the cats would have devoured most of what remained. The possibility of being found in a puddle of putrefying viscera terrified him so much that he had agreed with his neighbor, a widow with a steely temperament and a sentimental heart, that he would send her a text every night. He had given her a key so that if he did not text her for two days in a row, she could come and take a look around his house. The text message was just two words: *Still alive.* She was under no obligation to reply but, feeling a similar fear, always did so with three words: *Shit, me too.* The most dreadful thing about death was the idea of eternity. Dead forever, how terrible.

Richard was afraid the cloud of anxiety that often enveloped him was closing in again. Whenever it appeared, he took his pulse and either could not find one or discovered it was racing. In the past he had suffered from panic attacks, which were so similar to heart attacks that he ended up in the hospital, but in recent years they had not returned, thanks to the green pills and because he had learned to control them. He focused on visualizing the black cloud above his head being pierced by powerful spears of light, like the divine rays in religious pictures. Thanks to that image and some breathing exercises, he would manage to disperse the cloud, but this time there was no need to have recourse to that technique, because he soon accepted the novelty of his situation. He saw himself from afar, as if in a film in which he was not the protagonist but a spectator.

For years now he had lived in a perfectly controlled environment where there were no surprises or upheavals, and yet he had not completely forgotten the fascination of the few adventures he had known in his youth, particularly his mad passion for Anita. He smiled at his apprehension, because driving a few blocks through Brooklyn in bad weather was not exactly an adventure. At that moment he clearly saw how small and limited his existence had become. Then he really did feel afraid, afraid of having wasted so many years shut in on himself, afraid of the speed with which time was passing and old age and death were approaching. His glasses misted over with perspiration or tears; he tore them off and tried to wipe them on his sleeve. It was growing dark and visibility was poor. Clutching the wheel with his left hand, he tried to put his glasses back on with the right, but the gloves made him fumble, and the glasses fell down between the pedals. A curse issued from deep in his guts.

At that moment, when he was briefly distracted as he groped on the floor for his glasses, a white car that was almost invisible in the snow stopped at an intersection in front of him. Richard crashed into the back of it. The impact was so unexpected and overwhelming that for a fraction of a second he lost consciousness. He recovered at once, but felt as he did earlier that he was outside his body, with his heart racing, bathed in sweat, his skin burning hot, his shirt stuck to his back.

Despite this physical discomfort, his mind was on another plane, separated from this reality. The character in the film kept on muttering curses inside the car while he, a spectator in another dimension, was evaluating the situation coolly and calmly. He was sure it was only a minor accident. Both vehicles had been going very slowly. He had to find his glasses, get out of the car, and talk to the other driver in a civilized manner. After all, this was what auto insurance was for.

As he clambered out of the car he slipped on the icy sidewalk, and if he had not clung to the door he would have ended up flat on his back. He realized that even if he had braked he probably would have crashed, as he would have glided on along the ice for three or four yards before coming to a halt. Since the other vehicle, a Lexus SC, had been hit from behind, the force of the collision had knocked it forward. With the wind against him, Richard struggled the few yards separating him from the other driver, who had also emerged from the car. At first he thought it was a child too young to have a driver's license, but as he drew closer he saw it was a tiny young woman. She was wearing pants, black rubber boots, and a parka that was far too big for her. Her face was obscured by the hood.

"It was my fault. I'm sorry, I didn't see you. My insurance will pay for the repairs," said Richard.

The young woman glanced at the broken light and the dented, half-open trunk. She tried in vain to close it properly, while Richard went on about the insurance.

"If you want we can call the police, but there's no need. Here, take my card, it's easy to find me."

She did not seem to hear him. Visibly agitated, she continued beating on the trunk with her fists until she was finally convinced she could not close it. Then she rushed back to the driver's seat as quickly as the gusts of wind allowed, followed by Richard, who was insisting on giving her his contact details. She got into the Lexus without even looking at him, but he tossed his card into her lap just as she put her foot down on the accelerator without even closing the door, which banged into Richard, leaving him on his backside in the street. The vehicle turned the corner and disappeared. Richard struggled to his feet, squeezing the arm hit by the door. Conclusion: it had been a disastrous day; all he needed now was for the cat to die.

Lucia, Richard, Evelyn

By nine thirty that night, Richard, who was used to rising at five each morning to go to the gym, would normally have been in bed counting sheep, with Dois purring alongside him. But the day's unfortunate events had left him in such turmoil that he prepared for the torment of insomnia by watching something mindless on TV. That would clear his worries. He had reached the obligatory sex scene, where the director had struggled with the script as desperately as the actors were struggling in bed to excite the viewer but instead merely freezing the action. "Come on, get on with the story!" he shouted at the screen, feeling nostalgic for the days when movies hinted at fornication by showing a door closing discreetly, a lamp being switched off, or a cigarette burning down in an abandoned ashtray.

Just then his doorbell rang unexpectedly. Richard glanced at his watch: 9:40 p.m. Not even the Jehovah's Witnesses, who for the past couple of weeks had been in the neighborhood trying to

drum up possible converts, would risk canvassing so late. Puz-
zled, he went to the front door without switching on the outside light and peered through the glass. All he could see in the
darkness was a muffled shape. He was going to retreat when a
second loud ring startled him. Hastily he turned on the light and
opened the door.

Standing in the dimly illuminated entrance, framed by the
darkness, was the girl in the parka. Richard recognized her at
once. Hunched up, her head sunk between her shoulders and
face covered by the hood, she looked even smaller than she had a
few hours earlier. Richard murmured a "Yes?" but her only reply
was to hand him the card he had thrown into her car, which contained his name, academic title, and office and home addresses.
He stood there with the card in his hand, not knowing what to
do for a minute that seemed to last forever. Eventually, becoming
aware of the wind and snow sweeping in through the open door,
he reacted and stepped to one side, inviting the girl in. Closing
the door behind her, he studied her again in amazement.

"Y-you didn't have to come here. You need to call the insurance company directly," he stuttered.

She said nothing. Standing in the doorway without looking
at him, she seemed like some insistent visitor from beyond the
grave. Richard went on speaking about the insurance, but she
did not react.

"Do you speak English?" he finally asked.

A few more seconds' silence. Richard repeated his question
in Spanish, because her size suggested she might be from Central America, although she could also be from Southeast Asia.
She responded in an unintelligible murmur that sounded somewhat monotonous. Losing patience, Richard decided to ask her

into the kitchen, where there was more light and they might be able to communicate. She followed him, eyes on the floor and stepping exactly where he did, as if balancing on a tightrope. In the kitchen, Richard pushed aside the papers on the table and offered her a seat on one of the stools.

"I'm so sorry I rear-ended you, I hope you weren't hurt," he said.

When again there was no reaction, he translated his comment into mangled Spanish. She shook her head. Richard continued with his despairing efforts to discover why she had come to his house so late at night. As the slight accident did not justify her terrified state, he surmised she was running away from someone or something.

"What's your name?" he asked.

Struggling to pronounce every syllable, she managed to get out "Evelyn Ortega." Feeling that the situation was getting beyond him, Richard realized he needed help in dealing with this inopportune visitor. Hours later, when he was able to analyze all that had happened, he was surprised that the only thing that had occurred to him was to call Lucia, since she of course spoke Spanish. In the time he had known her, she had proved to be a competent professional, and yet he had no reason to think she might be able to handle such an unforeseen event as this.

THE SOUND OF THE TELEPHONE made Lucia Maraz jump. The only call she could possibly expect at ten o'clock at night would be from her daughter, Daniela, but this was Richard asking her to come urgently upstairs. After spending the whole day shivering, Lucia had finally gotten warm in her bed and had no intention of leaving her nest to respond to the peremptory call from the man who had not only condemned her to live in an igloo but the night before had ignored her plea for company in the storm. There was no direct access from the basement to the rest of the property; she would have to get dressed, struggle through the snow, and climb twelve slippery steps up to the front of the house. Richard was not worth all that effort.

A week earlier they had argued because the water in the dog's bowl was frozen in the morning, but not even this convincing proof had induced him to raise the thermostat. Richard had merely lent her an electric blanket that had not been used for decades. When she plugged it in, it emitted a cloud of foul smoke and blew one of the fuses. The cold was Lucia's most recent complaint, but there had been others. At night she could hear a chorus of mice in the walls, which according to her landlord was impossible since the cats dealt with all the rodents, and so the noises must have come from rusty pipes or dry rot.

"I'm sorry to bother you so late, Lucia, but I need you to come. I've got a serious problem," Richard announced on the phone.

"What sort of problem? Unless you're bleeding to death, it'll have to wait until tomorrow."

"A hysterical Latin American woman has invaded my house, and I don't know what to do with her. Maybe you could help. I can barely understand her."

"All right, get out a shovel and come and dig me out of here," Lucia said, relenting, her curiosity aroused.

A short while later, Richard, bundled up like an Inuit, had rescued his lodger and taken her and Marcelo upstairs to his house, which was almost as cold as the basement. Cursing how miserly he was when it came to heating, Lucia followed him to the kitchen, which she was familiar with from previous brief visits. Shortly after arriving in Brooklyn she had been there, intending to cook him a vegetarian meal, but Richard turned out to be hard to please. She considered vegetarianism an eccentricity of people who had never been really hungry, but nevertheless took great care in preparing his meal. Richard ate two platefuls, thanked her politely, and never returned the favor. This was when Lucia had been able to see how restricted her landlord's way of life was. Among the few pieces of unremarkable furniture in dubious condition, pride of place went to a shiny grand piano. On Thursday and Saturday afternoons she could hear from her lair the sounds of Richard and three other musicians performing together for the sheer pleasure of playing. In her opinion, they were quite good, but she had no ear for music and next to no musical culture. She had waited several months for Richard to invite her to one of these afternoon sessions to hear the quartet, but the offer never came.

Richard occupied only the first floor, and his bedroom was the smallest in the house, seeming more like a cell with bare walls and a tiny window. The living room appeared to be a stockroom for the printed word, while the kitchen, also piled high with books, was recognizable as such thanks to a sink and an unreliable gas stove that had the habit of turning itself on without any human intervention and was impossible to fix because there were no spare parts for it anymore.

THE PERSON RICHARD INTRODUCED as Evelyn Ortega was extremely short and was seated at the rough wooden table that served as both desk and dining space, her legs dangling from the stool. Ensconced in a garish yellow parka with the hood up and firefighter's boots, she did not appear to be hysterical so much as stunned. She ignored the newcomer's arrival, but Lucia went over and held out her hand, without letting go of Marcelo or taking her eyes off the cats, who were observing the dog closely, hackles raised.

"Lucia Maraz. I'm Chilean, the tenant from the basement," she said.

A trembling childlike hand poked out of the yellow parka and feebly shook Lucia's.

"A pleasure to meet you," said Lucia.

"I bumped into the back of her car when I was returning from the vet's. One of the cats was poisoned with antifreeze. I think she's very scared. Can you talk to her? I'm sure you'll understand her."

"Why?"

"You're a woman, aren't you? And you speak her language better than I do."

Lucia addressed the young visitor in Spanish to find out where she came from and what had happened to her. The stranger woke from her catatonic state and pushed back the hood but did not raise her eyes from the floor. She was a very small, thin young woman, her face as delicate as her hands, her skin the color of pale pine, and her black hair coiled at the nape of her neck. Lucia guessed she must be a native Central American, possibly Maya, although the characteristics of the race— an aquiline nose, pronounced cheekbones, and almond-shaped eyes—were not very prominent in her. On the principle that foreigners understand English if you shout at them loudly enough, Richard told her she could trust Lucia. In this case it worked, because the girl responded in a singsong voice that she was from Guatemala. She stammered so badly that she could barely string her words together; by the time she had finished a sentence it was hard to remember how it began.

Lucia managed to understand that Evelyn had taken the car belonging to her employer, someone called Frank Leroy, without permission, while he was traveling and his wife, Cheryl, was taking a nap. With difficulty, the young Guatemalan added that after Richard had crashed into her she had been forced to abandon her plan of going home without mentioning what she had done. It was not Cheryl she was frightened of, but Frank Leroy; he was a vicious, dangerous character. Her mind in turmoil, she had driven all over the neighborhood trying to come up with a solution. The dented trunk would not shut properly and had even sprung wide open on a couple of occasions; she had been obliged to pull over and improvise tying it up with the belt from her parka. She had spent the rest of the afternoon and evening parked in different spots, but only stayed a short time to avoid drawing attention to herself. During one of these stops she finally noticed the card Richard had given her, and had come to his house as a last resort.

While Evelyn remained seated on the kitchen stool, Richard took Lucia aside and whispered that their visitor either had mental problems or was drugged.

"Why do you think that?" she asked, also in a whisper.

"She can hardly speak, Lucia."

"Don't you realize she has a bad stammer?"

"Are you sure?"

"Of course I am! And besides, she's terrified, poor thing."

"How can we help her?" asked Richard.

"It's very late, there's nothing we can do now. How about if she stays here tonight, and tomorrow we take her back to her employers' house and explain about the accident? Your insurance will pay for the damage. They'll have no reason to object."

"Except that she took the car without permission. They're bound to throw her out."

"We'll see tomorrow. For now we have to calm her fears," Lucia decided.

The interrogation she gave the young girl cleared up some aspects of her relationship with her employers, the Leroys. Evelyn did not have fixed hours in their house: she in theory worked from nine to five, but in practice spent the whole day with the child she was looking after and even slept next to him so that she could attend to him if need be. In other words, she worked the equivalent of three normal shifts. According to Richard and Lucia's calculations, she was paid much less in cash than she was entitled to. To them it seemed like forced labor or slavery, but this did not matter to Evelyn. More important was that she had somewhere to live and was safe. Mrs. Leroy treated her very well, and Mr. Leroy only occasionally gave her orders. The rest of the time he ignored her. He treated his wife and child in exactly the same way. He was a violent man and everyone in the house, especially his wife, trembled in his presence. If he found out she had taken the car . . .

"Calm down, Evelyn, nothing's going to happen to you," Lucia told her.

"You can sleep here. This isn't as bad as you think. We'll help you," added Richard.

"For now what we need is a drink. Do you have anything, Richard? Beer for example?" asked Lucia.

"You know I don't drink."

"I suppose you do have some weed. That would help. Evelyn is dead on her feet, and I'm dying of cold."

Richard decided this was not the moment to be a prig and brought a tin of weed brownies out of the fridge. A couple of years earlier, due to his ulcer and headaches, he had been given a prescription that allowed him to buy marijuana for medicinal purposes. After splitting one of the brownies in three, Richard and Lucia each took a piece and gave one to Evelyn Ortega to lift her spirits. Lucia thought it best to explain what was in the brownie, but the girl ate it on trust, without any questions.

"You must be hungry, Evelyn. I'm sure that with all this confusion you haven't eaten. We need something hot," Lucia decided, opening the fridge. "There's nothing here, Richard!"

"I buy what I need for the week on Saturdays, but today I couldn't go because of the snow and the cat."

Lucia remembered the soup, the remains of which were still in her basement apartment, but did not have the heart to go outside again, descend to the catacombs, and return balancing a heavy pot on the icy stairs. Scraping together what little she could find in Richard's kitchen, she prepared toast with gluten-free bread and served it with mugs of lactose-free milk, while Richard strode up and down the kitchen muttering to himself, and Evelyn compulsively stroked Marcelo's back.

Forty-five minutes later, the three of them were relaxing in a pleasant daze in front of the lit fire. Richard was sitting on the floor with his back against the wall, and Lucia lay down on a blanket, her head across his legs. This familiarity would normally never have happened, since Richard did not encourage physical contact, least of all on his thighs. For Lucia, this was the first time in months she had smelled a man and felt his warmth, the rough texture of a pair of jeans on her cheek, and the softness of an old cashmere cardigan within reach. She would have preferred to be in bed with him but blocked out that image with a sigh, resigned to enjoying him fully dressed while she imagined the remote possibility of embarking down the winding path of sensuality with him. I'm a bit dizzy, it must be the brownie, she decided.

Evelyn was slumped on the only big cushion, with Marcelo on her lap, and looked as diminutive as a jockey. The piece of brownie she had eaten had had the opposite effect on her as it had on Richard and Lucia. While they relaxed with their eyes half-closed, struggling to stay awake, Evelyn began to pour out her tragic life story in stammering speech. It turned out she knew more English than it had at first seemed but hadn't managed to get the words out because she had been too nervous. Now calmer, she was able to make herself understood with surprising eloquence in Spanglish, that mixture of Spanish and English that is the official language of many Latinos in the United States.

Outside, the snow settled gently on the white Lexus as Evelyn told them of her past. Over the next three days, as the storm wearied of punishing the land and dissolved far out to sea, the lives of Lucia Maraz, Richard Bowmaster, and Evelyn Ortega would become inextricably linked.

Evelyn

Guatemala, 1992–2008

reen, an entire world of green, the buzzing of mosqui-
toes, the screeching of cockatoos, a murmur of reeds
in the breeze, sticky fragrant ripe fruit, wood smoke
and roasted coffee beans, constant heat, and moisture on her
skin and in her dreams. This was how Evelyn Ortega remembered her small village, Monja Blanca del Valle. Brightly painted
walls, textile looms, flowers and birds, color piled on color, a
rainbow of hues. And everywhere, at all times, her grandmother,
Concepcion Montoya, the most decent and hardworking Catholic woman, according to Father Benito, who knew everything
because he was not only a Jesuit but a Basque, and proud of
it, as he used to say with the irony typical of his homeland but
that no one there seemed to appreciate. Father Benito had seen
a lot of the world, and all of Guatemala. He knew the life the
peasants led, because he was so deeply rooted in it. He would
not have changed his own life for anything. He loved his com-

munity, his great clan, as he called it. Guatemala was the most beautiful country in the world, he used to say, the Garden of Eden blessed by God but mistreated by humanity, and he would add that his favorite village was Monja Blanca del Valle, which owed its name to the national flower, the whitest and purest of orchids.

The priest had witnessed the massacre of indigenous peoples in the eighties, with its systematic torture, mass burials, villages reduced to ashes where not even domestic animals survived. He saw how the soldiers, their faces blackened to avoid being recognized, crushed all attempts at revolt, every spark of hope in other human beings as poor as they themselves, just to keep things as they had always been. Far from hardening him, this experience softened his heart. He overlaid the atrocious images of that past with the fantastic spectacle of the country he loved, with its infinite variety of flowers and birds, its landscapes of lakes, forests, and mountains, its cloudless skies. The villagers accepted him as one of their own, because he truly was. They said he was still alive thanks to the miraculous Virgin of the Assumption, Guatemala's patron saint. What other explanation could there be, when it was rumored that he had hidden guerrilla fighters and they had heard him mention agrarian reform from the pulpit? For far less than that, others had had their tongues cut out and their eyes gouged from their sockets. The ever-present skeptics muttered that the Virgin had nothing to do with it: the priest must have been sent by the CIA, or protected by the narcos, or was simply an army informer. They never dared suggest any of this within his hearing, because the Basque Jesuit, despite having a fakir's body, would have been able to break their nose with a single blow. No one had greater moral authority than this priest with the harsh foreign accent. If he respected Concepcion Montoya as a saint, it must have been for a reason, thought Evelyn, although she had lived, worked, and slept for so long beside her grandmother that to her she seemed a lot more human than divine.

After Miriam, Evelyn's mother, left to head north, that indomitable grandmother had looked after her and her two older brothers. Evelyn was still a newborn when her father emigrated in search of work. They had no news about him for several years, until they heard rumors he had settled in California and had another family, although nobody could confirm it. Evelyn was six when her mother also disappeared without saying goodbye. Miriam fled the village very early one morning, afraid her determination would not survive a last embrace with her children. That was what their grandmother explained to them whenever they asked, and she added that thanks to their mother's sacrifice they could eat every day, go to school, and receive parcels from Chicago, containing toys, Nike sneakers, and sweets.

The day Miriam left was marked on the faded Coca-Cola calendar for 1998 still nailed to the wall of Concepcion's hut. Her elder two children, Gregorio, age ten, and Andres, who was eight, grew tired of waiting for Miriam to return and made do with her postcards and with hearing her choked-up voice on the post office telephone at Christmas or on their birthdays as she apologized yet again for not keeping her promise of coming back to see them. Evelyn continued believing that one day her mother would return with enough money to build her grandma a decent house. All three children had idolized their mother, but none as much as Evelyn, who could not clearly recall either her appearance or her voice, but constantly imagined them. Miriam sent photographs, but she had changed a lot over the years, put on weight, dyed her hair with yellow streaks, shaved off her eyebrows and painted new ones higher on her forehead, which made her look constantly surprised or scared.

The Ortegas were not the only ones without a father or mother: two-thirds of the children in their school were in the same situation. In the past it had been only the men who emigrated in search of work, but in recent years the women had been leaving as well. According to Father Benito, the emigrants sent back billions of dollars each year to maintain their families, and in so doing ended up contributing to the stability of the government and the indifference of the rich. Few of the village children finished school: the boys left to look for work or ended up in gangs or on drugs, while the girls got pregnant, moved away for work, or were recruited as prostitutes. The school had very few resources and were it not for the evangelical missionaries who competed unfairly with Father Benito thanks to funds from abroad, it would not even have had workbooks or pencils.

Father Benito was in the habit of installing himself in the village's only bar with a beer that lasted all night and talking to the locals about the ruthless repression launched against the indigenous peoples, which had lasted for thirty years and sowed the seeds of disaster. "Everyone has to be bribed, from the topmost politicians to the lowest policeman, not to mention all the delinquency and crime," complained the priest, who was prone to exaggerate. There was always somebody there to suggest that if he did not like Guatemala he should go back to his own country. "What are you saying, you wretch, haven't I told you a thousand times that this is my country?"

AT THE AGE OF FOURTEEN, Gregorio Ortega, Evelyn's eldest brother, quit school for good. Left to his own devices, he wandered the streets with other boys, his eyes glassy and his brain befuddled from sniffing glue, gasoline, paint stripper, or anything else he could get hold of. He spent his time stealing, fighting, and pestering girls. When he grew bored he stood by the roadside and asked a truck driver for a lift. They took him to other towns where no one knew him, and when he returned he brought ill-gotten money. If she caught him, Concepcion Montoya gave him a good hiding, which her grandson accepted because he still depended on her to feed him. From time to time the police picked him up in a roundup of young drug users, gave him an even worse thrashing, and put him in a cell on bread and water, until he was rescued by Father Benito when he happened to pass by on his rounds. The priest was an incurable optimist who against all evidence to the contrary kept his faith in the capacity of human beings to reform. The police would give the boy one last kick in the backside and hand him over, scared, covered in bruises, and riddled with lice. The Basque threw him into his pickup with a volley of insults and took him to the only taco stall in the village to fill his stomach, all the while prophesying in his doom-laden Jesuit manner that the boy would have a terrible life and an early death if he continued with his aberrant behavior.

Neither his grandmother's beatings, his time in jail, nor the priest's dire warnings served as a lesson to Gregorio. He went on drifting. The neighbors who had known him all his life avoided him. If he had no quetzales in his pocket, he would turn up at his grandmother's looking sheepish, feigning humility, and eat the same beans, chilies, and corn that were on offer every day in her home. Concepcion had more common sense than Father Benito and soon gave up trying to preach about impossible virtues to her grandson. He had no head for learning and no wish to take up a trade; there was no honest work anywhere for boys like him. She had to confess to Miriam that her son had abandoned his studies but avoided wounding her with the whole truth, since there was very little his mother could do from afar. Every night Concepcion prayed on her knees with her two other grandchildren, Andres and Evelyn, that Gregorio would survive until he was eighteen, when he would be called up for compulsory military service. Although she had a deep loathing of the armed forces, she thought that perhaps conscription could set him back on the right path.

GREGORIO ORTEGA DID NOT MANAGE to benefit from his grandmother's prayers or from the candles lit in the church in his name. Only a few months before he was due to be called for military service, he succeeded in being accepted into the MS-13, better known as the Mara Salvatrucha, the most vicious of Guatemala's gangs. He had to take the blood oath: loyalty to his comrades above everything else—family, women, drugs, and money. He went through the tough initiation ceremony: a tremendous beating meted out by members of the gang to test his spirit, which left him more dead than alive. Several of his teeth were broken and he passed blood for two weeks, but once he had recovered he won the right to his first MS-13 gang tattoo. Over time, as he accumulated crimes and won respect, he hoped to end up like the most fanatical gang members, his entire body and face covered in tattoos. He had heard that in Pelican Bay prison in California there was a Salvadorean who was blind because he had had the whites of his eyes tattooed.

In its twenty-something years of existence, the MS-13, which had started out in Los Angeles, had spread its tentacles to the rest of the United States, Mexico, and Central America. The Mara Salvatrucha had more than sixty thousand members, all of them dedicated to killing, extortion, kidnapping, and the trafficking of arms, drugs, and human beings. They had such a brutal reputation that other gangs tended to use them to do their dirty work. In Central America, where they enjoyed greater impunity than in the United States or Mexico, the gang members marked their territory by leaving a trail of mangled dead bodies. Neither the police nor the army dared confront them. In the village, Concepcion Montoya's neighbors knew that her eldest grandson had joined the MS-13, but only spoke of it in whispers behind closed doors, for fear of reprisals. At first they wanted nothing to do with the unfortunate grandmother and her other grandchildren. Nobody wanted any trouble. Ever since the years of repression they had grown accustomed to living in fear and found it hard to imagine things could be any different. The MS-13 was another plague, another punishment for the sin of existing, another reason to tread carefully. Concepcion faced their rejection with head held high, pretending not to notice the silence surrounding her in the street or at the market, where she went on Saturdays to sell her tamales and the secondhand clothes Miriam sent from Chicago. Gregorio soon left the region; for some time he was no longer to be seen, and so the fear he aroused in the village gradually subsided. They had more pressing problems.

Concepcion forbade her grandchildren to mention their elder brother. Don't go looking for trouble, she warned.

When a year later Gregorio returned for the first time, he had two gold teeth, a shaved head, and tattoos of barbed wire on his neck and numbers, letters, and skulls on his knuckles. He seemed to have grown several inches, and where before he'd had the build and skin of a youngster, now he sported a gang member's muscles and scars. In the Salvatrucha he had found a family and an identity. He did not have to go around begging; he could have whatever he wanted—money, drugs, alcohol, guns, and women, all within easy reach. He could scarcely recall the days of his humiliation. Striding into his grandmother's hut shouting that he was back, he found her shucking corn with Evelyn, while Andres, who had not grown much and looked young for his age, was doing his homework at the far end of the only table in the hut.

Andres leapt up, gawping with fear and admiration at his elder brother. Gregorio greeted him with an affectionate push, then shadowboxed him into a corner, showing off the tattoos on his fists. He approached Evelyn to give her a hug but stopped short. The gang had taught him to mistrust and be scornful of women in general, but his sister was an exception. Unlike the rest of them, she was good and pure, a girl who had not yet matured. When he thought of the dangers lying in wait for her simply because she had been born female, he was glad he would be able to protect her. No one would dare do her any harm, because they would have to face the gang and him.

His grandmother managed to find her voice and asked why he had reappeared. Gregorio studied her contemptuously, and after an overlong pause replied that he had come to ask for her blessing. "May God bless you," she stammered, the words she

said every night to her grandchildren before sleep, adding in a
whisper: "and may God forgive you." The boy took a bundle of
quetzales out of the pocket of his loose jeans precariously slung
around his hips and proudly handed it to his grandmother, his
first contribution to the family income. Concepcion Montoya not
only refused to accept the banknotes but asked him not to come
again, as he set a bad example for his brother and sister. "You
ungrateful old piece of shit!" cried Gregorio, flinging the money
to the floor. He left muttering curses, and several months went
by before he saw his family again. On the rare occasions when he
was passing through the village he waited for his brother and sister hidden on a street corner to avoid being recognized, a victim
of the same insecurity that had been the cross he'd had to bear
in childhood. He had learned to hide this weakness; in the gang
it was all boasting and machismo. He would intercept Andres
and Evelyn in the throng of kids leaving school, grab them by
the arm, and drag them into a dark alleyway to give them money
and find out if they had heard anything from their mother. The
rule in the gang was that they should reject affection, chop off all
sentimentality: the family was a tie, something weighing them
down. There should be no memories or nostalgia, for they were
to become men, and men don't cry, don't complain; they don't
love, relying only on themselves. The only thing that counted
was courage; honor was defended with blood, and respect was
earned by blood. Yet despite himself, Gregorio was still linked to
his brother and sister by the memory of the years they had spent
together. He promised Evelyn a fifteenth-birthday party with
no expense spared and gave Andres a bike. For several weeks,
Andres hid it from his grandmother, until she heard about it and
forced him to confess the truth. Concepcion boxed his ears for

accepting money from someone who was a gang member, even if he was his brother, and sold the bike in the market the next day.

The combination of fear and admiration that Andres and Evelyn felt toward Gregorio would turn into paralyzing shyness in his presence. The chains with crosses dangling around his neck, his green aviator's glasses, his American boots, the tattoos spreading like a plague across his skin, his reputation as a killer, his wild life and lack of regard for pain and death, his secrets and crimes—all of this kept them in awe of him. They talked of their terrifying brother in forbidden whispers as far as possible out of their grandmother's earshot.

Concepcion was worried that Andres would follow his brother's example, but he did not have the temperament to join a gang: he was too clever, too careful and timid; his dream was to head north and prosper. He planned to earn money in the United States and live like a pauper so as to save and send dollars to Evelyn and his grandmother. Later he would give them a good life in the north, where they would live with their mother in a proper cement house with running water and electricity. To get them there he would find them a responsible smuggler who would secure passports with visas and the vaccination certificates for hepatitis and typhus that the gringos sometimes asked for. Then they would leave Guatemala safely, otherwise the journey through Mexico on foot or on a freight train roof was an acid test: they would have to face attackers armed with machetes and police with dogs, or if they fell off the railcar they could lose their legs or their lives. After that, anyone crossing the US border could die of thirst in the desert or be shot by ranchers, who went out to hunt migrants as if they were hares. These were the tales told by the youngsters who had made the journey and been deported on the Bus of Tears. They returned ravenous and exhausted, their clothes in rags, but they were not defeated: within a few days, they recovered and set off once more. Andres knew one who had tried eight times and was preparing to go again, but he himself did not have the courage to do so. He was willing to wait, because his mother had promised she would find him a guide as soon as he finished school, before he was called up for the army.

The grandmother was tired of hearing Andres's plan, but Evelyn delighted in every last detail, even though she didn't want a life elsewhere. Her village and her grandmother's shack were the only world she knew. She had no clear memory of her mother and no longer lived in expectation of her postcards or the occasional telephone call. She had no time to dream. She got up at dawn to help her grandmother, going to the well for water, sprinkling the beaten-earth floor to keep down the dust, fetching firewood for the kitchen, heating black beans if there were any left from the previous day, making corn tortillas, frying slices of the plantains that grew in their yard, then straining the sweetened coffee for Concepcion and Andres. She also had to feed the chickens and pig and hang out the clothes left soaking overnight. Andres did none of this: it was women's work. He went to school before his sister to play soccer with the other boys.

Evelyn and her grandmother understood each other without the need for words, in a shared routine of repeated gestures and methodical domestic chores. On Fridays the two of them began work at three in the morning, preparing the filling for tamales. The next day they wrapped the mixture in plantain leaves, cooked them, and took them to the market to sell. Along with all the other small businesses, Concepcion paid protection money to the gang members and crooks who operated with impunity in the region; she also occasionally had to bribe the local police. Since she earned so little this was a tiny sum, but it was always demanded with threats, and if she did not pay, the delinquents would throw her tamales into the gutter and slap her around. Between this and the cost of the ingredients, she barely made enough to feed her grandchildren. If it had not been for the money Miriam sent, they would have been destitute. On Sundays and holy days, if they were lucky enough to count on Father Benito's presence, the grandmother and her granddaughter went to sweep the church and arrange the flowers for the mass. The devout village women gave Evelyn sweets: "My, oh my, how pretty our Evelyn is becoming. You'll have to hide her, Dona Concepcion, so that no heartless man can ruin her," they would say.

AT FIRST LIGHT ON THE SECOND FRIDAY IN FEBRUARY, the body of Gregorio Ortega was found swinging from the bridge over the river, covered in dried blood and excrement. Around his neck was a piece of cardboard with the fearsome initials "MS" that everyone knew. Blue flies had already begun their disgusting banquet before the arrival of the first onlookers and three uniformed police officers. Over the next few hours the body began to stink, and by midday everyone was leaving, driven away by heat, putrefaction, and fear. The only ones left near the bridge were the police awaiting orders; a bored photographer sent from a nearby town to cover "the bloodshed," as he called it (even though this was hardly news); and Concepcion Montoya with her two grandchildren, who stood there silent and unmoving.

"Take the kids away from here," ordered the officer who seemed to be in charge of the others. "This isn't something for them to see."

But Concepcion remained rooted to her spot like an old tree in the earth. She had witnessed this kind of brutality before: her father and two brothers had been burned alive during the civil war in the eighties. After that she had thought no human cruelty could surprise her, but when a neighbor came running to tell her what was on the bridge, she dropped a pan, spilling all the tamale ingredients on the ground. For a long while now she had been expecting to hear that her eldest grandson had ended up in prison or died in a fight, but she had never anticipated such a gruesome ending for him.

"Come on, old woman, move on before I get angry," the officer insisted, pushing her away.

Rousing themselves finally from their stupor, Andres and Evelyn took their grandmother by her arms, uprooting her, and pulled her away. Concepcion had suddenly aged, dragging her feet and hunched over like an old woman. She walked with her eyes on the ground, repeating to herself, "May God bless him and forgive him, may God bless him and forgive him."

It fell to Father Benito to call Gregorio's mother, inform her of her son's tragedy, and try to console her on the telephone. Miriam sobbed without being able to understand what had happened, since the priest had followed Concepcion's precise instructions and did not supply her with any details. All he said was that it had been an accident related to organized crime, like so many random killings that took place in Guatemala on a daily basis. Gregorio was simply another victim of the raging violence. There was no point in her coming for the funeral, he said, as she would not arrive in time, but money was needed for the coffin, a plot in the cemetery, and other expenses. He would make sure he gave her son a Christian burial and would say masses for the salvation of his soul. He did not tell Miriam that Gregorio's body was in a morgue some thirty miles away, and would only be handed over to the family after the official report had been completed. This could take months, unless they paid something under the table, in which case the autopsy would be quietly forgotten. This was what part of the money was for; once again, he would take this unpleasant task on himself.

On the back of the sign around Gregorio's neck was written that this was how traitors and their families died. No one knew what Gregorio's treachery could have been. His death served as a warning to other gang members in case their loyalty was weakening, a challenge to the national police with their boasts of having crime under control, and a threat to the population at large. Father Benito learned of the message from one of the police and considered it his duty to warn Concepcion of the danger her family was in. "So what do you want us to do, Father?" was her response. She decided that Andres should accompany Evelyn to school and back, and that instead of taking the shortcut along the green path through the banana plantation they should walk along the side of the road, even though this added twenty minutes to their journey. However, Andres did not have to follow her instructions, because his sister refused to go back to school.

By then it was obvious that the sight of her brother hanging from the bridge had left a lasting mark on Evelyn's brain and her tongue. That year she would be turning fifteen. Her body was starting to acquire a grown-up woman's curves and she was at last beginning to overcome her shyness. Before Gregorio's murder she had been speaking up in class, knew the latest pop songs by heart, and was just like the other girls in the village square who would glance at the boys with feigned indifference. But after the terror of that Friday, she lost her appetite and the ability to string words together. She stammered so badly that not even her grandmother's love enabled her to be understood.

Lucia and Richard listened in horrified silence to the story of Evelyn's ordeal. She was crying quietly, overwhelmed by those memories. Unable to comfort her, Lucia tried to distract her with her own story.

Lucia

Chile, 1954–1973

The two pillars of Lucia Maraz's childhood and youth were her mother, Lena, and her brother, Enrique, before the latter was taken from her by the military coup in 1973. Her father had died in a traffic accident when Lucia was tiny, and it was as if he had never existed, although the idea of a father continued to float like a mist around his two children. Among the few memories Lucia had, so vague that perhaps they were not real ones but scenes her brother invented, was a trip to the zoo. She was on her father's shoulders, clinging on with both hands to his thick black hair as they strolled between the monkey cages. In another equally hazy memory she was on a carousel astride a unicorn while he stood beside her, an arm around her waist to steady her. Her brother and mother were nowhere to be seen in either of these images.

Lena Maraz had loved her husband from the age of seventeen with unswerving devotion. When she received the news of his death she was only able to weep for him a few hours until she discovered that the person she had just identified covered with a sheet on a metal table in a public hospital was in fact a total stranger and her marriage a monumental fraud. The same highway police officer who had informed her of what had happened later returned with a detective inspector to ask questions that seemed cruel under the circumstances and bore no relation to the accident. They had to repeat their information twice before Lena understood what they were trying to tell her. Her husband was a bigamist. In a provincial city almost a hundred miles from the capital where she lived, there was another woman as much in the dark as she was, who believed she was his legitimate spouse and the mother of his only child. For years, Lena's husband had lived a double life, shielded by his job as a traveling salesman, which offered a good pretext for his prolonged absences. Since he had married Lena first, his second relationship had no legal standing, but the son had been recognized and bore his father's surname.

Lena's mourning was transformed into a storm of resentment and retrospective jealousy. She spent months scouring the past for lies and omissions, piecing things together to explain every suspect act, every false word, every broken promise, doubting even the way they had made love. In her desire to find out about the other wife she went to the province to spy on her, only to discover she was an ordinary-looking young woman who dressed badly and wore glasses: someone very different from the courtesan of her imagination. Lena observed her from a safe distance and followed her in the street but never approached her. Some weeks later, the woman phoned to suggest they meet to talk about the situation as they had both suffered in a similar way and both had children by the same father. Lena told her they had nothing in common, that the man's sins were his own business and he must surely be paying for them in purgatory. Then she hung up on her. Lena's life was consumed by rancor until she finally realized that her husband was still harming her from the grave, and it was her anger rather than his betrayal that was destroying her. She adopted a draconian remedy and cut the faithless wretch out of her life at a stroke. She tore up every photo of him she could lay her hands on, got rid of his things, stopped seeing the friends they had in common, and avoided all contact with the Maraz family, although she herself kept his name as it was also her children's.

Enrique and Lucia were given a simple explanation: their father had died in an accident, but life went on, and it was unhealthy to go on thinking of those no longer there. They had to turn the page. It was enough for them to include him in their prayers so that his soul could rest in peace. Lucia was only able to imagine how he looked thanks to a couple of black-and-white photographs her brother rescued before Lena found them. In them their father was a tall, thin man with intense eyes and brilliantined hair. In one he was very young, wearing the uniform of the Chilean navy, where he had studied and worked as a radio engineer for a while. In the other, taken several years later, he was with Lena and holding a few-months-old Enrique in his arms. He had been born in Dalmatia and emigrated to Chile with his parents as a young child, as was the case with Lena and hundreds of other Croatians who entered Chile as Yugoslavs and settled in the north of the country. He met Lena at a folk festival, and the discovery of how much they had in common created the illusion of love, but they were fundamentally very different. Lena was serious, conservative, and religious, while he was cheerful, bohemian, and irreverent. She stuck to the rules without questioning them, was hardworking and thrifty; he was lazy and a wastrel.

Lucia grew up knowing nothing about her father; the topic was taboo in her house. Lena never expressly forbade it but avoided the subject with pursed lips and knitted brow. Her children learned to control their curiosity. It was not until the final weeks of Lena's life that she could talk freely about him and answer Lucia's questions. "You've inherited your sense of responsibility and strength from me; you can thank your father for being likable and mentally alert, but you have none of his defects."

In Lucia's childhood the lack of a father was like having a locked room in the house, a hermetically sealed door that might contain who knew what secrets. What would it be like to open that door? Who would she find in that room? However much she studied the man in the photographs, she was unable to relate to him; he was a stranger. Whenever asked about her family, the first thing Lucia said, adopting a doleful expression to avoid any further questions, was that her father had died. That aroused pity—the poor girl was a half orphan—and no one asked anything more. In secret she envied her best friend, Adela, the only daughter of separated parents. She was spoiled like a princess by her father, a surgeon specializing in organ transplants who was constantly traveling to the United States, bringing back dolls that spoke English and had sparkly red shoes like those Dorothy wore in *The Wizard of Oz*. He was affectionate and great fun, and took Adela and Lucia to the tearoom in the Hotel Crillon to have ice-cream sundaes topped with whipped cream, to the zoo to see the seals, and to the Parque Forestal to ride horses, but the outings and the toys were the least of it. What Lucia most enjoyed was to hold hands with her friend's father in public, pretending that Adela was her sister and that they shared this fairy-tale father. With the fervor of a novice, she prayed that this perfect man would marry her mother so that she could have him as her stepfather, but the heavens ignored this wish, as they did so many others.

At that time, Lena Maraz was still a young, beautiful woman, with broad shoulders, a long neck, and sparkling, spinach-colored eyes. Adela's father never dared try to court her. Her severe suits with masculine jackets and chaste blouses could not entirely hide her seductive curves, but her demeanor commanded respect and distance. If she had so wished, she could have had more than enough suitors, but she clung to her widowhood with the haughtiness of an empress. Her husband's lies had created in her a definitive mistrust for the entire male gender.

THREE YEARS OLDER THAN HIS SISTER, Enrique Maraz did retain a few idealized or invented memories of his father, but over time this nostalgia faded. He was not interested in Adela's father, with his gifts from America or ice cream at the Hotel Crillon. He wanted a father of his own, someone he could resemble when he was older, someone he could identify with when he looked in the mirror when he was of an age to start shaving, someone to teach him the basic lessons of manhood. His mother kept telling him he was the man of the house, responsible for her and his sister, because it was a man's role to protect and look after the family. When he once ventured to ask her how he could learn

that without a father, she replied curtly that he should improvise, because even if his father were alive, he would be no model.
Enrique would have nothing to learn from him.

The brother and sister were as different from one another as
their parents had been. Whereas Lucia got lost in the maze of a
feverish imagination and boundless curiosity, constantly wearing her heart on her sleeve, weeping for suffering humanity and
mistreated animals, Enrique was a cerebral type. From childhood on he demonstrated an ideological fanaticism that at first
provoked laughter but soon became irritating. No one could
bear this kid who was far too vehement, thought too highly of
himself, and was too preachy. In his Boy Scout days he went
around for years in short trousers trying to convince anybody
who had the misfortune to bump into him of the virtues of discipline and fresh air. Later on he transferred this pathological
insistence to the philosophy of Gurdjieff, liberation theology,
and the revelations brought on by LSD, until he found his definitive vocation in Karl Marx.

Enrique's incendiary diatribes as a young man disturbed
his mother, who thought the Left did nothing but make a huge
racket, and did not impress his sister, a carefree schoolgirl more
interested in ephemeral boyfriends and rock singers than anything else. With his wispy beard, long hair, and black beret,
Enrique imitated the famous guerrilla fighter Che Guevara, who
had been killed in Bolivia a couple of years earlier. He had read
Che's writings and constantly quoted him, even when it was not
relevant, to his mother's explosive annoyance and his sister's
fascinated admiration.

Lucia was finishing high school at the end of the sixties when
Enrique joined the groups supporting Salvador Allende, the

Socialist Party's candidate for the presidency, who was the devil incarnate to many in Chile. In Enrique's view, the only salvation for humanity lay in overthrowing capitalism by a revolution that pulled the whole edifice down. This meant that elections were a circus, but since they provided a unique opportunity to vote for a Marxist, they had to be taken advantage of. The other candidates were promising reforms within a well-known framework, whereas the Left's program was radical. The Right unleashed a fear campaign prophesying that Chile would end up like Cuba, that the Soviets would snatch Chilean children and brainwash them, destroy churches, rape nuns and execute priests, steal the land from its legitimate owners, and put an end to private property, and that even the most humble peasant was going to lose his hens and end up a slave in a Siberian gulag.

Despite the campaign of fear, Chile opted for the left-wing parties, who got together in a coalition known as Popular Unity, led by Salvador Allende. In 1970, to the horror of those who had traditionally held power and of the United States, which viewed the election in terms of Fidel Castro and his Cuban revolution, the Popular Unity Coalition won. Allende himself was probably the most surprised of all. He had run for president three times before and liked to joke about his epitaph reading *Here lies the future president of Chile.* The second-most-surprised person was Enrique Maraz, who overnight found he had nothing to fight against. That changed almost as soon as the initial euphoria died down.

The triumph of Salvador Allende, the first Marxist elected by a democratic vote, attracted the interest of the entire world, and in particular the CIA. However, it proved impossible for him to govern with the support of parties of widely differing tendencies and in the teeth of an all-out war declared by his political enemies. This rapidly became obvious, and unleashed a storm that would last three years and shake Chilean society to its very foundations. No one could remain indifferent.

To Enrique Maraz, the only possible revolution was the Cuban one; Allende's reforms simply served to postpone that indispensable upheaval. His far-left party sabotaged the government with the same fervor as the Right. Shortly after the election, Enrique abandoned his studies and departed from his mother's home without leaving an address where she could find him. They had sporadic news of him, when he turned up on a visit or phoned, always in a hurry, but his activities remained secret. He still had his beard and long hair but had given up the beret and boots, and seemed more thoughtful. He no longer leapt into damning attacks on the bourgeoisie, religion, and Yankee imperialism. He had learned to listen with feigned politeness to what he saw as his mother's reactionary opinions and his sister's nonsense.

Lucia had decorated her room with a poster of Che Guevara her brother had given her, but only because the guerrilla fighter was sexy, and to annoy her mother, who thought he was a delinquent. She also had several records by Victor Jara. She knew his protest songs by heart and also some of the slogans of the "Marxist-Leninist vanguard of the working-class and oppressed sectors," as Enrique's party defined itself. She would join in huge marches in defense of the government, shouting until she was hoarse that the people united would never be defeated. Days later, with equal enthusiasm, she would go with her girlfriends to equally large protest demonstrations against the same government she had defended a few days earlier. She was much less interested in any cause than in the fun of shouting at the top of her voice in the street. Enrique reproached her one day when he caught sight of her in the distance at an opposition march, saying her ideological coherence left a lot to be desired. The fashion then was miniskirts, platform boots, and thick black eye makeup, all of which Lucia adopted. Also in vogue were hippies and flower children, whom some young Chileans imitated, dancing in a stoned haze with their tambourines and making love in the parks, just as they did in London or California. Lucia never went that far, because her mother would never have allowed her to mix with those bucolic degenerates, as she called them.

Since the only topic of conversation in the country was politics, which produced violent breakups between families and friends, Lena imposed a law of silence on the matter in her own house, just as she had done regarding her husband. To Lucia, who was at the height of adolescent rebelliousness, the ideal way to anger her mother was mentioning Allende. Lena would get back in the evening exhausted from her day at work, the dreadful public transportation, traffic held up by strikes and demonstrations, not to mention endless lines to buy a scrawny chicken or the cigarettes she could not live without, and yet she would recover sufficiently to bang on saucepans in her backyard with her women neighbors as an anonymous way of protesting about shortages in particular and socialism in general. The noise of these saucepans began with a single clang in one yard, taken up by others until it became a deafening chorus that spread through the middle- and upper-class neighborhoods as if heralding the apocalypse. Lena would come home to find her daughter sprawled in front of the TV or chatting with her friends on the phone with her favorite songs blasting in the background. Although she was worried about her irresponsible daughter, who had a woman's body but a child's brain, she was far more concerned about Enrique, fearing that her son was one of those hotheads who sought power through violence.

THE DEEP CRISIS DIVIDING CHILE became unsustainable. Peasant farmers invaded land to set up agricultural cooperatives, banks and industries were expropriated, the copper mines in the north, which were in the hands of American corporations, were nationalized, shortages became endemic. There were no needles or bandages in the hospitals, no spare parts for machinery or milk for babies; everyone lived in a state of paranoia. Business owners sabotaged the economy by withdrawing essential items from the market. In response, the workers formed committees, threw out the bosses, and took over industries. In the city center, pickets could be seen around bonfires guarding offices and stores from right-wing gangs. In the countryside, the peasants kept watch day and night to protect themselves from the former landowners. There were armed gunmen on both sides. Despite the bellicose atmosphere, the Left increased its percentage of the vote in the March 1973 legislative elections. It was then that the opposition, which had been plotting for three years, understood that sabotage was not enough to overthrow the government. They turned to arms.

On Tuesday, September 11, 1973, the military rose against Allende's government. That morning, Lena and Lucia heard helicopters and squadrons of planes roaring low above the rooftops. When they looked out, they saw tanks and army trucks in the nearly deserted streets. None of the television channels was functioning: all they showed was a geometric pattern. On the radio people heard the military pronouncement, but only understood what that meant several hours later when the state TV channel resumed broadcasting and four generals in combat uniforms appeared on the screen in front of a flag of Chile to announce the end of communism in the beloved homeland and issue edicts that the population was called on to respect. Martial law was declared; Congress was indefinitely suspended, as were civil rights, until the honorable Armed Forces restored law, order, and the values of Western, Christian civilization. They explained that Salvador Allende had hatched a plan to execute thousands upon thousands of opponents in an unprecedented genocide, but that they had stepped in first and succeeded in preventing this.

"What's going to happen now?" Lucia asked her mother nervously, because Lena's joyous outburst and the way she opened a bottle of champagne to celebrate the occasion seemed to her daughter misplaced: the news meant that somewhere her brother, Enrique, could be in desperate straits. "Don't worry, daughter, soldiers in Chile respect the constitution; they'll call elections soon," Lena replied, little imagining that more than sixteen years were to go by before this happened.

Mother and daughter remained shut up in their apartment until the curfew was lifted a couple of days later and they could emerge briefly to buy provisions. There were no lines in the stores anymore, and they saw mountains of chickens, although Lena did not buy any, because they seemed to her too expensive. She did though stock up on cartons of cigarettes. "Where were the chickens yesterday?" Lucia asked. "Allende was keeping them in his private warehouse," her mother said.

They learned that the president had died when the government palace was bombarded, an event they saw repeated on television until they were tired of it. They heard rumors of bodies floating through the city in the Mapocho River, big bonfires where banned books were burned, and thousands of suspects being thrown into army trucks and taken to hastily prepared detention centers like the National Stadium, where only days before, soccer matches had been played. Lena's neighbors were as euphoric as she was, but Lucia was scared. A chance comment she overheard reverberated inside her like a direct threat to her brother: "They're going to put those damned communists into concentration camps, and anyone who protests will be shot, just like those bastards were planning to do to us."

When word got around that the body of Victor Jara, his hands mutilated, had been tossed into a poor district of Santiago as a lesson, Lucia cried disconsolately for hours. "It's just gossip, sweetheart, it's all exaggerated. They go out of their way to invent things to dishonor the armed forces, who have saved our country from the clutches of communism. How can you think something like that could happen in Chile?" Lena told her. On television there were cartoons and military edicts; the country was calm. The first seed of doubt was sown in Lena's mind when she saw her son's name on one of the blacklists instructing people to hand themselves in at the police barracks.

THREE WEEKS LATER, several armed men in civilian clothes raided Lena's apartment. They had no need to identify themselves. They were looking for her two children: Enrique was accused of being a guerrilla fighter, and Lucia a sympathizer. It had been months since Lena had received news of her son, and even if she had, she would not have told these men. Because of the curfew, Lucia had spent the night at a friend's place, and her mother was smart enough not to allow herself to be cowed by the threats and slaps she received during the raid on her home. With astounding calm she informed the intruders that her son had distanced himself from the family and they knew nothing about him, and that her daughter was with a tour in Buenos Aires. The men left with a warning; they would come back for her unless her children appeared.

Lena guessed that her phone was being tapped and so waited until five in the morning, when the curfew was lifted, to go and warn Lucia at her friend's house. Immediately after that she went to see the cardinal, who had been a close family friend before he ascended the celestial stairs of the Vatican. Although she had never before asked any favors, she no longer felt any sense of pride. The cardinal, overwhelmed by the situation and the long lines of petitioners, was good enough to see her and to obtain asylum for Lucia in the Venezuelan embassy. He advised Lena to leave the country as well, before the secret police carried out their threat. "I'm staying here, Your Eminence. I'm not going anywhere until I know what's happened to my son, Enrique," she said. He replied, "If you find him, come and see me, Lena, because the boy is going to need help."

Richard

That snowy January morning, Richard was the first to awaken. It was six o'clock and still dark outside. After spending hours drifting between sleeping and waking, he had finally slept as if anesthetized. All that was left of the fire was a few embers; the house was an icy mausoleum.

He had spent Saturday night wedged against the wall, his legs numb from the weight of Lucia's head, awake some of the time, the rest dreaming in a dazed fashion thanks to the magic brownie. Still, he could not recall being so happy in a long while. The quality of the brownies varied a lot, which made it hard to calculate how much you could consume to produce the desired effect without becoming high as a kite. It was better to smoke it, but that gave him asthma. The last stash had been very strong; he would need to divide it into smaller pieces. The weed helped him relax after a hard day's work or to drive away ghosts of the vindictive kind. Of course, being a rational man, he did not believe in ghosts. And yet he saw them. In Anita's world, which he had shared for several years, life and death were linked inextricably, and good and bad spirits roamed everywhere. Long ago he had admitted to himself that he was an alcoholic, which was why he had avoided liquor all these years. He did not think he was addicted to any other substances or had any major vices, unless cycling was an addiction or vice, and the small quantities of weed he used definitely did not fall under that category. The piece of brownie he had eaten had affected him powerfully; otherwise, he would have gotten up as soon as the fire went out in the hearth and gone to bed, instead of spending the night sitting on the floor and waking the next morning with sore muscles and a weakened will.

His back ached and his neck was stiff. Only a few years before, he and his friend Horacio Amado-Castro used to go camping upstate, spending the night in sleeping bags on the hard ground, but now he was too old for such a lack of comfort. Curled up alongside him, Lucia, however, had the placid expression of someone sleeping on feather down. Evelyn, stretched out on the cushion and wrapped up in her parka, boots, and gloves, was snoring lightly with Marcelo on top of her. It took Richard several seconds to recognize her and remember why this tiny young woman was in his house, their collision, the snowstorm. After hearing part of Evelyn's story the previous night, he once more felt the moral outrage that in the past had stirred him to defend migrants and still made his father's blood boil. Richard had ultimately distanced himself from taking action, ending up enclosed in his academic world, far from the harsh reality of the poor in Latin America. He felt certain that Evelyn's employers were exploiting and possibly mistreating her, which would explain her terror at such a slight accident.

He pushed Lucia aside somewhat brusquely to get her off his legs and out of his mind, then shook himself like a wet dog and struggled to his feet, his mouth parched. He reflected that the brownie had been a bad idea: it had led to the revelations of the previous night, to Evelyn's story, Lucia's as well—and God knew what he had told them. He did not recall having let slip any details about his own past, something he never did, but he must have mentioned Anita, because Lucia had commented that all those years after losing his wife, he still missed her. "I've never been loved like that, Richard, love has always been in half measures for me," she had added.

Richard looked down at Lucia and felt a sudden rush of tenderness. She was still asleep on the floor and her sprawling limbs gave her a vulnerable, adolescent look. This woman who was old enough to be a grandmother reminded him of his Anita when she was resting, his twentysomething Anita. For a second he was tempted to stoop down, take Lucia's head in his hands, and kiss her. Disconcerted by this dangerous impulse, he controlled himself at once.

Whenever Richard turned on his computer, a screen saver of Anita and Bibi appeared, their expressions accusatory or smiling at him depending on his mood. It was not a reminder; he had no need of that. If his memory were to fail him, Anita and Bibi would be waiting for him in the timeless dimension of dreams. Occasionally a vivid one would stick with him, and he'd spend the entire day with one foot in this world and the other in the shifting sands of a dreadful nightmare. Each night when he switched off the light before going to sleep, he would summon Anita and Bibi in the hope of seeing them. He knew he was the one who created these nocturnal visions, and so if his mind was able to punish him with nightmares, it could also reward him, although he had not discovered a sure way of producing those consoling dreams. Over time, his mourning had changed in tone and texture. In the beginning it was red and piercing; then it became gray, thick and rough like burlap. He became used to this dull pain and incorporated it into his everyday discomforts, along with heartburn. The guilt though remained the same, as cold and implacable as glass. His friend Horacio, always ready to celebrate the good and minimize the bad, had at one point accused him of being in love with misfortune. "Tell your super-ego to fuck off, man. The way you examine every single action, past and present, is twisted. The sin of pride. You're not that important. You have to forgive yourself once and for all, just like Anita and Bibi have forgiven you."

Half-jokingly, Lucia Maraz had once told him he was turning into a fearful old hypochondriac. "I already am one," he replied, trying to adopt her joking tone, and yet he felt hurt, because it was undeniably true. They were at one of those dreadful social events in their department, this time to bid farewell to a retiring professor. He came over to Lucia with a glass of wine for her and mineral water for himself. She was the only person he'd had any desire to talk to there. And she was right, he lived with a constant feeling of anxiety. He swallowed handfuls of vitamin supplements because he thought that if his health failed everything would go to hell and the whole edifice of his existence would come crashing down. He protected his house with burglar alarms, because he'd heard that in Brooklyn, as everywhere else, robbers were active in broad daylight. He protected his computer and his cell phone with such complicated passwords that every so often he forgot them. Then there were the elaborate car, health, and life insurance policies. In the end the only insurance he lacked was against his worst memories, which would assail him the moment he stepped outside his routines, threatening to overwhelm with disorder. He preached to his students that order is an art rational beings possess, a ceaseless battle against centrifugal force, because the natural dynamic of all living things is to expand, multiply, and end in chaos. As a proof you only had to observe human behavior, the voracity of nature, and the infinite complexity of the universe. To maintain at least a semblance of order, he never let himself go, but kept his existence under control with military precision. That was why he had his lists and a strict timetable, which made Lucia laugh out loud when she discovered them. The bad thing about working with her was that nothing escaped her.

"How do you see yourself in old age?" Lucia had asked him.

"I'm already in it."

"No, you've got a good ten years yet."

"I hope I don't live too long, that would be awful. The ideal would be to die still in perfect health, say at around seventy-five, when my body and mind are functioning properly."

"Sounds like a good plan," she said cheerfully.

To Richard it was a serious plan. At seventy-five he would have to find an effective way of putting an end to it all. When the moment arrived, he would travel to New Orleans, where he could hear the music of the French Quarter's quirky characters. He intended to finish out his days playing the piano with some stupendous musicians, who would allow him to join their band out of pity, and lose himself in the blare of the trumpet and the saxophone, the exuberance of the African drums. And if this was too much to ask, well then he wanted to leave this world silently, seated beneath a dilapidated ceiling fan in an old-fashioned bar, comforted by the rhythms of a melancholy jazz tune, quaffing exotic cocktails with no thought of the consequences, because he would have the lethal capsule in his pocket. It would be his last night, so he could permit himself a few drinks.

"Don't you ever feel the need for female company, Richard?" Lucia asked with a mischievous wink. "Someone in your bed, for example?"

"Not at all."

He saw no need to tell her about Susan. That relationship was not important either for Susan or for him. He was sure he was one among several lovers who helped her bear an unhappy marriage, which he considered should have ended years before. This was a topic they both avoided: Susan said nothing about it, and he did not ask. They were colleagues, good companions, linked by a sensual friendship and intellectual pursuits. Their encounters were straightforward: always the second Thursday of the month, and always in the same hotel; she was as methodical as he was. One afternoon a month was enough; each of them had their own life to live.

Three months earlier, the idea of finding himself with a woman at a reception of this kind, searching for topics of conversation and testing out the ground for the next step, would have made Richard's ulcer explode, but ever since Lucia had been living in his basement he had found himself imagining dialogues with her. He wondered why with her exactly, when there were other more suitable women available, such as his neighbor, who had suggested they become lovers because they lived so close to each other and because she occasionally looked after the cats. The only explanation for these imaginary conversations was that loneliness was starting to weigh on him: another symptom of old age, he told himself. There was nothing more pathetic than the sound of a fork on a plate in an empty house. Eating alone, sleeping alone, dying alone. What would it be like to have female company, as Lucia had suggested? To cook for her, wait for her in the evening, go out hand in hand with her, sleep curled up together, tell her what he was thinking, write her poems. Someone like Lucia. She was a mature, stable, intelligent woman who had a ready laugh. She was wise because she had suffered, but did not cling to suffering the way he did. And she was pretty. But she was also bold and bossy. A woman like her took up a lot of room: it would be like struggling with a harem; too much work, a bad idea. He smiled, thinking how presumptuous it was of him to suppose she might accept him. She had never given any sign of being interested in him, except the occasion when she had cooked for him, but back then she had just arrived and he was on the defensive or his mind was elsewhere. I behaved like an idiot, I'd like to start over with her, he concluded.

On a professional level, Lucia had proved to be an excellent choice. A week after her arrival in New York he asked her to give a seminar for the faculty and students. They had to hold the session in a big lecture hall because more people enrolled than they had expected. It fell to him to introduce her. The topic was CIA interventions in Latin America. Richard sat in the audience while Lucia spoke in English without notes, in that accent of hers he found so beguiling, detailing how the agency helped to overthrow democracies, replacing them with the kind of totalitarian government no North American would accept. When she finished, the first question was from a colleague who referred to the economic miracle in Chile under the dictatorship. From the tone of his comment, it was obvious he was justifying the repression. The hair stood up on the back of Richard's neck, but he forced himself to remain silent. Lucia did not need anyone to defend her, and replied that the supposed miracle had evaporated, while the economic statistics conveniently ignored the enormous inequality and poverty.

A visiting professor from the University of California mentioned the violence in Guatemala, Honduras, and El Salvador, and the thousands of unaccompanied children who crossed the US border either to escape or to search for their parents. She suggested reorganizing the Sanctuary Movement of the 1980s. Richard took the microphone in case there was anyone in the audience unaware of what she was referring to. He explained that it was an initiative by more than five hundred American churches, lawyers, students, and activists to help the Central American refugees, who were treated as delinquents and deported by the Reagan administration. Lucia asked if anyone there had taken part in the movement, and four hands were raised. During that period Richard had been in Brazil, but his father had become so involved that on a couple of occasions he was put in jail. Those were some of the most memorable moments in his elderly father's existence.

The seminar lasted two hours, and was so fruitful that Lucia was given a standing ovation. Richard was impressed not only by her eloquence but because to him she looked very attractive in her black dress and silver necklace, and with the pink highlights in her hair. She had the cheekbones and energy of a Tatar, and he remembered her as she'd looked years earlier, with a reddish mass of hair and tight jeans. Even though she had changed, he thought she was still striking, and had he not feared

being misinterpreted, he would have told her so. He congratu-
lated himself on having invited her to his department. He knew
she had been through difficult years: an illness, a divorce, and
heaven knew what else. It occurred to him to ask her to teach
Chilean politics for a year at the university as it might serve as
a diversion for her, but it would be even more useful for the
students. Some of them were colossally ignorant, arriving at col-
lege without being able to place Chile on a map, and most likely
unable to situate their own country in the world. They thought
the United States *was* the world.

Richard would have liked Lucia to stay longer than two
semesters, but it was hard to come up with the funds: the university administration was as slow in making decisions as the
Vatican. When he had sent her the contract, he'd offered to rent
her the basement apartment, which was unoccupied at the time.
He imagined Lucia would be delighted to have somewhere so
sought-after in the heart of Brooklyn, close to public transport
and at such a reasonable rent, but when she saw it, she could
scarcely conceal her disappointment. What a difficult woman,
thought Richard. They had started off on the wrong foot, but
since then things had improved between them.

He was convinced he had been both generous and understanding toward her. He had even accepted the eventual
presence of the dog, which according to her would be only
temporary, but which had already lasted more than two months.
Although pets were forbidden in the rental agreement, he had
turned a blind eye to this Chihuahua that barked like a German
shepherd and terrified the mailman and neighbors. He knew
nothing about dogs but could see that Marcelo was very odd,
with bulging toad's eyes that seemed not to fit in their sockets

and a tongue that lolled out because of all the missing teeth. The tartan wool cape the dog wore did nothing to improve his appearance. According to Lucia, Marcelo had turned up on her doorstep one night, close to death and without an identity collar. "Who could possibly be so cruel as to throw him out?" she said to Richard with a pleading look. That was the first time Richard had noticed Lucia's eyes. They were as black as olives, with thick eyelashes and fine laughter lines around them—cat eyes, although that was an irrelevant detail. What she looked like did not matter. To retain his privacy, ever since he had purchased the house he had followed the rule of avoiding all familiarity with his tenants, and he had no intention of making an exception for her.

RICHARD CALCULATED THAT IT WAS STILL too early to phone his father, although the old man woke at dawn and waited impatiently for his call. On Sundays they always had lunch together at a restaurant his father chose, because if it depended on Richard they would always have gone to the same place. "At least this time I'll have something different to tell you, Dad," murmured Richard, realizing how interested his father would be to hear about Evelyn Ortega, since he was always concerned about immigrants and refugees.

Joseph Bowmaster, by now very elderly but still completely lucid, had been an actor. He was born in Germany to a Jewish family with a tradition as antiquarians and art collectors that could be traced back as far as the Renaissance. They were refined, cultured people, but the fortune they had amassed was lost during the First World War. In the second half of the thirties, when Hitler appeared unstoppable, his parents sent Joseph to France on the pretext that he was making a close study of the Impressionists, but in fact to get him away from the imminent Nazi danger. They meanwhile made plans to emigrate illegally to Palestine, at that time controlled by Great Britain. To placate the Arabs, the British limited the immigration of Jews to the territory, but nothing could stop the most desperate.

Joseph stayed on in France but devoted himself to the theater rather than studying art. He had a natural talent for acting and for languages. As well as German, he was fluent in French and set himself to studying English. He was so successful that he could soon imitate several accents, from Cockney to BBC pronunciation. In 1940, when the Nazis invaded France and occupied Paris, he managed to escape to Spain, and from there to Portugal. For the rest of his life he would remember the kindness of those people who, at great risk to themselves, helped him in this odyssey. Richard grew up listening to the story of his father's wartime escape, and with the idea etched on his mind that to help the persecuted is an inescapable duty. As soon as he was old enough, his father took him to France to visit two families that had kept him hidden from the Nazis, and to Spain to thank those who helped him survive and to cross into Portugal.

By 1940, Lisbon had become the last refuge for hundreds of thousands of European Jews desperate to obtain documents to reach the United States, South America, or Palestine. While awaiting his opportunity, Joseph stayed in the old quarter of the city, a maze of narrow streets and mysterious houses, in a boardinghouse fragrant with jasmine and oranges. There he fell in love with Cloe, the owner's daughter, who was three years older than him, a post office employee by day and a fado singer by night. She was a dark beauty with a tragic expression befitting the sad songs she sang. Joseph lacked the courage to tell his parents he was in love with a Gentile, until they emigrated together, first to London, where they lived for two years, and then New York. By this time war was raging furiously in Europe, and Joseph's parents, precariously settled in Palestine, had no objection to their new daughter-in-law. All that was important was for their son to be safe from the genocide the Germans were perpetrating.

In New York, Joseph changed his surname to Bowmaster, which sounded English through and through, and thanks to his feigned aristocratic accent found parts in Shakespeare plays for the next forty years. Cloe on the other hand never learned English properly and had no success there with her country's plaintive fados. However, instead of being plunged into despair by her failure as an artist, she began to study fashion and became the family's breadwinner, because the amount Joseph earned in the theater never stretched to the end of the month. The diva-like woman Joseph had met in Lisbon turned out to possess a great practical sense and a capacity for hard work. She was also unswervingly loyal, devoting herself fully to her husband and Richard, their only child. Richard grew up spoiled like a prince in a modest apartment in the Bronx, shielded from the world by his parents' love.

Richard turned out to be as good-looking as Joseph, though not as tall and lacking the actor's extravagant temperament; rather, he was more melancholic, like his mother. Busy with their own lives, his parents loved him without smothering him, treating him with mild neglect, as was common in those days before children became projects. This suited Richard, because they left him in peace with his books, and no one demanded much of him beyond getting good marks at school, behaving properly, and being considerate. He spent more time with his father than with his mother, because Joseph had a flexible schedule, whereas Cloe was a partner in a women's clothing store and habitually stayed there sewing until late at night. Joseph took his son with him on his errands of mercy, as Cloe called them. They went to hand out food and clothing donated by the churches and synagogues to the poorest families in the Bronx, both Jewish and Christian. "You never ask people in need who they are or where they've come from, Richard. We're all the same in misfortune," Joseph would preach to his son. Twenty years later he proved this by confronting the police on the streets of New York to defend undocumented immigrants who had been rounded up in raids.

Whenever he recalled his happy childhood, Richard asked himself why he had not lived up to what he was taught as a child, following the example he was given, and instead failed as both a husband and a father.

During the night, with his defenses lowered, his demons had come and clawed at him. Years before, he had tried to keep them in a sealed compartment of his memory, but eventually gave this up because his angels disappeared along with them. Later, he learned to cherish even his most painful memories: without them it would have been as if he had never been young, or loved, or a father. If the price he had to pay for this was more suffering, then so be it. Sometimes the demons won the fight against the angels, and the result was a paralyzing migraine, which was also part of the price. He carried with him the heavy debt of the mistakes he had made, a debt he had shared with no one. But now, in the winter of 2016, circumstances were finally forcing him to open his heart. The slow exorcism of his past began on that night sprawled on the floor between two women and a ridiculous dog, while outside a snowy Brooklyn slept.

"COME ON, LADIES, WAKE UP!" he cried, clapping his hands.

Lucia opened her eyes. It also took her a while to figure out where she was.

"What time is it?" she asked.

"Time to get going."

"It's still dark! Coffee first. I can't think without caffeine. It's like the North Pole in here, Richard. For the love of God, turn the heating up, don't be so stingy. Where's the bathroom?"

"Use the one on the second floor."

Lucia got up in several stages, first on all fours, back bent, then with her hands on the floor and her backside in the air, as she had learned in yoga. Finally she stood up.

"I used to be able to do push-ups. Now if I stretch I get a cramp. Old age stinks," she muttered on her way to the stairs.

I can see I'm not the only one approaching decrepitude, thought Richard with a hint of satisfaction. Then he went to make coffee and feed the cats, while Evelyn and Marcelo woke up as if they had the whole day in front of them with nothing to do. He stifled his urge to make the girl hurry up, realizing she must be exhausted.

The second-floor bathroom was clean and did not seem to be used much. It was big and old-fashioned, with a claw-foot bathtub and brass faucets. In the mirror, Lucia saw a woman she did not recognize, with puffy eyes, blotchy red skin, and pink-and-white hair that made her look like a clown. The highlights had originally been beet colored, but now they were fading. She took a quick shower, dried herself on her T-shirt because there were no towels, put on her sweater, and combed her fingers through her hair. She needed her toothbrush and her makeup bag. "You can't go into the world without mascara and lipstick," she told the mirror. She had always seen vanity as a virtue, except during the months when she had chemotherapy and gave in to defeat until Daniela obliged her to return to life. Every morning she found the time to do herself up, even if she was going to stay at home and not see anyone. She would prepare herself for the day, applying her makeup and choosing her clothes like someone donning armor: it was her way of presenting herself, full of confidence, to the world. She loved brushes, rouge, lotions, colors, powders, materials, textures. She was unable to do without her makeup, her computer, her cell phone, and a dog. The computer was her work tool; the cell phone connected her to the world, especially Daniela; and the need to share her existence with an animal had begun in Vancouver and continued during the years she was married to Carlos. The dog Olivia had died of old age just when she herself got cancer. During that time she had to weep for the death of her mother, her own illness, and the loss of Olivia, her faithful companion. Marcelo was a gift from the gods, the perfect confidant. They talked to one another, and he made her laugh with his ugliness and the inquisitive look in his toad eyes. With this Chihuahua that barked at mice and ghosts, she could release the unbearable tenderness she felt inside but could not show to her daughter for fear of overwhelming her. Usually her grooming ritual was her time of meditation but that morning she could only think of Evelyn Ortega's story.

Evelyn

On Holy Saturday, March 22, 2008, and six weeks after Gregorio Ortega's death, it was his brother and sister's turn. The avengers waited until Concepcion had gone to church to arrange the flowers for Easter Sunday and then burst into the hut in broad daylight. There were four of them, unmistakable because of their tattoos and their brazen attitude. Arriving at Monja Blanca del Valle on two noisy motorbikes, they made themselves instantly conspicuous in a village where everyone either walked or rode bicycles. They stayed inside the hut for only eighteen minutes; that was all they needed. If neighbors saw them, none intervened or were willing to give testimony afterward. The fact that they committed their crime during Holy Week, a sacred time given over to fasting and penance, would be commented on for years as the most unforgivable of sins.

Concepcion Montoya returned to her house around one

o'clock, when the sun was beating down and even the cockatoos had fallen silent in their branches. She was not surprised at the silence or the empty streets, because this was siesta time and those who were not resting would be busy with preparations for the procession of the Risen Christ and the high mass Father Benito was to celebrate the next day, wearing his white alb and purple stole rather than the pair of filthy jeans and threadbare embroidered stole woven in Chichicastenango he used the rest of the year. Still dazzled from the bright sunlight out in the street, Concepcion needed a few seconds to adjust her eyes to the darkness inside the hut, and to catch sight of Andres near the door, curled up like a sleeping dog. "What's wrong with you, my boy?" she managed to ask before seeing the trail of blood staining the earthen floor, and the slash across his throat. A raw cry rose from deep inside her, tearing her apart. She knelt down, calling out to him, "Andres, Andresito," and then suddenly Evelyn flashed through her mind. She found the girl lying at the far end of the room, her thin body exposed, and with blood on her face, her legs, her torn cotton dress. Concepcion crawled over to her, appealing to God, moaning for him not to take her, to show mercy. She seized her granddaughter by the shoulders and shook her, noticing that one of her arms was dangling at an impossible angle. She searched for any signs of life; unable to find one, she rushed to the door, shouting hoarsely and crying out to the Virgin Mary.

A neighbor was the first to come to her aid, followed by other women. Two of them restrained the crazed grandmother, while others discovered that nothing could be done for Andres, but that Evelyn was still breathing. They sent a boy on a bike to tell the police and tried to revive Evelyn without moving her because of the twisted arm and the blood coming from her mouth and between her legs.

Father Benito arrived in his pickup ahead of the police. He found the hut full of people talking and trying to help in whatever way they could. They had laid Andres's body on the table, straightening the head and covering the slit throat with a shawl. After cleaning his body with wet cloths they had sent for a fresh shirt to make him look presentable. Meanwhile other women were applying cold compresses to Evelyn and doing their best to comfort Concepcion. The priest understood that it was already too late to preserve the evidence, because it had been handled and trodden on by these well-meaning neighbors, but also that it did not really make any difference, given the police's lack of concern. It was unlikely that anyone in authority was going to put themselves to any trouble over this poor family. When the priest arrived, the villagers moved apart out of respect and hope, as if the divine powers he represented could undo the tragedy. He only needed to glance at Evelyn to assess her condition. He told the men to put a mattress on his pickup and had the women slide a blanket under her so that four of them could carry her out and place her on the mattress. He ordered Concepcion to go with him, and the others to wait right there for the police, if they ever showed up.

Evelyn's grandmother and two of the women accompanied Father Benito to the clinic seven miles away that was run by evangelical missionaries. There were always one or two doctors on duty as it served several surrounding villages. Usually a terror at the wheel, Father Benito drove carefully for the first time in his life, because every pothole or bend elicited a groan from Evelyn. When they arrived they carried her into the clinic on the blanket as if it were a hammock and placed her on a stretcher.

She was seen by a doctor, Nuria Castell, who as Father Benito later discovered was far from evangelical: she was Catalan and agnostic. Evelyn's right arm had been torn out of its socket and to judge by all the bruises, she must have had several broken ribs. The X-rays would confirm that, said the doctor. She had also been beaten about the face and suffered a possible concussion. Although she was conscious and had opened her eyes, she muttered only incoherent words. She did not recognize her grandmother or realize where she was.

"What happened to her?" asked the Catalan doctor.

"Her house was attacked. I think she saw how they killed her brother," Father Benito said.

"They probably forced her brother to watch what they were doing to her before they killed him."

"Jesus!" shouted the priest, punching the wall with his fist.

"Be careful with my clinic. It's flimsy and we've just had it painted. I'll examine the child to see what internal injuries she's suffered," Nuria Castell told him with a resigned sigh born of experience.

Father Benito called Miriam and this time had to tell her the harsh truth. He asked her to send money for the funeral of another of her children, and to pay a coyote, or people smuggler, who could take Evelyn to the United States. She was in imminent danger, because the gang would try to get rid of her to avoid her identifying the attackers. In a flood of tears and unable to take in this latest tragedy, Miriam explained that to pay for Gregorio's funeral she had plundered the money she was saving to pay for Andres's trip to see her when he finished school, as she had promised. She only had a small savings left but would borrow as much as she possibly could for her daughter's sake.

Evelyn spent several days in the clinic until she could swallow fruit juices and cornmeal and was able to walk again. Her grandmother went back to the village to organize Andres's burial. Father Benito presented himself at the police station and made good use of his booming voice and his strong Basque accent to demand a copy of a signed and officially stamped report on what had happened to the Ortega family. No one took the trouble to go and interview Evelyn; even if they had, it would have been of little use, because she was still unable to speak. The priest also asked Nuria Castell for a copy of the medical report, thinking it might be useful someday. During this time the Catalan doctor and the Basque Jesuit met on several occasions. They had long discussions about the divine without reaching agreement but discovered that on a human level they were united by the same principles. "It's a pity you're a priest, Benito. Such a good-looking man staying celibate is a real waste," the doctor joked between two cups of coffee.

The MS-13 had carried out its threat to wreak revenge. Gregorio's betrayal must have been very serious to deserve such punishment, thought the priest, although possibly it had simply stemmed from an act of cowardice or a misplaced insult. It was impossible for him to know, as he had no idea what codes operated in their world.

"Rotten bastards," he muttered during one of his meetings with the doctor.

"Those gang members weren't born so rotten, Benito. They were once innocent kids, but they grew up in utter poverty, with no laws and no heroes they could emulate. Have you seen the children begging? Selling needles and bottles of water on the roads? Digging in the garbage dumps and sleeping out in the open with the rats?"

"Yes, I've seen them, Nuria. There's nothing I haven't seen in this country."

"At least in the gangs they don't go hungry."

"This violence is the result of an endless war against the poor. Two hundred thousand indigenous people massacred, fifty thousand disappeared, a million and a half displaced. Guatemala is a small country; just calculate what percentage of the population that means. You're very young, Nuria, what can you know of all this?"

"Don't underestimate me, Father. I'm well aware of what you're talking about."

"Soldiers committing atrocities against people who are just like them, from the same race and class, born into the same bottomless misery. It's true they were following orders, but they carried them out intoxicated by the most addictive drug: power with impunity."

"You and I have been lucky, Benito, because we've never tried that drug. If you had power and impunity, would you make the guilty suffer as much as they do their victims?" she asked.

"I suppose I would."

"Even though you're a priest and God tells you to forgive."

"I always thought that story about turning the other cheek was stupid. It only means you get a second slap," he retorted.

"And if you are tempted by vengeance, just imagine what it's like for mere mortals. I would castrate those who raped Evelyn, without anesthetic."

"My Christian faith keeps failing me, Nuria. I guess it must be because I'm just a dumb Basque like my father, God rest his soul. If I'd been born in Luxembourg perhaps I wouldn't be so indignant."

"We need more angry people like you in this world, Benito."

The priest's anger went back a long way. He had been struggling with it for years and thought that at his age, with all he had lived through and seen, it was time to accept reality. Age had not made him any wiser or gentler, only more rebellious. As a young man, he had rebelled against the government, the military, the Americans, the usual rich people. Now his rebellion extended to the police, corrupt politicians, narcos, traffickers, gangsters, and all the others responsible for this mess. He had spent thirty-five years in Central America apart from a couple of interruptions when he was sent as a punishment to the Congo and to a retreat for several months in Extremadura to atone for the sin of pride and to dampen his passion for justice after a spell in prison in 1982. He had served the church in Honduras, El Salvador, and Guatemala, what was now known as the Northern Triangle, the most violent part of the world not at war, and in all that time he had never learned to live alongside injustice and inequality.

"It must be tough being a priest with a character like yours," Nuria said with a smile.

"The vow of obedience weighs a ton, Nuria, but I've never questioned my faith or my vocation."

"What about the vow of celibacy? Have you ever fallen in love?"

"Constantly, but God helps me and it passes quickly, so don't try to seduce me, woman."

After burying Andres alongside his brother, Concepcion rejoined her granddaughter at the clinic. Father Benito took them to a friend's house in Solola, where they would be safe while Evelyn convalesced and he looked for a coyote he could trust to take her to the United States. Evelyn had her arm in a sling and every time she inhaled her ribs were a torture. Since Gregorio's death she had lost a lot of weight; in recent weeks her adolescent curves had vanished. She was so skinny and frail that it seemed the slightest gust of wind could sweep her into the skies. Not only had she said nothing about what happened that fateful Easter Saturday but she had not uttered a single word since she came to on the mattress in the pickup. The only hope was that she had not seen how they slit her brother's throat, that by then she had been unconscious. Dr. Castell ordered them not to try to ask her any questions; she was traumatized and needed peace and time to recover.

As they were leaving the clinic, Concepcion Montoya raised the possibility that her granddaughter had been made pregnant. This had happened to her when she had been raped by soldiers in her youth: Miriam was the result of that abuse. The Catalan doctor shut herself in a bathroom with the grandmother and told her in a whisper that she need not worry about that, because she had given Evelyn a pill invented by the North Americans to avoid getting pregnant. It was illegal in Guatemala, but no one would find out. "I'm telling you this so that you won't go thinking of some homemade remedy for the girl. She's suffered enough."

WHEREAS BEFORE EVELYN HAD STAMMERED, after the rape she simply stopped speaking. She spent hours languishing in the house of Father Benito's friends, showing not the slightest interest in all the novelties there: running water, electricity, two toilets, a telephone, and even a television set in her room. Concepcion intuited that this word sickness went beyond the doctors' competence and decided to act before it became lodged in her granddaughter's bones. As soon as Evelyn could stand properly on her feet and breathe without stabbing pains in her chest, Concepcion said goodbye to the kind people who had sheltered them and left with her granddaughter for Peten on a lengthy, bone-shaking minibus journey to visit the shaman Felicita, a healer and guardian of the traditions of the Maya. Felicita was famous: people came from the capital and from as far as Honduras and Belize to consult her on matters of health and destiny. She had been interviewed on a television program, where they estimated she was a hundred and twelve years old and must be the oldest person in the world. Felicita never denied this, but she still had most of her teeth and two thick braids hanging down her back, too many teeth and too much hair for someone so old.

It was easy for them to find the healer, because everyone they asked knew her. Felicita showed no surprise when they appeared: she was used to receiving souls, as she called her visitors, and always welcomed them warmly in her living house. She claimed that the wood of its walls, the beaten earth of its floor, and the straw of its roof were alive, breathing and thinking like all living beings. She would ask their advice for the most difficult cases, and the materials of the house would answer her in dreams. Her house was a round hut with only one room, where daily life went on alongside her ceremonies and cures. A curtain of serape blankets enclosed the small space where Felicita slept on a bed of rough boards.

The shaman greeted her new arrivals with the sign of the cross, asking them to sit on the floor, and served bitter coffee to Concepcion and mint tea to Evelyn. She accepted a fair price for her professional services and put the banknotes into a tin box without counting them. Grandmother and granddaughter drank in respectful silence and waited patiently while Felicita watered the medicinal plants in pots lined up in the shade, threw grains of corn out for the hens wandering about, and then put beans to cook on a fire in the yard. After she had completed her most urgent chores, the old woman laid a brightly colored woven cloth on the floor. On it she placed all the elements of her altar in strict order: candles, bundles of aromatic herbs, conch shells, and various Maya and Christian religious objects. She lit some sprigs of sage and cleansed the inside of her house with the smoke, walking in circles and chanting incantations to drive off the negative spirits in an ancient tongue. It was only then that she sat down opposite her visitors and asked what had brought them there. Concepcion explained the speech problem afflicting her granddaughter.

The healer's eyes glinted below the wrinkled lids as they examined Evelyn's face for a long couple of minutes. "Close your eyes and tell me what you see," she instructed the girl. Evelyn did as she was told but could not find a voice to describe the scene at the bridge or the terror she had felt when the tattooed men seized Andres and beat and threw her to the floor. She tried to speak, but the consonants stuck in her throat. With the despairing efforts of someone drowning, she produced a few spluttering vowels. Concepcion interrupted to describe what had happened to her family, but the healer shushed her. She explained that she channeled the universe's healing energy, that this was a power she had received at birth and cultivated with other shamans throughout her long life. This was why she had traveled great distances in a plane to visit the Seminoles in Florida and the Inuits in Canada, among others, although her greatest knowledge came from the sacred plant of the Amazon, which was the way into the spirit world. She lit some herbs in a clay pot painted with pre-Columbian symbols and blew the smoke in her patient's face. Then she made her drink some disgusting ayahuasca tea that Evelyn could barely swallow.

The potion soon began to take effect, and Evelyn could no longer stay sitting upright. She toppled onto her side, her head in her grandmother's lap. Her limbs relaxed, her body dissolved like salt in an opalescent sea, and she saw herself enveloped in fantastic, violently colored whirlwinds: sunflower yellow, obsidian black, emerald green. The nauseating taste of the tea filled her mouth and she retched and vomited into a plastic bowl Felicita placed in front of her. Eventually the nausea subsided, and Evelyn lay back on her grandmother's skirt, trembling all over. The visions came in rapid succession. In some of them, her mother appeared as she had last seen her; others were scenes from her childhood, bathing in the river with other children, or at age five riding on the shoulders of her elder brother; a jaguar with two cubs emerged, then again her mother with a man, possibly her father. All of a sudden she found herself beside the bridge where her brother was hanging. She cried out in terror. She was alone with Gregorio. The earth giving off a warm mist; the rustling of the banana trees; huge flies; black birds suspended in midflight; violent, carnivorous flowers floating in the rust-colored water of the river; and her brother crucified. Evelyn went on shrieking and shrieking as she tried in vain to run and hide. She could not move a muscle; she had been turned to stone. From afar she heard a voice reciting a litany in Mayan, and felt that she was being rocked and cradled.

After an eternity she slowly became calm and dared to look

up. She saw that Gregorio was no longer strung up like a carcass in a slaughterhouse but was standing intact on the bridge, without tattoos, exactly as he had been before he lost his innocence. And beside him was Andres, also intact, calling to her or waving goodbye with his hand. She blew them a kiss in the distance and her brothers smiled, before gradually fading against a purple sky and vanishing altogether. Time became warped, twisted; she no longer knew if it was before or after, or how the minutes and hours were passing. She surrendered completely to the power of the drug and, as she did so, lost all fear. The mother jaguar returned with her cubs, and Evelyn dared to stroke her on the back. The fur was rough, with a swamplike smell. The enormous animal accompanied her as she entered and left other visions, watching her with amber eyes, showing her the way when she got lost in abstract labyrinths, protecting her when any evil being came near.

Hours later, Evelyn emerged from this magic world. She found herself on a mat, covered in blankets, bewildered, and with her body aching all over. She had no idea where she was. When finally she managed to focus, she saw her grandmother sitting beside her, reciting the rosary, with another woman she did not recognize until she said her name: Felicita.

"Tell me what you saw," the shaman instructed her.

Evelyn made a supreme effort to speak and to pronounce words, but she was very tired and could only stammer "brothers" and "jaguar."

"Was it female?" asked the healer.

The girl nodded.

"Mine is the feminine power," Felicita said. "That's the power of life that the ancients had, both women and men. Now it is asleep in men, which is why there is war, but that power is going to reawaken, and then good will spread over the earth, the Great Spirit will reign, there will be peace, and evil deeds will cease. I am not alone in saying this. It's prophesied by all the wise ancient women and men among the native peoples I have visited. You also have the feminine power. That's why the mother jaguar came to you. Remember that. And don't forget that your brothers are with the spirits and are not suffering."

Exhausted, Evelyn fell into a deathlike, dreamless sleep. Hours later, she awoke on Felicita's mat refreshed, aware of all she had been through, and ravenous. She devoured the beans and tortillas offered by the shaman, and her voice when she thanked her came tumbling out, but sonorously. "What you have is not a sickness of the body, but of the soul. It may get better on its own; it may go away for a while and then return, because it is a very stubborn sickness; and it may never be cured. We shall see," said Felicita. Before saying goodbye to her visitors, she gave Evelyn a card of the Virgin Mary blessed by Pope John Paul during his visit to Guatemala, and a small stone amulet in the fierce shape of Ixchel, the jaguar goddess. "You will know suffering, my girl, but two powers will protect you. One is the sacred mother jaguar of the Maya, the other is the sacred mother of all Christians. Call on them and they will come to your aid."

THE REGION OF GUATEMALA CLOSE to the Mexican border was a center for contraband and trafficking. Thousands of men, women, and children tried to eke out a living on the margins of the law, but it was hard to find a coyote who could be trusted.

There were some who after receiving half their payment left their charges abandoned anywhere in Mexico, or transported them under inhuman conditions. Occasionally the smell would give away the presence of a container bearing the bodies of dozens of migrants who had died of suffocation or had been broiled in the relentless heat. Girls faced greater danger, as they could be raped or sold to pimps and brothels. Once again it was Nuria Castell who gave Father Benito a helping hand and recommended a discreet agency with a good reputation among the evangelicals.

The agency was run by the owner of a bakery who had a sideline in smuggling people across the border. She was proud of the fact that none of her clients had ended up being trafficked, kidnapped en route, or murdered; none of them had fallen or had been pushed from a train. She could offer some degree of security in a fundamentally risky business. Taking what safety measures she could, she left the rest to the Lord, who took care of his subjects from his kingdom in the heavens. She charged the usual price smugglers demanded to cover the risks and costs, plus her own commission. Communicating with these coyotes on her cell phone, she would monitor their trail, always knowing which point of their journey her clients had reached. According to Nuria, she had not lost anyone so far.

Father Benito went to see the woman, who turned out to be in her fifties, wearing thick makeup and with gold everywhere: on her ears, around her neck and wrists, and in her teeth. The priest asked for a reduction in the name of God, appealing to her better nature as a Christian, but she avoided mixing faith with business and would not budge: they had to pay the coyote part of his fee in advance, plus the whole of her commission.

The rest was to be paid by the relatives in the United States, or by the client—with interest, of course. "Where do you think I can find that amount of money, señora?" asked the Jesuit. "From your church's collection," she said sarcastically. In the end this was not necessary, because the money Miriam sent was enough to cover Andres's burial, the agent's commission, and 30 percent of the coyote's fee, with an IOU for the rest once Evelyn arrived safely. This debt was sacred: no one could avoid paying it.

The people smuggler chosen by the baker to help Evelyn Ortega was someone called Berto Cabrera, a thirty-two-year-old mustached Mexican with a beer paunch. He had been doing this for more than a decade and had made the trip dozens of times with hundreds of migrants. When it was a matter of people he was totally honest, although with other contraband his principles were more flexible. "Some people look down on what I do, but I'm performing a social service. I look after people, I don't take them in animal trucks or on top of trains," he explained to the priest.

Evelyn Ortega joined a group of four men who were heading north in search of work, together with a woman with a two-month-old baby who was going to join her boyfriend in Los Angeles. The baby would be a hindrance on the journey, but his mother had pleaded so earnestly that in the end the agency's owner relented. The clients met in the back of the bakery, where each was given fake identity papers and warned about the adventure they were about to embark on. From that moment on they could only use their new names; it was better for them not to know the other passengers' real ones. Head bowed, Evelyn did not dare look at anyone, but the woman with the baby came over and introduced herself. "My name now is Maria Ines Portillo. What about you?" she asked. Evelyn showed her identity card. Her new name was Pilar Saravia.

Once they had left Guatemala they would be Mexicans. There was no going back, and they had to obey the coyote's instructions without fail. Evelyn would be a student at a supposed school for deaf and mute children run by nuns in Durango. The other migrants learned the Mexican national anthem and some commonly used words that were different in the two countries. This would help them pass as authentic Mexicans if they were arrested by the migration police. The coyote forbade them to address people with the word "*vos*" as they did in Guatemala. To anyone in authority or in uniform they were to use "*usted*" as a precaution and out of respect; with others they could employ the informal "*tu*." Since Evelyn was meant to be mute, she was to say nothing at all. If the authorities questioned her, Berto would show them a certificate from the fictitious school. They were told to dress in their best outfits and to wear shoes or sneakers rather than flip-flops, as it would make them look less suspicious. The women would be more comfortable in pants but should not wear the torn jeans in fashion at the time. They would need to take sneakers, underwear, and a thick jacket; that was all that would fit into a bag or backpack. "You have to walk through the desert. You're not going to be able to carry much. We'll change your Guatemalan quetzales for Mexican pesos. Your transport costs are covered, but you'll need money for food."

Father Benito gave Evelyn a waterproof plastic envelope containing her birth certificate, copies of the medical and police reports, and a letter attesting to her good character. Someone had told him that this would help her gain asylum in the United States, and although this seemed to him a very remote possibility, he did not want to fail from lack of trying. He also made Evelyn memorize her mother's phone number in Chicago, and his own cell phone number. As he embraced her, he gave her the few banknotes he had.

Concepcion Montoya tried to stay calm when she bid her granddaughter farewell, but Evelyn's tears spoiled her good intentions and she ended up weeping as well.

"I'm very sad you're going," she sobbed. "You're my angel and I'm never going to see you again . . . little one. This is the last pain I have to suffer. If God gave me this destiny there must be a reason."

At this, Evelyn uttered the first complete sentence she had spoken in many weeks, and the last she would say for the next two months.

"Just as I am going, Grandma, so I will return."

Lucia

The night before, shaken to the core by Evelyn's story, Richard told her how sorry he felt about the suffering she had undergone. He was well aware of the violence in the Northern Triangle of Central America, but this firsthand account gave a face to that horror. When Richard had mentioned that Lucia too had once been a refugee, Lucia said her own experience could not be compared to what Evelyn had endured. Yet the girl wanted to know more.

When her life as a refugee began, Lucia Maraz had just turned nineteen and had been enrolled at the university to study journalism. They heard nothing more about her brother, Enrique, and over time, despite all their efforts to locate him, he became just one more among all those who had vanished without a trace in Chile. Lucia spent two months in the Venezuelan embassy in Santiago, waiting for a safe-conduct that would allow her to leave the country. The hundreds of guests, as the ambassador insisted on calling them to lessen the humiliation of their being asylum seekers, slept on the floor wherever there was room, and lined up at all hours outside the embassy's few bathrooms. In spite of the military surveillance outside, several times a week more fugitives managed to find a way in over the wall. Lucia had a newborn baby thrust into her arms, brought into the grounds hidden in a basket of vegetables in a diplomatic car, and was asked to look after him until the parents could join them.

The crowded conditions and collective anxiety could have led to disputes, but the new guests quickly accepted the rules of coexistence and learned to be patient. Lucia's safe-conduct took longer to arrive than normal for someone with no political or police record, but once it was in the hands of the ambassador, she was free to leave. Before being escorted by two members of the diplomatic staff to the door of the plane and from there to Caracas, she managed to hand the baby over to his parents, who had finally been able to obtain asylum. She also spoke on the phone to her mother, with the promise that she would be back soon. "Don't return until there's democracy in Chile," Lena replied in a firm voice.

Hundreds of Chileans began to arrive in rich and generous Venezuela. This soon turned into thousands upon thousands; before long their numbers were augmented by fugitives from the Dirty War in Argentina and Uruguay. This growing colony of refugees from the southern part of the continent gathered in certain neighborhoods, where the food and even the Spanish accents from their native countries predominated. A refugee aid committee found Lucia a room where she could live rent-free for six months and a job as a receptionist in an elegant plastic surgery clinic. The room and the job did not even last that long, because she met another Chilean exile, an anguished far-left sociologist whose harangues were a distressing reminder of her brother. He was handsome and slim as a bullfighter, with long, greasy hair; slender hands; and sensual lips that often curled into a sneer. He did nothing to hide his foul temper or his arrogance. Years later, Lucia was perplexed whenever she recalled him: she could not understand how she could have fallen in love with such an unpleasant character. The only explanation must have been that she was very young and very lonely. Her partner was so shocked by the Venezuelans' natural exuberance, which he saw as undeniable proof of their moral decadence, that he convinced Lucia they should emigrate together to Canada, where no one breakfasted on champagne or took advantage of the slightest opportunity to get up and dance.

In Montreal, Lucia and her unkempt theoretical guerrilla were received with open arms by another committee of well-meaning people, who installed them in an apartment equipped with furniture, kitchen utensils, and even the right-size clothes in the closet. This was in the depths of January, and Lucia soon thought the cold had penetrated into her bones forever. She lived hunched up, teeth chattering, wrapped in layers of wool, convinced that hell was not a Dantesque inferno but a Montreal winter. She survived the first months by seeking refuge in stores, in heated buses, in the underground tunnels connecting buildings, at her work, anywhere except the apartment she shared with her companion, where the temperature was adequate but the tension could have been cut with a knife.

MAY ARRIVED WITH AN EXPLOSION OF SPRING. By then the guerrilla's personal story had evolved until it became a hyperbolic adventure. It turned out he had not left the Honduran embassy in a plane thanks to a safe-conduct, as Lucia had thought, but had passed through Villa Grimaldi, the notorious torture center of the Chilean secret police. He emerged from there damaged in body and soul and escaped the country through dangerous Andean mountain passes in the south of Chile to neighboring Argentina, where he narrowly avoided becoming another victim of that country's Dirty War. With such a painful past it was normal that the poor man was traumatized and unable to work. Fortunately the committee completely understood, and offered him the means to undergo therapy in his own language and to take the time necessary to write a memoir about his sufferings. Lucia meanwhile immediately took on two jobs, because she did not think she deserved the committee's charity when there were other refugees in far more pressing situations. She worked twelve hours a day and when she got home she found herself cooking, cleaning, washing clothes, and trying to raise her companion's spirits.

Lucia stoically endured this for several months, until one night she came back to the apartment half-dead with fatigue and found it in darkness, airless and smelling of vomit. Her guerrilla had spent the day in bed, drinking gin, so badly depressed he found it impossible to get up: he was stuck on the first chapter of his memoirs. "Did you bring anything to eat? There's nothing here and I'm dying of hunger," the aspiring writer groaned when she switched on the light. It was then that Lucia finally realized how grotesque their relationship was. She ordered a pizza on the phone and took up her nightly chore of struggling with the mess that the guerrilla had created. That same night, while he was sleeping a deep, gin-induced sleep, she packed her bags and left. She had saved some money and had heard that a colony of Chilean exiles had begun to flourish in Vancouver. The next day she caught a train that took her all the way across to the west coast of Canada.

Lena Maraz visited Lucia in Canada once a year. She stayed with her daughter for three or four weeks, but never any longer because she was still trying to find Enrique. Over the years, her desperate search had become a way of being, a series of routines she fulfilled religiously and that gave her existence meaning. Shortly after the military coup, the cardinal of Santiago had opened an office, the Vicariate of Solidarity, to help those who were being pursued and their families. Lena would go there every week, always in vain. She met other people in the same situation as herself, made friends with the religious and volunteers, and learned how to pick her way through the bureaucracy of sorrow. She stayed in contact with the cardinal as best she could, because he was the busiest man in Chile. The military government only barely tolerated the mothers and subsequently grandmothers who paraded with photos of their children and grandchildren around their necks and stood in silence with placards demanding justice outside the barracks and detention centers. These troublesome old women refused to understand that the people they were asking after had never been detained. They had gone elsewhere or had never existed.

At dawn one wintry Tuesday, a patrol car came to Lena Maraz's apartment to inform her that her son had been the victim of a fatal accident, and that she could receive his remains the following day at an address they gave her. They also warned her she must arrive at exactly seven in the morning in a vehicle big enough to transport a coffin. Lena's knees buckled and she collapsed to the floor. For years she had been waiting for news of Enrique, and now, confronted with the fact of having found him, even if he was dead, she could not breathe.

She did not have the courage to go to the Vicariate, fearing that any intervention on their part might spoil this unique opportunity to recuperate her son, but imagined that perhaps the church or the cardinal himself had worked this miracle. Unable to face the shock on her own, she contacted her sister and they went together, dressed in mourning, to the address she had been given. In a square courtyard, its walls stained by the damp and by time, they were met by men who pointed to a pine coffin and instructed them to complete the burial before six that evening. The coffin was sealed. The men told them it was strictly forbidden to open it; they handed them a death certificate for the cemetery authorities, and gave Lena a receipt to sign that stated that the procedure was legal and correct. She was given a copy of the receipt and they helped her load the coffin onto the market truck the women had rented.

Lena did not drive directly to the cemetery as ordered, but instead went to her sister's house on a small plot of land on the outskirts of Santiago. The truck driver lent a hand to carry the coffin into the house and lay it on the kitchen table. Once he had left, they broke open the metal seal. They did not recognize the corpse: it was not Enrique, although the death certificate was in his name. Lena felt a mixture of horror at the state of the dead young man and relief it was not her son. That meant there was still hope of finding him alive. Thanks to her sister's insistence, she decided to run the risk of reprisals and called a Belgian priest who was one of her friends in the Vicariate. An hour later, he arrived on his motorbike, and brought a camera with him.

"Do you have any idea who this poor boy could be, Lena?"

"All I can say is that he's not my son, Father."

"We'll compare his photo with those in our archive to see if we can identify him and get in touch with his family," the priest said.

"Meanwhile, I'm going to give him a decent burial, because that's what I was told to do and I don't want them to come and take him from me," insisted Lena.

"Can I help you with that, Lena?"

"Thanks, but I can manage on my own. For the moment this boy can rest in a niche together with my husband in the Catholic cemetery. When you find his family, they can transfer him wherever they wish."

The photographs they took that day did not correspond to any of the ones in the Vicariate's archive. As they explained to Lena, maybe he was not even Chilean, but had come from another country, possibly Argentina or Uruguay. In Operation Condor, which linked the intelligence and repression services of the dictatorships of Chile, Argentina, Uruguay, Paraguay, Bolivia, and Brazil, and led to sixty thousand deaths, sometimes there were errors in the trafficking of prisoners, bodies, and identity documents. The youngster's photo was pinned up on the office wall in the Vicariate in case anybody recognized him. The logic of despair convinced Lena that somewhere another mother would be opening a sealed coffin that contained Enrique's body. She thought that if she could find the mother of the young man they had buried, in the future somebody would contact her and tell her of her own son's fate.

It only occurred to Lena several weeks later that the young

man they had buried might be Enrique and Lucia's half brother: the son her husband had with his other wife. This possibility tormented her so much it would not leave her in peace. She began to take steps to try to trace the woman she had rejected years before, full of remorse for having treated her so badly, because neither she nor the boy was guilty; they also had been victims of the same deceit. When her efforts and those of the Vicariate proved fruitless, she hired a private detective who according to his business card specialized in finding missing persons, but he could not find any sign of mother and son either. "They must have gone abroad, señora. Apparently lots of people seem to want to travel at the moment . . . ," the detective said.

After this, Lena suddenly aged. She retired from the bank where she had worked for many years, shut herself in her house, and only went out to insist on her pilgrimage. Occasionally she visited the cemetery and stood in front of the niche containing the remains of the unknown young man. She poured out her sorrows and asked him that if her son was anywhere near he should tell Enrique she needed a message or a sign to stop looking for him. As time went by she incorporated the youngster into her family, a discreet ghost. The cemetery's silence, its shady avenues and indifferent pigeons, offered her solace and peace. Although this was where she had buried her husband, in all these years she had never been to visit him. Now, with the pretext of praying for the boy, she also prayed for him.

LUCIA MARAZ SPENT THE REMAINING YEARS of her exile in Vancouver, a friendly city with a much better climate than

Montreal, where hundreds of exiles from the Southern Cone of Latin America settled in such closed communities that some of them lived as if they had never left their own country, refusing to mix with Canadians any more than was strictly necessary. This was not Lucia's case. With the tenacity she inherited from her mother she learned English—which she spoke with a Chilean accent—studied journalism, and worked doing investigative reports for political magazines and television. She adapted to Canada, made friends, adopted a dog that was to be with her for many years, and bought a tiny apartment because it was more convenient than renting. Whenever she fell in love, which happened more than once, she dreamed of getting married and putting down roots in Canada, but as soon as the passion cooled, her nostalgia for Chile immediately resurfaced. That was her home, in the south of the south, in that long, narrow country that still beckoned to her. She would go back, she was sure of it. Many Chilean exiles had returned and kept a low profile without being bothered. She knew that even her first love, the melodramatic guerrilla with greasy hair, had secretly gone back to Chile and was working in an insurance company without anyone remembering or even knowing about his past. Possibly though she would not be so lucky, because she had participated tirelessly in the international campaign against the military government. She had promised her mother she would not try to enter the country, because to Lena Maraz the possibility that her daughter would also become a victim of the repression was intolerable.

Lena's visits to Canada became less frequent, but her correspondence with her daughter grew so intense she began writing to her every day; Lucia wrote several times a week. Their letters crossed in midair like a conversation of the deaf, but neither of them waited for a reply before writing. This abundant correspondence was the diary of both their lives, the register of the everyday. Over time, the letters became indispensable to Lucia; what she did not write to her mother seemed not to have happened, a forgotten life. Thanks to this endless epistolary dialogue, with one in Vancouver and the other in Santiago, they developed such a close friendship that when Lucia finally returned to her mother in Chile they knew each other better than if they had lived together all that time.

During one of Lena's trips to Canada, while she was speaking about the youngster whose body she had been given instead of her Enrique, Lena decided to tell her daughter the truth about her father that she had kept hidden for so many years.

"If the young man they handed over to me in that coffin isn't your half brother, then somewhere there is a man more or less the same age as you who has your family name and the same blood in his veins as you," she said.

"What's his name?" asked Lucia, so taken aback at the news that her father had been a bigamist that she could hardly get the words out.

"Enrique Maraz, like your father and brother. I've tried to find him, Lucia, but he and his mother have vanished. I need to know if that boy in the cemetery is your father's son by that other woman."

"It doesn't matter, Mama. He's hardly likely to be my half brother; that only happens in TV soaps. What's most probable is what they told you at the Vicariate, that the identity of the victims gets mixed up. Don't burden yourself searching for that young man. You've been obsessed for years with Enrique's fate. Accept the truth, however horrible it may be, before you go crazy."

"I'm perfectly sane, Lucia. I'll accept your brother's death when I have some proof, and not before."

Lucia confessed that as children neither she nor Enrique had completely believed the story about their father's accident, which was so shrouded in mystery it seemed like fiction. How could they believe it, when they never saw any expression of grief or visited any grave, but had to make do with a brief explanation and a cautious silence. She and her brother used to invent alternative versions: that their father was alive somewhere else, that he had committed a crime and was on the run, or was hunting crocodiles in Australia; any explanation was more reasonable than the official one: he'd died and that was that, don't ask any more questions.

"You two were very young, Lucia. You couldn't understand how final death is; it was my duty to shield you from that pain. I thought it was better for you to forget your father. I know that was a sin of pride. I set out to replace him: to be both father and mother to my children."

"You did that very well, Mama, but I wonder if you would have behaved the same way if he hadn't been a bigamist."

"Most likely not, Lucia. In that case maybe I would have idealized him. I was motivated more than anything by rancor and shame. I didn't want to contaminate you with the ugliness of what had happened. That's why I didn't talk about him later on, when you were of an age to understand. I know you missed having a father."

"Less than you think, Mama. It's true it would have been better to have a father, but you brought us up wonderfully."

"The lack of a father leaves a hole in a woman's heart, Lucia. A girl needs to feel she is protected; she needs masculine energy to develop trust in men and later to be able to give herself in love. What's the female version of the Oedipus complex? Electra? You didn't have it. That's why you're so independent and jump from one love to the next, forever searching for the security of a father."

"Oh please, Mama! That's pure Freudian jargon. I'm not looking for my father in my lovers. And I'm no bed-hopper either. I'm a serial monogamist, and my loves last a long time, unless the guy is a hopeless case," said Lucia, and the two of them burst out laughing when they remembered the guerrilla she had abandoned in Montreal.

Lucia, Richard, Evelyn

Brooklyn

Ten minutes later Lucia came down from the bathroom to find Richard in the kitchen toasting bread, the coffeepot full, and three mugs on the table. Evelyn entered from the yard with Marcelo shivering in her arms, and proceeded to devour the toast and coffee Richard served her. Swaying on the stool with her mouth full, she looked so ravenous and young that Richard was touched. How old could she be? Most likely older than she looked. Maybe she was the same age as his Bibi.

"We're going to take you home, Evelyn," Lucia told her when they had finished their coffee.

"No! No!" cried Evelyn, standing up so suddenly that the stool toppled over and Marcelo fell to the floor.

"It was only a small dent, Evelyn. Don't be frightened. I'll explain what happened to your employer. What's his name again?"

"Frank Leroy . . . but it's not just because of the accident," stammered Evelyn, ashen faced.

"What else is there?" asked Richard.

"Come on, Evelyn, what are you so afraid of?" added Lucia.

Then, stumbling over the words and trembling severely, the young girl told them that there was a dead body in the car trunk. She had to repeat it twice for Lucia to understand. It took Richard even longer. Although he spoke Spanish, he was much more comfortable with the lilting Portuguese of Brazil. He could not believe what he was hearing: the enormity of her declaration froze him to the spot. If he had understood correctly, there were two alternatives: either the girl was raving mad or there really was a dead body in the Lexus.

"A body, you said?"

Evelyn nodded, her eyes on the floor.

"That's impossible. What kind of body?"

"Richard! Don't be ridiculous. A human body, of course," Lucia cut in. She was so astonished she had to struggle to suppress a nervous laugh.

"How did it get there?" asked Richard, still incredulous.

"I don't know . . ."

"Did you run over the person?"

"No."

Faced with the possibility that they really were dealing with an anonymous dead person, Richard started scratching with both hands at the hives that broke out on his arms and chest in moments of tension. A man of unchanging habits and routines, he was ill prepared for unforeseen events like this. Although he was not yet aware of it, his stable, cautious existence had come to an end.

"We have to call the police," he decided, picking up his cell phone.

The young Guatemalan girl gave a shriek of terror and began weeping with heartrending sobs for reasons that were evident to Lucia but not to Richard, even though he was well aware of the constant state of uncertainty most Latin American immigrants lived in.

"I suppose you're undocumented," said Lucia. "We can't call the police, Richard. We would be getting this poor girl into trouble. She took the car without permission. She could be accused of theft as well as homicide. You know how the police treat undocumented immigrants. They always go for the weakest link in the chain."

"What chain?"

"It's a metaphor, Richard."

"How did that person die? Who is it?" Richard asked.

Evelyn told them she hadn't touched the body. She had gone to the drugstore to buy diapers and had opened the trunk with one hand while holding the shopping bag in the other. It was when she tried to push the bag in that she had noticed the trunk was full. She saw an object covered in a rug; when she pulled it aside she saw there was a curled-up body underneath. She was so scared she fell back onto the sidewalk but stifled the scream fighting to come out and slammed the trunk shut. She put the bag on the backseat and locked herself in the car for a good while—she wasn't sure how long, at least twenty or thirty minutes—until she had calmed down enough to be able to drive back to the house. With a bit of luck her absence might have gone unnoticed, and no one would know she had used the car, but after the collision with Richard, with the trunk dented and half-open, that was impossible.

"We don't even know whether that person is dead. He could be unconscious," suggested Richard, wiping his brow with a dish towel.

"Not too likely, he'd be dead from hypothermia by now. But there's one way to find out," said Lucia.

"Good God, woman! You're not suggesting we look inside the trunk on the street . . ."

"Do you have a better idea? There's no one outside. It's very early, it's still dark, and it's Sunday. Who's going to see us?"

"No way. Count me out."

"Okay, lend me a flashlight. Evelyn and I are going to take a look."

Hearing this, the girl's sobs increased in volume by several decibels. Lucia put her arm around her, feeling sorry for this young girl and all the suffering she had been through in the past few hours.

"This has nothing to do with me! My insurance will pay for the damage to the car, and that's all I can do. I'm sorry, Evelyn, but you'll have to leave," said Richard in his broken Spanish.

"You're going to throw her out, Richard? Are you crazy? As if you don't know what it means to be undocumented in this country!" cried Lucia.

"I do know, Lucia. If not from my work at the center, I'd know from my father, who's forever harping about it," sighed Richard, caving in. "What do we know about this girl?"

"That she needs help. Do you have family here, Evelyn?"

A sepulchral silence: Richard went on scratching, thinking of what a tremendous mess he was in—the police, an investigation, the press, his reputation down the drain. And his father's voice deep inside him reminding him of his duty to help the persecuted: "I wouldn't be in this world, and you wouldn't have been born, if some brave souls hadn't hidden me from the Nazis," he had told him over and over, about a million times.

"We have to find out if that person is still alive. There's no time to lose," Lucia repeated.

She picked up the car keys Evelyn Ortega had left on the kitchen table, handed her the Chihuahua as a precaution against the cats, put on her hat and gloves, and asked again for the flashlight.

"Oh shit, Lucia, you can't go on your own! I'll have to go with you," said Richard resignedly. "We'll need to defrost the trunk to open it."

They filled a large pot with hot water and vinegar and between the two of them managed with great difficulty to carry it out, treading carefully on the slippery staircase and clinging on to the handrails to stay upright. Lucia's contact lenses began to freeze, feeling like shards of glass in her eyes. Richard often went in winter to fish in the frozen lakes of the north and had experience with extreme cold, but he was not prepared for it in Brooklyn. The light from the streetlamps cast yellow, phosphorescent circles on the snow. The wind blew in gusts, rising and falling as if weary with the effort, then moments later stirring up swirls of loose snow. When it died down, complete silence reigned, a threatening stillness. Cars covered with varying amounts of snow were parked along the street; Evelyn's white Lexus was nearly invisible. It was not directly outside his house as Richard had feared, but some fifteen yards away, which in fact made no difference. No one was around at that early hour. The snowplows had begun to clear the street the day before, and there were mounds of snow piled on the sidewalks.

Just as Evelyn had said, the trunk was tied with a yellow belt. They had a hard time untying it because of their gloves: Richard had become paranoid about fingerprints. They finally got the trunk open and saw a bundle partially covered with a bloodstained rug. When they pulled it back they found a woman dressed in workout clothes, her face hidden in her arms. She was curled up in a strange position and barely looked human, more like a disjointed doll. What little skin they could see was lavender. There was no doubt about it: she was dead. They stood for several minutes trying to work out what had happened: they could not see any blood on her but would have to turn her over to examine her properly. The poor creature was frozen as solid as a block of cement. However much Lucia pushed and pulled, she could not budge her. Richard shone the flashlight on her, almost sobbing with anxiety.

"I think she died yesterday," said Lucia.

"Why do you think that?"

"Rigor mortis. A body becomes stiff about eight hours after death, and the rigor lasts for thirty-six hours or so."

"So then it could have been the night before ."

"True. It could have been even earlier because the temperature is so low. Whoever put that woman in the trunk was counting on that, I'm sure. Maybe they couldn't dispose of the body because of Friday's blizzard. It's obvious they were in no hurry."

"It could be that the rigor mortis has finished and the body has simply frozen," suggested Richard.

"A human being is not the same as a chicken, Richard. It takes a couple of days in an icebox for a body to freeze completely. Let's say she could have died between the night before last and yesterday."

"How come you know so much about this?"

"Don't ask," she said categorically.

"In any case, that's up to the forensic pathologist and the police, not us," Richard concluded.

As if summoned by magic, they saw the headlights of a vehicle slowly turning the corner. They succeeded in lowering the lid of the trunk just as a police patrol car pulled up alongside them. One of the policemen stuck his head out of the window.

"Everything okay?" he asked.

"All okay, officer," replied Lucia.

"What are you doing outside at this time of day?" the man asked.

"Looking for my mother's diapers. We left them in the car," Lucia said, pulling the big bag from the backseat.

"Good morning, officer," said Richard, his voice reedy.

They waited until the car moved off and fastened the trunk again with the belt. Then they went back into the house, slipping on the ice on the stairs as they carried the diapers and the empty pot, and praying to the heavens that the patrolmen would not think of coming back to take a look at the Lexus.

THEY FOUND EVELYN, MARCELO, AND THE CATS in exactly the same position as they had left them. When they asked the girl about the diapers, she explained that Frankie, the boy she cared for, had cerebral palsy and needed them.

"How old is the boy?" asked Lucia.

"Thirteen."

"And he wears adult diapers?"

Evelyn turned red with embarrassment and explained that Frankie was very advanced for his age and the diapers had to be loose because the "little bird" often woke him up. Lucia translated for Richard: erection.

"I left him on his own yesterday. He must be desperate. Who's going to give him his insulin?" murmured Evelyn.

"He needs insulin?"

"If only we could call Señora Leroy . . . Frankie can't be left on his own."

"It's risky to use the phone," Richard said.

"I'll call from my cell with the number blocked," said Lucia.

The phone only rang twice before an angry voice began shouting at the other end. Lucia ended the call at once, and Evelyn sighed with relief. The only person who could answer on that number was Frankie's mother. If she was with him, Evelyn could relax; the boy would be well looked after.

"Come on, Evelyn, you must have some idea of how that woman's body ended up in the car trunk," said Richard.

"No. The Lexus belongs to my boss, Mr. Leroy."

"He must be searching for his car."

"He's in Florida. He's supposed to come back tomorrow."

"Do you think he could have had something to do with this?"

"Yes."

"In other words, you think he could have killed that woman," Richard insisted.

"When Mr. Leroy gets angry, he's like a devil . . . ," said the young Guatemalan, bursting into tears.

"Let her calm down," Lucia told Richard.

"You realize we can't go to the police now, don't you, Lucia? How would we explain that we lied to the patrolman?"

"Forget the police for the moment!"

"My mistake was calling you, Lucia. If I'd known this girl had a dead body hanging over her I would have gone to the police right away," said Richard, more pensive than angry. He served Lucia more coffee. "Milk?"

"Black and no sugar."

"Shit, what a mess we've got ourselves into!"

"These things happen in life, Richard."

"Not in mine."

"Yes, I've realized that. But see how life refuses to leave us in peace? Sooner or later it catches up with us."

"The girl will have to take her dead body elsewhere."

"You tell her," said Lucia, pointing to Evelyn, who was sobbing silently.

"What are you thinking of doing?" Richard asked the girl.

Evelyn shrugged sorrowfully, mumbling excuses for having gotten them into trouble.

"You have to do something," Richard insisted, without great conviction.

Lucia tugged at his sleeve and led him over to the piano, away from Evelyn.

"The first thing is to dispose of the evidence," she said in a low voice. "Before we do anything else."

"I don't understand."

"We've got to get rid of the car and the body."

"You're mad!" he exclaimed.

"You're involved in this too, Richard."

"I am?"

"Yes, from the moment you opened the door to Evelyn last night and then called me. We have to decide where we're going to dump the body."

"You've got to be kidding. How can you even think of such a crazy idea?"

"Look, Richard: Evelyn can't go back to her employers' house, and she can't go to the police either. Do you want her to drive around everywhere with a dead body in somebody else's car? For how long?"

"I'm sure all this can be sorted out."

"With the police? No way."

"Let's drive the car to another neighborhood, and that'll be that."

"It would be found at once, Richard. Evelyn needs time to get to somewhere safe. I suppose you've realized how terrified she is. She knows more than she's telling us. I think she has a very specific fear of her employer, that Mr. Leroy. She suspects he killed that woman and is coming after her. He knows she took the Lexus and won't let her escape."

"If that's so, we're in danger too."

"No one suspects she is with us. Let's drive the car as far away as possible."

"That would make us accomplices!"

"We already are, but if we do things properly no one will know. They can't connect us to any of this, not even to Evelyn. The snow is a blessing, and we have to take advantage of it while it lasts. We have to leave today."

"Where to?"

"How should I know, Richard! Think of something. We have to head for somewhere cold so that the body doesn't start to smell."

AFTER RETURNING TO THE KITCHEN, they drank coffee while considering the possibilities. They did not consult Evelyn Ortega, who sat watching them timidly. She had dried her tears but had slipped back into the mute attitude of someone who has never had any control over what happens in her life. Lucia suggested that the farther away they went, the greater the probability they would emerge unscathed from this adventure.

"I once went to Niagara Falls and crossed the border into Canada without showing any documents. And they didn't search the car."

"That must have been fifteen years ago. Nowadays they always ask to see your passport."

"We could reach Canada in no time, then abandon the car in a wood; they have lots of woods up there."

"They can also identify the car in Canada, Lucia. It's not the far side of the moon."

"By the way, we need to identify the victim. We can't abandon her somewhere without at least knowing who she is."

"Why?" asked a perplexed Richard.

"Out of respect. We're going to have to take another look in the trunk, and it's better we do so now, before there are people out and about," Lucia decided.

They almost dragged Evelyn out of the house and had to push her over to the car.

"Do you know her?" Richard asked, after he had untied the belt and shone the flashlight into the trunk.

He had to repeat the question three times before Evelyn dared open her eyes. She was trembling, overwhelmed by that same atavistic terror she had felt by the bridge in her village, a terror that had been lurking in the shadows throughout the eight years that followed, so searing that it was as if the livid, bloody body of her brother Gregorio were present right there on that street.

"Make an effort, Evelyn. It's really important we know who this woman is," Lucia insisted.

"It's Miss Kathryn," the young woman finally murmured. "Kathryn Brown . . ."

Lucia and Richard quickly retied the lid of the trunk closed and made their way back to the house.

"Who is Kathryn?" Richard asked Evelyn.

"Frankie's physical therapist; she used to come every Monday and Thursday. She taught me exercises for the boy."

"That means she was someone who was known in the house. What did you say your employers' names were?"

"Cheryl and Frank Leroy."

"And it looks as though Frank Leroy is responsible for—"

"Why do you think that, Richard? We can't assume anything without proof," said Lucia.

"If that woman had died a natural death she would not be in the trunk of Frank Leroy's car."

"It could have been an accident."

"Yes, like she stuck her head in the trunk, wrapped the rug around her, the lid closed on top of her, she starved to death, and no one noticed. Not very probable. No doubt about it, Lucia:

someone killed her, and was planning to get rid of the body when the snow was cleared. By now he must be wondering what the hell happened to his car and his dead body."

"Come on, Evelyn, think about it: how do you guess that young woman ended up in the trunk of the Lexus?" Lucia asked her.

"I don't know . . ."

"When was the last time you saw her?"

"She used to come on Mondays and Thursdays," Evelyn repeated.

"And last Thursday?"

"Yes, she arrived at eight in the morning, but left almost immediately because Frankie had problems with his glucose levels. The señora was very angry. She told Kathryn to leave and not come back."

"They had an argument?"

"Yes."

"What did Mrs. Leroy have against her?"

"She said she was brazen and vulgar."

"Did she tell her that to her face?"

"She used to tell me. And her husband."

Evelyn explained that Kathryn Brown had been looking after Frankie for a year. From the start she got on badly with Cheryl Leroy, who thought she was indecent because she came to work in low-cut T-shirts with her breasts half-exposed. She was rude and common, with the manners of a platoon sergeant, Cheryl used to say, and besides, there were no signs of improvement in Frankie. She had given Evelyn instructions that she should always be present when the Brown woman was working with him, and to tell her at once if she saw any signs of abuse. She did not trust Kathryn and thought she was very rough with the exercises. Once or twice she had wanted to fire her, but her husband was against it, as he was with all her initiatives. In his view, Frankie was simply a spoiled brat and Cheryl was jealous of the physical therapist because she was young and pretty. For her part, Kathryn Brown also spoke badly of Mrs. Leroy behind her back. She thought Cheryl treated her son like a baby, and that children needed authority. Frankie ought to be eating on his own: if he could use a computer he could hold a spoon and brush his teeth, but how was he going to learn with that alcoholic, drugged mother of his who spent all her time in the gym, as if that could keep old age at bay? Her husband was going to leave her, that was for sure.

Evelyn would listen to the accusations from both sides with her mind a blank. She never repeated any of it. Her grandmother had washed her brothers' mouths out with soap whenever they said anything dirty, and hers whenever she repeated gossip. She found out about her employers' arguments because the walls of the house kept no secrets. Frank Leroy, who was so cold with his employees and his son, so controlled even when the boy suffered an attack or tantrum, would fly into a rage with his wife at the slightest excuse. That Thursday Cheryl, who was worried about Frankie's hypoglycemia and suspected it was the physical therapist who had caused it, disobeyed her husband's orders and fired her.

"Sometimes Mr. Leroy threatens his wife," Evelyn told them. "He once put a pistol in her mouth. I wasn't spying, I promise. The door was half-open. He said he was going to kill her and Frankie."

"Does he hit his wife? Or Frankie?" asked Lucia.

"He doesn't touch the boy, but Frankie knows he doesn't love him."

"You haven't answered if he hits his wife."

"Sometimes she has bruises on her body, never the face. She always says she fell."

"And do you believe her?"

"She falls over from the pills or the whiskey, and I have to pick her up and put her to bed. But the bruises come from fights with Mr. Leroy. I feel sorry for her, she's not happy at all."

"How could she be, with a husband and son like that . . ."

"She adores Frankie. She says that with love and rehabilitation he's going to get better."

"That's impossible," muttered Richard.

"From what I see, Frankie is the señora's only joy. They love each other so much! You should see how happy Frankie is when his mother is with him. They spend hours playing, and often the señora sleeps with him."

"She must be very anxious about her son's health," commented Lucia.

"Yes, Frankie's health is very delicate. Could we call the house again?"

"No, Evelyn. It's too risky," Lucia said. "We know his mother was with him last night. We can assume that if you're not there, she'll take care of him. Let's go back to our most pressing problem: what to do with the body."

Richard caved in so quickly that later on he was amazed at his own inconsistency. Reflecting on it, he concluded he had spent years fearful of any change that might threaten his security, and yet perhaps it was not fear but anticipation: maybe he harbored a secret desire for divine intervention to descend and disrupt his perfect, monotonous existence. Evelyn Ortega, with this corpse in her trunk, was the exaggerated reply to this latent wish. He needed to call his father because today he would not be able to take him out for their customary Sunday lunch. For a brief moment he was tempted to tell him what they were going to do to help Evelyn, because he was sure that old Joseph would be applauding from his wheelchair. He'd tell him later on, in person, so that he could see the look of approval on his father's face. For whatever reason, he put up only minimal resistance to Lucia's arguments, and went off to look for a map and a magnifying glass. The idea of getting rid of the body, which only a short time earlier he had flatly rejected, now seemed to him inevitable, the only logical solution to a problem that all of a sudden was his as well.

PORING OVER THE MAP, Richard remembered the lake in the Catskills he used to visit with Horacio. His friend had a log cabin there, where in the summer he vacationed with his family, and where he and Richard went in winter to fish in a hole on the icy lake. They would always avoid the busiest areas, because for them angling was a meditative sport, a special opportunity to enjoy silence and solitude, and to strengthen a friendship that went back almost forty years. That part of the lake was difficult to get to and did not attract the winter hordes. He and Horacio would drive across the frozen surface in an off-road vehicle, dragging a small trailer containing all they needed for the day: a saw and other tools to cut the ice, rods and hooks, batteries, a lamp, a kerosene stove, gasoline, and provisions. They made holes and with infinite patience fished for some rather small trout that when grilled were little more than skin and bones.

Richard missed Horacio and looked after his affairs in his absence. His friend had gone back to Argentina when his father died, thinking he would return after a few weeks, but two years had passed and he was still caught up in his family's businesses and only came to the United States a couple of times a year. Richard had the keys to his empty lakeside cabin and used his vehicle, a Subaru Legacy with a roof rack for skis and bicycles, which Horacio refused to sell. It was at Horacio's insistence that Richard had applied to be a faculty member at the Center for Latin American and Caribbean Studies at New York University. He had been an assistant professor for three years, and associate professor another three, before getting tenure, with all the security this implied. And when Horacio quit his position as chairman, Richard replaced him. He also bought his friend's house in Brooklyn at a bargain price. As Richard used to say, the only way to repay Horacio for everything he had done would be to donate his lungs to him for a transplant while still alive. Like his father and his siblings, Horacio was a chain-smoker and had a constant cough.

"The woods surrounding that part of the lake are fairly dense. No one goes there in winter and I doubt they do in summer either," Richard explained to Lucia.

"How are we going to organize this? We'd have to rent a car to get back," said Lucia.

"That would leave a trail. We can't draw attention to ourselves. We can take the Subaru to return in. Normally we could go and come back in one day, but with this weather it will take us two."

"What about the cats?"

"I'll leave them food and water. They're used to being left alone for a few days."

"Something unexpected might happen."

"Like for example us being sent to jail, or getting murdered by Frank Leroy?" Richard asked with a wry smile. "If that happens, my neighbor will come and look after the cats."

"We have to take Marcelo," Lucia said.

"No way!"

"What do you want me to do with him?"

"We can leave him with my neighbor."

"Dogs aren't like cats, Richard. They get anxious over separations. He has to come with us."

Richard flung his hands in the air. He found it hard to understand how anyone could be so dependent on animals in general and in particular on such a grotesque Chihuahua. The cats were independent; he could go away for weeks secure in the knowledge they would not miss him.

Lucia followed him to one of the unoccupied rooms on the first floor, where he kept his tools and a carpentry bench. This was the last thing she would have imagined; she'd assumed that like all the other men in her life, he was unable even to hammer a nail in the wall, but it was clear that Richard enjoyed manual work. The tools were mounted on pegboards on the wall, each with its own spot clearly outlined in chalk so that it would be obvious where to replace it. Everything was arranged as neatly as in the pantry, where each object had its exact position. The only evident chaos in the house was limited to the papers and books that had taken over the living room and kitchen, although possibly this chaos was only superficial and they were in fact

classified according to a secret system that only Richard understood. He must be a Virgo, she decided.

RICHARD GOT OUT THE SHOVEL and cleared away the snow in
front of the basement door so that Lucia could rescue what was
left of her Chilean *cazuela*, the food for Marcelo, and her toiletries. Back in Richard's kitchen they shared the tasty soup and
prepared another pot of coffee. Distracted by all the commotion, Richard ate two platefuls, even though there were chunks
of beef floating among the potatoes, green beans, and pumpkin.
He had succeeded in controlling the upsets of his digestive system thanks to a strictly disciplined life. He avoided gluten, was
lactose intolerant, and did not drink alcohol for a much more
serious reason than his ulcer problem. His ideal would be to eat
only plants, but he needed protein, and so each week he added
to his diet certain types of seafood that had no mercury in them,
six organic eggs, and four ounces of hard cheese. He followed
a biweekly plan with two fixed menus each month. This meant
he bought only what was strictly necessary and cooked it in the
preestablished order so that nothing was wasted. On Sundays
he improvised with whatever fresh produce he could find at the
market; this was one of the few flights of fancy he allowed himself. He did not eat meat from mammals out of a moral decision
not to eat animals he would be unable to kill, or fowl because of
his horror of industrial farming and because he would not have
been able to wring a chicken's neck either. However, he enjoyed
cooking, and occasionally, if a dish turned out especially well,
he fantasized about sharing it with someone, for example, Lucia

Maraz, who was far more interesting than any of his previous basement tenants. He had been thinking about her increasingly often and was now pleased to have her in his house, even if it was thanks to the extraordinary pretext offered by Evelyn Ortega. In fact, he was far more pleased than the circumstances warranted; something strange was happening to him, he had to be careful.

Fortified by the *cazuela*, they went out into the street again. Richard studied the broken lock on the trunk for several minutes while Lucia protected him from the falling snow under a black umbrella. "I can't fix it, I'm going to secure the lid with a piece of wire," he concluded. Beneath the disposable latex gloves he had insisted on wearing so as to leave no fingerprints, his hands were blue and his fingers stiff, and yet he worked with a surgeon's precision. Twenty-five minutes later he had painted the bulb in the smashed indicator red, and had fastened the lid so skillfully that the wire was invisible. Teeth chattering, the two of them went back into the house, where the still-hot coffee awaited them.

"The wire will last the whole trip and won't cause you any problems," Richard announced to Lucia.

"Cause me any problems? No, Richard, you're going to drive the Lexus. I'm a poor driver, and even worse if I'm nervous. The police could pull me over."

"Then Evelyn can drive. I'll go ahead in the Subaru."

"Evelyn doesn't have any documents."

"Not even a license?"

"I've already asked her. She has a license in someone else's name. A fake one, of course. We can't run any more risks than we have to. You'll drive the Lexus, Richard."

"Why me?"

"Because you're a white male. No cop is going to ask for your documents, even if a human foot is sticking out of the trunk. But a pair of Latinas driving in the snow is suspicious right away."

"If the Leroys reported the disappearance of the car we're in trouble."

"Why would they do that?"

"To claim insurance."

"What do you mean, Richard? One of them is a murderer, so the last thing they would do is to report something like that."

"What about the other one?"

"You always imagine the worst!"

"I really don't like the idea of traversing New York State in a stolen car."

"Neither do I, but we've got no alternative."

"Look, Lucia, has it occurred to you that it could have been Evelyn who killed that woman?"

"No, Richard, it hasn't occurred to me, because it's a stupid idea. Do you think that poor girl is capable of killing a fly? And why would she bring the victim to your house?"

On the map Richard showed her the two routes to the lake. One was shorter but had tollbooths where there might be checks; the other involved secondary roads that were full of bends. They chose the latter route, and could only hope the roads had been cleared by the snowplows.

Evelyn

Mexico, 2008

Berto Cabrera, the Mexican coyote hired to take Evelyn to the north, called his clients to the bakery at eight in the morning. When they were all assembled, they formed a tight circle holding hands and he raised a prayer to the heavens. "We are pilgrims in a church without borders. Grant us, Lord, that we travel with your divine protection against both attackers and guards. We ask this in the name of your son, Jesus of Nazareth." All the travelers said amen, except for Evelyn, who was still sobbing and unable to speak. "Keep your tears, Pilar Saravia, you're going to need them later on," Cabrera advised her. He gave each of them their bus ticket, told them it was forbidden to look at or talk to each other, to make friends with other passengers, or to sit in window seats, because first-timers always did that, and the border guards paid special attention to them. "And you, my girl, are coming with me. From now on, I'm your uncle.

Stay silent and with that moron's face of yours no one is going to be suspicious. Agreed?" Evelyn nodded.

A bakery delivery truck took them on the first stage of their journey, to Tecun Uman, a border town separated from Mexico by the Suchiate River. There was a constant flow of people and goods across the river and the bridge linking the two banks. It was a porous frontier. The Mexican federal police tried half-heartedly to intercept drugs, weapons, and other contraband but ignored the migrants as long as they did not attract attention to themselves. Scared by the busy throng of people, the chaos of bicycles and tricycles, and the roar of motorbikes, Evelyn clung to the coyote's arm. He had told the others to make their way separately to the Hotel Cervantes. He and Evelyn boarded one of the local pedicabs, a bicycle with a covered trailer for passengers that was the commonest form of transport. They soon met up with the rest of the group in the run-down hotel, where they rested overnight.

The next morning, Berto Cabrera took them down to the river, where there was a line of boats and rafts made from truck tires and a few planks. They were used to transport all kinds of goods, animals, and people. Cabrera hired two of these rafts, each pulled by a young man with a rope tied around his waist and propelled with a long pole by another man standing on it. In less than ten minutes they were in Mexico, where a bus took them to the center of Tapachula.

Cabrera explained to his clients that they were now in the state of Chiapas, the most dangerous area for migrants not protected by a coyote, because they were at the mercy of bandits, robbers, and police who could strip them of all they possessed, from their money to their sneakers. It was impossible to fool them, because they knew every hiding place, and even inspected people's private orifices. As for police extortion, anyone who could not pay was thrown into a cell, beaten up, and deported. The greatest risk, the coyote told them, was the "godmothers," volunteers who claimed to be assisting the authorities as an excuse to rape and torture; they were savages. People disappeared in Chiapas. They were not to trust anyone, civilians or officials.

They passed a cemetery, where solitude and the silence of death hung in the air. Then suddenly they heard the hiss of a train getting ready to set off, and the burial ground came to life as dozens of migrants who had been hiding there emerged. Adults and children appeared from among the tombs and bushes and started to run, jumping on stepping stones across the filthy water of a sewage canal, desperate to reach the railcars. Berto explained that the train was known as the Beast, the Iron Worm, or the Train of Death, and that some migrants would have to ride thirty or more such trains to cross Mexico.

"I won't tell you how many fall off and are crushed by the wheels," Cabrera warned them. "My cousin Olga Sanchez converted an abandoned tortilla factory into a shelter for people brought to her with arms or legs amputated by the train. She's saved a lot of lives in her Hostel of Jesus the Good Shepherd. My cousin Olga is a saint. If we had more time we could go and see her. But you are traveling in luxury, you won't be clinging onto trains, although we can't catch a bus here. Can you see those guys with dogs checking documents and luggage? They're from the federal police. The dogs can sniff out drugs and people's fear."

The coyote took them to a truck-driver friend, who for a suitable price installed them among crates of electrical goods.

At the back of the container was a narrow space where they could sit huddled together, although they could not stretch their legs or stand up. There was no light and little air, and the heat was stifling. The truck threw them around so much they were afraid the crates would fall on top of them. The coyote, who was comfortably seated up in the cabin, had forgotten to tell them they would be kept prisoner in the back for hours, though he did warn them to ration the water and refrain from urinating, as there would be no relief stop. The men and Evelyn took turns to fan Maria Ines with a piece of cardboard and gave her some of their water rations, since she had to breastfeed her baby.

The truck took them safely as far as Fortin de las Flores in Veracruz, where Berto Cabrera placed them in a derelict house on the outskirts of the town. He left them jugs of water, bread, mortadella, soft cheese, and crackers. "Wait here, I'll be back soon," he said, and disappeared. Two days later, when they had run out of provisions and there was still no news of him, the group became split, with the men convinced they'd been abandoned, while Maria Ines argued they should give Cabrera more time because he had been so strongly recommended by the evangelicals. Evelyn had no opinion, but none of them asked her anyway. In the few days they had been together, the four men had become protective toward the young mother, her child, and the strange skinny girl who always seemed to be in a world of her own. They knew she was not really deaf and mute because they had heard her say a few stray words, but they respected her silence since it could be a religious promise or her final refuge. The women ate first and were given the best places to sleep in the only room that still had a roof. At night the men took turns to make sure one stayed on guard while the others rested.

AT DUSK ON THE SECOND DAY, three of the men left to buy food, and to scout around to determine how they could continue the journey without Cabrera. The other man stayed to look after the women. Since the day before, Maria Ines's baby had refused to take any milk, and had cried and coughed so hard he could scarcely breathe. Unable to calm him, his mother grew increasingly anxious. Remembering her grandmother's remedies in such cases, Evelyn soaked a couple of T-shirts in water and wrapped them around the baby until his fever had abated; Maria Ines meanwhile could do no more than weep and talk of returning to Guatemala. Evelyn walked up and down with the boy in her arms, cradling him with a lullaby she invented with no real words but full of the noises of birds and the wind, which eventually sent him to sleep.

Later that night the others returned with sausages, tortillas, beans and rice, beers for the men, and soft drinks for the women. After this feast they all felt more cheerful and started making plans to continue on to the north. They had discovered there were migrants' houses along the route, and some churches that offered aid. They could also count on the Beta Groups, Mexican National Institute of Migration employees whose job was not to impose the law but to help travelers with humanitarian advice, and to rescue them and supply first aid in case of accidents. Most curious of all, said the men, was the fact that they did all this for free and did not take bribes. So the group was not completely unprotected. They had their meager funds, which they were prepared to share, and promised to go on together.

The following day they found that the baby had recovered his appetite even though he still had difficulty breathing and decided they would move on as soon as the heat dropped. There was no way they could take the bus, because it was very expensive, but they could ask truck drivers for a lift and as a last resort climb on board the freight trains.

They had already gathered their belongings and what was left of the food into their backpacks when Berto Cabrera appeared in a rented van, wreathed in smiles and loaded down with bags. They greeted him with a string of reproaches, which he countered in a friendly way, explaining he had to change the original plans because there was more surveillance on the buses and because some of his contacts had failed. In other words, they would have to hand out more bribes. He knew people at all the checkpoints along the route, who were paid a certain amount for each migrant. Their boss kept half, and the rest was distributed among his men, and so everyone was a winner in this squalid trade. Berto had to be very careful during the process, for if he came across an uncooperative patrol they would end up deported. There was a much greater risk of this with guards he did not know.

They could have made the journey to the border in a couple of days, but the baby's fever returned and they had to take him to a hospital in San Luis Potosi. They lined up, took a number, and waited for hours in a room crammed with patients until finally Maria Ines was called. By this time the child was limp. He was attended by a doctor with dark fatigue lines under his eyes and wrinkled clothes, who diagnosed whooping cough and kept the baby there on a course of antibiotics. The coyote was furious, because this was ruining his plans, but the doctor was insistent: the baby had a very serious infection in the respiratory tract. Cabrera had to back down. He assured the disconsolate mother that he would return within a week and that she would not lose the money she had paid in advance. Maria Ines sobbed and accepted, but the rest of the group refused to go on without her. "May God grant the little one doesn't die, but if he does, Maria Ines is going to need company in her grief," they unanimously decided.

They spent a night in a run-down hotel, but the coyote complained so much about the extra cost that they ended up sleeping in a churchyard together with dozens of other migrants in the same situation. There they were given a plate of food, and were able to shower and wash clothes, but at eight in the morning they had to leave and were only allowed to return after sundown. The days seemed very long as they wandered around the town, always on the alert, ready to run. The men tried to earn some cash washing cars or on building sites without attracting the attention of the police, who were everywhere. According to Cabrera, the North Americans were providing the Mexican government with millions of dollars to stop the migrants before they reached the border. Every year more than a hundred thousand people were deported from Mexico on the aptly named Bus of Tears.

Since Evelyn could not speak even to beg and might fall into the hands of one of the many pimps who preyed on unaccompanied girls, Cabrera took her with him in his vehicle. Silent and invisible, Evelyn waited in the van while he conducted dubious deals on his cell phone and had a good time in seedy dives with women for hire. He would come staggering back glassy-eyed at dawn, find her curled up on the seat, and realize the girl had spent the whole day and night with no food or water. "What a sonofabitch I am!" he would mutter, and take her off with him to find somewhere open where she could go to the toilet and eat her fill. "It's your own fault, dummy. If you don't talk you'll die of hunger in this crazy world. How are you going to survive on your own in the north?" he scolded her, with an involuntary hint of tenderness.

Four days later, Maria Ines's baby was discharged from the hospital, but the coyote decided there was no way they could run the risk of taking him with them, because he might die on the way. The toughest part was still to come: crossing the Rio Grande and then the desert. He gave Maria Ines the choice between staying in Mexico for a while, doing whatever work she could find—which would be difficult, because who would take her on with a baby?—or returning to Guatemala. She chose to go back, and said goodbye to her companions, who had already become her family.

AFTER PUTTING MARIA INES and her baby on the bus, Berto Cabrera drove his clients toward Tamaulipas. He told them that on a previous trip he had been held up in a hotel doorway by two men in suits and ties who looked like officials and who stole his money and cell phone. From then on he was wary of the roadside hotels where coyotes and their passengers often stayed, because Mexican migration officials, the federal police, and detectives all had them in their sights.

They spent that night in the house of someone Cabrera knew, stretched out in a huddle on the ground under blankets from the van. The next morning they set off for Nuevo Laredo, the last stage of their journey in Mexico. A few hours later they found themselves in Plaza Hidalgo in the center of the city, together with hundreds of migrants from Mexico and Central America as well as all kinds of traffickers offering their services. Nine organized gangs of smugglers operated in Nuevo Laredo, each of them employing more than fifty coyotes. They had dreadful reputations: they stole, they raped, and some had links to gangs of thieves and pimps. "They're not honest people like me. In all the time I've been in this profession no one has been able to say a bad word about me. I care about my honor, I'm a responsible person," Cabrera told them.

They bought phone cards and were able to talk to their relatives to tell them they had reached the border. Evelyn called Father Benito but stammered so badly that Cabrera grabbed the phone from her. "The girl is fine, don't worry. She says she sends greetings to her grandma. We'll soon be crossing to the other side. Do me a favor and phone her mother and tell her to be ready," he said.

He took them to eat tacos and burritos at a street stall and from there to San Jose Church to keep his promise to Father Leo, who he explained was as much a saint as Olga Sanchez. The priest often went without sleep, offering help at any time of the day or night to the endless line of migrants and other needy people, providing water, food, first aid, his telephone, and spiritual comfort in the form of jokes and edifying stories he made up on the spot. On every journey, Berto Cabrera passed by his church to give him 5 percent of whatever he had charged his passengers, less costs, in exchange for his blessing and prayers for his clients' safety. As Berto said, roaring with laughter, this was his insurance, the quota he paid heaven for protection. Of course he also paid the Zetas cartel not to abduct his passengers. If that happened, the Zetas charged a ransom for each of them, which their families had to pay if they wanted to save their lives. Express kidnappings, they were called. As long as Cabrera could count on the saint's prayers and paid the Zetas, he felt more or less reassured. That was how it had always been.

They found the priest barefoot, with his trousers rolled up and wearing a filthy T-shirt as he sorted edible fruit and vegetables from the overripe ones they were given at the market. The sweet smell of putrefaction from a big puddle of fruit juice on the floor attracted a cloud of flies. Father Leo was pleased to see Cabrera not simply for his economic contribution but also because he helped convince other coyotes to purchase this tremendous insurance guaranteed by the Lord.

Evelyn and her companions took off their sneakers, waded into the swamp of fruit and rotting vegetables, and helped rescue what could be used in the church kitchen while the priest rested in the shade for a while and brought his friend Cabrera up to date on the latest problems the North Americans had created. Now, as well as using night-vision binoculars and apparatus that could detect body heat, they had sowed the desert with seismic sensors that detected any footsteps on the ground. The two men commented on the latest "events," a euphemism for the latest assaults. They also avoided using words like "gang" or "narco," as they had to be cautious.

From San Jose Church, Berto Cabrera took them to one of the camps on the banks of the Rio Grande. These were wretched cardboard villages filled with tents, mattresses, stray dogs, and garbage, a temporary home to beggars, delinquents, drug addicts, and migrants awaiting their opportunity. "We'll stay here until the moment comes to hop across to the other side," he told them. His charges plucked up the courage to protest that this had not been the bargain: the woman in the bakery in Guatemala had promised they would sleep in hotels. "Have you forgotten we've already stayed in hotels? Here on the border you have to make do. If anyone doesn't like it, they can go back where they came from," retorted the coyote.

From the camp they could see the US side, guarded night and day by cameras, lights, and men in military vehicles, launches, and helicopters. Loudspeakers warned anybody venturing into the river that they were in American territory and had to turn back. In recent years the Americans had reinforced the border with thousands of guards equipped with the latest technology, but the desperate migrants always found a way to outwit the surveillance. Seeing the fear on his clients' faces when they saw how broad and rough the greenish waters were, Cabrera explained that the only people who drowned were the idiots who tried to swim across or get pulled by a rope. Hundreds died this way every year, their bloated bodies eventually caught on the boulders, stuck among the reeds near the banks, or floating out into the Gulf of Mexico. The difference between life and death was information: to know where, how, and when to cross. And yet, as he warned them, the greatest danger was not the river, but the desert beyond. There the temperatures were so hellish they melted stones, there was no water, and they could be preyed upon by scorpions, wildcats, and hungry real coyotes. Getting lost in the desert meant they would die within a day or two. Rattlesnakes, as well as coral, moccasin, and darting indigo snakes, came out to hunt at night, the time when the migrants set off, because the daytime heat was lethal. They would not be able to use flashlights, as that would give their position away: they had to rely on prayers and good luck. Cabrera repeated that they were traveling in luxury and would not be abandoned in the desert at the mercy of the snakes. His own participation ended when they crossed the Rio Grande, but in the United States his colleague was waiting to lead them to safety.

The four men and Evelyn grudgingly settled into the camp beneath a makeshift cardboard roof that offered them some protection against the suffocating heat of the day and gave an illusion of security at night. Unlike other migrants, who slept wrapped in plastic bags and ate once a day in any nearby church, or earned a few pesos doing whatever work they could find, they had some money to buy food and bottled water. Cabrera meanwhile went to seek out an acquaintance, who he thought was probably lying drugged somewhere, to get them across the river. Before leaving he gave them instructions to stay together and not to let the girl out of their sight for a moment: they were surrounded by unscrupulous people, especially the users, who were capable of killing to steal their sneakers or backpacks. There was not much food in the camp, but there was more than enough liquor, marijuana, crack, heroin, and a wide variety of unnamed pills that could be deadly when mixed with alcohol.

Lucia, Richard, Evelyn

Brooklyn

Richard

Brazil, 1985–1987

On the trips Richard Bowmaster had made over the years with Horacio Amado-Castro, they would usually head for somewhere remote that they reached first in the Subaru and then on their bikes, carrying backpacks and a tent. Richard felt the absence of his friend like a kind of death. Horacio had left a void in the space and time of his existence; there was so much he wanted to share with him. He would have come up with a precise and rational solution to the problem of the dead body in the Lexus, and would have carried such a dire task out without hesitation, in a lighthearted way. Richard on the other hand could feel the threatening peck of his ulcer, a frightened bird inside his stomach. "What do you gain by thinking about the future? Things follow their course and you can't control anything, so relax, brother," was the advice he had heard a hundred times from his friend. Horacio accused Richard of spending his life talking to himself, muttering, remembering, repenting, planning. He said that only human beings were so focused on themselves, slaves to their egos, navel-gazing, on the defensive even though no danger threatened them.

Lucia argued something similar. She gave as an example the Chihuahua, Marcelo, who lived eternally grateful in the present, accepting whatever might happen without worrying about any future misfortune that might add to all those he had previously encountered in his life as an abandoned dog. "Too much Zen wisdom for such a small creature," Richard replied when she listed all these virtues. He admitted he was addicted to negative thoughts, as Horacio claimed. At the age of seven he was already concerned the sun would be extinguished someday and all forms of life on the planet would come to an end. The only encouraging sign was that this had not happened yet. Horacio on the other hand was not even worried about global warming: when the poles melted and the continents were submerged, his great-grandchildren would have died of old age or would have grown fish's gills. Richard thought Horacio and Lucia would get on well together, with their irrational optimism and inexplicable tendency toward happiness. He was more comfortable in his reasoned pessimism.

On his camping forays with Horacio, every ounce of weight counted, and every item of food was calculated to keep them going until their return. A born improviser, Horacio made fun of Richard's obsessive preparations, but experience had shown how essential they were. On one trip they had forgotten matches and after spending a night stiff and hungry they had been forced to go back. They discovered that making a fire by rubbing two sticks together is a Boy Scout fantasy. With the same care as he had taken in planning those adventures with his friend, Richard now organized the short journey to the lake. He made an exhaustive list of all they might need in an emergency, from provisions to sleeping bags and spare batteries for their flashlights.

"The only thing missing is a portable toilet, Richard. We're not going to war; there are restaurants and hotels everywhere," said Lucia.

"We can't be seen in public places."

"Why not?"

"People and cars don't just disappear, Lucia. There's likely to be a police investigation. They could identify us if we leave a trail."

"No one notices anyone, Richard. And we look like a mature couple on vacation."

"In the snow? In two vehicles? With a tearful young girl and a dog dressed like Sherlock Holmes? And you with that outlandish hair of yours. Of course we attract attention."

Richard placed all their luggage in the trunk of the Subaru, left enough food for the cats, and before giving the order to set off called the clinic to find out how Três was doing. The cat was stable but had to remain under observation for a few more days. Next he called his neighbor to tell her he would be away for a short while, and to ask her to look in on the other three cats. He checked again that the wire holding the Lexus's trunk was secure and scraped the snow and ice off the windshields of both vehicles. He imagined that the car's documents were in order but wanted to make sure. In the glove compartment he found what he was looking for, plus a remote control and a key ring with a single key on it.

"I suppose the remote opens the Leroys' garage."

"Yes," said Evelyn.

"And the key is to your house."

"It's not from the house."

"Do you know where it's from? Have you seen it before?"

"Señora Leroy showed it to me."

"When was that?"

"Yesterday. She spent Friday in bed. She was very depressed, she said her whole body ached. She's like that sometimes, she finds it impossible to get up. Besides, where was she going to go in that storm? But yesterday she felt better and decided to go out. Before she left she showed me the key. She said she found it in Mr. Leroy's suit pocket. She was very nervous. Maybe because of what happened to Frankie on Thursday. She told me to check his sugar levels every two hours."

"And?"

"Frankie was frightened by the storm on Friday, but yesterday he was fine. His sugar was stable. There's a gun in the car too."

"A gun?" spluttered Richard.

"Mr. Leroy keeps it for protection. For his work, he says."

"What is his work?"

"I don't know. Señora Leroy told me her husband would never divorce her, because she knows too much about what he does."

"An ideal couple, apparently. I imagine he has a permit. But there's no gun in here, Evelyn. Just as well, one problem less," said Richard, checking the glove compartment a second time.

"That Frank Leroy must be a real bandit," Lucia grumbled.

"We ought to leave soon, Lucia. We'll go in tandem. If possible, keep me in sight, but stay far enough back to be able to brake, the road surface is icy. Keep your headlights on so that you can see and be seen by other drivers. If the traffic gets backed up, put your flashers on to warn those behind you—"

"I've been driving for fifty years, Richard."

"Yes, but badly. One more thing: the ice is worse on bridges, because they're colder than the ground," he added, and with a resigned wave got ready to set off.

Lucia sat behind the wheel of the Subaru, with Evelyn and Marcelo as copilots. She had traced the route in red on the map, because she did not really trust the GPS and was afraid of losing sight of Richard, who had given her instructions to meet up with him at various points on the way if they were separated. They both had cell phones to keep in contact. It was impossible for the journey to be any more secure, she told Evelyn to reassure her. As they left Brooklyn she tailed close behind Richard; there was no traffic, but the snow was an obstacle. She missed listening to her favorite music, Judy Collins and Joni Mitchell, but realized that Evelyn was praying in a low voice and so it would not be respectful to distract her. Marcelo, who was not used to traveling in a car, lay groaning on the young woman's lap.

DESPITE THE GREEN PILL he had taken before they left, Richard was very anxious. If the police stopped him and inspected the car, he was done for. What reasonable explanation could he give? He was in someone else's possibly stolen car, and in the trunk was the body of the unfortunate Kathryn Brown, whom he had never met. It had been there for many hours, but given the frigid temperatures it was probably stiff. In theory he would

have liked to see her face to remember it later on and to examine her body to see how she had died, but in practice neither he
nor Lucia, much less Evelyn, had any desire to reopen the trunk.
Who really was the woman traveling in the car with him? From
what Evelyn had told them about the Leroys, the young woman
could have been murdered to keep her mouth shut if she had
discovered something that incriminated Frank Leroy. As Evelyn
had said, his mysterious activities and violent conduct gave rise
to sinister speculation. How had he managed to get fake documents for Evelyn? He must have had illegal ways of doing so.
Lucia had told him the young Guatemalan had a Native American identity document.

He wished he could call his father to ask for advice, or more
exactly to boast a little, to show he wasn't a good-for-nothing
but could embark on a crazy adventure like this, and yet it would
be unwise to mention what he was up to over the phone. He was
sure his father would enjoy meeting Lucia; those two would get
on very well. "Providing of course we come out of this alive . . .
I'm getting paranoid, as Lucia says. Help us, Anita, help us, Bibi,"
he implored out loud, as he often did when on his own, as a
way of feeling accompanied. "Now I need protection rather than
company.

He could sense the presence of Anita so strongly that he
turned to see if she was sitting in the seat alongside him. It
would not have been the first time she had appeared, but she
always came and went so fleetingly that he doubted his own fac-
ulties. He rarely allowed himself to be carried away by fantasy,
considering himself rigorous in his reasoning and scrupulous in
checking facts, but Anita had always escaped those parameters.
At sixty, launched on a crazy mission, half paralyzed with cold

as he had not turned the heating on to preserve the frozen dead body in the trunk, and with the window wound halfway down to prevent the windshield from misting or freezing over, Richard reflected yet again on his past, with the knowledge that his happiest years had been those with Anita before disaster struck.

He had been truly alive then. By now he had forgotten their everyday problems, the language and cultural misunderstandings they had encountered frequently, as well as the constant interference from his in-laws; the nuisance of uninvited friends roaming his house at all hours; Anita's rituals, which he considered pure superstition; and above all her explosive reaction whenever he drank too much. He did not remember her in moments of crisis, when her golden eyes turned the color of pitch, or her frenzied jealousy, her blind rages, or when he had to cling to her in the doorway like a jailer to prevent her from leaving. Now he simply remembered her as he first knew her: passionate, vulnerable, and generous. Anita, with her savage love and ready tenderness. They were happy. The fights never lasted long, and the reconciliations went on for entire days and nights.

RICHARD HAD BEEN A SHY, studious boy with chronic stomach ailments. This saved him from having to take part in the brutal sports of American schools and inevitably led him into academic life. He studied political science, specializing in Brazil because he spoke Portuguese, having spent many of his childhood vacations with his maternal grandparents in Lisbon. He wrote his doctorate on the actions of the Brazilian oligarchy and their allies that led to the 1964 overthrow of the political and economic model adopted by the charismatic left-wing president João Goulart. He was ousted in a military coup backed by the United States following the "Doctrine of National Security" to combat communism, as was the case with so many governments on the continent, before and after Brazil. Goulart's presidency was replaced by a succession of military dictatorships that lasted for twenty-one years, with periods of harsh repression, involving the imprisonment of opponents, censorship of the press and culture, torture, and disappearances.

Goulart died in 1976, after more than a decade of exile in Uruguay and Argentina. The official version put his death down to a heart attack, but popular rumor had it that he had been poisoned by his political enemies, who were afraid he might return from abroad to stir up the dispossessed. Since no autopsy was ever carried out, these suspicions could not be proven, but years later this gave Richard the pretext to interview Maria Thereza, Goulart's widow, who had returned to her country and agreed to receive him for a series of conversations. Richard found himself in the presence of a lady with all the poise and self-assurance guaranteed by being born beautiful. She answered his questions but could not shed any light on the doubts surrounding her husband's death. Even so, that woman, the representative of a political ideal and a period that were already part of history, created in Richard an ongoing love for Brazil and its people.

He arrived there in 1985, just before his twenty-ninth birthday. By then the dictatorship had softened, some political rights had been restored, there was an amnesty program for people accused of political offenses, and censorship had been relaxed. More importantly, the government had allowed the opposition to triumph in the 1982 legislative elections.

Richard was present for the first free presidential election. For a student of politics like himself it proved to be a fascinating moment. The military government and its followers were rejected, and the opposition candidate won, but in one of history's low blows, he died before he could take office. It was his vice president, Jose Sarney, a big landowner close to the military, who was called upon to usher in the "New Republic" and consolidate the transition to democracy. Brazil was facing huge problems on all fronts: it had the largest foreign debt in the world and was mired in a recession; economic power was concentrated in a few hands while the rest of the population suffered inflation, unemployment, poverty, and inequality that condemned many to permanent hardship. There was more than enough material for the topics Richard wanted to research and the articles he intended to publish, but alongside these intellectual challenges was the permanent temptation to enjoy his youth to the fullest in the hedonistic atmosphere in which he found himself.

He rented a student apartment in Rio de Janeiro, exchanged his harsh Portuguese accent for the softer Brazilian one. He learned to drink caipirinhas, the national drink of cane liquor and lime that hit his stomach like battery acid, and cautiously ventured out into the city's vibrant life. As the most attractive girls were on the beaches or dance floors, he began to swim in the sea and decided to learn to dance, something he had never felt the need to do before. When Anita Farinha's dance academy was recommended to him, he enrolled to learn the samba and other popular dances, but like so many white men he was too stiff and self-conscious. Although he was the academy's worst student, his efforts proved worthwhile, because it was there that he met his true love.

ANITA FARINHA ATTRACTED Richard at first sight, with the exuberant shape of her body, her narrow waist, sturdy legs, and rounded butt that swayed with every step she took, although there was no hint she was flirting. Music and grace were in her blood. In the academy her splendid nature was evident, but outside work Anita was a formal, reserved young woman who behaved impeccably and was extremely close to her extended, noisy family. She practiced her own religion, but not fanatically: a mixture of Catholic and animist beliefs, seasoned with female mythology. Every so often she went with her sisters to a ceremony of candomble, an African slave religion that had been limited to black Brazilians in the past but was now gaining followers among the white middle class. Anita had her guardian *orixa*, her divine guide in the realization of her destiny: Yemaya, the goddess of motherhood, life, and the oceans. She explained this to Richard the only time he accompanied her, but he took it as a joke. Like many of Anita's customs, this paganism seemed to him exotic, enchanting. She laughed with him, because she only half believed in it. It was better to believe in everything than in nothing: that way she ran less risk of angering the gods, just in case they did exist.

Richard pursued her with a crazy determination totally unexpected in someone so levelheaded, until he had been accepted by the thirty-seven members of the Farinha family and finally succeeded in marrying her. To achieve this he had to make countless courtesy calls without mentioning the reason for them. He was accompanied by his father, who traveled to Brazil especially for that purpose, as it would have been improper for Richard to have gone to Anita's family alone. Joseph Bowmaster wore strict mourning clothes due to the recent passing of Cloe, the woman he loved so dearly, but wore a red flower in his buttonhole to celebrate his son's engagement. Richard would have preferred a private wedding, but Anita's family and close friends alone came to more than two hundred guests. On Richard's side there was only his father; his friend Horacio Amado-Castro, who arrived from the United States by surprise; and Maria Thereza Goulart, who had developed a maternal affection for the handsome American student.

The president's widow, who was still young and beautiful—she had been twenty-two years younger than her husband—captured all the guests' attention and was a valuable support for Richard in the face of Anita's overwhelming clan. It was she who made him see the obvious: by marrying Anita he was also marrying her family. The wedding was not arranged by the bride and groom but by Anita's mother, sisters, and sisters-in-law, all of them gossipy, affectionate women who lived in permanent communication and poked their noses into every aspect of each other's lives. They attended to everything, from the wedding banquet menu to the butter-colored lace mantilla Anita had to wear because it had belonged to her deceased great-grandmother. The role of the men in the family was a more decorative one; their domain, if they had one, was outside the home. All of them were so friendly toward Richard that it took him a long while to realize that the Farinhas as a whole did not trust him. None of this affected him, because the love he shared with Anita was the only thing that really mattered. At that moment he could never have imagined the control the Farinha family would exert over his marriage.

The couple's happiness redoubled with the birth of Bibi.

Their daughter arrived in the second year of their marriage, just as Yemaya had predicted in the *buzios*, the fortune-telling conch shells. She was such a gift that Anita feared the price the goddess would demand for this wonderful child. Richard laughed at the quartz bracelets and other safeguards against the evil eye that his wife wore. Anita forbade him to boast of their happiness; it was dangerous to stir up envy.

The best moments of this period, which years later still set Richard's heart racing, were when Anita curled up on his chest like a gentle cat or sat astride his knees and buried her nose in his neck, or when Bibi was taking her first steps with all her mother's grace, a broad smile displaying her milk teeth. Anita in an apron chopping fruit in summer; Anita at her academy writhing like an eel to the sound of a guitar; Anita purring fast asleep in his arms after they had made love; Anita heavy with her watermelon belly, leaning on him to climb the stairs; Anita in the rocking chair with Bibi at her breast, singing softly in the orange glow of evening.

Richard never allowed himself to doubt that those years were the best for Anita as well.

Lucia, Richard, Evelyn

Their first stop was at a gas station half an hour after leaving Brooklyn to buy chains for the Lexus's tires. Although Richard had snow tires on the Subaru, he had warned Lucia of the danger of black ice, the cause of most of the serious accidents in winter. "More reason to stay calm. Relax, man," she had replied, echoing Horacio's advice without realizing it. She was instructed to wait for Richard at a turnoff a quarter of a mile down the road while he bought the chains.

Richard was served by a gray-haired grandma with the red hands of a lumberjack, who turned out to be stronger and more skillful than he first thought. She attached the chains herself in less than twenty minutes, apparently without even noticing the cold, all the while bellowing out her life story: she was a widow and ran the business on her own, eighteen hours a day and seven days a week, even on a Sunday like this one, when no one even dared go out. She did not have a replacement for his back light.

"Where are you going in weather like this?" she asked when he paid. "To a funeral," Richard replied with a shudder.

The two cars soon left the highway and traveled a couple of miles down a rural road, but had to double back when they reached a point where the snowplows had not yet passed through. They met very few vehicles and none of the enormous freight trucks or passenger buses that linked New York to Canada. They all seemed to have obeyed the order not to operate until Monday, when the traffic was supposed to return to normal. The frosty pine woods stretched up into the infinite white of the sky; the road was no more than a gray pencil line between mounds of snow. Richard envied the women and the dog, who were traveling in the Subaru with the heat at full blast. He had put on a balaclava and so many layers of clothes he could hardly bend his elbows or knees.

As time went by, the green pills Richard had taken began to kick in, and the anxiety he had felt before they set out started to fade. The questions surrounding Kathryn Brown became less urgent: it all formed part of a novel whose pages had been written by other people. He was curious about what came next, wanting to know how the novel would end, but he was in no hurry to reach his destination. Sooner or later he would arrive and accomplish his mission. Or rather, he would accomplish the mission Lucia had given him. She was in charge; he simply had to obey her. He was floating.

The panorama was unchanging: time went by on the car's clock, the miles mounted, but he was not getting anywhere, he was held up in the same spot, immersed in a white space, hypnotized by the monotony. He had never driven in such a harsh winter. As he had told Lucia, he was aware of the dangers of the road, as well as of the more immediate danger of being overcome by sleep, which was already making his eyelids droop. He switched on the radio, but the poor reception and the static irritated him, and so he decided to drive on in silence. He made an effort to return to reality, to the vehicle, the journey. He took a few sips from the lukewarm coffee in the thermos, thinking that in the next town he would need to go to the toilet and drink a strong, piping-hot coffee with two aspirins.

In the rearview mirror he could see the distant lights of the Subaru, disappearing on the bends and then reappearing shortly afterward. He was afraid Lucia must have been as tired as he was. It was hard to remain in the present, for his thoughts kept getting enmeshed with images from the past.

IN THE SUBARU, Evelyn was still praying softly for Kathryn Brown in the way they did for the dead in her village. Because death had surprised Kathryn when she was least expecting it, the young woman's soul had been unable to fly up to heaven, but was stuck on the way. No doubt it was still trapped in the trunk. That was a sacrilege, a sin, an unpardonable lack of respect. Who would send Kathryn off with the appropriate rites? A soul in torment is the worst thing in the world. Evelyn felt responsible: if she had not taken the car to go to the drugstore she would never have discovered what had happened to Kathryn Brown, but now that she had done so, they were both trapped. Many prayers and nine days of mourning were needed to free her soul. Poor Kathryn, no one had wept for her or said farewell. In Evelyn's village they sacrificed a cock to accompany the deceased to the other side and drank rum to toast the journey to heaven.

Evelyn prayed and prayed, one rosary after another, while

Marcelo grew weary of moaning and fell asleep with his tongue lolling out and eyes half-open because the lids only covered the top half. For a while Lucia accompanied Evelyn in the litany of Our Fathers and Hail Marys she had learned as a child and could still recite without hesitation, even though she had not prayed for forty years or more. The monotonous repetition made her feel sleepy, and so to stay awake she started telling another part of her life story and to ask about Evelyn's. They had begun to trust one another, and Evelyn was stammering much less.

Dusk would fall soon and as Richard had feared it began to snow again before they reached the town where they were planning to go to the toilet and get something to eat. They had to slow down. He tried to reach Lucia on his cell phone, but there was no signal, so he pulled over at the roadside with his warning lights on. Lucia came to a stop behind him and they were able to scrape the windshields and share a thermos of hot chocolate and muffins. They had to convince Evelyn that this was not the moment for them to fast for Kathryn and that her prayers were enough. However many layers of clothes Richard had on, he was shivering with cold. He took advantage of the stop to stretch his numb legs and to jump and clap his hands to warm up a little. He checked that there were no problems with either car, showed Lucia the map once more, and gave the order to carry on.

"How much farther is it?" she asked.

"Quite a long way. There'll be no time to eat."

"We've been driving for six hours, Richard."

"I'm tired as well, and I'm dying of cold, I can feel it in my bones. I'm probably going to catch pneumonia, but we have to reach the cabin in daylight. It's isolated and if I don't spot the turnoff we could continue on straight past it."

"What about the GPS?"

"It won't show the turnoff. I've always done the journey from memory, but I need to be able to see. What's happened to the Chihuahua?"

"Nothing."

"He looks dead."

"He gets like that when he's asleep."

"What an ugly animal!"

"I hope he didn't hear you, Richard. I need to pee."

"It'll have to be here. Watch out you don't freeze your butt off."

The two women crouched down beside the vehicle, while Richard relieved himself behind the Lexus. Realizing he had been abandoned, Marcelo raised his muzzle, took a look outside, and decided to contain himself. No one was going to convince him to step out into the snow.

THEY SET OFF AGAIN, traveling seventeen more miles until they reached a small town with one main street and the usual stores, a gas station, two bars, and low, one-story dwellings. Richard finally realized there was no way they could reach the lake in daylight and decided they should spend the night there. The wind and cold had worsened, and he needed to get warm: his teeth had been chattering so much his jaw hurt. He was worried about spending the night in a hotel because he did not want to attract attention, but it would be worse to continue in darkness and get lost. His cell phone now had reception, so he was able to tell Lucia about the change of plan. There was not much chance they would find a decent lodging, but they came upon a motel, which had the advantage that the rooms gave directly onto the parking lot, so they would not be noticed. At the reception desk, which smelled strongly of creosote, Richard was informed that the motel was being refurbished and that there was only one room available. He paid $49.90 in cash and then went to call the two women.

"It's all there is. We're going to have to share a room," he told them.

"At last you're going to sleep with me, Richard!" exclaimed Lucia.

"Mmm . . . I'm worried about leaving Kathryn in the car," he said, quickly changing subjects.

"You want to sleep with her?"

The room smelled the same as the reception area and had the makeshift aspect of a poor stage set. The ceiling was low, the furniture rickety; everything was covered in a depressing veneer of cheapness. There were two beds, an ancient TV set, a bathroom with indelible stains, and a permanent trickle from the toilet, but there was also an electric kettle, a hot shower, and good heating. In fact, the room was stifling, and within a few minutes Richard was no longer cold, and had to remove the layers of heavy clothing. The coffee-colored carpet and the black-and-blue patterned bedspreads were in urgent need of a proper cleaning, but although the sheets and towels were threadbare, they were clean. Marcelo scuttled into the bathroom and peed at length in a corner, to Lucia's amusement and Richard's horror.

"What do we do now?" asked Richard.

"I suppose that among all the rations you packed there must be some paper towels. I'll go and get them, you've suffered enough from the cold."

Even so, a short while later Richard, who had gotten over his fear of catching pneumonia, announced he would set off in search of food. In weather like this there was no way anyone would deliver a pizza, and the motel had no kitchen, only a bar where the snacks consisted of olives and stale potato chips. He imagined that however humble the town was, there had to be a Chinese or Mexican restaurant. They still had some provisions but preferred to keep them for the following day. When Richard returned forty minutes later with Chinese food, and coffee in their two thermoses, he found Lucia and Evelyn watching news about the storm on the television.

"On Friday the lowest temperatures since 1869 were registered in New York State. The blizzard lasted almost three hours, but the snow is going to continue for the next few days. The storm has caused millions of dollars' worth of damage, and it has a name: Jonas," Lucia told him.

"It'll be worse up at the lake. The farther north, the colder it gets," said Richard, removing his coat, vest, scarf, cap, balaclava, and gloves.

He spotted a tiny fly on his undershirt, but when he went to brush it off it jumped and disappeared. "A flea!" he cried, desperately patting himself all over. Lucia and Evelyn barely looked up from the television.

"Fleas! There are fleas in here!" Richard insisted, scratching himself.

"What did you expect for forty-nine dollars and ninety cents, Richard? Anyway, they don't bite Chileans," she said.

"Nor Guatemalans," added Evelyn.

"They bite you because you're light blooded," Lucia teased.

The cartons from the Chinese restaurant looked depressing,

but the contents were less inedible than they feared and helped restore their spirits, even though they contained so much salt that any other taste was obliterated. Even the Chihuahua, who was very picky because he had trouble chewing, wanted to try the chow mein. Richard went on scratching for a while until he grew resigned to the fleas; he preferred not to even think about the cockroaches that would crawl out of the corners as soon as they switched off the lights. He felt sheltered and safe in this sad motel, linked to the two women in their adventure, feeling his way toward friendship and moved at finding himself so close to Lucia. He was so unfamiliar with this peaceful sense of happiness he did not even recognize it.

Lucia had asked for something she could add to her and Evelyn's coffee, and he had bought a bottle of Mendez tequila, which was all he could find in the hotel bar. For the first time in years he felt the desire for a drink, more out of companionship than necessity, but he rejected the idea. Experience had taught him to be very careful with alcohol: he would start just wetting his lips and end up falling back headfirst into addiction. It would be impossible to sleep; it was still very early, despite being completely dark outside.

Since they could not agree on what to watch on TV, and the only thing they had forgotten to pack was something to read, they ended up continuing to tell each other their life stories, as they had done the previous night, although this time without the magic brownie, but with the same ease and sense of trust. Richard wanted to know about Lucia's failed marriage, because he had known her husband, Carlos Urzua, in the academic world. Although he admired Carlos, he did not tell her so, imagining he was probably not so admirable on a personal level.

Lucia

D uring the twenty years of her marriage, Lucia Maraz would have wagered her husband was faithful to her simply because she thought he was too busy to plan the necessary subterfuges for hidden affairs. In this as in so many other things, time was to prove her wrong. She was proud of having given him a stable home and an exceptional daughter. His participation in that particular project was unintentional at the start and casual later on, not because he was wicked but through weakness of character, as Daniela insisted when she was of an age to judge her parents without condemning them. From the outset, Lucia's role was to love him, and his was to let himself be loved.

They had met in 1990. Lucia had returned to Chile after almost seventeen years in exile and found a job as a TV producer with great difficulty, as thousands of young, better-qualified professionals were looking for work. There was little sympathy for those who came back: people on the left accused them of being cowards for leaving; those on the right saw them as communists.

The capital, Santiago, had changed so much that Lucia did not recognize the streets she had grown up in. Their former names, deriving from saints and flowers, had been replaced by those of military men and heroes from past wars. The city gleamed with the cleanliness and order of barracks; the social-ist realism murals had disappeared, replaced by white walls and well-tended trees. Parks for children had been created on the banks of the Mapocho River, and no one remembered the gar-bage or the bodies the river had once carried away. In the center, the gray buildings, the traffic of buses and motorbikes, the drab poverty of office workers, the weary passersby, and the boys jug-gling at the streetlights to beg a few pesos were in stark contrast to the shopping malls of the rich neighborhoods. These were as brightly lit as circuses and offered to satisfy the most extravagant tastes: Baltic caviar, Viennese chocolate, tea from China, roses from Ecuador, perfumes from Paris, all available for those who could pay. Two nations coexisted in the same space: the small, affluent one with cosmopolitan pretensions, and the large one that included everyone else. The middle-class districts exuded an air of modernity on credit, those of the upper classes one of imported refinement. The store windows there were similar to those on Park Avenue, and the mansions were protected by electric fences and guard dogs. Near the airport, however, and along the highway into the city, there were wretched slums hid-den from the tourists' gaze by walls and huge billboards show-ing blond girls in underwear.

There seemed to be little left of the modest, industrious

Chile that Lucia had known: ostentatious wealth was the fashion. But all one had to do was to leave the city to recover something of the country as it once was: fishermen's villages; popular markets; inns serving fish soup and freshly baked bread; simple, hospitable people who talked with the same accent as before and laughed hiding their mouth behind their hand. Lucia would have liked to live in the provinces, far from the noise of the capital, but she could only do her research in Santiago.

She realized she was a foreigner in her own land, disconnected from the network of social relationships without which almost nothing was possible, lost in what remained of a past that did not fit into the bustling present-day Chile. She did not understand the keys or codes: even the sense of humor had changed, and the language was peppered with euphemisms and caution, because there was still the aftertaste of the censorship of the tough times. No one asked her about the years she had been away, no one wanted to know where she had been or what her life had been like. That parenthesis in her existence was completely erased.

HAVING SOLD HER HOUSE IN VANCOUVER and saved some money, she was able to install herself in a small but well-situated apartment in Santiago. Her mother was offended that she did not want to live with her, but at thirty-six Lucia needed to be independent. "That might be how they do things in Canada, but here unmarried daughters stay with their parents," Lena argued. Lucia was just about able to live on her salary as a producer and began work on her first book, on the "disappeared." She had given herself a year to complete it but quickly understood that the research would be much harder than she had thought. Defeated in a plebiscite, the military government had ended a few months earlier, and a restricted, vigilant democracy was taking its first steps in a country wounded by its recent past. There was a watchful atmosphere, and the kind of information she was looking for was part of the secret history.

Carlos Urzua was a well-known and controversial lawyer who collaborated with the Inter-American Commission on Human Rights. Lucia went to interview him for her book after trying to arrange an appointment for several weeks, because he was away a lot and was extremely busy. His office in a nondescript building in the center of Santiago consisted of three rooms crammed with desks and metal cabinets with files spilling out of drawers, weighty legal tomes, and black-and-white photographs of people, nearly all of them young, tacked on a bulletin board together with dates and times. The only signs of anything more modern were two computers, a fax machine, and a photocopier. In one corner, typing on an electric typewriter at the speed of a pianist, sat Lola, his secretary, a plump, pink-cheeked woman with the innocent look of a nun. Carlos received Lucia from behind his desk in the third room, which differed from the others only because it had a ficus tree in a container that miraculously survived in the dark shadows of the office. Urzua was impatient.

The lawyer was fifty-one but radiated an athlete's vitality. He was the most attractive man Lucia had ever seen and produced in her an instantaneous, devastating passion, a primeval, wild heat that soon turned into a fascination with his personality and the work he did. For several minutes she was completely lost, trying to focus on her questions, while he waited, tapping his pencil on the desk in exasperation. Afraid he would dismiss her on some pretext or other, Lucia explained as tears welled in her eyes that she had lived outside Chile for many years and that her obsession with investigating the topic of the disappeared was a very personal one, because her own brother was among them. Disconcerted by this turn of events, Urzua pushed a box of tissues in Lucia's direction and offered her coffee. She blew her nose, ashamed at her lack of control in front of this man who must have come across thousands of cases like hers.

Lola brought instant coffee for her and a tea bag for him. As she was handing Lucia the cup, she laid a hand on her shoulder and left it there for a few seconds. This unexpected kind gesture brought on another flood of tears, which succeeded in softening Carlos, and after that they were able to talk. Lucia stretched out her coffee as long as she could: he had information she could not obtain elsewhere. He answered her questions for more than three hours, trying to explain the inexplicable, and finally, when they were both exhausted and night had fallen outside, he offered her access to the material in his archives. Lola had left some time earlier, but Carlos told Lucia to come back another day, when his secretary would provide her with the information she needed.

There was nothing romantic about the situation, but Carlos was aware of the impression he had made on Lucia and since she seemed attractive he decided to accompany her home, even though on principle he avoided becoming involved with complicated women and still less with tearful ones. He had enough emotional traumas with the misfortunes he had to deal with every day in his work. At Lucia's apartment he agreed to taste her recipe for pisco sour. Later on, he would always jokingly say that she befuddled him with alcohol and captivated him with her witch's arts. That first night passed in a mist of pisco and mutual surprise at finding themselves in bed together. The next morning Carlos left very early, saying goodbye with a chaste kiss, and after that she heard nothing more from him. He did not phone her and never returned her calls.

Three months later, Lucia Maraz turned up at Urzua's office unannounced. Lola the secretary, who was at her post typing as furiously as on the previous occasion, recognized her at once and asked when she was going to go through the archive material. Lucia said nothing about Carlos's ignoring her calls, because she presumed Lola already knew. Lola showed her into her boss's office, gave her a cup of instant coffee with condensed milk, and told her to be patient, because he was in court. Less than half an hour later Carlos arrived, shirt collar unbuttoned and jacket in hand. Lucia stood up to greet him and told him straight out she was pregnant.

She had the impression he did not remember her at all, although he assured her she was mistaken, of course he remembered who she was, and had very fond memories of that night of pisco sour: his delayed reaction was due to his surprise. When she explained this was probably her last chance to become a mother, he coldly asked her for a DNA test. Lucia was on the verge of leaving, determined to bring the child up on her own, but was halted by the memory of her own childhood without a father, and so agreed to his demand. The test proved Carlos's paternity beyond any reasonable doubt, and his mistrust and annoyance gave way to genuine enthusiasm. He announced that they should get married, because this was also his last opportunity to overcome his terror of marriage, and because he wanted to be a father, although he was old enough to be a grandfather.

Lena predicted that the marriage would last no more than a few months due to the fifteen-year difference in age and because as soon as the child was born Carlos Urzua would vanish; a lifelong bachelor like him would not be able to bear the howls of a newborn. Lucia prepared herself for that eventuality with a philosophical sense of reality. In Chile at that time there was no divorce law—and there would not be one until 2004—but there were complicated ways to annul a marriage with false witnesses and obliging judges. This method was so common and effective that the number of couples who remained married for life could be counted on two hands. She suggested to the future father that once the child was born they should separate as friends. She was in love but understood that if Carlos felt trapped he would end up hating her. He flatly rejected what seemed to him an immoral idea, and so she was left with the belief that over time and thanks to the habit of intimacy he could come to love her as well. She set herself the goal of achieving this at all costs.

THEY SETTLED IN THE RAMSHACKLE HOUSE Carlos had inherited from his parents, in a neighborhood that had deteriorated while Santiago expanded toward the slopes of the nearby mountains where the well-off preferred to live, far from the toxic smog that often covered the city. On her mother's advice, Lucia postponed research for her book, as the topic was so grim it could affect the mind of the child in her womb. No one gains from

starting life in the belly of a mother who is searching for dead
bodies, declared Lena. This was the first time she had referred
to the disappeared as being dead; it was akin to placing a grave-
stone over her son.

Carlos agreed with his mother-in-law's theory and was firm
in his decision not to help Lucia until after the birth. He maintained that the months of pregnancy ought to be ones of happiness and gentle rest, but Lucia's filled her with boundless energy,
and instead of knitting booties she dedicated herself to painting
the house inside and out. In her spare time she took several practical courses and then upholstered the living room furniture and
replaced the kitchen plumbing. Her husband would return from
the office to find her clutching a hammer and with a mouthful
of nails, or dragging her belly behind the dishwasher, blowtorch
in hand. With equal enthusiasm she attacked the yard, which
had been abandoned for a decade, and with pick and shovel converted it into an untidy garden, where rosebushes thrived alongside lettuce and onions.

She was busy with one of her building projects when her
water broke. At first she thought she had wet herself without
realizing it, but her mother, who was visiting her, called a taxi
and rushed her to the maternity clinic.

Daniela was born at seven months. Carlos attributed this
early birth to Lucia's irresponsible behavior, since only a few
days earlier, while she was painting white clouds on the sky-
blue ceiling of the baby's room, she had fallen off the stepladder.
Daniela spent three weeks in an incubator and two more under
observation at the clinic. This still-raw little being, resembling
a hairless monkey and connected to tubes and monitors, gave
her father an empty feeling in the stomach similar to nausea,

but when finally she was installed in her crib at home and determinedly grasped his little finger, he was won over forever. Daniela was to become the only person Carlos Urzua would submit to, the only one he was capable of loving.

Lena Maraz's pessimistic prophecy did not come true, and her daughter's marriage lasted two decades. For fifteen of those years Lucia kept the romance alive without the slightest effort on her husband's part, a great feat of imagination and tenacity. Before the marriage, she had known four important loves. The first was the self-styled *guerrillero* she met in Caracas, dedicated to the theoretical struggle for the socialist dream of equality, which as she quickly discovered did not include women; and the last, an African musician with rippling muscles and dreadlocks decorated with plastic beads, who confessed to her he had two legitimate wives and several children in Senegal. Lena dubbed her daughter's tendency to adorn the object of her infatuation with imagined virtues her "Christmas tree syndrome": Lucia chose an ordinary fir tree and decorated it with baubles and tinsel that over time fell off until all that remained was the skeleton of a dried-out tree. Lena put this down to karma: getting over the Christmas tree stupidity was one of the lessons her daughter had to learn in her current incarnation to avoid repeating the same mistake in the next one. Though a fervent Catholic, Lena had adopted the idea of karma and reincarnation in the hope that her son, Enrique, would be born again and could live a full life.

For years, Lucia attributed her husband's indifference to the tremendous pressures of his work, little suspecting he spent a good deal of his time and energy with casual lovers. They lived together in a friendly way, but with their separate activities, sep-

arate worlds, and separate rooms. Daniela slept in her mother's
bed until she was eight. Lucia and Carlos would make love whenever she crept into his room so as not to wake the child; this left
her feeling humiliated, as it was almost always on her initiative.
She made do with crumbs of affection, too proud to ask for more.
She managed on her own, and he thanked her for it.

Lucia, Richard, Evelyn

S tuck in their motel room smelling of creosote and Chinese food, Lucia, Richard, and Evelyn could have found the final hours of Sunday endless, but in fact they flew by as they told each other about their lives. The first to succumb to sleep were Evelyn and the Chihuahua. The young Guatemalan girl took up a tiny amount of space in the bed she had to share with Lucia, but Marcelo sprawled over all the rest, stretched out with his legs stiff in front of him.

"I wonder how the cats are," Lucia said to Richard around ten, when they too finally began to yawn.

"They're fine. I called my neighbor from the Chinese restaurant. I don't want to use my cell phone because they can trace the call."

"Who's going to be interested in what you say, Richard! Besides, you can't tap cell phones."

"We've already discussed that, Lucia. If they find the automobile—"

"There are billions of calls crossing in space," she interrupted him. "And thousands of vehicles disappear every day. People abandon them, they get stolen, they're dismantled for spare parts or are turned into scrap, they're smuggled to Colombia—"

"And they're also used to dump dead bodies at the bottom of a lake."

"Is your conscience bothering you?"

"Yes, but it's too late for me to change my mind. I'm going to take a shower," announced Richard, heading for the bathroom.

Lucia looks really good with her crazy hair and those snow boots, he thought as the boiling water scalded his back, the perfect remedy for the day's fatigue and the flea bites. They might argue over details, but they got on well; he liked her combination of sharpness and affection, the way in which she flung herself fearlessly into life, that expression of hers somewhere between amused and mischievous, her lopsided smile. In comparison he was a zombie stumbling into old age, but she brought him back to life. He told himself it would be good for them to grow old together, hand in hand. His heart began to pound when he imagined what Lucia's weird hair would look like on his pillow, her boots beside his bed and her face so close to his that he could lose himself in her Turkish princess's eyes. "Forgive me, Anita," he murmured. He had been alone a long time and had forgotten that rough tenderness, that empty feeling in the pit of the stomach, the rushing blood and sudden surges of desire. Can this be love? he thought. If it is, I wouldn't know what to do. I'm caught. He chalked it up to his fatigue; doubtless his mind would clear in the light of day. They were going to get rid of the car and of Kathryn Brown; they were going to say goodbye to Evelyn Ortega, and after that Lucia would return to being simply the Chilean woman in the basement. But he didn't want that moment to arrive. He wanted all the clocks to stop so that they would never have to part.

After the shower he put on his T-shirt and trousers, since he didn't have the nerve to get his pajamas out of the backpack. Lucia had laughed at the amount of stuff he had packed for just two days and would think it ridiculous he had included his pajamas. Now that he thought about it, it *was* ridiculous. He returned to the room refreshed, aware it was going to be hard to sleep; any variation in his routines gave him insomnia, especially if he did not have his hypoallergenic ergonomic pillow. He decided it would be better never to mention that pillow to Lucia. He found her lying in the narrow space the dog had left free.

"Move him off the bed, Lucia," he said, approaching with the intention of doing so himself.

"Don't even think it, Richard. Marcelo is very sensitive. He'd be offended."

"It's dangerous to sleep with animals."

"Why's that?"

"For health reasons, to begin with. Who knows what diseases he might—"

"What's bad for your health is to wash your hands obsessively, the way you do. Good night, Richard."

"Have it your way. Good night."

An hour and a half later, Richard began to feel the first symptoms. His stomach was heavy and he had a strange taste in his mouth. He locked himself in the bathroom and turned on all the faucets to drown out his intestines' explosive roar. Opening the window to let out the smell, he sat shivering on the toilet, cursing ever having eaten the Chinese food and wondering how it was possible he was the only one of the three to be suffering. His churning stomach caused him to break out in a cold sweat. Shortly afterward, Lucia knocked on the door.

"Are you all right?"

"That food was poisoned," he muttered.

"Can I come in?"

"No!"

"Open up, Richard, and let me help you."

"No! No!" he shouted with what little strength he had left.

Lucia struggled with the door, but he had bolted it. At that moment, he hated her: all he wanted was to die right there, crap stained and full of fleabites; to die alone, completely alone, without any witnesses to his humiliation. He wanted Lucia and Evelyn to disappear, for the Lexus and Kathryn to vanish into thin air, for his stomach cramps to calm down, to get rid of all the mess once and for all, to shout out in helplessness and rage. Through the door, Lucia assured him there was nothing wrong with the food; it had done nothing to Evelyn or her; it would pass, it was just nerves; she offered to make him tea. Richard did not answer: he was so cold his jaw seemed locked shut. Ten minutes later, just as she had predicted, his intestines settled down, and he could stand and examine his green face in the mirror, then give himself another lengthy hot shower, which calmed his convulsive trembling. A bone-chilling wind was blowing in through the window, but he did not dare shut it or open the door, because of the disgusting smell. He intended to stay in there as long as he could, and yet realized that the idea of spending the night in the bathroom was impractical. Weak at the knees and with his teeth still chattering, he finally emerged, closed the door behind him, and dragged himself over to the bed. Barefoot, her hair disheveled, and wearing a loose T-shirt that reached down to her knees, Lucia brought him a steaming cup of tea. Feeling humiliated to the core, Richard apologized for the foul stench.

"What are you talking about? I can't smell anything, and neither can Evelyn and Marcelo—they're both fast asleep," she replied, handing him the cup. "You can rest now and tomorrow you'll be just like new. Make room, I'm going to sleep with you."

"What did you say?"

"Move over, I'm going to get into your bed."

"Lucia . . . you couldn't have chosen a worse moment; I'm ill."

"My, but you're playing hard to get, aren't you? We're off to a bad start: you're the one who's supposed to take the initiative, and instead you insult me."

"I'm sorry, I simply meant that—"

"Stop being such a crybaby. I won't disturb you. I sleep all night without moving."

With that she slipped between the sheets and in no time was stretched out comfortably in the bed. Sitting up, Richard blew on his tea and sipped it, taking as long as possible. He was completely at a loss as to how to interpret what was going on. In the end, he lay down quietly beside Lucia; he felt weak, achy, and enchanted, completely aware of the unique presence of this woman: the shape of her body; her comforting warmth; her strange mop of hair; the inevitable, exciting contact of her arm on his, her hip, her foot. What Lucia had said was true: she slept on her back with her arms folded across her chest, as solemn and silent as a medieval knight sculpted on his marble tomb. Richard thought he was not going to close his eyes in the hours to come, that he would stay awake breathing in Lucia's unknown, sweet smell, but he had barely completed the thought before he fell contentedly asleep.

MONDAY DAWNED CALM: the storm had finally dissipated miles out in the ocean, but snow covered the land like a thick down blanket that muffled all sound. Lucia was asleep alongside Richard in the same position as the previous night, and Evelyn was sleeping in the other bed with the Chihuahua curled up on the pillow. When he awoke, Richard noticed the room still smelled of Chinese food, but it no longer bothered him. During the night he had at first been worried as he was not accustomed to being with a woman, much less sleeping with one. But to his surprise he quickly fell asleep, drifting off weightlessly into sidereal space, an empty, infinite abyss. Earlier in his life, when he drank too much, he often fell into an abyss, but that was a heavy stupor far removed from the blessed peace of the past few hours in the motel with Lucia beside him. He saw from his cell phone that it was already a quarter past eight in the morning; he was astonished he had slept so many hours after the embarrassing episode in the bathroom. He got up cautiously to go and bring fresh coffee for Lucia and Evelyn. He needed to get some air and ponder all that had happened the previous day and night. He was in turmoil, shaken by a hurricane of new emotions. He had woken with his nose pressed to Lucia's neck, an arm around her waist, and an adolescent's erection. Her intimate warmth, tranquil breathing, and tousled hair: everything was so much better than he had imagined, and produced in him a mixture of intense eroticism and the overwhelming tenderness of a grandfather.

He thought vaguely of Susan, whom he met regularly in a Manhattan hotel as a prophylactic measure. They enjoyed each other's company, and once they had sated their bodily appetites, they talked about everything apart from feelings. They had never spent the night together, but if they had enough time they would go out to eat in a very discreet Moroccan restaurant, and part afterward as good friends. If they happened to bump into each other in one of the university buildings they would say hello with a casual friendliness that was not a facade to conceal their clandestine relationship but a true reflection of what they both felt. They appreciated one another, but the temptation to fall in love had never arisen.

What he felt for Lucia could not compare to that: it was the opposite. With her, Richard felt as if decades had been ripped from the calendar and he was eighteen again. He had thought he was immune, and yet there he was, like a youngster prey to his hormones. If she so much as guessed this, she would mock him pitilessly. In those divine hours of the night he was accompanied for the first time in twenty-five years; he felt so close to her as they breathed in unison. It was very easy to sleep with her, and very complicated what was happening to him now, this mixture of happiness and terror, of anticipation and the wish to run away, the urgency of desire.

This is madness, he decided. He wanted to talk to her, clear things up, find out if she felt the same, but he was not going to rush into it; that might scare her off, ruin everything. Besides, with Evelyn present there was very little they could say, yet the wait was becoming impossible: by the next day they might no longer be together and the moment would have gone to say what he had to say. If he had the courage, he would have come straight out and told her he loved her, that last night he had wanted to hold her and never let her go. If only he had the slightest idea of how she felt, he would tell her. What did he have to offer? He was bringing a huge burden with him, and although at his age everyone brought baggage, his weighed as much as a slab of granite.

This was the second time he could observe Lucia sleeping. She looked like a child and had not even noticed he had gotten up, as if they were an old couple who had shared a bed for years. He wanted to wake her with kisses, ask her to give him a chance, beg her to take him over, move into his house, occupy every last inch of his life with her ironic, bossy affection. He had never been so sure of anything. He imagined that if Lucia were to love him it would be a miracle. He wondered how it had taken him so long before he became aware of this love that now overwhelmed him, filling every fiber of his being: What had he been thinking of? He had wasted four months by being such an idiot. This torrent of love could not have suddenly come into being, it must have been growing ever since she came to New York in September. His chest was aching with fear, like a delicious wound. Bless you, Evelyn Ortega, he thought, it was thanks to you this miracle happened. A miracle, there's no other way to describe what I feel.

Richard opened the door to get some cold air and try to calm down: he was being swept away by this sudden, uncontrollable avalanche of feelings. But he had not even taken a step outside before he came face-to-face with a moose. He was so startled he fell backward with a yelp that woke Lucia and Evelyn. Apparently not as shocked as he was, the animal lowered its huge head to try to get inside the room, but the size of its flat antlers made this a difficult maneuver. Evelyn, who had never seen such a monster, curled up in terror; Lucia searched desperately for her cell phone to take a photo. The moose might have succeeded in getting in had it not been for Marcelo, who took charge of the situation with his gruff guard-dog bark. The moose retreated, shaking the foundations of the wooden building when its antlers collided with the doorway, and then trotted off, accompanied by a chorus of nervous laughter and furious barking.

Sweating from the discharge of adrenaline, Richard announced he was going for coffee while they dressed. He did not get very far. A few steps from the doorway, the moose had deposited a pile of fresh excrement: two mounds of soft brown balls into which his boot sank to the ankle. Cursing, Richard hobbled on one foot to the reception, which fortunately had a window that faced the parking lot, to ask for a hose to clean himself. He had been so careful about no one seeing or recalling them on this rash pilgrimage of theirs, and now this nosy animal had brought all his plans crashing to the ground. If there is one thing that's memorable, it's an idiot covered in crap, Richard concluded. This was a bad omen for the rest of their journey. Or would it be a good one? Nothing bad can happen, he decided, I'm protected by the ridiculousness of having fallen in love. He burst out laughing, because if it were not for the discovery of love, which painted the world in the brightest colors, he would have imagined there was a curse on him. As though the question of poor Kathryn Brown were not enough, he had come up against atrocious weather, fleas, food poisoning, his ulcer, and his own and the moose's shit.

Evelyn

Mexico–US border, 2008

F aced with the boredom and suffocating heat of Nuevo
Laredo, the days seemed endless to Evelyn Ortega. But
no sooner had night brought cooler air than the camp
was transformed into a den of clandestine activity and vice.
Cabrera had warned her and the others not to mix with anyone and to be careful not to show any money, but that proved
impossible. They were surrounded by migrants like themselves,
but in much more desperate straits. Some of them had been
there for months suffering hardships: they had tried to cross
the river several times without success, or had been arrested
on the other side and deported back to Mexico, since sending
them to their countries of origin in Central America would have
been more expensive. Most of them could not pay a coyote. The
most pathetic were the children traveling on their own; not even
the meanest person could refuse to help them. Evelyn's group
shared their provisions and fresh water with two of them who

went everywhere hand in hand: a boy aged eight and his sister, a girl of six. A year earlier in El Salvador they had escaped from the house of an uncle and aunt who abused them, then wandered through Guatemala living off charity. They had been going from place to place in Mexico for months, joining with other migrants who adopted them for a while. They were hoping to find their mother in the United States but had no idea which city she lived in.

At night, to avoid being robbed of all they had, Cabrera's group took turns to sleep. On the second day, a Saturday, there were rain showers that soaked their cardboard roof, so that they were left in the open like the rest of the wretched itinerant population. When the moonless night arrived, the camp seemed to waken out of its lethargy, as if this was what everyone had been waiting for. While many migrants prepared to confront the river, the criminals and police swung into action. Fortunately, Cabrera had negotiated a safe-conduct for his group with both the gangs and the men in uniform.

The next night, when the sky was cloudy and no stars were visible, Cabrera's contact showed up. He was a short, bony man, with yellow skin and the vague gaze of a hardened addict, who introduced himself as the Expert. Cabrera assured them that despite his doubtful appearance no one was better qualified. He might have been a poor devil on land, but in the water he could be trusted completely: nobody knew the currents and whirlpools like him. When he wasn't high he spent his time studying the movement of the patrols and their powerful searchlights. He knew when to enter the water, crossing between two sweeps of the beams, and how to reach a precise spot among the weeds so as to remain unseen. He charged in dollars and per person, a cost the coyote had to pay because without the man's knowledge and confidence it would be almost impossible for them to reach the United States. "Can you swim?" asked the Expert. None of them could give a positive answer. He said that if they still had any possessions they could not take any of them, only their identity documents and money. He told them to take off their clothes and sneakers and put them in black plastic garbage bags, which he then tied to the inner tube of a truck tire, which was to be their raft. He showed them how to hold on with one arm and swim with the other, trying not to splash to avoid making any noise. "Anyone who lets go is screwed," he warned.

Berto said goodbye to his group with hugs and final recommendations. Two of the men were the first to enter the water, in their underpants. They clung to the tire and headed off, guided by the Expert. They were soon out of sight in the darkness of the river. Fifteen minutes later, the Expert reappeared on the bank pulling the inner tube behind him. He had left the two men hidden among the reeds on a small island in midriver to wait for the rest of the group. Berto Cabrera gave Evelyn one last regretful embrace: he doubted the poor girl would overcome all the obstacles she faced. "I can't see you able to walk eighty-five miles across the desert, little one. Follow my associate's instructions, he'll know what to do with you."

THE RIVER WAS MORE DANGEROUS than it looked from the bank, but none of them hesitated: they had only a few seconds to avoid the search beams. Evelyn tiptoed into the water in her panties and bra, with her male companions on either side of her and the Expert ready to help if she faltered. She was afraid she might drown but was even more worried they might all be discovered through her fault. Stifling a cry of alarm as she plunged into the cold water, she found that the riverbed was slimy, with branches, garbage, and perhaps even water snakes. The rubber tube was slippery, her good arm was barely long enough to stretch around it, and she kept her other arm tight against her chest. Within a few seconds she could no longer touch bottom and the current sent her tumbling. She went under, then resurfaced swallowing water and trying desperately to cling on. One of the men managed to grab hold of her waist before the current swept her away. He motioned for her to use both arms to hang on, but Evelyn felt a stabbing pain in her sore shoulder. Her companions lifted her and laid her facedown on the tire. She closed her eyes and let herself go, abandoning herself to her fate.

The crossing took very little time, and they soon found themselves on a small island, where they met up with the other two. Crouching among the bushes on sandy ground, they stared at the riverbank on the US side. It was so close they could hear the conversation between a pair of patrolmen standing guard next to a vehicle with a powerful light aimed directly at their hiding place. More than an hour went by without the Expert's showing any sign of becoming impatient. In fact he seemed to have fallen asleep, while their teeth chattered with cold and they were only too aware of the insects and reptiles crawling over them. Around midnight, the Expert roused himself as if he had an internal alarm, and at that precise moment the patrol vehicle switched off its beam and they heard it move off. "We have less than five minutes before their replacement arrives. There is less current here, we'll go together and splash our way across, but on the other bank you mustn't make the slightest noise," he instructed them. They plunged into the river again, clinging to the inner tube, which sank level with the water because of the weight of their six bodies, and propelled it straight ahead of them. Soon they could stand and used the reeds to pull themselves up the muddy bank, all of them giving Evelyn a helping hand. They had reached the United States.

Moments later they heard another vehicle engine, but by now they were protected by the undergrowth, beyond the reach of the searchlights. The Expert led them to dry land. They stumbled forward in single file, holding hands so as not to get lost in the darkness, pushing their way through the reeds until they came to a small clearing. Their guide switched on a flashlight. Pointing it at the ground, he gave them their plastic bags and indicated for them to get dressed. He took off his wet T-shirt and used it to bind Evelyn's arm against her chest: she had lost the bandage in the river. It was then she realized she no longer had the plastic folder with the papers Father Benito had given her. She searched for it in the feeble gleam from the flashlight, hoping she might have dropped it there, but when she could not see it, she understood it must have been carried away by the current when her companion rescued her. The belt with the folder must have come loose when he grabbed her by the waist. She had lost the prayer card blessed by the pope but was still wearing around her neck the jaguar goddess amulet that was meant to keep her from harm.

They were just finishing getting dressed when out of nowhere Cabrera's associate appeared, like a phantom of the night. He was a Mexican who had lived in the United States so many years he spoke Spanish with a strange accent. He offered them thermoses of coffee with added liquor, which they drank in grateful silence. The Expert slipped away without a word of goodbye.

The Mexican told the men to follow him in single file but said Evelyn should walk on her own in the opposite direction. Horrified, she tried to protest but could not make so much as a sound, rendered mute at having gotten this far and then being betrayed. "Berto told me your mother is in the States. Give yourself up to the first guard or patrol that comes across you. They won't deport you, because you're a minor," the Mexican told her. He was sure no one would think she was more than twelve years old. Evelyn did not believe him, but her companions had heard this was the law in the United States. They embraced her briefly, then followed the Mexican, and were quickly swallowed up by the darkness.

WHEN EVELYN MANAGED TO REACT, all she could think of doing was to curl up shivering among the bushes. She tried to pray but could not remember any of her grandmother's many prayers. One, two, maybe three hours went by; she had lost all sense of time and even the ability to move. Her body was stiff and she could feel a dull ache in her shoulder. Suddenly she sensed a furious beating in the air above her head and guessed it must be bats flying in search of food, as they did back in Guatemala. This made her shrink back still farther into the vegetation, because everyone knew bats sucked human blood. In order not to think about vampires, snakes, or scorpions, she concentrated on a plan to get out of there. Other groups of migrants must have been coming through; it was simply a question of staying awake so that she could join them. She invoked the mother jaguar and the mother of Jesus, as Concepcion had taught her, but neither came to her aid. These holy women must lose their powers in the United States, Evelyn thought, feeling utterly abandoned.

There were only a few hours of darkness left, but they stretched out interminably. Slowly, Evelyn's eyes grew accustomed to the moonless night that at first had seemed to her impenetrable, and she began to make out the vegetation around her: tall, dry grasses. The night was one long torment for Evelyn, until finally the first light of day came. All this time she had been unaware of either migrants or border guards anywhere near her. As the sky lightened, she plucked up her courage to explore around her. She was so stiff she found it hard to get to her feet and walk a couple of steps. Although she felt hungry and thirsty, at least her shoulder no longer hurt. She got some idea of how hot the day would be from the mist rising from the ground like a bridal veil. The night had been silent, interrupted only by warnings from loudspeakers in the distance, but at dawn the land awoke in a buzzing of insects, the crackle of twigs beneath the tiny paws of rodents, the rustle of reeds in the breeze, and a constant coming and going of sparrows through the air. Here and there she saw splashes of color among the bushes: the vermilion of a flycatcher, a yellow warbler, or a jay with its bright blue feathers. All of these were modest compared with those of her Guatemalan village. She had grown up amidst a profusion of birds, plumages of a thousand colors, seven hundred species: according to Father Benito, it was a bird-watcher's paradise. She listened for the severe warnings in Spanish from the loudspeakers and tried in vain to calculate the distance to the border posts, the watchtowers, and the road, if there was one. She had no idea where she was. One by one, her mind filled with the stories passed by word of mouth among migrants: the dangers of the north, the merciless desert, ranchers who shot randomly at anyone entering their properties in search of water, guards with heavy weapons, attack dogs trained to detect the smell of fear, prisons where years could go by without anyone hearing of you. If they were like the ones in Guatemala, Evelyn would rather be dead than end up in one of those cells.

The day crept by hour after hour, with awful slowness. The sun climbed in the sky, burning the land with a dry heat like hot coals that was very different from what Evelyn was used to. She was so thirsty that she no longer felt hungry. As there were no trees to provide her with shade, she scraped a hole in the ground among some bushes, using a stick she found to scare off the snakes, and settled there as best she could. Then she drove the stick into the ground so that its moving shadow could show her the passage of time, as she had seen her grandmother do. She heard vehicles going by at regular intervals, as well as low-flying helicopters, but when she realized they always followed the same path she stopped paying attention to them. Confused, her head woozy, she could feel thoughts racing through her brain. Thanks to the stick she guessed it was midday, and that was when the first hallucinations began. They had the shapes and colors of the time she had been given the ayahuasca potion: armadillos, rats, jaguar cubs without their mother, Andres's black dog that had died years earlier but now came to visit her in perfect health. She dozed off, exhausted by the brutal heat, dizzy from weariness and thirst.

The afternoon passed slowly by without any drop in temperature. A long, thick, black snake crawled over her leg in a ghastly caress. Petrified, she waited without drawing breath as she felt the reptile's weight on her, the brush of its satiny skin, the undulation of every muscle of the hoselike body that slid lazily across her. It was unlike any snake she had seen back in her village. When the reptile finally moved on, Evelyn jumped to her feet and gulped down mouthfuls of air. Terror made her feel giddy; her heart was pounding. It took hours for her to recover and relax her guard; she no longer had the strength to stay on her feet scanning the ground. Her lips were cracked and bleeding, her tongue was a swollen mollusk in her mouth, her skin burned with fever.

At last night fell and it began to grow cooler. By now Evelyn was exhausted. She no longer cared about snakes, bats, armed guards, or nightmarish monsters; all she felt was the overpowering need to drink water and rest. Curled up on the ground, she gave in to despair and solitude, wishing only to die soon, in her sleep and never have to wake again.

EVELYN DID NOT DIE ON THAT SECOND NIGHT on US territory as she had feared. Awaking at dawn in the same position, she was unable to remember anything about what had happened since she left the camp at Nuevo Laredo. She was dehydrated and it took her several attempts to stretch her legs, get to her feet, put her sore arm in the sling, and totter a few steps like an old woman. Every fiber of her body ached, but what most dominated her was thirst. She had to find water. She could not focus her eyes or think properly, but she had always lived in the midst of nature, and experience taught her water must be nearby: she was surrounded by reeds and undergrowth, which she knew grew on damp soil. Driven on by thirst and anxiety, she set off aimlessly, leaning on the same stick that had previously served as a sundial.

She had only zigzagged some fifty yards when she was halted by the sound of an engine very close by. Instinctively, she threw herself down and lay flat among the tall grasses. As the vehicle passed by she could hear a man's voice speaking English, and another answering voice, crackling as if it came from a radio or telephone. She stayed without moving for a long while after the sound of the engine had died away, but finally thirst forced her to crawl on through the bushes in search of the river. Thorns scratched her face and neck. A branch tore her T-shirt and jagged stones cut her hands and knees. She stood up but kept low, feeling her way as she did not dare raise her head to find out exactly where she was. It was early morning, but the glare from the sky was already blinding.

Suddenly she heard the rushing of the river as clearly as if it were another hallucination. This encouraged her to speed up and abandon all precaution. First she felt the mud under her feet and then, pushing apart the reeds, she found herself on the bank of the Rio Grande. She cried out and waded into the water up to her waist, drinking desperately from her cupped hands. The cold water trickled inside her like a blessing. She drank mouthful after mouthful, oblivious to the dirt and the dead animals floating in these waters. Where she stood the river was shallow, and so she could bend down and completely submerge her body, feeling an infinite pleasure as the water flowed around her cracked skin, bad arm, and scratched face. Her long black hair floated out around her like seaweed.

She had just clambered out of the river and was slowly recovering on the bank when the patrolmen found her.

AFTER BEING DETAINED, Evelyn was interviewed by a female immigration officer in a small cubicle. The woman found herself confronted by a timid, trembling young girl who refused to look up and had not touched the fruit juice or crackers she had put on the table to win her trust. She tried to reassure her by briefly stroking her head, but this only frightened the girl further. She had been told that the detainee had mental problems and so she had asked for extra time to conduct the interview. Many of the minors who passed through there were traumatized, but without an official order it was impossible to carry out a psychological evaluation. She had to trust her intuition and experience.

Faced with the girl's stubborn refusal to speak, the official at first thought perhaps she spoke only Mayan and wasted several precious minutes until she realized Evelyn understood without a problem but had a speech impediment. She gave her paper and a pencil to write down her replies, praying she knew how to write; most of the children who arrived at the detention center had never been to school.

"What is your name? Where do you come from? Do you have any family here?"

In clear handwriting, Evelyn wrote her name, those of her village and country, her mother's name, and a telephone number. The officer gave a sigh of relief.

"This makes things much easier. We'll call your mother so

that she can come and get you. You'll be allowed to go with her temporarily until a judge decides on your case."

Evelyn spent three days in the detention center, without speaking to anyone, despite being surrounded by women and children from Mexico and Central America, including many from Guatemala. They were given two meals a day, milk and diapers for the youngest children, camp beds, and military blankets. These were essential because the air-conditioning kept the building at a frigid temperature that led to a constant epidemic of coughs and colds. It was a transit facility: no one stayed there very long and the detainees were transferred as quickly as possible to other facilities. Those minors who had relatives in the United States were handed over without any serious investigation, as there was not enough time or staff to examine every case.

It was not Miriam who came to look for Evelyn but a man called Galileo Leon, who said he was her stepfather. She had never heard of him and resolutely refused to go with him, because she knew about pimps and traffickers who lay in wait for juveniles like her. Sometimes children were claimed by perfect strangers, who took them away after simply signing a form. An official had to call Miriam on the phone to clarify the situation, and this was how Evelyn learned that her mother had a husband. She was soon to discover that as well as a stepfather she had two half brothers, aged four and three.

"Why didn't the girl's mother come to fetch her?" the duty officer asked Galileo Leon.

"Because she would lose her job. And don't think this is easy for me either. I'm losing four days of earnings thanks to this kid.

I'm a painter and my clients won't wait," the man replied, in a humble tone that contrasted with his words.

"We're going to hand over the girl to you under presumption of credible fear. Do you understand what that means?"

"More or less."

"The judge will have to decide if the reasons why the girl left her country are valid. Evelyn will need to prove a specific, concrete danger, for example that she was attacked or had been threatened. You can take her with you on parole."

"Does that mean I have to pay?" the man asked in alarm.

"No. It's a nominal amount that gets written in the book but that the migrant is not charged. She will be told by mail at her mother's house when she has to appear in front of an immigration court. Before the hearing Evelyn will have a meeting with an asylum counselor."

"A lawyer? We don't have the money for one . . . ," said Leon.

"The system is rather slow because there are so many children seeking asylum. The reality is that not even half of them get to see a counselor, but if they do, it is free."

"Outside I was told they could find me one for three thousand dollars."

"Don't believe them, they're traffickers and swindlers. All you need to do for now is wait for the notification from the court," said the duty officer, considering the matter closed.

He took a copy of Galileo Leon's driver's license to add to Evelyn's file, even though this was next to useless because the center did not have the capacity to follow the trail of every child. Then he said a rapid goodbye to Evelyn; he had several more cases to deal with that day.

GALILEO LEON HAD BEEN BORN in Nicaragua. At eighteen he had immigrated illegally to the United States, but had obtained residency thanks to the 1997 amnesty law. He was a small man of few words and rough manners. At first glance he did not inspire confidence or affection.

Their first stop was at a Walmart to buy Evelyn clothes and toiletries. She thought she was dreaming when she saw the size of the store and the infinite variety of goods on offer, each in different colors and sizes, a labyrinth of aisles crammed full to overflowing. Fearing she might get lost forever, she clung to her stepfather's arm. He found his way around like an experienced explorer and led her directly to each section, telling her to choose underwear, T-shirts, three blouses, two pairs of jeans, a skirt, a dress, and proper shoes. Even though she was not far from her sixteenth birthday, her size corresponded to that of a ten- or twelve-year-old American girl. Bewildered, Evelyn always wanted to choose the cheapest item, but since she was unfamiliar with the currency she took far too long.

"Don't look at the prices. Everything here is cheap, and your mom gave me money for clothes," explained Galileo.

From there he took her to a McDonald's to eat hamburgers with French fries and a huge sundae topped with a cherry. In Guatemala it would have been enough for an entire family.

"Did no one ever teach you to say thank you?" asked her stepfather, more out of curiosity than as a reproach.

Without daring to look at him, Evelyn nodded, licking the last spoonful of ice cream.

"Are you scared of me or something? I'm no ogre."

"Than . . . thank . . . I'm . . . ," she stuttered.

"Are you stupid or do you have a stammer?"

"Stam . . . stamm—"

"Okay, I see. Sorry," Galileo interrupted her. "If you can't even talk Spanish properly, I don't know how you'll manage in English. What a mess! What are we going to do with you?"

They spent the night in a motel for truckers next to the highway. The room was filthy but had a hot shower. Galileo told her to get washed, say her prayers, and go to sleep in the bed on the left. He always slept nearest to the door; it was one of his little obsessions. "I'm going out for a smoke, and by the time I get back I want to see you asleep," he said. Evelyn obeyed as quickly as she could. She showered rapidly, then crept into bed fully dressed and wearing her sneakers. She pulled the bedcover up to her nose, pretending to be asleep and planning to escape the moment he touched her. She felt very tired, her shoulder ached, and her chest was tight with fear, but she prayed to her grandmother and that gave her strength. She knew her grandma would have gone to the church to light candles for her.

After more than an hour, Galileo returned. He took off his shoes, went into the bathroom, and closed the door. Evelyn heard the toilet flush, and out of the corner of her eye she saw him come back into the room in his shorts, undershirt, and socks. She got ready to leap out of bed. Her stepfather draped his trousers over the only free chair, bolted the door, and switched off the light. The blue reflection of a neon sign with the motel's name shone in through the net curtains, and in the semidarkness Evelyn saw him go down on his knees next to the bed he had chosen. Galileo Leon murmured prayers for a long while. By the time he eventually climbed into bed, Evelyn was sound asleep.

Lucia, Richard, Evelyn

Upstate New York

Richard

Brazil, 1987–1990

They left the motel at nine with only a coffee inside them. They were all hungry, so Lucia demanded they have breakfast somewhere: she needed hot food on a normal plate, not in a carton with chopsticks. They ended up at a Denny's, the women tucking into a banquet of pancakes while Richard stirred a bowl of insipid oatmeal. Leaving Brooklyn the day before, they had agreed to stay apart in public, but as the hours went by, they forgot their caution. They felt so comfortable with one another that even Kathryn Brown had been incorporated into the group without a fuss.

The road looked in better shape than on the previous day. During the night there had been only a light dusting of snow, and although the temperature was still several degrees below freezing, the wind had dropped and the snow had been cleared from the highways. They could travel more quickly; if they kept up the same speed, Richard calculated they would reach the cabin around midday and would have plenty of daylight in which to dispose of the Lexus. However, an hour and a half later, as he was driving around a bend, he found himself a hundred yards from the flashing blue and red lights of several police patrol cars blocking the route. There was no detour, and if he did a U-turn he would only attract their attention.

The contents of his breakfast rose into his mouth, filling it with bile. Nausea and a phantom return of his diarrhea panicked him. He felt in the top pocket of his jacket, where he normally kept his pink pills, but could not find them. In his rearview mirror he saw Lucia crossing her fingers for luck. In front of him were halted vehicles, an ambulance, and a fire engine. A highway trooper motioned for him to join the line. Removing his balaclava, Richard opened the window and asked him in the calmest voice he could muster what was wrong.

"A multiple pileup."

"Any fatality, officer?"

"I am not authorized to give that information," the trooper replied, and walked off.

Richard collapsed with his head on the steering wheel, waiting with the other drivers and counting the seconds. His stomach and esophagus were on fire. He could not recall having had such a ferocious acid attack as this before. He was afraid his ulcer might have burst and he was bleeding internally. It was just his rotten luck that he would run into a traffic pileup right at that moment, when he had a dead body in the car trunk and desperately needed a toilet. What if it was appendicitis? The oatmeal had been a mistake; he had forgotten it loosened the bowels. "If these damned cops don't clear the road I'm going to crap myself right here. That's all I need. What's Lucia going to think: that I'm a wreck, an idiot with chronic diarrhea," he said aloud.

On the dashboard clock the minutes went by at a snail's pace. All of a sudden his cell phone rang.

"Are you okay? You looked as if you passed out," Lucia said, her voice reaching him from another planet.

"I don't know," he replied, raising his head from the wheel.

"It's psychosomatic, Richard. You're nervous. Take your pills."

"They're in my bag in your car."

"I'll bring them to you."

"No!"

He saw Lucia climb out of one door of the Subaru and Evelyn out of the other, Marcelo in her arms. Lucia approached the Lexus with a completely natural air and rapped on the window. He lowered it, intending to shout at her, but as she handed him the pills one of the patrolmen came striding over.

"Miss! Stay in your vehicle!" he ordered her.

"I'm sorry, officer. Do you have a match?" she asked him, making the universal gesture of raising a cigarette to her lips.

"Get into your vehicle! You too!" the man shouted at Evelyn.

They had to wait thirty-five minutes before the accident was cleared, the Subaru with its engine on to keep the heating going, the Lexus an icebox. Once the ambulances and the fire engine had departed, the police allowed the cars lined up in both directions to get going. As they passed the accident they saw an upturned van with its four wheels in the air, an unrecognizable car with a completely crumpled hood that had rammed into it from behind, and a third car piled up on the second. It was a clear day, the storm had passed, and perhaps none of the three drivers involved had considered the possibility of black ice.

Richard had taken four antacid tablets. The taste of bile remained in his mouth and his stomach was still burning. He drove hunched over the wheel, bathed in a cold sweat, his sight clouded with pain, increasingly convinced he had internal bleeding. He warned Lucia on his cell phone that he could not go on and pulled up at the first stop he found. She came to a halt behind him just as he was opening the door and vomiting spectacularly onto the road.

"We have to get help. There must be a hospital somewhere near here," said Lucia, handing him a tissue and a bottle of water.

"No hospital. It'll pass, but I need a toilet . . ."

Before Richard could contradict her, Lucia told Evelyn to drive the Subaru and she got in behind the wheel of the Lexus. "Drive slowly, Lucia. You saw what can happen if the car skids," said Richard, before collapsing onto the backseat in a fetal position. It occurred to him that in exactly the same posture, separated from him only by the back of the seat and a plastic partition, lay the body of Kathryn Brown. Half dazed by pain and weakness, he found himself sharing with her some of his worst memories and wondering if her spirit had already sensed much of what had happened to him in the past.

IN THE DAYS WHEN RICHARD LIVED in Rio de Janeiro people drank as a matter of course. It was a social obligation, part of the culture, a necessity at every meeting, even business ones, a comfort on a rainy evening or at a hot noon, a stimulus for political discussion, and a cure for a cold, sadness, frustrated love, or a disappointment in soccer. Richard had not been back to Rio for years, and yet he guessed it must still be the same: certain customs take generations to die out. At the time he drank as much alcohol as his friends and acquaintances, not considering it anything out of the ordinary. Very occasionally he drank himself into a stupor, but that was always unpleasant. He preferred to float, to see the world with no jagged edges, a friendly, warm place. He had not given his drinking much importance until Anita declared it was a problem and began obsessively counting how many glasses he downed, discreetly at first but later humiliating him in public with her comments. He had a good head for liquor: he could drink four beers and three caipirinhas without any drastic consequences—on the contrary, he lost his shyness and thought he was wonderful. Yet from then on he restrained his drinking to assuage his wife and his ulcer, which had the habit of springing unpleasant surprises. Although he wrote frequently to his father, he never mentioned his drinking, because Joseph was abstemious and would not have understood.

After giving birth to their daughter, Bibi, Anita became pregnant three more times, but on each occasion suffered a miscarriage. She dreamed of having a large family like her own; she was one of the younger daughters among eleven children and also had countless cousins, nephews, and nieces. Every new loss deepened her despair, and got it into her head that it was a sign from the gods or a punishment for some unknown fault. Gradually she began to lose her strength and joyousness.

Without these essential virtues dancing lost all meaning for her, so that in the end she sold her academy. The women in the Farinha family—grandmother, sisters, aunts, and cousins—all closed ranks, taking turns to be with her. Anita clung closely to Bibi, watching over her anxiously all the time for fear of losing her. Her family tried to distract her by getting her to write a book with the recipes of several generations of Farinhas, in the belief that nothing bad can resist the remedy of work and the comfort of food. Then they made her arrange eighty albums of family photographs in chronological order, and when she had done that invented other pretexts to keep her busy. Richard reluctantly allowed them to take his wife and child to her grandparents' ranch for a couple of months. The sun and wind revived Anita's spirits; she returned from the countryside weighing four kilos more and regretting that she had sold the academy because she wanted to dance again.

They made love as they had in the days when that was all they ever did. They went out to listen to music and dance. Richard tried a few steps with his wife until he could see that all eyes were fixed on her, whether it was because they recognized the queen of the Anita Farinha Academy or simply out of admiration or desire, then he gallantly gave way for other men who were lighter on their feet. He retreated to drink at their table and watch her tenderly, vaguely wondering about his existence.

He was of an age to plan the future, but with a glass in his hand it was easy to postpone that concern. He had completed his doctorate more than two years earlier but had not made anything of it apart from a couple of articles published in academic journals in the United States. One was on the land rights of indigenous people in the 1988 Brazilian constitution, the other on gender violence. He made his living giving English classes. Out of curiosity rather than ambition he occasionally applied for one of the job vacancies he saw in the *American Political Sci-*

ence Review. He considered his time in Rio de Janeiro as a nice pause in his destiny, a prolonged vacation. He would soon have to carve out a professional career for himself, but that could wait a while longer. The city was conducive to pleasure and leisure. Anita had a small house near the beach and they got by on the money from the sale of her academy and his English classes.

BIBI WAS ALMOST THREE when the goddesses finally answered the prayers of Anita and the rest of the women in her family. "I owe it to Yemaya," said Anita when she told her husband she was pregnant. "Is that so? I thought you owed it to me," he laughed, lifting her in a bear hug. There were no problems during the pregnancy and she reached full term, but the birth itself was difficult and in the end a caesarean was needed. The doctor warned Anita she should not have any more children, at least for a few years, but that did not upset her too much because now she had Pablo in her arms. He was a healthy boy with a voracious appetite, the little brother for Bibi that the whole family had been waiting for.

At dawn a month later, Richard leaned over the crib to pick up the child and hand him to Anita. He was surprised Pablo had not cried from hunger in the night, as he usually did every three or four hours. He was sleeping so peacefully that Richard hesitated to disturb him. A wave of tenderness engulfed him to the core. The overwhelming sense of gratitude he often felt in the presence of Bibi made his eyes sting and brought a knot to his throat. Anita took the baby with her night gown open to put him on her breast. It was then she realized he was not breathing.

A visceral scream like that of a tortured animal shook the house, the neighborhood, the whole world.

An autopsy was required to determine the cause of death. Richard tried to keep this from Anita, because the idea that their tiny Pablo would be systematically cut open would be too horrible for her to bear. The pathologist's report attributed it to sudden infant death syndrome, or crib death. An entirely unpredictable misfortune. Anita fell into a deep, dark sorrow, an unfathomable cavern from which her husband was excluded. Richard found himself rejected by his wife and banished to the farthest corner of his home as an encumbrance by the rest of the Farinha family, who invaded his privacy to take care of Anita, look after Bibi, and make decisions without consulting him. The relatives took over his small family, thinking he was incapable of understanding the magnitude of the tragedy because he did not share their sensibilities. Deep down, Richard was relieved, because it was true that he was a stranger to this kind of mourning. He increased the number of hours he taught, left the house early, and found excuses to come back late. In need of distraction, he started drinking more.

THEY WERE ONLY A FEW MILES from the turnoff to the cabin when they heard a siren and a police car pulled out from where it had been concealed behind some bushes. Lucia saw the lights whirling between her and the Subaru behind. For a moment she seriously considered putting her foot down and risking her life on it, but a cry from Richard forced her to change her plan. She slowed and pulled off onto the shoulder of the road. "Now we really are done for," groaned Richard, struggling upright. Lucia lowered the window and waited breathlessly while the patrol car came to a halt behind her. The Subaru slowed down as it went past, but she managed to signal to Evelyn to continue on without stopping. The policeman came up a moment later.

"Your license and registration," he demanded.

"Have I done something wrong, officer?"

"Your documents, please."

Lucia searched in the glove compartment and passed him the Lexus's documents and her international driver's license, which she was afraid might have expired as she could not remember when she had obtained it in Chile. The policeman studied them slowly and glanced at Richard, who had sat up and was straightening his clothes in the backseat.

"Step out of the car," he ordered Lucia.

Lucia obeyed. Her legs began to give way beneath her. It flashed through her mind that this must be how African-Americans felt when they were stopped by the police, and that if Richard had been driving their treatment would have been very different. At that moment Richard opened the rear door and almost crawled out.

"Wait inside the vehicle, sir!" yelled the policeman, his right hand moving toward his gun holster.

Richard was on his knees retching. He vomited the rest of his oatmeal all over the man's boots. The policeman jumped back in disgust.

"He's sick, he has an ulcer, officer," Lucia explained.

"What is your relationship to him?"

"I'm . . . I'm . . . ," Lucia stammered.

"She's my housekeeper. She works for me," Richard managed to groan between two bouts of retching.

The stereotypes automatically fell into place for the policeman: a Latina employee driving her boss, probably to the hospital. The guy seemed genuinely ill. Curiously, the woman had a foreign license; this was not the first time he had seen an international permit. Chile? Where on earth was that? He waited for Richard to straighten up, then told him to get back into the car, but by now his voice had softened. He went around to the rear of the Lexus, called Lucia over, and pointed to the trunk.

"Yes, officer. It just happened. There was a pileup on the highway, you might know about it. I was hit by a car that didn't manage to brake, but it was nothing, only a slight dent and the rear light casing. I painted the bulb with nail polish until I can find a replacement."

"I'm going to have to issue you a ticket."

"I need to take Mr. Bowmaster to see a doctor."

"I'll let you go this time, but you must replace the light within twenty-four hours, do you understand?"

"Yes, officer."

"Do you require help with your sick passenger? I can escort you to the hospital."

"Many thanks, officer, but that won't be necessary."

Lucia's heart was beating wildly as she slid back behind the wheel. The police car moved off. I'm going to have a heart attack, she thought, but thirty seconds later she was wracked with nervous giggles. If she had been fined, her identity and the car's details would have been registered in the police report, and then Richard's worst fears would have come true in their full horror.

"That was a close one," she said, wiping away tears of laughter, but Richard remained unamused.

The Subaru was waiting for them a half mile farther on. A short while later, Richard spotted the entrance to Horacio's cabin, little more than an almost invisible track covered with several inches of snow that snaked between the pines. For about ten minutes they made their way slowly through the woods without seeing any signs of human life, praying their vehicles would not get stuck. Suddenly they saw the sloping roof of a cabin straight out of a fairy tale, with icicles hanging from it like Christmas decorations.

Still weak from vomiting, but in less pain, Richard undid the padlock on the gate. They parked the cars and got out. He had to push as hard as he could to open the front door, which was swollen from the dampness. As soon as they stepped inside a foul smell assaulted them. Richard explained the house had been shut up for more than two years, and that bats and other creatures must have taken it over.

"When are we going to get rid of the Lexus?" asked Lucia.

"Today, but give me half an hour to recover," said Richard, flinging himself down on the battered living room sofa. He did not dare ask her to lie down with him or embrace him to warm him up.

"Yes, get some rest. But if we stay here for long we're going to freeze to death," she told him.

"We have to switch on the electricity generator and fill the heaters with fuel. There are cans of kerosene in the kitchen. The pipes are frozen so we'll melt snow to cook with. We can't use the hearth, someone might see the smoke."

"You're in no state to do anything. Come on, Evelyn," said

Lucia, covering Richard with a stiff moth-eaten blanket she found.

Within a short while, the women had lit two heaters but had been unable to make the decrepit generator start. After he managed to get to his feet, Richard also failed. In the cabin there was only a kerosene camping stove, which he and Horacio used when they went ice fishing. In their luggage Richard had included three flashlights, sleeping bags, and other items essential for an exploration up the Amazon, as well as a few packets of the dried vegetarian food he took with him on his long cycling trips. "Food for donkeys," commented Lucia good-humoredly as she tried to boil water on the tiny stove, which turned out to be as uncooperative as the generator. However, after being soaked in boiling water the donkey food turned into a decent meal, although Richard was unable to touch it and had nothing more than some clear soup and half a cup of tea to stay hydrated since he could not keep anything more down. After that he collapsed once more, wrapped in the blanket, while Lucia and Evelyn shared a cup of tea and talked quietly so not to disturb him.

Evelyn

Chicago–New York, 2008–2011

It was ten years since Evelyn Ortega's mother, Miriam, had seen the three children she had left with their grandmother in Guatemala, but she recognized her daughter the moment she arrived in Chicago thanks to photos and because she looked so much like Concepcion Montoya. Thankfully she doesn't take after me, Miriam thought as Evelyn climbed out of Galileo Leon's pickup. The grandmother was of mixed blood: she had the best of both the Maya and white races, and had been a beauty in her youth before she was captured by the soldiers. Evelyn had inherited her fine features, which had skipped a generation. Miriam on the other hand was coarser looking, stocky and with short legs, as her father had probably been, that "rapist straight down from the mountains," as Concepcion always called him. Miriam's daughter seemed still a child, with her thick black braid hanging down to her waist and her delicate face. Miriam ran toward her and hugged her tight, repeating her name over and over, weeping with joy at having Evelyn at last and with sadness for her other two murdered children. Evelyn allowed herself to be embraced without making any move to return her mother's effusive greeting: this plump woman with yellow hair was a stranger to her.

That initial encounter set the tone for the relationship between mother and daughter. In order to avoid the embarrassment of getting her words entangled, Evelyn spoke as little as possible, and Miriam took this silence as a reproach. Although Evelyn never brought the matter up, Miriam used every excuse she could find to make it plain that she had not chosen to abandon her children but had been forced to. They would all have gone hungry if she had stayed in Monja Blanca del Valle making tamales with Evelyn's grandmother. Couldn't Evelyn see that? When she herself was a mother she would understand what a huge sacrifice Miriam had made for her family's sake.

Another matter floating in the air was the fate of Gregorio and Andres. Miriam thought that if she had been in Guatemala, she would have brought up the boys with a firm hand. Gregorio would not have strayed onto the path of criminality and Andres would not have died through his brother's fault. Whenever this came up, Evelyn did find the words to defend her grandma, who she insisted had taught them how to behave. Her brother had gone bad because of his own weakness, not because his grandmother had spared him the back of her hand.

The Leon family lived in a trailer park. There were about twenty similar trailers, each with a small yard, in their case shared with a parrot and a big, harmless dog. Evelyn was given a foam mattress that at night she put down on the kitchen floor. They had a tiny bathroom and a sink out in the yard. Despite the cramped conditions, they all got along well, partly because they worked different shifts. Miriam cleaned offices at night and houses in the morning. She was away from midnight until the following noon. Galileo had no fixed hours for his painting contracts, and when he was at home he was as quiet as if he had done something wrong, so as to avoid his wife's flaring bad temper. A neighbor had looked after the children without over-charging, but when Evelyn arrived she was given that responsi-bility. Miriam was at home in the afternoon, which meant that for the first year Evelyn could attend English classes for immi-grants that were offered by a local church and later finish high school. After that she began working with her mother. Miriam and Galileo were Pentecostals; their lives revolved around their church's services and social activities.

Galileo explained to Evelyn that he had found redemption in the Lord and a family in his brothers and sisters in faith. "I led the life of a sinner until I went to the church and there the Holy Spirit descended on me. That was nine years ago." Evelyn found it hard to believe that such a meek man could have done a great deal of sinning. According to Galileo, a bolt from the heavens threw him to the floor during a religious service and as he writhed in a trance Satan was driven out of his body while the enthusiastic congregation sang and prayed for him at the tops of their lungs. Ever since then, his life had taken a new direction, he said. He had met Miriam, who shouted a lot but was a good woman who helped keep him on a righteous path. God had given him two children. The Almighty was like family to him, and he spoke to him like son to father; it was enough for him to ask for something with all his heart for it to be granted. He had made public witness of his faith and been baptized by immersion in a local swimming pool. He was hoping Evelyn would do the same, but she kept postponing the moment out of loyalty to Father Benito and her grandmother, who would be offended if she changed religion.

The harmony that reigned among the trailer's inhabitants was endangered during the rare visits made by Doreen, Galileo's daughter born of a fleeting youthful romance with an immigrant from the Dominican Republic who lived by smuggling and fortune-telling. Miriam said that not only had Doreen inherited her mother's knack for hoodwinking fools but she was an addict who went about enveloped in a fateful dark cloud that made everything she touched turn to dog shit. Although twenty-six, she looked fifty, and had never done an honest day's work in her life but boasted of handling vast amounts of money. No one dared ask where she got it from—they suspected her methods were unlawful—but apparently the cash slipped through her fingers as quickly as it had come. This meant she often came to her father to demand a loan without any intention of ever paying it back. Miriam loathed her and Galileo was afraid of her. In her presence he squirmed like a worm and gave her whatever he could, which was always less than what she wanted. Miriam did not have the courage to stand up to her either, saying Doreen had bad blood, without specifying what she meant by that, and looking down on her because she was black. Nothing in Doreen's appearance seemed capable of inspiring fear: she was skinny, wasted, with rat's eyes and yellow teeth and fingernails, permanently hunched due to her weak bones. Yet she gave off a frightening, barely contained rage, like a pressure cooker about to explode. Miriam ordered her daughter to stay off that woman's radar; nothing good could come from her.

Her mother's warning was unnecessary, because Evelyn found it impossible even to breathe whenever Doreen came near. Out in the yard the dog would begin to howl a warning several minutes before she appeared. This alerted Evelyn to the fact she should make herself scarce, but she did not always manage to do so in time. Doreen would catch her: "Where are you going so fast, you stuttering retard?" She was the only one who insulted Evelyn in this way: all the others had become accustomed to figuring out the meaning of Evelyn's stumbling sentences before she finished them. Galileo Leon was quick to give his daughter money so that she would leave, and each time he begged her to accompany him to church, even if only once. He still lived in hope that the Holy Spirit would graciously descend to save her from herself, as it had done with him.

MORE THAN TWO YEARS went by without Evelyn's receiving the notification from the court that she had been informed about at the detention center. Miriam lived in fear of the mail, although she thought that by now her daughter's file had probably gotten lost in the dusty recesses of the immigration service and she would be able to live without documents for the rest of her days without being bothered. Evelyn had finished her last year at high school and had graduated in her cap and gown like all the rest of her class, without anyone asking to see any proof of who she was.

The recent economic crisis had stirred up old resentments against Latinos in the United States. Thousands of Americans, swindled by finance companies and banks, lost their houses or jobs and made immigrants their scapegoats. "I'd like to see an

American of whatever color work for the little they pay us," Miriam used to say. She earned less than the legal minimum wage and had increased her hours to cover her household expenses, because prices always rose while wages stayed the same. At night, Evelyn went with her and two other women to clean offices. A formidable team, they would arrive in a Honda Accord with their cleaning equipment and a transistor radio to listen to evangelical preachers and Mexican songs. They made a point of working together to protect themselves from any nocturnal danger: attacks in the street or sexual harassment in the locked buildings. They earned themselves a reputation as Amazons one night when they used their brooms and buckets to give a hiding to an office worker who had stayed on late and tried to take advantage of Evelyn in a restroom. The security guard, another Latino, turned a deaf ear to the noises for a while, and by the time he eventually intervened, the Don Juan looked as if he had been hit by a truck. Even so, he did not report his assailants to the police, preferring to accept his humiliation in silence.

Miriam and Evelyn worked side by side. They shared the domestic chores, the rearing of the smaller children, looking after the parrot and the dog, doing the shopping and the rest of the daily tasks, and yet they lacked the easy intimacy of mother and daughter; they seemed always to be on a visit with each other. Miriam did not know how to treat her silent daughter oscillating between ignoring her and showing her affection through gifts. Evelyn was a lonely soul and had made no friends either at school or in church. Miriam thought no boy would be interested in her, because she still looked like an underfed urchin. Many immigrants arrived with their bones poking out but within a few months that changed due to a diet of mainly fast food. Evelyn though was uninterested in food by nature. She detested fat and sugar, and missed her grandmother's beans. Miriam was unaware that Evelyn froze whenever anyone came within a yard of her; the trauma of her rape was seared in her memory and body. She associated physical contact with violence, blood, and above all with her brother Andres and his slit throat. Her mother knew what had happened, but no one had told her the full details and Evelyn could never bring herself to talk about it. She was content to be left alone, because it saved her the effort of speaking.

Miriam had no complaints: her daughter fulfilled her duties on time and never stood around idle. In this she was following the example of her grandmother, for whom laziness was the mother of all vices. Evelyn only relaxed when she was with her two siblings and the children at the church, who did not judge her. While her parents attended the service, she minded a group of twenty children in an adjoining room. This saved her from having to listen to the lengthy sermons given by the pastor, a fervent Mexican who succeeded in whipping up the congregation to the point of hysteria. Evelyn invented games to keep the children amused. She sang to them, got them to dance with the aid of a tambourine, and was able to tell them stories without too much of a stutter, provided no adults were around. The pastor suggested she should study to become an elementary school teacher; it was obvious the Lord had given her that talent, and to waste it would be spitting in the face of heaven. He promised to help her get residence papers, but although he had such a powerful influence in celestial affairs, these counted for nothing in the arid offices of the immigration service.

Evelyn's court hearing would have been postponed indefi-

nitely had it not been for Doreen. For the past few years, Galileo
Leon's daughter had been going downhill until little was left of
her former arrogance, and yet her rage was undiminished. She
usually turned up covered in bruises that bore witness to her ferocious character: the slightest provocation was an excuse to start
a fight. She had a pirate's scar on her back that was the result of
a knife attack. She showed it to the children as a badge of honor,
boasting that she had been left for dead, bleeding on the ground
among garbage cans in an alleyway. Evelyn only seldom had to
face her, because her strategy of flight normally succeeded. If
she was on her own with the younger children she would rush
them away with her as soon as the dog began to howl. On this
particular day however her plan failed, because the two children
had scarlet fever. Their illness had begun three days earlier with
sore throats, and now they were covered in a rash. It was impossible to force them out of bed on a cold day in early October.
Doreen entered kicking the door and threatening to poison the
goddamned dog. Evelyn prepared herself for the string of insults
that would rain down on her as soon as Doreen found out her
father was not in and there was no money in the house.

From the small children's bedroom Evelyn could not make
out what Doreen was up to but could hear her rummaging and
cursing impatiently. Fearing her reaction if she did not find what
she was looking for, Evelyn plucked up courage and went into
the kitchen to intercept her before she burst in on the children.
To disguise her intention, she started making a sandwich, but
Doreen did not give her time. She charged like a fighting bull
and, before Evelyn could even see what was going on, grabbed
her by the throat, shaking her with all the strength of an addict.
"Where's the money? Tell me, you retard, or I'll kill you!" Evelyn

struggled helplessly to free herself from her fierce claws. When they heard Doreen shouting, the terrified little ones came running. They burst into tears at the very moment that the dog, who rarely came into the trailer, seized the attacker by the jacket and began to growl and tug at it. Doreen pushed Evelyn away and turned to kick the animal. Evelyn slipped and fell backward, hitting her head on the corner of the kitchen table. Doreen kicked out at her and the dog, but in the midst of her fury she had a flash of lucidity and, realizing what she had done, ran out of the house, still cursing. Drawn by the commotion, a woman neighbor came in to find Evelyn on the floor and the two children weeping inconsolably. She called Miriam, Galileo, and the police, in that order.

Galileo Leon arrived minutes after the police and found Evelyn trying to stand, helped by a woman in uniform. The world was whirling round. She could hardly see because of black streaks clouding her eyes, and her skull was throbbing so much she found it hard to explain what had happened. However, as they sniveled and sobbed, the younger children kept repeating the name Doreen. Galileo could not prevent them from taking Evelyn to the hospital in an ambulance and the police from writing a report.

In the emergency room they put several stitches in Evelyn's scalp, kept her in for observation for a few hours, then sent her home with a bottle of analgesics and the recommendation to rest. Unfortunately, because of the police report, that was not the end of the matter. The following day, the police came looking for her, and questioned Evelyn for two hours about her relationship with Doreen. They returned a couple of days later and took her away again, but this time the questions were about her entry into the United States and her reasons for leaving her own country. Terrified and hesitant, Evelyn tried to explain what had happened to her family but made little sense, and so the police officers began to lose patience. In a corner of the room was a man in civilian clothes who took notes but did not open his mouth even to say his name.

Because Doreen had a police record for drugs and other offenses, three policemen came to the trailer with a sniffer dog and searched every corner without finding anything of interest. Since Galileo Leon managed to make himself scarce, Miriam was left to endure the shame of watching the police tear up the linoleum from the floor and rip open her mattresses in search of drugs. Several neighbors gathered to get a good look, and after the police left they stayed around waiting for the second act in the drama. As expected, when Galileo reappeared, his wife launched into a furious tirade. It was all his fault and his whore daughter's. How many times had she told him she didn't want to see her in her house? He was a poor good-for-nothing with no backbone and of course no one had the slightest respect for him. On and on she went with her epic litany, which began in the house, continued in the yard and then the street, and ended up in the church, where the couple was escorted by a crowd of witnesses to ask the pastor's advice. Within a few hours Miriam had run out of steam. Her anger subsided once Galileo timidly promised he would keep his daughter well away from the house.

THAT SAME DAY, at about eight o'clock in the evening, when Miriam was still red in the face from her outburst, there was a knock on the trailer door. It was the man who had been taking notes at the police station. He presented himself as coming from the immigration service. The atmosphere froze, but they could not prevent him from entering. Accustomed to the effect he caused, the official tried to lessen the tension by speaking in Spanish. He said he had been brought up by Mexican grandparents, that he was proud of his origins and navigated easily between the two cultures. They listened to him stupefied, because he was whiter than white, had blue fish eyes, and mercilessly mangled the Spanish language. When he saw that none of them appreciated his attempt to win them over, he came to the real point of his visit. He knew that Miriam and Galileo had residency in the United States, but Evelyn Ortega's situation was not so clear. He had the detention center file with the date of her arrest at the border, and since she had no birth certificate he concluded she was eighteen and therefore eligible for deportation.

There was a deathly silence while Miriam tried to calculate whether the man had come simply to uphold the law or was fishing for a bribe. All of a sudden the normally reticent Galileo spoke out in a firm voice none of them had heard from him before.

"This girl is a refugee. No one is illegal in this life, we all have the right to live in this world. Money and crime do not respect borders. I ask you, sir, why we human beings should do so?"

"I don't make the laws. My job is to see that they are followed," replied the other man, taken aback.

"Take a good look at her. How old do you think she is?" said Galileo, pointing to Evelyn.

"She looks very young, but I need the birth certificate to prove it. In her file it says the water swept away all her documents when she was crossing the river. That was three years ago: you could have obtained a copy by now."

"Who was going to do that? My mother is an illiterate old woman, and in Guatemala that kind of thing takes a long time and costs money," said Miriam, once she had recovered from her shock at her husband arguing like a legal expert.

"What the girl says about gangs and her murdered brothers is common, I've heard it many times. There are lots of similar stories from immigrants. The judges have heard them as well. Some of them believe them, others don't. Asylum or deportation will depend on which judge you get," was the man's parting shot.

Reverting to his usual docile attitude, Galileo Leon favored waiting for the law to run its course: it may be slow, but it gets there, he said. Miriam, however, was of the opinion that if the law does get there, it never favors the weakest, and so immediately launched a campaign to have her daughter disappear. She did not ask Evelyn's opinion when she contacted her acquaintances in the subterranean network of undocumented immigrants or when she agreed to send her to work in the house of some people in Brooklyn. She had been tipped off by another woman member of the church, whose sister knew someone who had been a maid with that family and said they did not care about papers or any other details of that kind. As long as the girl performed her duties, no one was going to inquire about her legal status. When Evelyn wanted to know what those duties would be, she was told she would have to look after a sick child, nothing more.

Miriam showed her daughter New York on a map, helped her pack her belongings in a small suitcase, gave her an address in Manhattan, and put her on a Greyhound bus. Nineteen hours later, Evelyn presented herself at the Latin American Pentecostal Church, a two-story building that from outside had little of the dignity of a temple. She was received by a volunteer from the congregation, who read the letter of introduction from the Chicago pastor, offered to put her up for a night in her own apartment, and the next day explained how she could travel by subway to the Church of the Tabernacle of the New Life in Brooklyn. There another woman almost identical to the first gave her a soft drink and a leaflet outlining the church's religious services and social activities, as well as instructions on how to reach her new employers' address.

At three in the afternoon on an autumn day in 2011, when the trees were starting to grow bare and the street was strewn with a rustling, short-lived covering of fallen leaves, Evelyn Ortega rang the bell of a three-story corner house with a garden full of broken statues of Greek heroes. And that was where she ended up working peacefully for the following years with her fake documents.

Lucia, Richard, Evelyn

Upstate New York

Lucia

Chile, 2007–2008

Richard's guts felt better, but he fell asleep immediately, overcome by fatigue after this long, drawn-out day, and perturbed by the combination of uncertainty and newly discovered love gnawing away at him. Meanwhile, Lucia and Evelyn cut a towel into strips and went outside to get the fingerprints off the Lexus. According to the Internet instructions Lucia had obtained earlier on her cell phone, it was enough to wipe them with a cloth, but she had insisted on using alcohol just to be on the safe side, as they could still be identified even if the vehicle was at the bottom of a lake. "How do you know?" Richard had asked her before he fell asleep. As usual she replied, "Don't ask." In the blue-tinged light of the snow they systematically rubbed the visible parts of the car inside and out, except for the trunk's interior. Then they went back inside the cabin to warm up with a cup of tea and to chat, while Richard rested. They had three hours before it grew dark.

Evelyn had been silent since the previous night, doing whatever she was asked to do as distantly as if she were sleepwalking. Lucia guessed she was immersed in her past, reliving the tragedy of her short life. Understanding that the situation was much more nerve-racking for Evelyn than for her or Richard, she had given up any attempt to distract or console her. Evelyn was paralyzed with terror. The threat from Frank Leroy hung over her, and that was even worse than being arrested or deported. And yet there was another reason, which Lucia had sensed since they had left Brooklyn.

"You told us how your brothers died in Guatemala, Evelyn. Kathryn died a violent death as well. I imagine that must bring back dreadful memories."

Without raising her eyes from the steaming cup, the young girl nodded.

"My brother was killed too," said Lucia. "I loved him a great deal. We think he was arrested, but we heard nothing more about him. We weren't able to bury him, because they did not hand over his remains."

"Is . . . is . . . is it certain he died?" asked Evelyn.

"Yes, Evelyn. I spent years investigating the fate of those who were arrested and never appeared again, like Enrique. I wrote two books about it. They died from torture or were executed. Their bodies were blown up or thrown into the sea. A few mass graves have been found, though not many."

With great difficulty, stumbling over the words, Evelyn managed to say that at least they had buried her brothers, Gregorio and Andres, with proper respect, even though few of their neighbors had attended the funeral due to fear of the gangs. They had lit candles and burned aromatic herbs in her grandmother's house. They sang and wept for the boys, drank to them with rum, and buried them with some of their possessions so they would not miss them in their other life. As was the custom, they prayed a novena for them, since children spend nine months in their mother's womb before they are born, and because the deceased take nine days to be reborn in heaven. Her brothers had graves in consecrated ground, where her grandmother went to lay flowers on Sundays and take them food on the Day of the Dead.

"Like my brother Enrique, Kathryn will have none of that . . . ," murmured Lucia, moved by the thought.

"Souls who have not found rest come back to frighten the living," said Evelyn in one long rush.

"I know. They come to visit us in our dreams. Kathryn has already appeared to you, hasn't she?"

"Yes, last night."

"I'm truly sorry we can't say farewell to Kathryn with the rites of your people, Evelyn. But I'm going to have masses said for her for nine days. I promise."

"Did . . . your mo . . . mother p-p-pray for you . . . your brother?"

"She prayed for him up to the last day of her life, Evelyn."

LENA MARAZ BEGAN TO SAY GOODBYE to the world in 2007, more out of weariness than any illness or due to old age. She had been searching for her son, Enrique, for almost thirty-five years. Lucia would never forgive herself for not realizing how depressed her mother was. She thought that if she had stepped in much sooner, she might have been able to help her. She only became aware of this toward the end, because Lena did her best to hide the fact and Lucia, caught up in her own affairs, did not spot the symptoms. In the final months, when Lena could no longer pretend that life interested her, she consumed only a little clear soup and mashed vegetables. Reduced to mere skin and bone, she lay in bed utterly worn out, indifferent to everything apart from Lucia and her granddaughter, Daniela. She was preparing to starve to death, to depart in the most natural way, according to her faith and beliefs. She asked God not to be long in taking her, and to please allow her to preserve her dignity to the end. While her vital organs began slowly to shut down, her mind had never been so clear or more open, sensitive, and alert. She accepted the progressive weakening of her body with grace and good humor until there came a point when she lost control of some of the functions that to her were absolutely private. It was then that she wept for the first time. Daniela was the one who succeeded in convincing her that the diapers and more intimate care she received from Lucia, herself, and a male nurse who came once a week were not a punishment for sins of the past but an opportunity to reach heaven. "You can't go to heaven with that arrogance of yours still intact, Grandma. You have to practice a little humility," she would say in a tone of friendly reproach. This seemed reasonable to Lena, who resigned herself to not trying to fight her condition. However, soon there was no way to get her to swallow more than a few spoonfuls of yogurt and some sips of chamomile tea. When the nurse mentioned the possibility of feeding her through a tube, both daughter and granddaughter refused to submit her to such an outrage. They had to respect Lena's irrevocable decision.

From her bed Lena could appreciate the patch of sky visible through her window. She was grateful for her bed baths, and occasionally she asked them to read her poems or play the romantic songs she had danced to in her youth. Imprisoned as she was in her deteriorating body, she was free of the abysmal sorrow she felt for her son. As the days went by, what at first had been no more than a feeling, a fleeting shadow, a kiss brushing her forehead, began to take on increasingly clear outlines. Enrique was at her side, waiting with her.

Nothing could prevent her encroaching death, but Lucia, horrified at seeing her mother wasting away, became her jailer. She even deprived her of the cigarettes that were her only pleasure, thinking they cut her appetite and so were killing her. Daniela, who had the gift of understanding other people's needs and the kindness to try to meet them, sensed that this abstinence was her grandmother's worst torment. She had finished high school that year, was planning to go to study in Miami in September, and meanwhile was taking intensive English courses. She dropped in to see Lena every afternoon, so that Lucia would be free to do a few hours' work. At the age of seventeen, Daniela was tall and beautiful, with the features of her Slavic ancestors. She played solitaire or got into bed with her grandmother and did her English homework while Lena dozed, snoring throatily as the end approached. Lucia had no idea that Daniela gave her grandmother the forbidden cigarettes, which she smuggled in her bra. It was only several years later that Daniela confessed these sins of compassion to her mother.

The slow onset of death eased Lena's stubborn rancor toward

the husband who had betrayed her, and she was able to talk to her daughter and granddaughter about him in the faint whisper she had left.

"Enrique has forgiven him, now it's your turn, Lucia."

"I don't feel resentful toward him, Mama, I hardly knew him."

"Exactly, daughter. It's his absence that you have to forgive."

"In reality I never needed him, Mama. Enrique was the one who wanted a father. He was very hurt; he felt abandoned."

"That was when he was a boy. Now he understands his father didn't behave like that because he was evil, but because he was in love with that woman. He didn't realize how much damage he did to all of us, including her and her son. Enrique understands that."

"What kind of man would my brother be now, at fifty-seven?"

"He is still twenty-two, Lucia. And he is still a passionate idealist. Don't look at me like that, daughter. My life is slipping away, not my mind."

"You talk as though Enrique were here."

"He is."

"Oh, Mama . . ."

"I know they killed him, Lucia. Enrique won't tell me how. He wants to convince me it was rapid, that he did not suffer too much because when he was arrested he was already wounded and losing a lot of blood, and so he was spared torture. You could say he died fighting."

"Does he talk to you?"

"Yes, he talks to me. He's with me."

"Can you see him?"

"I can feel him. Sense him. He helps me when I'm choking. He arranges my pillows, mops my brow, refreshes my mouth with ice chips."

"That's me, Mama."

"Yes, it's you and Daniela, but it's also Enrique."

"You say he's still a young man?"

"No one grows old after they have died, daughter."

In her mother's last days, Lucia understood that death was not an end, was not the absence of life, but a powerful oceanic wave of clear, luminous water that was carrying her off to another dimension. Lena was loosening her ties to the earth, letting herself be borne on the wave, free of any anchor and the weight of gravity; light, a translucent fish driven on by the current. Lucia no longer struggled against the inevitable, and relaxed. Seated beside her mother, she took slow, deliberate breaths until she was filled with an immense calm, a desire to go with her, to let herself be pulled along until she too dissolved in the ocean. For the first time in her life, she felt her own soul as an incandescent light within her, sustaining her, an eternal light that could not be affected by the urgencies of existence. She found a point of absolute calm at the very center of herself. There was nothing to do but wait. To shut out the clamor of the world. She realized this was how her mother was experiencing the approach of death, and this helped banish the terror she had been overwhelmed by when she saw how her mother was being consumed and gradually snuffed out like a candle.

Lena Maraz died on one of those February mornings when the suffocating heat of the Chilean summer is felt from the early hours. She had been semiconscious for several days, her breathing reduced to a sporadic gargle, as she clutched Enrique's hand. Her granddaughter prayed that her heart would give out once and for all, to spare her from this desolate miasma. Lucia on the other hand understood that her mother had to travel this last part of the journey at her own pace, without being rushed. She had spent the night stretched out alongside her awaiting the final outcome, with Daniela on the living room sofa. To them, the night seemed very short. At first light, Lucia splashed her face with cold water, drank a cup of coffee, and then woke Daniela so that they could resume their posts on either side of the bed. For an instant Lena seemed to return to life. She opened her eyes and stared at her daughter and granddaughter. "I love you very much, little ones. Let's go now, Enrique." She closed her eyes, and Lucia could feel her mother's hand grow limp between hers.

DESPITE THE LIT STOVES, the cold penetrated the cabin and they had to cover up with all the clothes they could find. They put a cardigan over Marcelo's tartan coat: his fur was sparse and he suffered from the cold. The only one who was hot was Richard, who woke from his siesta sweating and feeling renewed. A feathery snow had begun to fall, and he announced it was time they got a move on.

"Where exactly are we going to get rid of the car?" asked Lucia.

"There's a bluff less than a mile from here. The lake there must be at least forty feet deep. I hope the track is passable, because that's the only way in."

"I assume the trunk is properly closed . . ."

"For the moment the wire has held, but I can't be sure the trunk will stay shut at the bottom of the lake."

"Do you know how to avoid the body floating up if the trunk opens?"

"Let's not even consider the possibility," said Richard, who had not even thought of it.

"You have to slit the stomach so that water gets in."

"What are you saying, Lucia!"

"That's what they did with the bodies they threw into the sea," she said, her voice breaking.

The three of them remained silent, absorbing the horror of what had just been revealed and certain that none of them would be capable of doing such a thing.

"Poor, poor Miss Kathryn . . . ," Evelyn finally murmured.

"I'm sorry, Richard, but we can't go through with this," said Lucia, who like Evelyn was on the verge of tears. "I know it was my idea and I forced you to come here, but I've changed my mind. We have done all this on the spur of the moment, we didn't make a proper plan, think deeply enough about it. Of course, there wasn't time for that—"

"What are you trying to tell me?" Richard interrupted, aghast.

"Ever since last night Evelyn can't stop thinking about Kathryn's spirit, wandering in torment. And I can't stop thinking that the poor woman has a family. She must have a mother . . . and my own mother spent half her life searching for my brother, Enrique."

"I know, Lucia, but this is different."

"What do you mean, different? If we go on with this, Kathryn Brown will be a disappeared person, just like my brother. There will be people who love her and will look for her all the time. The suffering caused by that uncertainty is worse than the certainty of her death."

"What shall we do then?" asked Richard, after a long pause.

"We could leave her where she will be found . . ."

"What if they don't find her? Or if her body is so decomposed it can't be identified?"

"It can always be identified. Nowadays all you need is a tiny piece of bone to identify a corpse."

Pale-faced, Richard paced the living room clutching his stomach, searching for a solution. He understood Lucia's reasons and shared her scruples; he didn't want to condemn Kathryn's family to an endless search either. They should have talked it over before they got this far, but there was still time to put things right. The responsibility for Kathryn Brown's death lay with the murderer, but her disappearance would be his fault. He could not take on this fresh guilt—he had more than enough on his conscience about the past. They had to leave the body somewhere far from the cabin and lake, where it would be safe from preying animals and would be found in two or three months' time with the spring thaw. That would give Evelyn the chance to find somewhere safe. It would be extremely hard to bury Kathryn. Digging a hole in the frozen earth was something he could not have done even if he were well, still less so with his ulcer raging. He raised the problem with Lucia, only to find she had already come up with an idea.

"We can leave Kathryn in Rhinebeck," she said.

"Why there?"

"I don't mean the town but the Omega Institute."

"What's that?"

"Briefly, it's a spiritual center, although it's a lot more than that. I've been there for retreats and conferences. It's set among almost two hundred acres of pristine nature, in an isolated spot, near Rhinebeck. No one ever goes there during the winter months, because the retreat is closed."

"But there must be maintenance staff."

"Yes, for the buildings, but the woods are covered in snow and don't need any special care. The road to Rhinebeck and its surroundings is good. There's quite a lot of traffic, so we wouldn't attract attention, and once we entered the institute no one would see us."

"I don't like it, it's very risky."

"I do, because it's a spiritual place, with good energy, in the middle of spectacular woods. I'd like my ashes to be scattered there. Kathryn would like it as well."

"I never know if you're talking seriously, Lucia."

"Completely seriously. But if you have a better idea . . ."

By now it was snowing again, and they realized it was high time they disposed of the car before the track became impassable. They had no time to discuss it anymore; they were in agreement that Kathryn's body should be found, and so they would have to transfer her to the Subaru before they got rid of the Lexus.

Richard gave them disposable gloves, with strict instructions not to touch the Lexus without them. He positioned the car alongside the Subaru and then cut the wire with a pair of pliers. Kathryn Brown had been there at least two or three days and nights, but very little had changed: she still looked fast asleep under the rug. When he touched her she was frozen but seemed less stiff than when Lucia had tried to move her in Brooklyn. Seeing her body brought a sob to Richard's throat: in the radiance from the snow this young woman curled up like a child looked as vulnerable and tragic as Bibi. He closed his eyes and gulped down lungfuls of freezing air to rid himself of this pitiless flash of memory and force himself back into the present. It was not Bibi, the daughter he adored; this was Kathryn Brown, a woman he did not even know. While a paralyzed Evelyn looked on murmuring prayers, Richard and Lucia began the task of removing the body from the car trunk. They finally managed to turn Kathryn over and saw her face for the first time. Her eyes were wide open. The round, blue eyes of a doll.

"Go inside, Evelyn. It's better you don't see this," Lucia told her, but the girl stood rooted to the spot.

Kathryn was a slender, short young woman with cropped, chocolate-colored hair and the look of an adolescent. She was wearing a yoga outfit. There was a black hole in the middle of her forehead, as precise as if it had been painted on, and some dried blood on her cheek and neck. They stared sorrowfully at her for two long minutes, trying to imagine what she could have been like in life. Even in the contorted position she was in, Kathryn retained some of the elegance of a dancer at rest.

Lucia took hold of her legs, while Richard grasped her under her arms. They lifted her and struggled until they succeeded in transferring her to the Subaru. They pushed her into the trunk, covered her with the same rug, and put a tarpaulin on top in case the trunk had to be opened for any reason.

"She died of a single shot from a low-caliber pistol," Lucia said. "The bullet stayed lodged in the brain, there's no exit hole. She died instantaneously. The murderer is a good shot."

Still shaken by the vivid memory of the moment when he had lost his beloved Bibi more than twenty years earlier, Richard was crying without noticing the tears freezing on his cheeks.

"Kathryn must have known her killer," Lucia added. "They were face-to-face, possibly conversing. She was not expecting the bullet. You can tell from her challenging look, it's obvious she was not afraid."

Evelyn called them over. She had overcome her paralysis and was cleaning the marks off the trunk of the Lexus.

"Look," she said, pointing to a pistol in the bottom of the trunk.

"Is that Leroy's?" asked Richard, carefully picking it up by the barrel.

"It looks like it."

Holding the weapon between his thumb and index finger, Richard went back inside the cabin and laid it on the table. If the bullet had come from Frank Leroy's pistol, they now had to face yet another unwelcome decision: Whether or not to hand over the firearm to the police. To protect a guilty person or perhaps incriminate an innocent one.

"What shall we do with the gun?" Richard asked Lucia once the two women had joined him in the cabin.

"I say we leave it in the Lexus. Why complicate our existence still further, we have enough problems as it is."

"It's the most important proof we have against the murderer. We can't throw it into the lake," Richard objected.

"Well, we'll see. The most urgent thing right now is to get rid of the car. Are you up to it, Richard?"

"I feel a lot better. We need to take advantage of the light, it grows dark early."

THE TRACK THAT PROVIDED the only access to the bluff was almost invisible in the snow, which made everywhere look the same. Richard's plan was to take both vehicles, tip the Lexus over the cliff, and return in the Subaru. In normal conditions it was possible to cover the short distance on foot in twenty minutes. The snow was a hindrance but had the advantage that it would cover their tracks within a few hours. He decided he would go first in the Lexus, carrying a shovel, and Lucia would bring up the rear in the other car. She argued it would be more logical for the Subaru, which had four-wheel drive, to clear the path. "No, let's do it my way, I know what I'm doing," said Richard, impulsively kissing her on the tip of her nose. Taken by surprise, Lucia gave a little yelp. They left Evelyn with the dog and instructions to keep the curtains closed and to light only one lamp if necessary. The less light the better. Richard calculated that if all went well they would be back within the hour.

The tree branches were bent toward the ground by the weight of snow. Guided by the distance between them, Richard drove slowly along the twisting track that only he could make out because he had traveled up it before. Lucia followed behind. On one occasion they had to retreat several feet when they lost the trail, and a short distance farther on the Lexus became stuck in the snow. Richard got out to dig around the wheels with the shovel, then instructed Lucia to push with the other car. This was not easy, because it kept skidding. It was then Lucia understood why the Subaru had to go behind: it was hard to push, but it would have been almost impossible to pull. This maneuver cost them half an hour, while the sky grew darker and the temperature dropped.

Finally they came out to where they could see the lake, an immense silver mirror reflecting the gray-blue sky with the intense stillness of a painted Dutch landscape. The track came to an abrupt end, and Richard got out to explore. He walked this way and that, observing the bluff, until he found what he was looking for some thirty yards from where they had come to a halt. He explained to Lucia that this was the exact spot where the water was deep enough, and that they had to push the Lexus themselves, as it would be very dangerous to drive the car that far. Lucia again understood why Richard had wanted the Lexus to go first; the space here was so narrow it could not have gotten around the other car. Pushing the Lexus proved complicated: their boots sank into the soft ground; the wheels became stuck in the deep snow and they had to clear them with the shovel.

To Lucia, the bluff did not look very high, but Richard insisted this was deceptive: from that height the impact and the car's weight would smash the ice. Thanks to the mildness of the winter up until then, the ice on the lake's surface was not yet thick. They managed with difficulty to line the car up perpendicular to the shore. Richard put it into neutral, and between the two of them they gave it one last push. The car moved slowly forward and its front wheels plunged over the abyss, but the rest got stuck on the edge with a dull thud. The Lexus was left swaying on its chassis, with three-quarters stuck and the rest dangling in midair. They pushed again with all their might but could not budge it.

"That's all we needed! Behave, you stupid animal!" Lucia exclaimed, giving the car a kick before collapsing on the ground, panting.

"We should have started from farther back so that it would pick up speed," said Richard.

"Too late. What are we going to do now?"

For several long minutes, covered in snow, they tried to

recover their breath. They could see what a disaster it was but could not come up with a solution. Suddenly the front of the car dipped several degrees and with a grinding sound slid forward a few inches. Richard guessed that the heat from the engine was melting the snow underneath. They quickly took advantage of this, giving it a push. A moment later the Lexus plunged over the cliff with the force of a mortally wounded pachyderm. They watched from the summit as it hit the ice nose-first. For an instant it seemed as if it might stay there sticking up vertically like some strange metallic sculpture, but then they heard a tremendous crack, the surface of the lake splintered into a thousand pieces like a mirror, and the car slowly sank with a farewell sigh, throwing up a wave of freezing water together with shards of blue ice. Dumb with amazement, Lucia and Richard watched as the Lexus was swallowed up by the dark waters until it had completely disappeared into the lake.

"The surface will have frozen over again in a couple of days," said Richard when the last ripple had subsided.

"Until the spring thaw."

"The lake is deep here, I don't think anyone will find it. Nobody comes up this way," Richard said.

"God willing," said Lucia.

"I doubt God will approve of anything we've done," he said with a smile.

"Why not? Helping Evelyn is an act of compassion, Richard. We can count on divine approval. If you don't believe me, ask your father."

"No act of compassion will save me from my own hell," he murmured.

Richard

T he weeks and months following little Pablo's death were a nightmare from which neither Anita nor Richard could escape. Bibi's fourth birthday was extravagantly celebrated by the Farinha family in her grandparents' house, to avoid the sadness that reigned in her own home. The little girl was passed between her grandmother and many aunts; she had always seemed too wise, serene, and well behaved, and yet at night she wet her bed. She would wake up soaked, stealthily take off her pajamas, and tiptoe naked into her parents' room. She slept between the two of them, and in the morning occasionally found the pillow wet with her mother's tears.

The delicate balance Anita had succeeded in maintaining during the years of her miscarriages was destroyed by the death of her baby. Neither Richard nor the unswerving affection of the Farinha family could help her, but between them they managed to drag her to see a psychiatrist, who prescribed a whole cocktail of medicines. The therapy sessions took place almost in silence: she refused to speak, and the psychiatrist's efforts constantly came up against her profound sense of grief.

As a desperate last resort, Anita's sisters took her to see Maria Batista, a respected *lyalorixa*, the mother of candomble saints. At transcendental moments in their lives all the women in the family had made the journey to Bahia to visit Maria Batista's *terreiro*. She was a voluminous elderly lady with a permanent smile on a face the color of molasses. She dressed in white from her sandals to her turban, with symbolic necklaces cascading down from her neck. Experience had made her wise. She spoke quietly, and stared into the eyes and stroked the hands of all those who came to her to be guided along the uncertain path.

Aided by the *buzios*, her cowrie shells, she peered into Anita's destiny. She did not say what she saw, as her role was to offer hope and solutions and give advice. She explained that suffering has no purpose and is futile unless it can be used to cleanse the soul. If she wanted to escape from the prison of memory, Anita must pray and ask for help from Yemaya, the *orixa* of life. "Your boy is in heaven and you are in hell. Come back to the world," she told her. She advised the Farinha sisters to give Anita time; her reservoir of tears was bound to dry up at some point, and her spirit would heal. Life is persistent. "Tears are good, they clean inside," she added.

Anita returned from Bahia as disconsolate as she had been when she traveled there. Indifferent to her solicitous family and husband, she turned in on herself. Apart from Bibi, she cut herself off from everyone. She took her daughter out of day care in order to always keep her within sight, to protect her with an oppressive, fearful love. Stifled by this tragic embrace, Bibi

took it upon herself to stop her mother from slipping irrevo-
cably down into madness. She was the only one who could dry
her tears and lighten her pain with caresses. She learned not to
mention her little brother, as if she had forgotten his brief existence, and pretended to be happy so as to entertain her. She and
her father were living with a ghost. Anita spent most of the day
dozing or motionless in an armchair, watched over by one of the
other women in her family because the psychiatrist had warned
about the risk of suicide. Every hour went by exactly the same
for Anita; the days crawled slowly past and she had more than
enough time to weep for Pablo and her unborn children. Maybe,
as Maria Batista had said, the tears would eventually have dried
up, but there was not time enough for that to occur.

RICHARD WAS AFFECTED more by his wife's boundless despair
than by the death of the baby. He had wanted and loved his son,
but not as deeply as Anita, as he had not managed to grow close
to him. Whereas Pablo's mother nurtured him at her breast, cradling him in a constant loving litany, united to him by the powerful cord of maternal instinct, Richard was only just getting to
know his son when he lost him. He had had four years to fall in
love with Bibi and learn to be her father, but only one month
with Pablo. Of course he was shocked at his sudden death, but
it was Anita's reaction that shook him even more. They had
been together for several years and he had grown accustomed
to her mood swings: in a matter of minutes she could change
from laughter and passion to anger or sadness. He had found
ways to cope with Anita's unpredictable states of mind without

growing upset. He put them down to her tropical temperament, although he only described her in this way well out of her ear-shot, to avoid her accusations of his being racist. However, he found he could not help her in any way over her grieving for Pablo. She could barely tolerate her own family, and still less him. Bibi was her only comfort.

In the meantime, the streets and beaches of the erotic city of Rio de Janeiro teemed with life. In February, the hottest month, people went around almost naked. The men wore shorts and often little else; the women, light dresses showing off their cleavages and legs. Beautiful, youthful, tanned, sweating bodies; bodies and more bodies on exuberant display. Richard saw them everywhere. His favorite bar, where he automatically headed in the evening to refresh himself with beer or numb himself with cachaça, was one of the regular haunts of Rio youth. Around eight it began to fill up, and by ten the noise was as loud as a clanking locomotive. The air was dense with the smell of sex, perspiration, alcohol, and perfume. Cocaine and other drugs were passed around in a discreet corner. Richard came so often he did not have to order his drink: the barman had it ready for him as soon as he approached the counter. He had become friends with several loyal customers like himself, who had then introduced him to others. The men drank, shouted conversation above the din, watched soccer on the screen, argued about goals or politics. Whenever they went too far and reacted angrily, the barman stepped in and threw them out. The girls were divided into two groups: the untouchables, who came in on a man's arm, and the others, who came in groups to indulge in the art of seduction. If a woman appeared on her own, she was nor-mally old enough to ignore the crude remarks and always found someone who would flirt with her in a friendly way, with the gallantry typical of Brazilian men that Richard found impossible to imitate, confusing it with sexual harassment. For his part he was an easy target for those girls who wanted to have fun. They accepted the drinks he offered, laughed and joked with him, and in the intimacy of the crowded bar caressed him until he was forced to respond. At those moments, Richard forgot Anita. They were innocuous games that presented no danger to his marriage, as would have been the case if Anita had acted in a similar fashion.

The young woman who Richard was never to forget was not one of the most beautiful of the girls he met during those caipirinha nights, but she was lively, with an uninhibited laugh, and keen to try whatever she was offered. She became Richard's best party companion, yet he kept her out of the rest of his life. It was as if she were a tailor's dummy that only came to life when she was next to him in the bar sharing alcohol and cocaine. He thought she meant so little to him that to simplify he called her Garota, the generic name for the beautiful girls from Ipanema made famous by the lyrics of the old Vinicius de Moraes song. She showed him the drugs corner and the poker table in the back room where the bets were low and you could lose without any serious consequences. She was tireless; she could spend the night drinking and dancing, then in the morning go straight to work as an administrator in a dental clinic. She gave Richard endlessly differing versions of the life she had invented for herself, in a frenetic, tangled Portuguese that to him sounded like music. By the second drink he would complain about his sad domestic life; by the third he was blubbering on her shoulder. Garota sat on his lap, kissed him until he almost suffocated, and rubbed herself against him with such exciting movements that he went home with stains on his trousers and a concern that was never quite remorse. Richard planned his days around his meetings with this girl who gave his existence color and flavor. Forever joyous and willing, Garota reminded him of the Anita of the early days, the one he had fallen in love with at the dancing academy, who now was slipping rapidly away in the mists of her misfortune. With Garota, Richard was once again a young man with no worries; with Anita he felt weighed down, old, and judged.

It was only a short distance between the bar and Garota's apartment. The first few times, Richard went in a group. At three in the morning, when they threw the last customers out of the bar, some went to sleep it off on the beach or continue partying in somebody's house. Garota's apartment was the most convenient for this, as it was less than five blocks away. On several occasions, Richard woke with the first light of day somewhere it took him a few seconds to place. He would stand up dizzy and confused, unable to recognize the jumble of men and women sprawled on the floor or in armchairs.

Seven o'clock one Saturday morning found him on Garota's bed fully dressed and with his shoes on. She was naked, arms and legs spread wide, head dangling and mouth wide open, a trickle of dried blood on her chin and eyelids half-closed. Richard had no idea what had happened or why he was there. The previous few hours were a complete blank. The last thing he remembered was a poker game in a cloud of cigarette smoke. How he came to be in this bed was a mystery. On several other occasions alcohol had betrayed him: his mind had emptied while his body carried on automatically. He was sure there must be a name and a scientific explanation for the condition. After a couple of minutes he recognized the woman but still could not explain the blood. What had he done? Fearing the worst, he shook and shouted at her without being able to remember her name, until finally she stirred. Relieved, he plunged his head in cold water in the sink until he ran out of breath and the world stopped spinning. He rushed out of the apartment and reached home with stabbing pains in his temples, his body shattered, and a devastating heartburn raging in his stomach. He thought up a last-minute excuse for Anita: he had been arrested by the police after a stupid row in the street, had spent the night in jail, and had not been allowed to phone home.

The lie proved unnecessary, because he found Anita in a drugged sleep brought on by her pills and Bibi playing silently with her dolls. "I'm hungry, Papa," she said, clinging to his legs. Richard made her cocoa and got her a bowl of cereal. He felt unworthy of the little girl's love; he felt stained, disgusting, and was unable to touch her before he had a shower. Afterward he sat her on his lap and buried his nose in her angel's hair, inhaling her smell of curdled milk and innocent sweat. He swore silently to himself that from this moment on his family would be his first priority. He was going to devote himself body and soul to rescuing his wife from the dark well in which she was sunk and make it up to Bibi for all the months he had neglected her.

His intentions lasted seventeen hours. From then on, his nocturnal escapades became more frequent, longer, and more intense. "You're falling in love with me!" Garota pointed out, and in order not to disappoint her he admitted it, even though love had nothing to do with how he behaved. His lover was disposable, she could have been replaced by dozens of others similar to her—frivolous attention seekers, girls afraid of being alone. The following Saturday morning he woke up in her bed again. It was nearly nine o' clock. It took him a few minutes to find his clothes in the messy apartment, but he was in no hurry: Anita would probably be only half-conscious due to her pills, and wouldn't get up until around noon. He was not worried about Bibi either, because this was the time of day that the maid arrived, and she would look after her. The vague sense of guilt he felt was becoming almost imperceptible. Garota was right, he was the only victim of this state of affairs because he was tied to a wife who was mentally ill. If he showed any sign of concern about deceiving Anita, she would repeat the old refrain: what the eyes don't see, the heart doesn't feel. Anita either was unaware of his flings or pretended not to notice, and he had the right to enjoy himself. Garota was a fleeting pleasure, nothing more than a footprint in the sand, thought Richard. Little did he imagine that she would become a scar he could never erase from his memory. His infidelity worried him less than the effects of alcohol. It took him hours to recover after a night on the town. He could spend the whole day with his stomach aflame and his body aching all over, unable to think clearly, his reflexes dulled. He floundered about as heavily as a hippopotamus.

That morning it took him a while to find his car, which was parked on a side street. He was also slow to put the key in the ignition and turn the engine on. A mysterious conspiracy left him moving in slow motion. There was little traffic at that hour, and despite his throbbing head he remembered the way back home. Twenty-five minutes had gone by since he woke up next to Garota. He urgently needed a cup of coffee and a long, hot shower. As he entered the driveway, his mind was on the coffee and shower.

Afterward he tried to find a thousand explanations for the accident. None of them was sufficient to blot out the precise image that stayed etched forever in his brain.

BIBI HAD BEEN WAITING for him at the front door. When she saw his car come around the corner she ran out to greet him, as she always did inside the house when he arrived. Richard did not see her: he felt the bump but did not realize he had run over Bibi. He braked at once, and it was then he heard the maid's screams. He tried to convince himself he had hit a dog, because the truth already stealing into the back of his mind was too terrible to bear. A ghastly fear that instantly wiped away his hangover made him leap from the driver's seat. When he could not see the cause of the accident he felt relieved for a moment. Until he bent down.

He was the one who had to pull his daughter out from under the car. The accident had not spoiled anything: the pajamas with their teddy bear design were still clean, she was still holding a rag doll in her hand, her eyes were still open with the expression of irresistible delight she always greeted him with. His heart beating wildly with hope, he picked her up with infinite care and clutched her to him, kissing her and calling her name. In the distance, from another universe, he could make out the cries of their maid and the neighbors, the horns from the blocked traffic, and later the police and ambulance sirens. When he eventually came to understand the magnitude of the disaster, he wondered where Anita had been at that moment, why he had not heard or seen her among the confused crowd milling around him. A long while later he learned that when she heard the squeal of brakes and all the noise, she had been on the second-floor window and from up there, frozen to the spot, she had witnessed everything. She saw her husband stoop down beside the car, saw the ambulance disappear up the street with its wolflike howl and ill-omened red light. From her window, Anita Farinha knew without a doubt that Bibi had stopped breathing, and she accepted this final stab of fate for what it was: her execution.

Anita went to pieces. She kept up an endless stream of incoherent utterances, and when she stopped eating was transferred to a psychiatric clinic run by Germans. Two nurses were placed at her bedside, one during the daytime and the other at night. They were so similar in their plump build and imposing authority that they looked like twins descended from a Prussian colonel. For a fortnight, these terrifying matrons took it upon themselves to feed Anita a thick liquid smelling of vanilla through a tube down her throat, to dress her against her will, and to almost carry her for walks around the patients' yard. These walks and other forced activities, such as watching documentary films of dolphins or panda bears, intended to combat any destructive thoughts, had no appreciable effect on her. The head of the clinic suggested electroshock therapy, which he said was an effective and low-risk way of bringing her out of her state of apathy, as he termed it. The treatment would be administered under anesthetic and the patient was not even aware of it. The only slight drawback would be a temporary loss of memory, which in Anita's case would be a blessing.

Richard listened to the explanation but decided to wait, finding it impossible to subject his wife to several sessions of electroshock therapy. For once the Farinha family supported him. They also agreed that her stay in that Teutonic institution should be no longer than strictly necessary. As soon as it was possible to remove the tube and feed her spoonfuls of nutritious baby food, they took the patient back to her mother's home. If previously her sisters had been set on taking turns to care for her, after Bibi's accident they did not leave her on her own for a minute. There was somebody with her day and night, watching and praying.

Once again Richard found himself excluded from the female world where his wife was languishing. He could not even get near her to try to explain what had happened and beg for forgiveness, even though forgiveness was impossible. Although no one accused him of it to his face, he was treated like a murderer. And that was exactly how he felt. He lived alone in his house while the Farinha family kept Anita with them. They've kidnapped her, he would tell his friend Horacio whenever he called from New York. To his father though, who also called regularly, he never confessed what a disaster his life had become. Instead he reassured him with an optimistic version according to which he and Anita, with help from a psychiatrist and the family, were getting over their grief. Joseph knew that Bibi had died after being run over but did not suspect it was Richard who had been driving the car.

The maid who had previously done the cleaning and looked after Bibi left on the day of the accident and never returned, not even to claim her wages. Garota also vanished, partly because Richard could no longer buy the drinks, and partly out of a superstitious fear: she thought that Richard's tragedies were the result of a curse and that usually this was contagious. Meanwhile, the mess around Richard grew and grew. Rows of empty bottles littered the floor; in the fridge produce that had lost its original identity became covered with green mold, while dirty clothes seemed to multiply as if by magic. His unkempt appearance scared off his English pupils, who quickly stopped coming. For the first time, he found himself without funds; the rest of Anita's savings had gone to pay the clinic. He began drinking cheap rum at home on his own because he owed money at the bar. He spent his time sprawled in front of the television, which was never switched off, trying to avoid silence and darkness, where his children's transparent presence would float on the air. At the age of thirty-five he considered himself half-dead: he had already lived half his life and the other half was of no interest to him.

IT WAS DURING THIS DESPERATE PERIOD that Horacio, by now the director of the Center for Latin American and Caribbean Studies at New York University, decided to devote more attention to Brazil and coincidentally offer Richard a helping hand. They had been friends since their bachelor days, when Horacio was just setting out on his academic career and Richard was writing his doctoral thesis. Back then, Horacio had gone to visit him in Rio de Janeiro, where his friend received him with such generous hospitality despite his meager student budget that he stayed for two months. They took their backpacks and traveled to the state of Mato Grosso to explore the Amazon rain forest, forming one of those male friendships that has nothing sentimental about it but proves immune to distance and time. Later on, Horacio again visited Rio to be the best man at Richard and Anita's wedding. They did not see much of each other over the following years, but their mutual affection was safely stored in their memories. They knew they could count on each other. When he heard what had happened to Pablo and Bibi, Horacio started calling his friend a couple of times a week to try to raise his spirits. Over the phone, Richard's voice was unrecognizable. He slurred his words and repeated himself with the mindless insistence of a drunkard. Horacio understood Richard needed as much help as Anita.

Horacio was the one who told Richard about the vacant post at the university even before it appeared in the relevant journals, advising him to apply right away. The competition for the job would be intense, and he could not help him with that, but if Richard got through the necessary steps and had luck on his side, he might end up at the top of the list. His doctoral thesis was still referred to, and that was a point in his favor, as were the articles he had published. But since then more time had gone by than was customary; Richard had wasted years of his professional career lying about on the beach and drinking caipirinhas. He sent in his application without much hope, but to his great surprise two weeks later a letter arrived summoning him for an interview in April. Horacio had to send him the money for the airfare to New York. Richard prepared for the journey without telling Anita, who was still in the German clinic at the time, and convinced himself he was not doing this for selfish reasons. If he was offered the post, Anita would be much better looked after in the United States, where she could rely on the university's health insurance to cover her care. Besides, the only way to reclaim her as his wife was to rescue her from the clutches of the Farinha family.

Following an exhaustive interview process, Richard was

offered a university contract starting in August. He calculated there was time enough for Anita to get better and to organize their move. In the meantime he had to ask Horacio for another loan to take care of all the necessary expenses. He promised to pay him back out of the proceeds from the sale of the house, provided Anita agreed, as the property was in her name.

Thanks to his family fortune, Horacio Amado-Castro had never lacked money. At the age of seventy-six, his father still exercised a patriarchal tyranny from Argentina in the same steely manner as ever, although he was resigned to the misfortune that one of his sons had married a Protestant Yankee and two of his grandchildren did not speak Spanish. He visited them in New York several times a year, refreshing his vast love of culture with outings to museums, concerts, and the theater, as well as supervising his investments in several banks there. His daughter-in-law detested him but treated him with the same hypocritical politeness as he did her. For years the patriarch had wanted to buy a house that would do Horacio proud. The cramped Manhattan apartment where the family lived, on the tenth floor in a development of twenty identical redbrick buildings, was a hovel unworthy of a son of his. As soon as he was in his grave, Horacio would of course come into his share of his fortune, but everyone in the family went on to a ripe old age and he personally intended to live to be a hundred. It was stupid for Horacio to wait until then to live a comfortable life when he could do so beforehand, his father would say, clearing his throat and puffing on one of his Cuban cigars. "I don't want to owe anything to your father. He's a despot and he hates me," said the Protestant Yankee, and Horacio did not dare contradict her. Eventually though, the old man found a way to convince his stubborn daughter-in-law. One day he arrived with an adorable little dog for his grandchildren, a ball of fluff with sweet eyes. They called her Fifi, little imagining that the name would soon be far too small for her. She was a Canadian Eskimo, a sled dog that grew to weigh over a hundred pounds. Realizing it would be impossible to deprive the children of her, his daughter-in-law gave in and the grandfather made out a substantial check. Horacio looked for a house with a yard for Fifi near Manhattan, and ended up buying a brownstone in Brooklyn shortly before his friend Richard Bowmaster arrived to work at NYU.

Considering his wife to be in no shape to grasp the situation, Richard accepted the post in New York without consulting her. He was sure he was doing what was best for her, quietly getting rid of almost all their possessions and packing up the rest. He found it impossible to throw away Bibi's toys or Pablo's baby clothes. Instead, he put them into three boxes, intending to entrust them to his mother-in-law shortly before leaving. He prepared Anita's suitcases quite ruthlessly, knowing it was all the same to her. For months now she had only worn her gym clothes and had hacked off her hair with a pair of kitchen scissors.

His plan to find some excuse or other to rescue his wife and leave Rio without any melodrama failed when Anita's mother and sisters guessed his intentions the moment he turned up with the three boxes. They sniffed out his plans like trained bloodhounds and were determined to prevent the journey. They pointed out how fragile Anita was: How was she going to survive in that dangerous city, with that complicated language, without family or friends? If she was depressed surrounded by her own family, how was she going to feel among American strangers? Richard refused to listen; his mind was made up.

To avoid offending them he made sure not to say as much, but he thought it was time for him to consider his own future and not pay so much attention to his unreachable wife. For her part, Anita showed complete indifference toward her fate. It was all the same to her what she did, or where she was.

Armed with a bag containing her various medications, Richard led his wife to the plane. Anita boarded meekly without looking back or making any farewell gesture to her family, who were all standing in tears behind the airport's glass wall. During the ten-hour flight she stayed awake, refusing to eat anything, and never once asked where they were going. Horacio and his wife were waiting for them at the airport in New York.

Horacio did not recognize his friend's wife. He remembered her as beautiful and sensual, all curves and smiles, but the person who appeared before him had aged ten years, dragged her feet along the ground, and looked furtively from left to right as though expecting an attack. She did not return their greetings or allow his wife to accompany her to the restroom. God help us, this is much worse than I thought, Horacio murmured to himself. His friend did not look good either. Taking advantage of the free alcohol on board, Richard had been drinking for most of the journey. He had a three-day growth of stubble, his clothes were in tatters, he stank with a drunkard's sweat, and without Horacio's aid he would have probably been stranded in the airport with Anita.

The Bowmasters installed themselves in a university apartment that Horacio had arranged, intended for members of the faculty. This was a real find as it was in the center of Greenwich Village, had a low rent, and had a waiting list. After dropping their suitcases in the hallway and handing over the keys, Horacio shut himself in one of the rooms with his friend and gave him some advice. There were hundreds, if not thousands, of applicants for every vacant academic post in the United States, he told him. The chance to teach at New York University did not come up twice, and so he needed to make the most of it. Richard had to control his drinking and create a good impression from the outset. There was no way he could turn up in the filthy, messy state he was in now.

"I recommended you, Richard. Don't make me look bad."

"Of course I won't. I'm half dead from the journey and leaving Rio, or rather, the escape from Rio. I'll spare you the Farinha family tragedy over our departure. Don't worry, in a couple of days you'll see me at the university as good as new."

"What about Anita?"

"What about her?"

"She's very frail, I'm not sure she can stay on her own, Richard."

"She'll have to get used to it, like everyone else. She doesn't have her family here to spoil her. I'm all she has."

"Then make sure you don't let her down, brother," said Horacio as he left.

Evelyn

Brooklyn, 2011–2016

E velyn Ortega began to work for the Leroy family in 2011. The house of statues, as she always called the family residence, had in the 1950s belonged to a Mafia boss and his numerous relatives, including two old spinsters and a Sicilian great-grandmother who refused to come out of her room when naked Greeks were brought into the garden. Frank Leroy was amused by the property's murky past and the weather-worn statues covered in pigeon droppings. His wife, Cheryl, would have preferred a modern apartment to this pretentious mansion, but her husband was the one who made all the decisions, big and small, and they were never open for discussion. The house of statues had many conveniences the mobster had installed for his family's comfort. There was wheelchair access, an internal elevator, and a two-car garage. It was also well situated on a quiet street in a neighborhood that had become respectable.

It took Cheryl Leroy no more than five minutes with Evelyn

Ortega before she offered her the job. They urgently needed a nanny and could not worry about details. The previous one had left five days earlier and never returned. She must have been deported; that's what happens when you employ people without documents, Cheryl told herself. Normally it was her husband who dealt with hiring, paying, and firing staff. Through his office he had many contacts and could find Latino and Asian immigrants ready to work for next to nothing, but he made it a rule not to confuse work and family. And anyway, his contacts were hopeless when it came to finding a trustworthy nanny; they had been through several dreadful experiences. This was one of the few things the couple agreed on, and so Cheryl had begun looking for nannies through the Pentecostal Church, which always had a list of reliable women eager to find employment. This young girl from Guatemala probably had no papers either, but for the moment Cheryl preferred to ignore that fact: there would be time for that later. She liked her honest face and respectful manners. She sensed she had found a gem, someone very different from the others who had passed through her house. Her only doubts were about her age, because she seemed barely an adolescent gone through puberty, and her size. Cheryl had read somewhere that the indigenous women of Guatemala were the smallest people on earth, and now she had the proof right before her eyes. She wondered if this tiny scrap of a girl, with a quail's bones and a bad stammer, would be able to manage her son, Frankie, who must have weighed more than she did and was uncontrollable when he had one of his fits.

For her part, Evelyn thought Señora Leroy was so tall and blond she must have been a Hollywood actress. She had to look up at her as if she were a tree. Cheryl had muscular arms and

calves, eyes as blue as the sky above Evelyn's Guatemalan village, and a yellow ponytail that bounced with a life of its own.
She was tanned an orange color Evelyn had never seen before
and spoke with a faltering voice like her grandmother Concepcion, although she was not old enough to be short of breath. She
seemed very skittish, a foal ready to bolt off.

Her new employer introduced her to the rest of the domestic staff. These were the cook and her daughter, who did the
cleaning, the two of them working from nine to five on Monday,
Wednesday, and Friday. She also mentioned Ivan, whom Evelyn
would meet another day as he was not part of the household but
did jobs for them. She explained that her husband, Mr. Leroy,
had only minimal contact with the staff. She showed her up to
the third floor in an elevator, convincing Evelyn that she had
ended up with millionaires. The elevator was a birdcage made of
wrought iron in a floral design, wide enough to fit a wheelchair.
Frankie's room was the one the Sicilian great-grandmother had
occupied half a century earlier. It was spacious, with a sloping
roof and a skylight as well as a window shaded by the top of a
maple tree in the garden. Aged about eight or nine, Frankie was
as blond as his mother and as pale as a consumptive. He was
strapped by the waist to a wheelchair in front of the TV. His
mother explained that the straps were to stop him from falling out or hurting himself if he had a convulsion. He needed
constant supervision as he had a tendency to choke, and if that
happened someone had to shake him and hit him on the back to
help him recover his breathing. He wore diapers and had to be
fed but never caused trouble and was a little angel who immediately made himself cherished. He suffered from diabetes, but
this was carefully controlled; Señora Leroy herself checked his

blood sugar levels and administered the insulin. She explained all this to Evelyn in a hurry before she ran off to her gym.

Confused and tired, Evelyn sat beside the wheelchair. She took one of the boy's hands, trying to straighten his clawlike fingers, and told him without a stammer in Spanglish that they were going to be good friends. Frankie responded with grunts and spasmodic flaps of his arms that she took to be a welcome. This was the start of a relationship of peace and war that was to become all-important for both of them.

IN THE FIFTEEN YEARS they had been together, Cheryl Leroy had grown resigned to her husband's brutal authority. She stayed with him because she had become accustomed to being unhappy, because she depended on him financially, and because of her sick son. She had also admitted to her psychiatrist that she put up with him since she was addicted to comfort—how could she give up her spiritual growth workshops, her reading group, and the Pilates classes that kept her in shape, although not as much as she would have liked. She hated it when she compared herself to successful, independent women as well as the ones who paraded around naked in the gym. She never took all her clothes off in the changing room and was expert at wielding her towel going into or out of the shower or sauna so as not to show the welts on her body. However she looked at it, her life was a failure. It pained her to take stock of her shortcomings and limitations. She had not lived up to her youthful ambitions and now, as the signs of aging became more pronounced, she often found herself in tears.

She felt very much alone, and the only person she had was her beloved Frankie. Her mother had died eleven years earlier, and her father, with whom she had always gotten on badly, had remarried. They lived in Texas and had never invited Cheryl to go and visit them, or made any attempt to come to see her in Brooklyn. Nor did they ask about their grandson with cerebral palsy. Cheryl had only seen her father's wife in the photos they sent her each Christmas, in which they both appeared wearing Santa Claus hats, her father smiling smugly and his wife looking dazed.

Despite her efforts, everything seemed to be slipping away from Cheryl: not just her body but her future. Before reaching forty she had viewed old age as a distant enemy; at forty-five, she felt it lurking in wait for her, an obstinate, implacable foe. She had once dreamed of a professional career, had hopes of rescuing her marriage, and was proud of her physique and beauty. Now all this was in the past. She was a broken, defeated woman. For several years she had been taking drugs to treat depression, anxiety, and insomnia. Her psychiatrist, the only man who had not made her suffer and listened to her, had prescribed a wide variety of palliatives over the years. She had obeyed him like a well-brought-up little girl, just as she had meekly obeyed her father, the transitory boyfriends of her youth, and her husband.

Cheryl was so afraid of her spouse that she tensed whenever she heard his car entering the garage or his footsteps inside the house. It was impossible to predict Frank Leroy's mood, because it changed from one moment to the next for no obvious reason. She prayed for him to be distracted or busy, or only to have dropped in to change clothes and go out again. She always counted the days to his next trip and had confessed to her psychiatrist that she longed to be a widow. He had listened without showing the least surprise, having heard the same from other patients with fewer motives than Cheryl Leroy to wish their spouse dead. He had come to the conclusion that it was a normal female sentiment. His waiting room was filled with repressed, furious women.

She felt incapable of taking care of her son on her own. She had not worked for many years, and her family counseling diploma was an ironic joke: it had not even helped her manage her relationship with her husband. Before they were married, Frank Leroy had told her he wanted a full-time wife. At first she rebelled, but the heaviness and sloth she felt during her pregnancy had made her give way. Once Frankie was born she abandoned all ideas of working, as the boy needed her constant attention. For a couple of years she looked after him on her own day and night, until a nervous crisis sent her to consult her psychiatrist. He recommended she hire help as she was in a position to pay for it. It was only then that, thanks to a succession of nannies, Cheryl gained some freedom for her limited activities. Frank Leroy was unaware of most of these, not because she tried to hide them, but because he was not interested. He had other things on his mind. He more than did his bit maintaining the family, paying the wages, the bills, and his son's astronomical expenses.

It became clear soon after Frankie was born that there was something wrong, but several months went by before the seriousness of his condition was established. The specialists tactfully explained to his parents that Frankie would probably never walk, speak, or be able to control his muscles or sphincter. However, with proper medication, rehabilitation, and corrective surgery for his misshapen limbs, the boy could make progress. Refusing to accept this dire verdict, Cheryl not only tried everything that traditional medicine could offer but went searching for alternative therapies and quack doctors, including one who claimed to cure by telepathic waves over the phone from Portland. Cheryl learned to interpret her son's gestures and noises; it was the only means she had of sharing any kind of communication with him, and the main way she found out how the nannies behaved when she was not there.

To Frank Leroy, his son was a personal insult. No one deserved a catastrophe like this. Why had they resuscitated him when he was born a blue baby? It would have been kinder to let him go rather than condemn him to a life of suffering and his parents to one of caring for him. He wanted nothing to do with the boy; let his mother look after him. No one could convince him that the cerebral palsy or the diabetes were accidents. His wife had given him a damaged child and could not have any more, because after the birth, which had almost cost her her life, she'd had a hysterectomy. He thought Cheryl was a disastrous wife, a bundle of nerves, obsessed with looking after Frankie. She was frigid and had an annoying habit of playing the victim. The woman who had attracted him fifteen years earlier was a Valkyrie, a strong and determined swimming champion. How could he have suspected that within that Amazon's breast beat the heart of a coward? She was almost as tall and strong as he was, and was capable of standing up to him, as she had proved in the early days when they were passionate opponents. They began with blows and ended up making love violently in a dangerous, exciting game. After her operation, the fire went out of Cheryl. To Frank, his wife had become a neurotic rabbit capable

of driving him into a frenzy. Her passivity seemed like a provocation. She did not react to anything, but put up with it tear-
fully, a further aggravation that only served to increase Frank's
anger. He would go too far and afterward be worried because
the bruises could raise suspicion. The last thing he wanted was
problems. He was tied to her because of Frankie, who could
survive for years. Frank Leroy was trapped in the marriage
not only because of his son but above all because he wanted to
avoid a very costly divorce. His wife knew too much. Cheryl had
managed to find out about his business affairs and could blackmail and even destroy him. When it was a matter of defending
Frankie or her own rights, Cheryl did stand up to him, and was
prepared to fight tooth and nail.

They may have loved each other once, but the arrival of
Frankie had killed off any hope they might have had in that
regard. When Frank Leroy learned he was to have a son, he
threw a party that cost as much as a wedding. He himself was
the only boy among several girls, the only one who could pass
on the family name to his descendants. His son would continue
the lineage, as Grandfather Leroy said, proposing a toast at the
party. To talk of a family lineage was a rich joke to describe three
generations of good-for-nothings, as Cheryl told Evelyn during
one of her bouts of drinking and tranquilizers. The first Leroy
from this branch of the family had been a Frenchman who in
1903 escaped from a Calais jail, where he was serving a sentence
for robbery. He reached the United States with nothing more
than his shamelessness, and prospered thanks to his imagination and lack of scruples. He succeeded in living on his luck for
years until he was sent back to prison, this time for a massive
swindle that left thousands of retirees in poverty. His son, Frank

Leroy's father, had been hiding for five years in Puerto Vallarta, Mexico, escaping from American justice for his crimes and for tax evasion. To Cheryl, the fact that her in-laws were far away and unable to return was a blessing.

As the grandson of this French scoundrel and the son of another similar crook, Frank Leroy had a simple philosophy: the end justifies the means if you can benefit from it. Any deal that is profitable for you must be a good one, however disastrous it is for others. Some win, others lose. That was the law of the jungle, and he never lost. He knew how to make money and how to hide it. Thanks to creative accounting, he managed to seem almost a pauper as far as the Internal Revenue Service was concerned, but when it suited him he could put on a show of opulence. This was how he won the trust of his clients, who were men as unscrupulous as him. He inspired envy and admiration. He was as much of a rogue as his father and grandfather, but unlike them he had class and a cool head. He did not waste his time on trifles and avoided risks. Safety first. His strategy was to act through others who fronted for him. They could end up in jail; he never would.

FROM THE OUTSET, Evelyn treated Frankie as a rational individual, on the basis that despite appearances he was intelligent. She learned how to move him without breaking her back, to bathe and dress him, to feed him without hurry in order to avoid his choking. Evelyn was so capable and affectionate with him that Cheryl was quickly convinced she could also hand over the control of her son's diabetes to her. Evelyn measured his sugar intake before every meal and regulated his insulin injections, which she herself administered several times a day. She had learned a fair amount of English in Chicago, but there she had lived among Latinos and had few opportunities to practice it. At first at the Leroys' she felt her lack of English when she tried to communicate with Cheryl, but they soon developed a friendly relationship that did not rely on too many words for them to understand one another. Cheryl came to depend on Evelyn for everything, and the young girl seemed to intuit her thoughts. "I don't know how I lived without you, Evelyn. Promise me you'll never leave," her employer would often say when she felt over-whelmed by anxiety at her husband's violence.

Evelyn told Frankie stories in Spanglish that he listened to closely. "You have to learn Spanish so we can tell each other secrets no one else will understand," she said. At first the boy only grasped an idea here and there, but he liked the sound and rhythm of that melodious language and soon came to master it. Even though he could not form words, he answered Evelyn using the computer. When she first met Frankie, she had to cope with his frequent fits of anger, which she put down to his feel-ing isolated and bored. Then she remembered the computer her little brothers played with in Chicago and thought that if they could use it at such a young age, all the more reason why Frankie could: he was the smartest child she had ever met. She had little or no knowledge of computers, and the idea of having one of those fabulous machines at her disposal seemed fantastic, but as soon as she suggested it, Cheryl rushed out to buy her son one. They hired a young Indian immigrant to teach Evelyn the basics of computing, and she in turn showed Frankie.

His life and spirits improved remarkably thanks to this intel-

lectual challenge. He and Evelyn became addicted to information and all sorts of computer games. Frankie typed with great
difficulty as his hands barely obeyed him, but he spent hours
glued to the screen. He quickly surpassed the basics the young
instructor had taught them and soon was teaching Evelyn what
he discovered for himself. He could communicate, read, entertain himself, and investigate whatever aroused his curiosity.
Thanks to this machine and its infinite possibilities he proved
that he did indeed have a superior intelligence, and his vast
mind found the perfect foil for his challenges. The entire universe opened up before him, and one thing led to another. He
would start with *Star Wars* and end up with a Madagascan dor-
mouse lemur by way of *Australopithecus afarensis*, a forebear
of *Homo sapiens*. Later on he set up an account on Facebook,
where he led a virtual life with invisible friends.

To Evelyn, this reclusive world of gentle intimacy with Frankie
was a balm that helped erase the violence she had endured. Her
recurring nightmares ceased, and she was able to remember
her brothers alive, as she had seen them in the last vision she
had with the shaman in Peten. Frankie became as important to
her as her distant grandmother. Every sign of progress he made
was a personal triumph for her. His possessive affection and the
trust Cheryl placed in her were enough to make her happy. She
did not need anything more. She spoke to Miriam on the phone,
and occasionally saw her on FaceTime, where she could observe
how her little brothers were growing up, but not once in those
years did she make arrangements to go and see her in Chicago.
"I can't leave Frankie, Mama, he needs me," she would explain.
Nor did Miriam feel any great need to visit this daughter who
in fact was a stranger to her. They sent each other photos and

Christmas and birthday presents, but neither of them made any effort to improve a relationship that had never really gotten off the ground. At first Miriam was afraid her daughter was going to suffer all alone in a cold city with people she did not know. She also thought she was being paid very little for the work she was doing, even though Evelyn never complained. In the end, Miriam convinced herself that Evelyn was better off with the Leroys than with her own family in Chicago. Her daughter had grown up, and she had lost her.

IT TOOK SOME TIME for Evelyn to understand the strange dynamic within the Leroy household.

The cook and her daughter warned her not to poke her nose into the Leroys' affairs, because more than one employee had lost their job from being too curious. They had been in the house three years and still knew nothing of what their employer did. Maybe he did not have a job but simply was rich. They only knew that he brought in goods from Mexico and shifted them from state to state, but what kind of goods remained a mystery. No one could get a word out of Ivan Danescu, his right-hand man. He was as dry as week-old bread and it was obviously smart to stay away from him. Their employer always got up early, had a cup of coffee standing up in the kitchen, then went off to play tennis for an hour. After coming back, he took a shower and disappeared until evening or for several days at a stretch. If he remembered, he would go take a look at Frankie from the doorway before he left. Evelyn learned to avoid him and not to mention the boy in front of him.

For her part, Cheryl Leroy got up late because she slept badly. She spent the day at her different activities and had dinner on a tray in Frankie's room. When her husband was away she used the opportunity to go out. She had only one male friend and almost no family; her activities outside the house were her many classes, her doctors, and her psychiatrist. She started drinking early in the afternoon, and by nightfall the alcohol had transformed her into a tearful child. It was then she turned to Evelyn for company. There was no one else she could rely on: this humble Guatemalan girl was her only support, her confidante. This was how Evelyn learned the details of her employers' destructive relationship, including the beatings, and how from the start Frank Leroy had been against his wife's friends, how he forbade her to receive anyone at home, not because he was jealous, as he told her, but to safeguard his privacy. His business affairs were very sensitive and confidential, and had to be protected at all costs. "After Frankie was born he became even stricter. He won't allow anyone to come here, because he's ashamed of his son," Cheryl told Evelyn.

Whenever her husband was away on a trip, Cheryl's nighttime outings were always to the same place, a modest Italian restaurant with checked tablecloths and paper napkins, where the staff knew her since she had been going there for years. Evelyn knew she did not eat on her own, because before leaving she would arrange on the phone to meet someone. "Apart from you, he's my only friend, Evelyn," she told her. He was a painter forty years older than she was; he was poor, an alcoholic, but very charming. Cheryl shared pasta made by the mamma in the kitchen, veal cutlets, and table wine. They had known each other for a long time. Before she was married she had inspired several of his paintings and was briefly his muse. "He saw me at a swimming competition and asked me to pose as Juno for an allegorical mural. Do you know who Juno was, Evelyn? She was the Roman goddess of vital energy, strength, and eternal youth. She was a warrior and a protective goddess. That's how he still sees me. He has no idea how much I've changed." It would have been pointless trying to explain to her husband how much her platonic affection for this elderly artist meant to her, or how those meetings in the restaurant were the only moments when she felt admired and loved.

IVAN DANESCU WAS SOMEONE who looked sinister and behaved accordingly. He was as enigmatic as his boss and his status in the household remained ill defined. Evelyn suspected her employer was almost as afraid of Danescu as the rest of them. She had seen Ivan raise his voice defiantly and Frank Leroy accept it without a word. She thought they sounded like accomplices. Since no one took any notice of the insignificant, stammering Guatemalan girl, she was able to flit about like a phantom, passing through walls and learning all the best-kept secrets. The others thought she barely spoke English and did not understand what she heard or saw.

Evelyn had seldom been alone with Danescu. After she had worked there a year, once Cheryl was sure she was going to stay and saw that Frankie loved her so much she herself was jealous, she suggested Evelyn learn to drive so that she could use the van. In a surprisingly friendly gesture, Ivan offered to teach her. On her own with him in the privacy of the vehicle, she discovered that the ogre, as the other employees called him, was a patient instructor and could even smile when he adjusted the seat for her to reach the pedals, although the smile was more like a grimace, as if he had teeth missing. She turned out to be a good student, learning the traffic laws by heart, and within a week could drive the van. Ivan took a photo of her against the white kitchen wall, and a few days later handed her a driver's license in the name of someone called Hazel Chigliak. "It's a tribal license, now you belong to a Native American tribe," he announced briefly.

At first Evelyn only used the van to take Frankie for a haircut, or to go to a heated pool or the rehabilitation center, but soon they started to go out for ice cream, on picnics, and to the movies. On TV, Frankie watched action films full of murders, torture, explosions, and shooting, but in the movie theater, sitting behind the back row in his wheelchair, he enjoyed the same sentimental stories of romance and heartbreak as his caregiver. They sometimes ended up holding each other's hand as they cried their eyes out. Classical music calmed him, and Latin rhythms made him deliriously happy. She would give him a tambourine or maracas to hold, and while he shook them she would dance around like a disjointed puppet, sending him into gales of laughter.

Over time they became inseparable. Evelyn regularly gave up her days off and it never occurred to her to ask for vacations, because she knew Frankie would miss her. For the first time since her child was born, Cheryl could relax. In the strange language of caresses, gestures, and sounds that they shared, as well as by means of the computer, Frankie asked Evelyn to marry him. "First you have to grow, little man, and then we'll see," she replied, deeply touched.

If the cook and her daughter were aware of what went on between Mr. Leroy and his wife, they never said a word. Evelyn did not mention it either, but she could not pretend she did not know about it, because she had become part of the family and very close to Cheryl. The beatings always took place behind closed doors, but the walls of that house were thin. Frankie's name always came up in these rows. Leroy's wish for him to die once and for all was so obvious that he used to fling it in his wife's face. He wished they would both die, she and her monster, that bastard clearly without a single Leroy gene, because in his family there were no retards. Neither of them deserved to live, they were a waste of space. And Evelyn would hear the dreadful crack of his belt.

After these beatings, Cheryl would spend several days without going out, hiding away in the house and silently allowing Evelyn to look after her. The Guatemalan girl comforted her with a daughter's loyal care. She treated the welts on her body with arnica, helped her to wash, brushed her hair, sat with her to watch soap operas on TV, and listened without commenting as Cheryl poured her heart out. Cheryl took advantage of these periods of seclusion to spend time with Frankie. She read to him, told him stories, held a brush between his fingers so that he could paint. His mother's intense affection could become stifling for Frankie: he would grow nervous and write to Evelyn on the computer for Cheryl to leave him alone. So as not to hurt his mother, he always sent the message in Spanish. The week would end with the boy out of control and his mother doped on anxiety and antidepressant pills. This meant more work for Evelyn, who never complained, because her existence seemed easy compared to her employer's.

She felt great compassion for Cheryl and wanted to protect her, but no one could intervene. Fate had given her a brutal husband and she would have to accept her punishment until the day she could take it no more; then Evelyn would be at her side to escape with Frankie far from Mr. Leroy. Evelyn had seen similar cases back in her own village. The man would get drunk, or fight with someone, or be humiliated at work, or lose a bet—anything could lead to him beating his wife or children. It was not his fault, it was the way men were and that was the law of existence, thought Evelyn. No doubt the reasons for Mr. Leroy's behaving so badly toward his wife were different, but the consequences were the same.

As the other employees had warned Evelyn, discretion was essential if she was to continue to live there. In spite of the fear Mr. Leroy aroused in her, she wanted to keep her job. In the house of statues she felt as safe as she had in her childhood home with her grandmother and enjoyed things she had never dreamed of, all the ice cream she could wish for, television, and a soft bed in Frankie's room. She was paid minimum wage but she had no expenses and could send money to her grandmother, who bit by bit was replacing the mud and reed walls of her hut with bricks and cement.

THAT FRIDAY IN JANUARY when the state of New York was paralyzed, the cook and her daughter did not turn up for work. Cheryl, Evelyn, and Frankie stayed cooped up in the house. The media had been forecasting the storm since the day before, but when it arrived it was worse than predicted. The wind lashed at the windows and Evelyn closed the blinds and curtains to protect Frankie as much as possible from the noise. She tried to take his mind off the storm by switching on the TV, but it proved useless because the rattle of the wind terrified him. When she finally managed to calm him, she put him to bed hoping he would fall asleep, unable to distract him with the TV anymore because the satellite signal was so awful. Anticipating a possible blackout, she had gathered up a flashlight and some candles and filled a thermos with soup. That day Frank Leroy had left at dawn in a taxi to the airport, heading for a golf club in Florida, content to ride out the storm if it struck. Cheryl spent the day in bed, sick and tearful.

On Saturday, Cheryl got up late in a panic, with the distraught expression of her bad days. But unlike on other occasions, she was so quiet that Evelyn grew worried. At around noon, after the gardener had arrived to clear the snow from the driveway, she left in the Lexus for an appointment with her psychiatrist. She returned a couple of hours later, very upset. Her hands were trembling so badly that Evelyn had to open the bottle of sedatives, count the pills, and serve her a large shot of whiskey. Cheryl took the pills with three big gulps of the drink. She said it had been a dreadful day, her head was about to burst, she didn't want to see anyone, least of all her husband. It would be best if that heartless sonofabitch never came back, if he disappeared and went straight to hell, it was no less than he deserved for being mixed up in what he was doing, not that she cared what happened to him or that bastard Danescu, the enemy in her own home. "Damn the pair of them, I hate them," she muttered, feverishly gasping for breath.

"I've got them where I want them, Evelyn. If I choose to, I

can talk, and then they'll have nowhere to hide. They're criminals, murderers. Do you know what they're up to? Human trafficking. They transport and sell people. They bring them from
other countries on false pretenses, and they put them to work as
slaves. Don't tell me you haven't heard about that!"

"I have heard something . . . ," the girl admitted, scared of the
expression on her employer's face.

"They make them work like animals. They don't pay them,
they threaten and kill them. Lots of people are involved in it,
Evelyn: agents, trucking companies, police, border guards,
and even corrupt judges. There's never any shortage of clients.
There's a lot of money in it, if you understand me?"

"Yes, señora."

"You were lucky they didn't get hold of you. You'd have
ended up in a brothel. You think I'm crazy, don't you, Evelyn?"

"No, señora."

"Kathryn Brown is a whore. She comes here to spy on us;
Frankie is only an excuse. My husband brought her here. Did
you know she sleeps with him? No, how could you, child. The
key I found in his pocket is to that whore's place. Why do you
think he has it?"

"Señora, please . . . how can you be sure where the key is from?"

"Where else could it be? And do you know something more,
Evelyn? My husband wants to get rid of me and Frankie . . . his
own son! He wants to kill us! That's what he's after, and that Kathryn Brown must be his accomplice, but I've got my eye on them. I
never lower my guard, I'm always watching, watching . . ."

At the limits of her strength, befuddled by alcohol and pills,
Cheryl let Evelyn lead her to her room, leaning heavily on the
walls as she went. Evelyn helped her undress and lie down.

Cheryl had no idea Evelyn knew about the relationship between Frank and the physical therapist. Evelyn had kept the secret inside her like a malignant tumor for months now, unable to let it out. Thanks to the fact she was regarded as invisible, she listened, observed, and drew conclusions. On several occasions, she had caught them whispering in the corridor. She had heard them planning vacations together and seen them shut themselves in one of the empty bedrooms. Mr. Leroy often appeared in Frankie's room when Kathryn was making him do exercises, and they always sent Evelyn out on some pretext or other. They made no attempt to be careful in front of the boy, even though they knew he could understand everything. It was as if they wanted Cheryl to find out about their relationship. Evelyn supposed Mr. Leroy must be in love with Kathryn, because he looked for excuses to be with her, and when he was, his tone of voice and his expression changed, and yet she found it hard to understand why Kathryn should want to be mixed up with such an evil-hearted person who was a lot older than her, a married man with a sick son. Unless of course she was attracted to all the money he was supposed to possess.

According to what Cheryl had told her, Frank could be irresistible when he put his mind to it. That was what he was like when he won her heart. If Frank Leroy got an idea about something, there was no stopping him, she told Evelyn. They had met in the elegant bar at the Ritz, where she had gone to have some fun with two female friends and he had come to clinch a deal. As she told Evelyn, they glanced at each other a couple of times, sizing each other up from afar, and that was enough for him to come over with two martinis and a determined expression on his face. "From that moment on, he wouldn't leave me alone. I couldn't escape, he trapped me like a fly. I always knew he would mistreat me, because it started before we were married, but back then it was like a game. I never thought it would get worse and worse, and increasingly frequent . . ." In spite of the terror and loathing he inspired in her, Cheryl admitted he was attractive, with his good looks, his exclusive clothes, his air of authority and mystery. Evelyn was unable to appreciate any of these qualities.

That Saturday afternoon as she was listening to Cheryl's incoherent rambling, Evelyn caught the smell from the adjoining room warning her she needed to change Frankie's diaper. Just like her hearing and intuition, her sense of smell had become sharper since working for the Leroys. Cheryl was supposed to have bought diapers but had been in such a state she had forgotten. Evelyn calculated that the dozing boy could wait while she rushed to the drugstore. Pulling on a sweater, a parka, rubber boots, and gloves, she left the house ready to face the snow but discovered that the van had a flat tire and Cheryl's Fiat 500 was at the shop being repaired. There was no point calling a taxi, because it would take an age to arrive in this weather. Waking up her employer was not an option either, because by now she would be comatose. Evelyn was about to give up on the diapers and resolve the problem with a towel when she saw the keys to the Lexus where they were always left on the hall table. That was Mr. Leroy's car, and she had never driven it, but she thought it must be easier than the van. The journey to the drugstore would not take long. Cheryl was in limbo and would not even notice she had gone, and the matter would be solved. She checked that Frankie was fast asleep, kissed him on the forehead, and whispered that she would be back soon. Then she carefully drove the car out of the garage.

Lucia

When her mother died in 2008, Lucia Maraz felt an inexplicable sense of insecurity, even though she had not depended on Lena since leaving for exile at the age of nineteen. In their relationship, she had offered Lena emotional protection, and in her final years economic support as well, as inflation ate away at her pension. Yet when Lucia found herself without her mother the sensation of vulnerability was as sharp as the sadness at her loss. Since her father had vanished from her life very early on, her mother and her brother, Enrique, were the only family she had. With neither of them there anymore, she realized the only person she had left was her daughter, Daniela. Carlos lived in the same house, but remained emotionally absent. Lucia began to feel the weight of her years for the first time. Though well into her fifties, she believed she was still thirty, suspended in time. Until then, growing old and dying had been abstract notions, something that happened to others.

She went with Daniela to pour Lena's ashes into the sea. Her mother had made the request without any explanation, and Lucia presumed she wanted to be in the same waters of the Pacific as her son. Like so many others, Enrique's body might have been thrown into the sea tied to a length of rail track, but the spirit that visited Lena in her final days did not confirm this. They hired a fisherman to take them out beyond the farthest rocks, where the ocean became the color of petroleum and there were no seagulls. Standing in the boat, bathed in tears, they improvised a farewell for the grandmother who had suffered so much, as well as for Enrique. They had never had the courage to bid him goodbye before then, as Lena had refused to acknowledge his death out loud until the end, although perhaps she had done so years earlier in a secret corner of her heart. Lucia's first book, published in 1994 and read by Lena, gave details of the murders under the dictatorship, none of which were subsequently denied. Lena had also accompanied Lucia when she testified before a judge as part of an investigation into the use of army helicopters. Lena must have had a fairly clear idea of her son's fate, but to acknowledge it meant renouncing a mission that had obsessed her for more than three decades. Enrique would have remained forever in a dense fog of uncertainty, neither dead nor alive, had it not been for the miracle of his appearance at his mother's side in her final days to lead her into the next life.

In the boat, Daniela held the ceramic urn while Lucia scattered handfuls of ashes and prayed for her mother, her brother, and the unknown young man who still lay in the Maraz family niche in the cemetery. Over all those years, no one had identified the body in the Vicariate's archives, and Lena had come to think of him as another member of her family. The breeze kept the ashes floating in the air like stardust, until they slowly fell onto the surface of the sea. Lucia suddenly understood that she should replace her mother; she was the eldest in her tiny family, the matriarch. At that moment she felt her age, but it did not overwhelm her until two years later, when she had to come to terms with her losses and it was her turn to confront death.

WHEN SHE LATER TOLD RICHARD BOWMASTER about this period in her life, Lucia left out the shades of gray and concentrated on the brightest and darkest events. The rest was almost erased from her memory, yet Richard wanted to know more. He was familiar with Lucia's two books, where Enrique's story provided the starting point and lent a personal touch to what was a lengthy political analysis, but he knew little of her private life. Lucia explained that her marriage to Carlos Urzua had never really been intimate, but her romantic vocation or simple inertia meant she could never make a decision. They were two people wandering around in the same space, so distant from one another that they got along well, since to fight there has to be proximity. Her cancer led to the end of their marriage, which had been in the making for years.

Following her grandmother's death, Daniela had left for the University of Miami in Coral Gables, and Lucia began a feverish correspondence with her, similar to the one she had had with her mother when she lived in Canada. Her daughter was overjoyed at her new existence, fascinated by the sea creatures, and keen to explore the vagaries of the oceans. Several people of both sexes were in love with her and she could enjoy a free-

dom she would never have had in Chile, where she would have
been constantly scrutinized by a narrow-minded society. One
day she announced to her parents over the phone that she did
not define herself as either a woman or a man and had poly-
amorous relationships. Carlos asked if she meant she was pro-
miscuously bisexual and warned her it would be better not to
advertise the fact in Chile, where few would understand. "I see
they've changed the name of free love. That has always failed,
and it won't work this time," he predicted to Lucia following the
conversation.

After Lucia fell ill with cancer in 2010, Daniela interrupted
her studies and sexual experiments. It was a year of losses and
separations for Lucia, a year of hospitals, fatigue, and fear. Carlos left her, claiming he did not have the courage to witness her
devastation. He felt ashamed, but his mind was made up. He
refused to see the scars crisscrossing her breasts, felt an atavistic repulsion toward the mutilated creature she was becoming, and instead left the responsibility of looking after her to
their daughter. Indignant at her father's behavior, Daniela confronted him in an unexpectedly fierce manner: she was the first
to mention divorce as the only decent way out for a couple who
did not love one another. Carlos adored his daughter, but his
horror at Lucia's double mastectomy was stronger than his fear
of disappointing her. He announced he was moving temporarily to a hotel because the tension at home was affecting him
too much and preventing him from working. Though well past
retirement age, he had decided he would only leave his office
feet first. Lucia and Carlos said goodbye with the tepid courtesy that had characterized the years they had lived together,
without any show of hostility but without clarifying anything.

Within a week, Carlos rented an apartment, and Daniela helped him settle in.

At first, Lucia felt the separation as a gaping void. She was accustomed to her husband's emotional absence, but when he left for good she found she had time to spare, the house seemed enormous, and the empty rooms were filled with echoes. At night she could hear Carlos's footsteps and the water running in his bathroom. This break with her established routines and small daily ceremonies gave her a great sense of abandonment, and added to the worry of the months she spent suffering from the effects of the drugs she was taking to overcome her illness. She felt wounded, fragile, naked. Daniela thought the treatment had destroyed both her body and her spirit's immunity. "Don't make a list of what you haven't got, Ma, but focus on what you do have," she would tell her. In Daniela's view, this was a unique opportunity for Lucia to cleanse her mind as well as her body, to rid herself of the unnecessary burdens of her rancor, complexes, bad memories, impossible desires, and all the rest of the garbage. "Where do you get this wisdom from, daughter?" Lucia asked her on one occasion. "From the Internet," replied Daniela.

Carlos left so definitively that even though he only lived a few blocks from Lucia it was as if he had moved to the far end of another continent. Not once did he ask about her health.

WHEN LUCIA ARRIVED IN BROOKLYN in September 2015, she was hoping that the change of surroundings would revive her. She was tired of routines; it was time to shuffle the cards of her destiny, to see if she would be dealt a better hand. She wanted New York to be the first stop on a long journey and was planning to look for other opportunities to travel the world while she still had the strength and funds to do so. Above all, she wanted to leave behind the losses and sorrows of recent years. The hardest part had been her mother's death, which affected her more than the divorce or cancer. Although at first she had felt her husband's departure as a stab in the back, she soon came to see it as a gift of freedom and peace.

It took more of an effort to recover from her illness, which was what had finally made Carlos flee. The months of chemo and radiation left her gaunt and bald, with no eyelashes or eyebrows, blue circles around her eyes, and numerous scars, but she was healthy and the prognosis was good. Her breasts were reconstructed with implants that inflated gradually as the muscles and skin adjusted to accommodate them. This was a painful process that she endured without complaining, buoyed by her vanity, feeling that anything was preferable to the flat chest scarred with knife wounds.

The experience of that year lost to illness gave her a burning desire to live, as if the reward for her suffering was to have discovered the philosopher's stone, that elusive substance of the alchemists that was capable of turning lead into gold and restoring youth. She had already lost her fear of dying when she witnessed her mother's elegant passage from life to death. Once more she experienced with complete clarity the irrefutable presence of the soul, that primordial essence that neither cancer nor anything else could destroy. Whatever happened, the soul would win out. She imagined her possible death as a threshold and was curious to know what she would find on the other side.

She was not afraid of crossing that threshold, but while she was in this world she wanted to live life to the fullest, without worrying about anything, to be invincible.

The medical treatments came to an end in late 2010. For months she had avoided looking at herself in the mirror, and until Daniela threw it into the garbage she had worn a fisherman's woolly hat pulled down over her eyebrows. Daniela had just turned nineteen when her mother was diagnosed and had postponed her studies to return to Chile and be with her. Although Lucia had begged her not to, she later understood that her daughter's presence during the ordeal was indispensable. When she first saw her arrive, she hardly recognized her. Daniela had left in wintertime, a pale young woman wearing too many layers. When she returned she was a caramel color, her head half shaven and the other half with long dyed strands of hair, wearing military boots and shorts that showed her hairy legs. She immediately began to take care of her mother and entertain the other hospital patients. She would appear on the ward blowing kisses to everyone reclining in armchairs plugged into chemical drips, handing out blankets, nutrition bars, fruit juices, and magazines.

She had been at the university for less than two years, yet talked as if she had navigated the oceans with Jacques Cousteau among blue-tailed mermaids and sunken galleons. She taught the patients the term "LGBT"—"lesbian, gay, bisexual, and transgender"—and explained the distinctions between them. The term had come into recent use among young people in the United States; in Chile no one even suspected what it meant, least of all the cancer patients on this ward. She told them she was of neutral or fluid gender because there was no obligation to accept being categorized as man or woman on the basis of your genitals. You could define yourself however you liked, and change opinion if some time later another gender seemed more appropriate. "Like indigenous people in certain tribes, who change their names at different stages in their lives, because the one they were given at birth no longer represents them," she added by way of explanation, which only added to the patients' general confusion.

Daniela stayed with her mother throughout her convalescence and during the long, irritating hours of each chemo session, as well as through the divorce process. She slept next to her, ready to jump out of bed and help her if need be, buoyed her up with her brusque affection, her jokes, her hearty soups, and her skill at navigating through the bureaucracy of ill health. She dragged her out to buy new clothes and made her follow a reasonable diet. And once she had left her father settled in his new bachelor life and her mother steady on her feet, she said goodbye without fuss and left as joyfully as she had arrived.

Prior to her illness, Lucia had led what she called a bohemian existence that Daniela viewed as unhealthy. She had smoked for years, never exercised, drank two glasses of wine every evening with dinner, and had ice cream for dessert. She was several pounds overweight, and her knees ached. When she was married she had ridiculed her husband's way of life: whereas she began the day propped up in bed with a milky coffee and two croissants reading the newspaper, he would drink a thick green liquid containing bee pollen, then run like a fugitive to his office, where Lola, his faithful secretary, would be waiting for him with clean clothes. Despite his age, Carlos Urzua kept fit and walked with no sign of a stoop. Thanks to Daniela's iron authority, Lucia had begun to imitate him, and the results were soon evident from the bathroom scales and a vitality she had not felt since adolescence.

When Lucia and Carlos saw each other to sign the papers for the divorce, which had only recently become legal in Chile, it was still too soon for Lucia to say she was in remission, but she had regained strength and her breasts had been reconstructed. Her hair had turned white, and she decided to leave it short, tousled, and in its natural color except for some purple streaks that Daniela added before leaving for Miami. When he saw her on the day of the divorce, weighing twenty pounds less, with a young girl's breasts beneath a low-cut blouse and neon hair, Carlos gave a start. Lucia thought he looked more handsome than ever and felt a fleeting stifled pang for their lost love. In reality she felt nothing for him apart from gratitude that he was Daniela's father. She thought it would have been a healthy sign if she was at least a little angry but could not even manage that. Not even a lingering disappointment remained of the passionate love she had felt for him for many years.

JULIAN CAME INTO LUCIA'S LIFE at the start of 2015, several years after she had grown resigned to the lack of love and thought her fantasies of romance had dried up in the chemotherapy reclining chair. Julian taught her that curiosity and desire were renewable resources. If her mother, Lena, had still been alive she would have warned Lucia about the ridiculousness of this kind of pretension at her age, and she would perhaps have been right, because with each passing day the opportunities for love lessened and those of looking ridiculous increased. And yet Lena would not have been entirely right, because when Julian appeared he offered Lucia love when she was least expecting it. Even though their love affair ended almost as quickly as it had begun, it served to show her that she still had embers inside her that could be rekindled. There was nothing for her to feel sorry about. She had no regrets about anything she had experienced and enjoyed.

The first thing she noticed about Julian was his appearance. Without being exactly ugly, it seemed to her he was not that attractive. All her lovers, especially her husband, had been good-looking. Not that this was intentional, more a matter of chance. As she told Daniela, Julian was the best proof of her lack of prejudice toward ugly men. At first glance he was an ordinary Chilean, with bad posture and an ungainly way of walking. His clothes looked as if they were borrowed: baggy corduroy trousers and a grandfather's knitted cardigans. He had the olive skin of his southern Spanish forebears, gray hair and beard, the soft hands of someone who had never worked with them. But underneath this loser's facade was someone of exceptional intelligence and an experienced lover.

Their first kiss and what followed that night were enough for Lucia to surrender to adolescent infatuation that was fully reciprocated by Julian. At least for a while. During the early months Lucia welcomed with open arms everything that had been lacking in her marriage. Her new lover made her feel cherished and desirable; thanks to him she rediscovered her joyful youth. At first Julian also appreciated her sensuality and sense of fun, but it was not long before the emotional intensity began to frighten him. He would forget their rendezvous, arrive late, or call at the last minute with an excuse. Or he'd drink an extra glass of wine and fall asleep in the middle of a sentence or between two caresses. He complained of how he had no time to read and how his social life had dwindled, resenting the attention he had to pay Lucia. He was still a considerate lover, more concerned to give than to receive pleasure, but she noticed he was holding back, no longer surrendering wholeheartedly to love. He was sabotaging the relationship. By this time Lucia had learned to recognize failing love as soon as it raised its gargoyle head. She no longer put up with it as she had done through the twenty years of her marriage in the hope that something would change. She was more experienced and had less time to waste. She realized she ought to call it quits before Julian did, even though she would miss his sense of humor terribly, his puns, the pleasure of waking up tired beside him knowing it would take only a whispered enticement or nonchalant caress for them to embrace once more. It was a break without drama, and they stayed friends.

"I've decided to give my broken heart a rest," she told Daniela on the phone, in a tone of voice that did not sound humorous, as she had intended, but more like a complaint.

"How kitsch can you get, Ma? Hearts don't break like eggs. And if yours is an egg, isn't it better for it to be broken and for feelings to pour out? That's the price for a life lived to the full," her daughter replied implacably.

A year later, in Brooklyn, Lucia still occasionally fell prey to a certain degree of nostalgia for Julian, but it was no more than a slight itch that did not really bother her. Could she find another love? Not in the United States, she thought—she was not the kind of woman who attracted Americans, as Richard

Bowmaster's indifference demonstrated. She could not imagine seduction without humor, but her Chilean irony was not only untranslatable but perceived as frankly offensive by North Americans. In English, as she told Daniela, she had the IQ of a chimpanzee. She could only laugh out loud with Marcelo, at his stumpy legs and lemur face. That dog permitted himself the luxury of being both completely self-centered and grumpy, just like a husband.

The sadness she felt at breaking up with Julian manifested itself in an attack of bursitis in her hips. She spent several months taking analgesics and waddling like a duck, but refused to see a doctor, convinced the condition would disappear once she had gotten over her bitterness. And so it would eventually prove, although she arrived at the airport in New York limping. Richard Bowmaster was expecting the active, cheerful woman he knew. Instead he had to greet a stranger wearing orthopedic shoes and using a cane, who sounded like a rusty hinge whenever she stood up from a chair. However, a few weeks later he saw her without the cane and wearing fashionable ankle boots. He could not have known it, but this miracle was thanks to Julian's brief reappearance.

In October, a month after Lucia installed herself in his basement, Julian came to New York for a conference, and they spent a wonderful Sunday together. They had breakfast in Le Pain Quotidien, took a stroll in Central Park that was even slower because she still dragged her feet, and went to a Broadway musical matinee hand in hand. Afterward they had dinner in a small Italian restaurant with a bottle of the best Chianti and drank to friendship. Their complicity was as fresh as on the first day. They effortlessly regained the secret language and double entendres that only they could understand. Julian apologized for having made her suffer, but she replied sincerely that she could hardly recall it. That morning, when they had met over their mugs of milky coffee and fresh bread, Julian had aroused a festive delight in her. She wanted to smell his hair, straighten his jacket collar, and suggest he buy a pair of trousers that fitted him. Nothing more. In the Italian restaurant she left her cane under the table.

Lucia, Richard, Evelyn

Upstate New York

By five in the afternoon, when Lucia and Richard met Evelyn back at the cabin, the winter day was already at an end, and a bright moon was shining. They were smeared with mud and snow from toppling the car into the lake, and had taken longer to return than calculated, because the Subaru had skidded out of control and ended up in a pile of snow. They had to use the shovel once again to clear the snow from around the wheels, then tore off some pine branches to place on the ground. Richard put the Subaru into reverse and at the second attempt it jerked backward. The tires gained traction on the branches and they were able to move forward again.

By that time night was falling and their earlier tracks were invisible. They had to drive on slowly, guessing where they were headed. They got lost a couple of times, but fortunately for them Evelyn had disobeyed their instructions and lit a kerosene lamp in the doorway that guided them over the last stretch.

After this adventure the cabin interior seemed like a welcoming nest, even though the stoves hardly managed to temper the cold that crept in through the gaps in the old wooden planks. Richard felt responsible for the poor state the primitive dwelling was in; over the two years it had been shut, it had deteriorated as if a century had passed. He resolved to come back every summer to air it out and have repairs made so that Horacio could not accuse him of negligence when he returned to the United States. *Negligence:* the word still made him shudder.

Given the snow and the darkness they decided to abandon their original plan of driving to a hotel. They also thought it unwise to travel around any more than necessary with Kathryn Brown in the trunk of the Subaru. They were not concerned about the state of the body, which would stay frozen, and so they settled down to spend their Monday night wrapped up as warmly as possible. Having been through so many stressful moments in the past few days, they resolved to set aside the problem of Kathryn for now and to take their mind off things by playing a game of Monopoly, which had been left behind by Horacio's children. Richard taught them the rules. Evelyn found the concept of buying and selling properties, hoarding money, dominating the market, and forcing rivals into bankruptcy completely incomprehensible. Lucia turned out to be an even worse player than Evelyn, with the result that they both lost miserably and Richard ended up a millionaire. But it was a hollow triumph that left him feeling he had cheated.

They managed to rustle up some dinner from what was left of the donkey food, filled the stoves with fuel, and laid out the sleeping bags on the three beds in the kids' room. They had no sheets, and the blankets smelled of damp. Richard made a mental note that on his next visit he should also replace the mattresses, which could have been concealing bedbugs or rodents' nests. They took off their boots and lay down fully dressed: it was going to be a long, cold night. While Evelyn and Marcelo fell asleep at once, Lucia and Richard continued talking until past midnight as they had so much to say to one another in this delicate stage of getting to know each other more closely. They began revealing their secrets, imagining the other's features in the semidarkness. They were trapped in their cocoons, their beds so close they could easily have kissed should either of them have dared.

Love, love. Until the day before, Richard had been thinking up clumsy dialogues with Lucia. Now he was bursting with sentimental verses he would never find the courage to write. To tell her for example how much he loved her, how grateful he was that she had appeared in his life. She had been blown in like gossamer by the wind of good fortune and here she was, present and close in the midst of the ice and snow, with a promise glinting in her large eyes. Lucia realized he was covered in invisible wounds, and he could clearly see the fine cuts life had inflicted on her. "Love has always been in half measures for me," she had confessed to him. That was over and done with. He was going to love her without any limits, absolutely. He wanted to protect her and make her happy so that she would never leave, for them to be together throughout that winter, then spring, summer, and forever. He wanted to create the deepest complicity and intimacy with her, to share the most secret parts of his being, to draw her into his life and soul. In fact he knew very little about Lucia and even less about himself, but none of that would matter if she was to reciprocate his love. In that case they would have the rest of their lives to discover one another, to grow and to age together.

Richard had not thought he could ever again be in love as he had been with Anita in his youth. He was no longer the man who loved Anita; he felt as if he had grown the scales of a crocodile, which seemed almost visible and heavy as armor. He was ashamed of having always protected himself from disenchantment, from being abandoned or betrayed; frightened of suffering the way he had made Anita suffer; terrified of life itself; cut off from the formidable adventure of love.

"I don't want to go on living this kind of half life," he told Lucia. "I don't want to be this cowardly man. I want you to want me, Lucia."

WHEN IN 1991 RICHARD turned up for the first day of his new job at New York University, Horacio Amado-Castro was amazed at his transformation. When he had met him at the airport only a few days earlier he had been a disheveled, incoherent drunk, and Horacio regretted inviting him to be part of the faculty. He had admired him when they were both students and young professionals, but that was years earlier and since then Richard had fallen very low. The death of his two children had wounded his soul, as it had Anita's. He guessed they would eventually separate: few couples survived the death of one child, and they had lost two. As if that were not tragedy enough, Richard had been the cause of Bibi's death. Horacio found it impossible to begin to imagine the guilt Richard must have felt; if anything similar happened to one of his own children, he would have preferred to die. He was afraid Richard would be unable to take up his academic post, and yet there he was, looking impeccable, freshly shaved and with hair recently cut, and wearing a smart summer suit and tie. His breath did smell of alcohol, but the effects of alcohol were not obvious from his behavior or his ideas. He was appreciated from the very first day.

Richard and Anita moved into an eleventh-floor apartment for faculty members in University Village. It was small but adequate, with functional furniture and in a very convenient location, as Richard could walk to his office in ten minutes. When they arrived, Anita crossed the threshold with the same automaton-like demeanor she had had for several months. She sat at the window and stared out at the tiny corner of sky she could see among the surrounding tall buildings, while her husband unloaded, unpacked, and made a list of provisions to shop for. This set the tone for the brief length of time they lived together in New York.

"They warned me, Lucia. Anita's family and her psychiatrist in Brazil warned me. How could I not see how fragile she was? She was destroyed by the loss of the children."

"It was an accident, Richard."

"No. I had spent the night partying and arrived befuddled by sex, cocaine, and alcohol. It wasn't an accident, it was a crime. And Anita knew it. She began to hate me. She wouldn't let me touch her. By bringing her to New York I separated her from her family and her country. In the United States she was adrift: she didn't know anyone or speak the language, and she was far apart from me, the only person who might have helped her. I failed her in every sense. I didn't think of her, only of myself. I wanted to leave Brazil, to escape the Farinha family, to embark on a professional career I had postponed too long. By the age I was then, I should have been an associate professor. I began very late and wanted to catch up. I was going to study, teach, and above all, publish. From the outset I knew I had discovered the perfect place for me, but while I was parading around the university rooms and corridors, Anita was spending the whole day sitting silently at the window."

"Was she seeing a psychiatrist?"

"That was available. Horacio's wife offered to accompany her and help her with the insurance bureaucracy, but Anita refused to go."

"So what did you do?"

"Nothing. I was caught up in my own world. I even played squash to stay fit. Anita stayed cooped up in the apartment. I have no idea what she did all day; she slept, I suppose. She didn't even answer the phone. My father used to go and see her. He took her boxes of chocolates and tried to persuade her to go out for walks, but she wouldn't even look him in the face. I think she detested him because he was my father. One weekend I came to this cabin with Horacio and left her alone in New York."

"You were drinking a lot at the time," Lucia concluded.

"A lot. I spent the evenings in a bar. I kept a bottle in my office drawer; no one suspected my glass contained gin or vodka rather than water. I would chew peppermints to conceal the smell on my breath. I thought it wasn't noticeable, that I had the constitution of an ox for drinking—all alcoholics deceive themselves in the same way, Lucia. It was fall, and the small square outside our building was strewn with yellow leaves . . . ," Richard whispered, his voice cracking.

"What happened, Richard?"

"A policeman came to inform us, because we never had a phone here in the cabin."

Lucia waited a long while without interrupting Richard's stifled sobs. She did not take her hand out of the sleeping bag to touch and comfort him; she understood there was no possible consolation for such memories. From rumors and comments by her colleagues at the university, she knew roughly what had happened to Anita; she suspected this was the first time Richard had talked about it. She was deeply moved at being the recipient of this harrowing disclosure, the witness to his purifying tears. She knew the strange healing power words had from what she had written and discussed concerning her brother Enrique's fate—how important it was to share one's pain and discover that others too had their fair share of it, that lives are often alike and feelings similar.

Thanks to the unfortunate Kathryn Brown, she and Richard had ventured far from their known and safe terrain, and as they did so they revealed who they really were. Their strange adventure was creating a mysterious bond between them. Lucia closed her eyes and tried to reach Richard with her thoughts. She put all her energy into crossing the few inches between them to enfold him in her compassion, as she had done so often with her mother in her dying days to lessen her anxiety, and her own.

The previous night she had climbed into Richard's bed to see how she felt beside him. She had needed to touch and smell him, to feel his energy. According to Daniela, when you sleep with someone the two energies are combined. This can be enriching for both, or can be very negative for the weaker of the two. "Just as well you didn't sleep in the same bed as my papa, because your aura would have been burned to a cinder," said Daniela. Sleeping with Richard, even when he was ill and in a flea-infested bed, had brought Lucia profound comfort. She was certain this man was for her. She had had an inkling of this for some time, possibly even before coming to New York; that was why she had accepted his offer, but she had been paralyzed by his apparent coldness. Richard was a mass of contradictions and would be incapable of taking the first step; she would have to take him by storm. He might reject her, but that would not be so serious, she had overcome greater reversals; it had to be worth trying. They had some years of life left and maybe she could convince him they should enjoy them together. The possibility of her cancer returning cast a shadow over her; all she could count on was the precious, fleeting present. She wanted to make the most of every day, because they were numbered and no doubt fewer than she hoped. There was no time to lose.

"She fell right next to the Picasso sculpture," said Richard. "It was in the middle of the day. She was seen standing in the window, then jumping, and crashing into the pavement among the leaves. I killed Anita just as I killed Bibi. I'm guilty for being a drunk, for my negligence, for loving them much less than they deserved."

"It's time for you to forgive yourself, Richard. You've been paying for that guilt a long time."

"Almost twenty-five years. And I can still feel the last kiss I gave Anita before leaving her on her own with her grief. A kiss that only brushed her cheek, because she turned her head from me."

"That's many years with your soul in winter and your heart locked away, Richard. That's not a life. And the fearful man of those years is not you. In these last few days, when you were forced out of your comfort zone you were able to discover who you really are. It may be painful, but anything is better than being anesthetized."

Richard had practiced meditation for years, and it had kept him sober. He had attempted to learn the principles of Zen, to be aware of the present moment, to start again with each new breath, but the ability to empty his mind escaped him. His life was not a succession of separate moments, it was a tangled story, a changing, chaotic, and imperfect tapestry he had woven day by day. His present was not a blank screen, it was packed with images, dreams, memories, shame, guilt, loneliness, pain, all his damned reality, as he told Lucia in whispers that night.

"But then you turn up and allow me to feel hurt for all I've lost, to laugh at my idiocy, and to weep like a small child."

"It was time you did, Richard. Enough wallowing in the sorrows of the past. The only cure for so much misfortune is love. It's not the force of gravity that keeps the universe in balance, but the binding power of love."

"How could I have lived so many years alone and disconnected? I've been asking myself that for days now."

"Because you *are* an idiot. What a way to waste time and life! You must have realized that I love you, haven't you?" she laughed.

"I don't know how you can love me, Lucia. I'm no one special, you're going to be bored with me. And I carry with me the exhausting weight of my mistakes and omissions, and they're a sackful of rocks."

"No problem. I've got the muscles to sling your sack across my shoulder and throw it into the frozen lake so it disappears forever along with the Lexus."

"Why have I lived, Lucia? Before I die I have to find out why

I am in this world. What you say is true: I've been anesthetized for so long I've no idea where to start to live again."

"I can help you if you'll let me."

"How?"

"It starts with the body. I suggest we bring the sleeping bags together and sleep curled up with one another. I need it as much as you do, Richard. I want you to put your arms around me, to feel safe and protected. How long are we going to tiptoe about so timidly, waiting for the other to take the first step? We're too old for that, but perhaps we're still young enough for love."

"Are you sure, Lucia? I couldn't bear it if—"

"Sure? I'm not sure of anything, Richard!" she cut in. "But we can try. What's the worst that can happen? More suffering? That it doesn't work out?"

"Let's not think that, I couldn't bear it."

"I scared you . . . I'm sorry."

"No, on the contrary, I'm sorry I didn't tell you before what my feelings are. This is so new, so unexpected, that I don't know how to deal with it, but you're much stronger and more clear-sighted than me. Come on, get into bed with me and let's make love."

"Evelyn is only a couple of feet away, and I'm a bit noisy. We'll have to wait, but in the meantime we can cuddle with each other."

"Do you know I spend hours talking to you in secret like a lunatic? That I picture you in my arms the whole time? I've wanted you for so long . . ."

"I don't believe a word of it. You only noticed me last night, when I pushed myself into your bed. Before that you weren't even aware of me," she said with a laugh.

"I'm so glad you did, you shameless Chilean," he said, crossing the short distance between them to give her a kiss.

They brought the sleeping bags together on one bed, joined the zips, and embraced each other fully dressed with unexpected desperation. That was all Richard was able to recall clearly later on. The rest of that magical night was preserved forever in a perfect nebula. Lucia on the other hand swore she remembered every last detail. In the following days and years she would tell him them little by little, always with a different version and more audacious with each retelling, until her story verged on the unbelievable, because they could not have performed all the acrobatics she described without waking Evelyn. "It's true, even if you don't believe me," she would maintain. "Perhaps Evelyn pretended to be asleep but was spying on us." Richard thought they must have kissed long and hard, then taken off their clothes in the restricted space of their sleeping bags, explored each other's body as best they could without making any noise, as stealthily and excitedly as two youngsters making love in some dark corner. What he did remember was that she climbed on top of him and he could run his hands over her, surprised at her taut, warm skin, at this body he could only dimly make out in the flickering candlelight, a body that was slenderer, more docile, and younger than it seemed when she had her clothes on. "These chorus girl's breasts are now mine, Richard, they cost me enough," Lucia whispered in his ear, suppressing her laughter. That was what was best about her, that laugh like clear water that cleansed him inside and swept his doubts away.

LUCIA AND RICHARD WOKE to the timid light of that Tuesday morning still in the warmth of their sleeping bags. They had been buried in them all night long in a tangle of arms and legs, so close there was no telling where one began and the other ended, breathing in unison, perfectly at ease in the love they were just beginning to discover. The convictions and defenses that had sustained them until now collapsed faced with the magic of true intimacy. When they poked their heads out, the freezing cold of the cabin hit them. The heaters had gone out. Richard was the first to pluck up the courage to peel himself away from Lucia's body and face the day. He checked that Evelyn and the dog were still asleep, and took advantage of those minutes to kiss Lucia, who was purring beside him. Then he got dressed, filled the heaters with fuel, put water on to boil, made tea, and took it to the two women. They drank it semireclining, while he took Marcelo outside for some fresh air. He was whistling as he went.

The day had arrived radiant, with the storm no more than a bad memory. Snow covered the world like meringue, and the icy breeze bore the impossible hint of gardenias. The cloudless sky took on the light blue color of forget-me-nots. "A good day for your funeral, Kathryn," Richard murmured. He was happy and full of energy, like a puppy. This happiness was so new he had no name for it. He probed the feeling carefully, touching it lightly and then retreating, exploring his heart's virgin territory. Had he imagined all those midnight secrets? Lucia's dark eyes so close to his? Perhaps he had invented her body between his hands, their lips joined as one, the joy, passion, and fatigue in the two sleeping bags that made their nuptial bed. He was sure they had been in each other's arms, because that was the only way he could have caught her slumbering breath, her provoca-tive warmth, the images of her dreams. Again he wondered if this was love; it was so different from the flaming passion he had felt for Anita. This new emotion was like the hot sand on a beach with the sun high in the sky. Could this subtle, unmistakable pleasure be the essence of mature love? There was plenty of time for him to find out. He walked back to the cabin with Marcelo in his arms, still whistling.

All that remained of their provisions were a few miserable leftovers, and so Richard proposed they go to have breakfast in the nearest town, and from there continue on to Rhinebeck. He had completely forgotten about his ulcer. Lucia had explained there were maintenance staff at the Omega Institute during the week, but if they were lucky there would be nobody there now because of the recent storms. The road would be clear and the journey should take them three or four hours; they were in no hurry to arrive. Complaining of the cold, Lucia and Evelyn crawled out of their sleeping bags and assisted Richard in tidying up before leaving the cabin.

Lucia, Richard, Evelyn

I n the unheated Subaru, with two windows cracked open and the three of them bundled up like Arctic explorers, Richard Bowmaster told his companions that a few months earlier he had invited a couple of experts in human trafficking to give a talk at his university. As Evelyn had explained, this was what Frank Leroy and Ivan Danescu were dedicated to. Nothing new in that, said Richard, supply and demand had existed ever since slavery was officially abolished, but the business had never been as profitable as it was now; it was a gold mine matched only by drug and arms dealing. The tougher the laws and the stricter the border controls, the more efficient and ruthless the organization of the business became, and the greater sums earned by the agents, as the traffickers were known. Richard suspected that Frank Leroy connected the criminals with clients in the United States. Men like him did not get their hands dirty; they knew nothing of the faces or lives of the migrants who ended up as slaves in agriculture, manufacturing, industry, or brothels. To him they were mere numbers, an anonymous freight to be transported, worth less than livestock.

Leroy maintained the facade of a respectable businessman, with an office on Lexington Avenue in Manhattan. There he dealt with clients keen to employ slaves, cultivated politicians and compliant authorities, laundered money, and resolved any legal problems. In the same way as he had obtained a Native American's driver's license for Evelyn Ortega, he could obtain fake identity papers for the right price, although the victims of human trafficking did not need them: they existed under the radar, invisible, silenced, in the shadows of a lawless world. He was bound to charge a hefty commission, but the people who moved this human cargo on a large scale paid it in order to be safe.

"Do you think Frank Leroy really intends to kill his wife and son, as Cheryl told you? Or were they simply threats?" Richard asked Evelyn.

"The señora is scared of him. She thinks he might inject Frankie with an overdose or suffocate him."

"That man must be a monster if that's what his wife thinks of him," Lucia exclaimed.

"She also believes Kathryn was considering helping him."

"Do you think that's possible, Evelyn?"

"No."

"What motive could Frank Leroy have for killing Kathryn?" Richard asked.

"Maybe Kathryn had found out something about him and was blackmailing him," speculated Lucia.

"She was three months pregnant," Evelyn said.

"What a shock! Why didn't you tell us before, Evelyn?"

"I try not to gossip."

"Was Leroy the father?"

"Yes. Miss Kathryn told me so. Señora Leroy doesn't know."

"It could be that Frank Leroy killed her because she was putting pressure on him, though that seems a very weak motive. It could have been accidental . . . ," suggested Lucia.

"It must have been on Thursday night, before he left for Florida," Richard said. "That means Kathryn died at least four days ago. If it weren't for the freezing temperatures . . ."

THEY ARRIVED AT THE OMEGA INSTITUTE at around two in the afternoon. Lucia had described a place where nature flourished, with woods dense with bushes and ancient trees, but in the winter many of them had shed their foliage and the park was less secluded than they had hoped. If there were any guards or cleaning personnel they would easily be spotted, but they decided to run the risk.

"This place is enormous. I'm sure we'll find the ideal site to leave Kathryn," said Lucia.

"Are there security cameras?" asked Richard.

"No. Why would they want security cameras somewhere like this? There's nothing here to steal."

"That's good. And afterward, what are we going to do with you, Evelyn?" Richard asked in the paternal tone he had come to adopt with her over the past two days. "We have to keep you safe from Leroy and the police."

"I promised my grandmother that just as I left, so I would return," she replied.

"But you left to escape the MS-13. How can you go back to Guatemala?" said Lucia.

"That was eight years ago. A promise is a promise."

"The men who killed your brothers are dead or in prison. Nobody lives for long in that gang, but there's still a lot of violence in your country, Evelyn. Even if no one remembers the vengeance on your family, a pretty young woman like you will be in a very vulnerable position. You understand that, don't you?"

"Evelyn is in danger here too," Richard interjected.

"I don't think she'll be arrested for not having documents. There are eleven million immigrants in the same situation," said Lucia.

"Sooner or later they're going to find Kathryn's body and there will be an in-depth investigation into the Leroys. The autopsy will show she was pregnant, and a DNA test could prove the baby was Frank Leroy's. The disappearance of the Lexus and Evelyn will come out."

"That's why she has to get as far away as possible, Richard," said Lucia. "If they find her she'll be accused of stealing the car and could be linked to Kathryn's death."

"In that case all three of us will be in a spot. We're accomplices in concealing evidence—disposing of a dead body for starters."

"We're going to need a good lawyer," said Lucia.

"However smart, no lawyer can get us out of this mess. Come on, Lucia, spit it out. I'm sure you've got a plan."

"It's just an idea, Richard . . . what's most important is to make sure Evelyn is safe somewhere where neither Leroy nor the police will find her. I called my daughter last night, and it occurred to her that Evelyn could disappear in Miami. There are millions of Latinos in the city, and more than enough work. She could stay there until things calm down, and once we're sure no one is looking for her, Evelyn could go back to her mother in Chicago. In the meantime, Daniela offered to put her up in her apartment."

"You're not thinking of getting Daniela involved in this, are you?" exclaimed Richard, horrified.

"Why not? Daniela loves adventures, and when she heard what we were up to she was only sorry not to be here to lend a hand. I'm sure your father would say the same."

"Did you tell Daniela all this on the phone?"

"On WhatsApp. Calm down, Richard, no one suspects us, there'd be no reason for them to investigate our cell phones. Besides, with WhatsApp there's no problem. As soon as we've dealt with Kathryn, we'll put Evelyn on a plane to Miami. Daniela will be waiting for her."

"A plane?"

"She can travel within the country with her Native American ID, but if that's too risky, we can put her on a bus. It's a long journey, a day and a half, I think."

THEY ENTERED THE OMEGA INSTITUTE along Lake Drive and passed the administration buildings in a white landscape of absolute silence and solitude. Nobody had been there since the start of the storm. No machines had come to clear the path, but the sun had begun melting the snow. There were no tracks from any recent vehicles. Lucia took them to the sports field, because she recalled seeing a box for sports equipment big enough to hold a body. Kathryn would be safe there from coyotes and other predators. But Evelyn said it would be a sacrilege to put Kathryn somewhere like that.

They continued on to the shore of a long, narrow lake where Lucia had paddled a kayak on her visits to the institute. It was frozen over, but they did not dare step out onto it. Richard knew how difficult it could be to judge the thickness of ice at a glance. There was a boathouse on the bank, a few canoes, and a jetty. Richard suggested they tie one of the light canoes to the Suba-ru's roof rack and drive along the narrow path bordering the lake in search of an out-of-the-way spot. They could leave Kathryn on the far bank, covered by the tarpaulin. Within a few weeks, when the thaw began, the canoe would float across the lake until someone found it. A funeral in water is poetic, he added, like a Viking ceremony.

Richard and Lucia were struggling with the chain mooring one of the canoes when a cry from Evelyn stopped them. She pointed to a nearby grove of trees.

"What is it?" asked Richard, thinking she must have seen a guard.

"A jaguar!" exclaimed Evelyn, ashen faced.

"That's not possible, Evelyn. They don't exist up here."

"I can't see anything," said Lucia.

"Jaguar!" Evelyn repeated.

In the white expanse of the wood the three of them thought they glimpsed a big yellow animal that turned and leapt away toward the gardens. Richard assured them it must be a deer or a coyote. There had never been any jaguars in that region, and if there had been other large cats, such as pumas, they had been wiped out more than a century earlier. It was such a fleeting vision that he and Lucia doubted they had seen it, but Evelyn, transfigured, began to follow the tracks of the supposed jaguar as though she were floating above the ground: light, ethereal, diminutive. The other two did not dare call out to her in case someone heard them, but followed behind, waddling like penguins to avoid slipping in the snow.

EVELYN FLOATED ON ANGEL'S WINGS along the path past the office, the store, the bookstore, and the café. She drifted on until she rounded the library and the lecture hall and left the large dining rooms behind. Lucia remembered the institute in the high season, green and filled with flowers, myriad birds, and red squirrels, with visitors moving in slow motion in the garden to the controlled rhythms of tai chi, others strolling between their classes in saris and monks' sandals, as well as youthful employees reeking of marijuana on their electric carts loaded with bags and boxes. The winter panorama was desolate and beautiful, with the phantasmagoric whiteness adding to the sense of vastness. The buildings were locked up, their windows sealed with wooden planks. There were no signs of life; it was as if no one had been there for fifty years. The snow muffled the sounds of nature and their crunching boots. They followed Evelyn as if in a dream, without making a noise. Though it was a clear day and still early, they felt as if they were enveloped in a theatrical mist. Evelyn went on past the cabin area and took a path to the left that ended in a steep flight of stone steps. She climbed them without hesitation or watching out for ice, as though she knew exactly where she was headed. The other two struggled along behind her. They passed a frozen fountain and a stone Buddha and found themselves on the top of the hill in the Sanctuary, a square, Japanese-style wooden pagoda flanked by covered eaves: the spiritual heart of the community.

They understood this was the spot Kathryn had chosen. Evelyn Ortega could not have known the Sanctuary was here, and there were no tracks left in the snow by the animal visible only to her. It was useless trying to find an explanation; as she had done so often, Lucia gave in to the mystery. Richard managed to continue with rational doubts for a few moments, then shrugged and gave in as well. Over the past two days he had lost confidence in what he thought he knew and in the illusion of being in control. He had accepted that he knew very little and controlled even less, but was no longer frightened by this uncertainty. During their night of shared secrets, Lucia had told him that life always asserts itself, but does so more fully if we accept it without resisting. Guided by an unshakable intuition or by the specter of a jaguar that had escaped from a secret jungle, Evelyn had led them directly to the sacred place where Kathryn would rest in peace, protected by kindly spirits, until she was ready to continue her final journey.

Evelyn and Lucia waited beneath the pagoda roof, sitting on a bench near two frozen ponds that in summer contained tropical fish and lotus flowers, while Richard went to fetch their car. There was a steep access road for maintenance and gardening vehicles that the Subaru, with its snow tires and four-wheel drive, climbed with ease.

They lifted Kathryn carefully out of the car, laid her on the tarpaulin, and carried her to the Sanctuary. Since the meditation room was locked, they chose the bridge between the ponds to prepare the body, which was still rigid in its fetal position, the big blue eyes open wide in astonishment. Evelyn took off the stone carved in the image of Ixchel, the jaguar goddess, the ancestral protective amulet she had been given by the shaman in Peten eight years earlier, and hung it around Kathryn's neck. Richard tried to stop her, considering it risky to leave this evidence, but relented when he understood it would be almost impossible to trace the stone to its owner. By the time the body was found, Evelyn would be far away. He contented himself with wiping it clean with a tissue soaked in tequila.

Following instructions given by Evelyn, who quite naturally took on the role of priestess, they improvised some primitive funeral rites. A circle was closing for her: she had been unable to say anything at her brother Gregorio's funeral and had been absent for Andres's burial. She felt that by saying goodbye to Kathryn she was also solemnly honoring her brothers. In her village the last moments and the passing of a sick person were faced without any great drama, because death was regarded as a threshold, just like birth. Those present were supporting the person as they crossed to the other side without fear, delivering their soul to God. In cases of violent death, a crime, or an accident, additional rites were needed to convince the victim of what had happened and to ask them to leave and not come back to frighten the living. Kathryn and the child she was carrying inside her had not had even the simplest vigil. Perhaps they had not even realized they were dead. No one had washed, perfumed, and dressed Kathryn in her finest clothes, no one had sung or worn mourning for her, served coffee, lit candles, or offered flowers. Nor was there a black paper cross signifying the violence of her departure. "I feel very sorry for Miss Kathryn, who hasn't even got a coffin or a place in a cemetery. And the poor little unborn child, who has no toy to take to heaven," said Evelyn.

While Evelyn prayed out loud, Lucia wet a cloth with snow and washed the dried blood from Kathryn's face. Instead of flowers, Richard cut a few sprigs from a bush and placed them between her hands. Evelyn insisted they also leave the bottle of tequila, because in vigils there was always liquor. They wiped the fingerprints from the pistol and left that alongside Kathryn. That could be the clinching proof against Frank Leroy. Kathryn's body would be identified as being his lover's, the gun that fired the shot was registered in his name, and it could be proved he was the father of the fetus. Everything pointed to his guilt, except for one thing: he had an alibi because he had been in Florida.

They rolled Kathryn into the rug, folded the four corners of the tarpaulin around her, and tied the bundle with the ropes Richard had in the car. Like all the buildings in the institute, the Sanctuary had no foundation, but was raised off the ground on stilts. This left a gap underneath into which they could slide Kathryn's body. They spent some time collecting stones to block the entrance. With the spring thaw the body would inevitably start to decompose, and the smell would reveal her presence.

"Let us pray, Richard, to join Evelyn in saying farewell to Kathryn," Lucia asked him.

"I don't know how to pray, Lucia."

"Everyone does it in their own way. For me, praying is relaxing and trusting in the mystery of existence."

"Is that God for you?"

"Call it whatever you like, Richard, but give Evelyn and me

your hands while we form a circle. We're going to help Kathryn and her little one go up to heaven."

Afterward Richard taught Lucia and Evelyn to make snow-balls and stack them one on top of another to form a pyramid, with a lit candle at its center, as he had seen Horacio's children do at Christmas. The fragile lantern composed of a flickering flame and frozen water cast a delicate golden light, surrounded by blue circles. A few hours later, after the candle had burned down and the snow had melted, there would be no trace left.

Lucia and Richard

Richard Bowmaster and Lucia Maraz conscientiously collected everything published about the Kathryn Brown case from the moment her body was found in March to a couple of months later, when they were able to consider their life-changing adventure at an end. The discovery of the body at Rhinebeck led to speculation about a possible human sacrifice by members of an immigrant cult in New York State. Xenophobia toward Latinos was already in the air, unleashed by Donald Trump's hateful presidential campaign. Although few people took him seriously as a candidate, his boast that he would build a wall like the Great Wall of China to seal the border with Mexico and deport millions of undocumented immigrants was beginning to take root in the popular imagination. This made it easy to give the crime a macabre explanation. Details of the discovery pointed toward the theory of a cult: like a pre-Columbian mummy the victim had been wrapped in a fetal position inside a bloodstained Mexican rug, with an image of the devil carved on a stone around her neck and a bottle with a skull on its label next to the body. The point-blank shot to the forehead suggested it had been an execution. And, according to some scandal-mongering newspapers, the body had been left in the Sanctuary of the Omega Institute to mock its spirituality.

Several Spanish-speaking churches put out emphatic denials of the existence of satanic cults in their communities. Soon however, the virgin sacrifice—as one tabloid called her—was identified as Kathryn Brown, a physical therapist from Brooklyn, aged twenty-eight, single, and pregnant. Forget the virgin. It also emerged that the tiny stone sculpture did not represent Satan but a goddess from Maya mythology, and the skull was a frequent decoration on the commonest bottles of tequila. At this, interest from public and press diminished until it faded away completely, making it harder for Richard and Lucia to follow the case.

The article that appeared in the *New York Times* during the last week in May, which Richard Bowmaster confirmed through other sources, had little to do with Kathryn Brown. It concerned a human trafficking network that involved Mexico, several Central American countries, and Haiti. Frank Leroy's name was mentioned in the article, along with that of other accomplices, and Kathryn's death warranted barely a couple of lines. Even though it was within the police department's jurisdiction, the FBI had investigated the Kathryn Brown case due to her links to Frank Leroy, who was briefly arrested as the main suspect for the crime but released on bail. For several years, the FBI had been on the trail of a vast human trafficking operation, and they were more concerned with laying their hands on Leroy for that than with the fate of his unfortunate lover. They were aware of Frank Leroy's involvement in the trafficking but did not have sufficient proof to prosecute; he had protected himself carefully against that eventuality. It was only by linking him to Kathryn Brown's murder that they were able to obtain a search warrant for his office and house, uncovering sufficient evidence to implicate him.

Leroy escaped to Mexico, where he had contacts and where his father had lived quietly for years as a fugitive. That could have been his destiny as well, were it not for a special FBI agent who had infiltrated their gang. This man was Ivan Danescu. It was thanks to him more than anyone that they were able to disentangle the criminal knot in the United States and its links with Mexico. Danescu was killed during a raid on a ranch in Guerrero where many of the victims were imprisoned, and where several of the network's bosses were holding a meeting. According to the press, Ivan Danescu accompanied the Mexican military in a heroic operation to free more than a hundred prisoners waiting to be transported and sold.

Between the lines, Richard read a different version, because he had studied the methods of both the cartels and the authorities. Any cartel boss arrested usually succeeded in escaping from prison with astonishing ease. The law was constantly flouted, since both police and judges yielded to threats or corruption, and anyone who resisted was killed. Very seldom were the guilty men who operated with impunity in the United States ever extradited.

"I'm convinced the military entered that ranch to kill, backed up by the FBI. That's what they do in operations against the narcos, and I don't see why it would be any different in this case.

Their plan to take them by surprise must have failed, and it ended in a shootout. That would explain the death of Ivan Danescu on the one hand and Frank Leroy on the other," Richard told Lucia.

THEY CALLED EVELYN, who had not heard the news, and agreed she should come up from Miami to Brooklyn, as she was obsessed with the idea of seeing Frankie again. She had not as yet dared to call Cheryl. Lucia had to convince Richard that now that Frank Leroy was dead, Evelyn was in no danger, and that both she and Cheryl deserved some closure on what had happened. She offered to make the initial contact, and faithful to her conviction that it was always best to take the bull by the horns, she immediately phoned Cheryl and asked to see her because she had something important to tell her. Terrified, Cheryl hung up. Lucia left a note in the mailbox at the house of statues: *I'm a friend of Evelyn Ortega's, she trusts me. Please see me, I have news of her.* She added her cell phone number and put the keys to the Lexus and Kathryn Brown's house in the envelope. The same night, Cheryl called her.

An hour later, Lucia went to see her. Richard waited in the car, so nervous his ulcer began to throb. They had decided it would be better if he didn't appear, as Cheryl would feel more at ease with another woman. Lucia discovered that Cheryl was exactly as Evelyn had described her: tall, blond, almost masculine, but a lot older looking than she had expected. She was agitated, fearful, and defensive. She was trembling when she showed Lucia into the living room.

"Tell me right away how much you want, so we can get this

over with," she said in a choking voice, standing with her arms folded.

It took Lucia half a minute to grasp what she had heard.

"Good Lord, Cheryl, I don't know what you're thinking. I haven't come to blackmail you, far from it. I know Evelyn Ortega and what happened to your car. I'm sure I know a lot more than you do about that Lexus. Evelyn wants to come in person to explain, but above all she wants to see Frankie. She misses him a lot; she adores your son."

At this, Lucia witnessed an astonishing transformation in the woman in front of her. It was as if the armor plating protecting her had been suddenly smashed, to reveal someone with no backbone, nothing to hold her up inside, a person held together by an accumulation of pain and fear, so weak and vulnerable that Lucia could scarcely resist the urge to hug her. A sob of relief escaped from Cheryl's chest. She collapsed onto the sofa, head in hands, crying like a baby.

"Please, Cheryl, calm down, everything is all right. All Evelyn ever wanted is to help you and Frankie."

"I know, I know. Evelyn was my only friend, I told her everything. She left when I most needed her. She vanished with the car without saying a word."

"I don't think you know the whole story. You don't know what was in the trunk of the car . . ."

"How wouldn't I know?" said Cheryl.

CHERYL TOLD LUCIA that the Wednesday before the January storm, when she was going through her husband's shirts for the laundry, she saw a grease stain on his jacket lapel. Before adding it to the pile she discovered a key hanging from a golden ring. A jealous itch told her it belonged to Kathryn Brown's house, which confirmed her doubts about her husband and that woman.

The next morning, when Kathryn was helping Frankie exercise, he suffered a hypoglycemic crisis and passed out. Kathryn brought him around with an injection and his blood sugar levels soon stabilized. No one was to blame for the incident, but the question of the key had stirred up Cheryl against Kathryn. She accused her of mistreating her son and sacked her on the spot. "You can't get rid of me. It was Frank who hired me. Only he can fire me, and I doubt he'll do that," Kathryn replied haughtily, despite which she picked up her things and left.

Cheryl spent the rest of Thursday with her stomach churning as she waited for her husband. When he arrived that evening there was no need to explain anything, because he already knew. Kathryn had called him. Frank grabbed Cheryl by the hair, dragged her into their bedroom, slammed the door so violently the walls shook, and punched her so hard in the chest it left her gasping desperately for air. When he saw this, Frank was afraid he had gone too far, and went to his own room in a fury. On the way he bumped into Evelyn, who was waiting anxiously for the chance to go to Cheryl's aid. Frank pushed her out of the way and stormed off. Evelyn ran to the bedroom and helped Cheryl lie down. She made her comfortable on the pillows, gave her painkillers, and put ice compresses on her chest, afraid Cheryl might have suffered some broken ribs, just as she herself had when attacked by the MS-13 gang members.

That Friday before anyone was awake, Frank Leroy left home

very early in a taxi to catch his flight before the airport closed
due to the blizzard. Cheryl spent the whole day in bed, drugged
with tranquilizers, and Evelyn looked after her. Cheryl remained
stubbornly silent, not shedding a tear, but as she lay there, she
decided she must act. She loathed her husband and it would
be a blessing if he left with Kathryn Brown, but that was not
going to happen in the normal course of events. The bulk of
Frank Leroy's wealth was in offshore accounts that she would
never have access to, but the remainder still in the United States
was in her name. This was something he had set up to protect
himself if he ran into any legal problems. To Frank, the best
solution was to get rid of her and Frankie. He had fallen in love
with Kathryn Brown and was in a sudden rush to be free. Cheryl
could not have suspected there was an even more powerful reason: his lover was pregnant. She only discovered that in March,
when the results of the autopsy were made public.

Cheryl thought she must confront her rival, since it was useless to try to reach any kind of agreement with her husband. The
two of them only communicated on trivial matters, and even
then they were at odds, but once she understood the advantages
of her offer, Kathryn Brown was bound to be more reasonable.
Cheryl was going to suggest she could keep her husband; she
would grant him a divorce and guarantee to remain silent, in
exchange for financial security for Frankie.

On Saturday Cheryl had left around midday. The pain from
the blow to her chest and what felt like a crown of thorns at her
temples ever since the beating on Thursday had grown worse.
With two glasses of liquor and a large dose of amphetamines
in her stomach, she told Evelyn she was going to her therapy.
"They're just clearing the streets, señora, you'd do better to

stay calm at home," Evelyn begged her. "I've never been calmer, Evelyn," Cheryl replied, then left in the Lexus. She knew where Kathryn Brown lived.

When she arrived she saw Kathryn's car out on the street. This meant she was thinking of going out soon, otherwise she would have left it in the garage to protect it from the snow. On an impulse, Cheryl felt in the glove compartment for Frank's pistol, a small semiautomatic thirty-two-millimeter Beretta, and put it into her pocket. Just as she had suspected, the key she had found was to the front door of the house, and she could slip in without making any noise.

Dressed in her sports gear, Kathryn Brown was about to go out, a canvas bag slung over her shoulder. She gasped in surprise when she suddenly found herself face-to-face with Cheryl. "I only want to talk to you," said Cheryl, but Kathryn pushed her toward the door, screaming insults. Nothing was turning out as Cheryl had intended. Pulling the pistol from her coat pocket, she pointed it at Kathryn, intending to force her to listen. Far from cowering, the young woman burst out laughing defiantly. Cheryl slipped off the safety catch and clutched the gun in both hands.

"You stupid bitch! You think you can scare me with your damn pistol? Wait and see when I tell Frank!" shouted Kathryn.

The shot rang out of its own accord. Cheryl had no intention of shooting her when she pulled the trigger, and as she swore to Lucia Maraz when she told her, she didn't even take aim. "The bullet hit her in the middle of her forehead by pure chance, because it was written, it was my karma and Kathryn Brown's," she said. It was so instantaneous, such a simple, clean act, that Cheryl did not register the sound of the shot or the recoil of the weapon in her hands. She could not understand why Kathryn fell backward or what the black hole in her face meant. It took her more than a minute to react and realize the other woman wasn't moving, then to stoop down and discover she had killed her.

After that, all her movements were made in a trance. She explained to Lucia that she could not remember what she did in any detail, even though she had never stopped thinking about what happened that cursed Saturday. "At that moment, the most urgent thing was to decide what I was going to do with Kathryn, because when Frank discovered her it would be terrible," she said. The wound had not bled much, and the stains were all on the rug. She opened the garage and drove the Lexus inside. Thanks to a lifetime of swimming and exercise, and thanks to her rival being so small, she was able to drag the body along on the rug and heave it into the trunk. She threw the pistol inside and put Kathryn's key in the glove compartment. She needed time to sort things out and had forty-eight hours before her husband was due to return. For more than a year now the fantasy had been going around in her head that she should call the FBI and testify against him in return for protection. Above all she had to calm down: her heart was about to shatter. She headed for home.

In March, during the investigation into Kathryn Brown's death, she was only briefly questioned. The prime suspect was her husband, whose alibi of being in Florida playing golf proved useless because the state of the cadaver made it impossible to determine the exact time of death. Perhaps if she had been questioned in the days immediately following the young woman's murder, Cheryl would have given herself away, but the interrogation did not take place until two months later. Those months gave Cheryl the chance to make peace with her conscience.

She had lain down to rest that Saturday at the end of January because she had a blinding headache, only to wake up several hours later with the terrifying sensation that she had committed a crime. The house was in darkness, Frankie was asleep, and Evelyn was nowhere to be found, something that had never happened before. She could easily have gone mad, envisaging all the possible explanations for the incredible disappearance of Evelyn, the car, and Kathryn Brown's body.

Frank Leroy got back the following Monday. Cheryl had spent the two intervening days in a state of absolute panic, and as she confessed to Lucia, had it not been for her sense of duty toward her son, she would have swallowed all her sleeping pills and put an end to her miserable existence once and for all. When Frank couldn't find the missing Lexus or his lover, he imagined all sorts of explanations, apart from her having been murdered. He only learned about it when her body was discovered and he was accused of the crime.

"I think Evelyn got rid of the evidence to protect Frankie and me," Cheryl told Lucia.

"No, Cheryl. She thought your husband had killed Kathryn and went to Florida as an alibi, without ever imagining someone might use the Lexus. The cold would preserve the body until the Monday when he returned."

"What? Evelyn didn't know it was me? So why did she . . . ?"

"Evelyn took out the Lexus to go the drugstore while you were asleep. My partner, Richard Bowmaster, collided with her. That's how he and I got mixed up in all this. Evelyn thought that when your husband returned he would know she had used the car and seen what was in the trunk. She was terrified of him."

"In other words . . . You didn't know what happened either," murmured Cheryl, the color draining from her face.

"No. I only knew Evelyn's version. She thought Frank Leroy was going to eliminate her, to silence her. She was also scared for you and Frankie."

"So what's going to happen to me now?" asked Cheryl, horrified at what she had confessed.

"Nothing, Cheryl. The Lexus is at the bottom of a lake, and no one suspects the truth. What we've said stays between the two of us. I'll tell Richard, because he deserves to know, but there's no need for anyone else to find out. Frank Leroy has already done you and many others enough harm."

Epilogue

At nine in the morning of the last Sunday in May, Richard and Lucia were drinking coffee in bed with Marcelo and Dois, the only one of the four cats that the dog had become friendly with. For Lucia this was early: what need was there to wake up so soon on a Sunday? For Richard it was part of the enjoyable decadence of life as a couple. It was a brilliant spring day, and in a while they would go and fetch Joseph Bowmaster to take him for lunch. That afternoon the three of them would then proceed to the bus terminal to wait for Evelyn, because the old man had insisted on meeting her. He could not forgive his son for neglecting to ask him to take part in that January's odyssey. "What would we have done with you in a wheelchair, Dad?" Richard kept saying, but Joseph saw that as an excuse rather than a reason; if they had managed to take a Chihuahua along, they could have taken him as well.

Thirty-two hours earlier, Evelyn had left Miami, where, in the months she had been living there, she had begun to create a more or less normal existence for herself. She still lived with Daniela but was thinking of becoming independent in the near future. She worked looking after children in a day care center and waiting on tables in the evenings. Richard was helping her financially, because as Lucia always said, you have to spend your money on something before you end up in the cemetery. Evelyn's grandmother Concepcion Montoya had put to good use the money orders Evelyn regularly sent her, first from Brooklyn and then Miami. She had replaced her shack with a brick house that had an extra room from which she could sell the secondhand clothing her daughter dispatched from Chicago. She no longer went to the market to sell her tamales, but only to buy provisions and chat with her neighbors. Evelyn thought she must be around sixty, but in the eight years since the deaths of her two grandsons and Evelyn's absence, suffering had aged her, as she could tell from a couple of photos that Father Benito had taken. These showed her in her elegant attire, the outfit she had worn for thirty years and would go on wearing until her dying day: the thick blue and black woven skirt, the *huipil* blouse embroidered with the colors of her village, the red and orange sash around her waist, and the heavy, colorful head-dress on her head.

According to Father Benito, Concepcion was still very active, but her body had shrunk and shriveled. She was as wrinkled as a monkey, and since she was always going around murmuring prayers under her breath, people thought she was crazy. That worked in her favor because no one asked her to pay protection money anymore and she was left in peace. Once every two weeks Concepcion spoke to her granddaughter on Father Benito's cell phone, because she refused to have one of her own, as Evelyn had offered. It was a very dangerous apparatus that worked without a plug or batteries and caused cancer. "Come and live with me, Grandma," Evelyn had begged her, but Concepcion thought this was a dreadful idea. What would she do in the north, and who would feed her chickens and water her plants while she was away? Strangers could come and take over her house; you had to be very careful. Yes, she would visit her granddaughter, but she would see when was a good moment. Evelyn understood that this moment would never arrive and hoped that someday soon her own situation would allow her to pay a visit to Monja Blanca del Valle, if only for a few days.

"We'll have to tell Evelyn the truth about what happened to Kathryn," Richard told Lucia.

"Why complicate things? It's enough that you and I know. And besides, it's not important anymore."

"What do you mean it's not important? Cheryl Leroy killed that woman."

"I hope you're not thinking she should pay for her crime, Richard. It was an accident."

"You're a disastrous influence in my life, Lucia. Before I met you I was an honest, serious man, an academic beyond reproach . . ." He sighed.

"You were such a bore, Richard, but even so, I fell in love with you."

"I never thought I would end up obstructing justice."

"The law is cruel and justice is blind. We tilted the balance slightly in favor of natural justice, because we were protecting Evelyn, and now we have to do the same for Cheryl. Frank Leroy was a criminal and he paid for his sins."

"How ironic they couldn't catch him for the crimes he committed and he had to escape for a crime he didn't commit," said Richard.

"You see? That's what I mean by natural justice," said Lucia, kissing him lightly on the lips. "Do you love me, Richard?"

"What do you think?"

"That you adore me and can't understand how you lived for so long without me, bored and with a hibernating heart."

"'In the midst of winter, I finally found there was within me an invincible summer.'"

"Did you just think of that?"

"No. It's by Albert Camus."

Acknowledgments

The idea for this novel came at Christmas 2015 in a brownstone in Brooklyn where a small group of us had met to drink a first cup of coffee in the morning. I was with my son, Nicolas, and my daughter-in-law, Lori; her sister Christine Barra; Ward Schumaker; and Vivienne Flesher. Someone asked what I was planning to write on the rapidly approaching January 8, the date when I have begun all my books for the past thirty-five years. Since I had nothing in mind, they began to throw out ideas that came to form the skeleton of this book.

As always, I was aided in my research by Sarah Hillesheim, and by Chandra Ramirez. Also by Lori Barra, Susanne Cipolla, Juan Allende, Elizabeth Lesser, and Beatriz Manz.

Roger Cukras was the inspiration for the romance of the mature couple Lucia and Richard.

My first readers and critics were my son, Nicolas; my editors Johanna Castillo and Nuria Tey; my agents Lluis Miguel Palomares and Gloria Gutierrez; the fierce reader from the Balcells agency Jorge Manazanilla; my brother Juan; and my wonderful friends Elizabeth Subercaseaux and Delia Vergara.

Also of course Panchita Llona, my mother, who at the age of ninety-six has not relinquished her grasp on the red pencil with which she has corrected all my books.

To all of them and many others who have lent me emotional support in my life and writing over the past two years, which have not been easy for me, I owe these pages.

About the Author

Born in Peru and raised in Chile, Isabel Allende is the author of numerous bestselling and critically acclaimed books, including *The House of the Spirits*, *Daughter of Fortune*, *Paula*, *My Invented Country* and *The Japanese Lover*. Her books have been translated into more than 35 languages and sold over 67 million copies worldwide. A lifelong activist and campaigner, she is the founder of the Isabel Allende Foundation, which promotes economic and social justice for women. In 2014, Barack Obama awarded Isabel Allende the Presidential Medal of Freedom, the US's highest civilian honour. She lives in California.

www.isabelallende.com